VAN TERRA

Rory North

For Laika.

Yes, the dog.

The Janus System

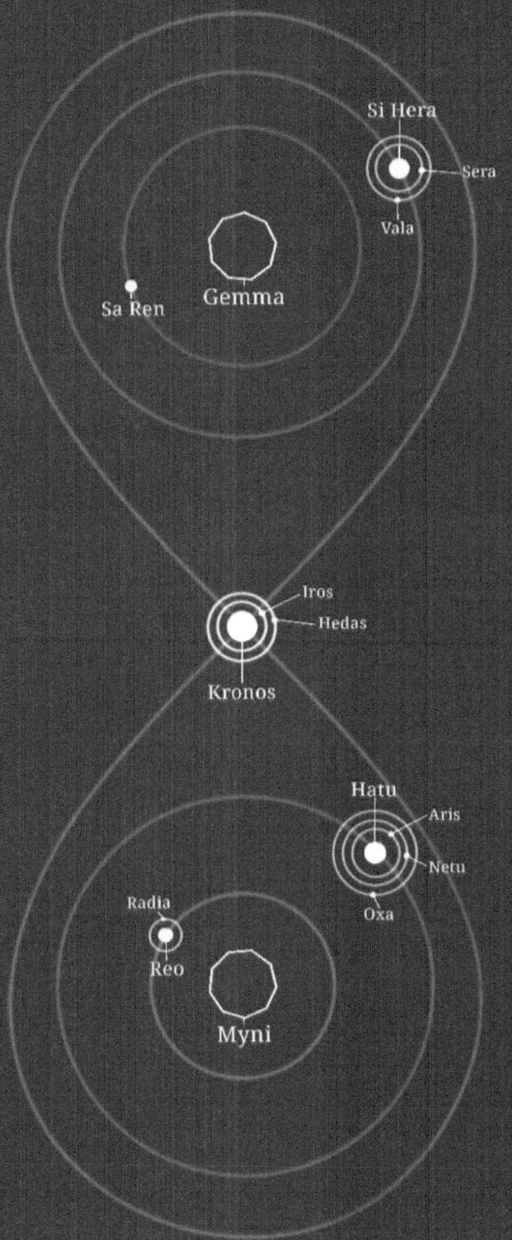

Chapter One
Fall From Good Graces

The long, shining white halls of the Governor's Palace didn't offer many places to hide. Grace pressed herself against a wall near an intersection, as close to the gold-laced marble as she could manage. Her wings prevented her from resting completely flat against it, but they folded up tight enough under her jacket for her to largely ignore their presence. Across the hall, a massive window offered a glimpse of the countless skyscrapers sprawled across the city-planet's surface. Above them stretched a dark sky barely touched by the morning light of the closest sun.

It felt wrong to be sneaking around her home like this. Though, even after four years of shelter here, it was hard to feel completely at home in the palace. She rarely saw the governor, the very man who'd taken her in. Her tutors and guards were swapped out every season. And security kept her as far as possible from the prying eyes of the public, from the reporters snooping around for news on the hero that had saved their governor's life.

Grace's personal staff were the source of her current predicament, actually. Her math tutor had failed to show up to her room for the morning's lesson, and she had received no answer when she tried calling the palace secretaries. She'd exited her rooms to find her usual guards missing from their post by her door.

In fact, this entire section of the palace seemed deserted. Grace couldn't help but assume something was seriously wrong, but no emergency alarms had gone off. There wasn't so much as a distant shout or footsteps.

She took a deep breath and forced herself around the corner. Another quiet hallway greeted her. She began to walk, resisting the urge to call out.

Most doors were closed, but an open one at her right led into a conference room. Grace paused. The room was empty of people, but a smartsphere sat on the table, projecting a holoscreen into the air. A news broadcast played quietly.

"—scene of the robbery. Several shots were fired, but no injuries have been reported."

Grace found herself staring at a photo of the infamous Van Terra, standing atop a convenience store roof, holding a blaster aimed toward the security camera the image had come from. The villain's black coat billowed in the wind around her. Her ponytail of long, black hair whipped about similarly.

Grace shuddered. There were a lot of villains stalking Kronos's streets, but Van Terra seemed the most interested in making people afraid of her.

"Hey, Grace."

Grace whirled around and found herself facing a semi-familiar face. Pale skin, lighter than Grace's light brown. Straight blonde hair pulled back in a short ponytail. And a simple black and white suit that was standard for a diplomat. The material had a glossiness that was exaggerated by the lights above.

An ambassador. One of many that came in and out of the palace. This woman was human, like Grace. And if she remembered correctly, the woman actually had been born on Earth. In Earth years, she looked to be in her late forties, far older than Grace's nineteen.

"Uh, hi?" Despite the woman's non-threatening appearance, Grace found herself taking instinctive steps backward. She racked her brain for the woman's name. "It's...Callisto, right?"

"Kara Callisto," the woman confirmed with a warm smile.

And then, behind her, at the other end of the hall, was a far more familiar face: one of Grace's bodyguards that had actually been kept in her rotation for more than a few seasons. A tall, bald, and bulky man with skin so pale it was practically white. His irises glittered like opals. He was a member of the Starr family, distantly related to the governor.

What was his name again? Coron? Caro? He never spoke to Grace, only followed silently like a shadow. She opened her mouth to call out to him. Maybe he knew what was going on.

Blindingly fast, the bodyguard drew a gun and took aim. Kara's instincts were much faster than Grace's, and the next thing Grace knew, she was being yanked sideways. The bullet missed her by inches, striking a wall somewhere behind her with a loud crack.

A flash of light warned of another shot. This time, the weapon that fired was the one in Kara's hand, a blaster with the same silver-white metal casing that most standard blasters had. Its yellow beam of energy pierced the bodyguard's chest, and he collapsed.

Grace was too stunned to make any sound, though her mouth hung open and her chest squeezed with the urge to scream. Dark blood pooled on the marble floor beneath the guard.

Kara grabbed Grace's arm. "Time to run."

Grace didn't protest as she was dragged around the corner into the next hallway, though she had a million questions, starting with *What on Kronos is happening?* and *Oh god, am I going to die?*

Instead of asking any of those, she went with, "Why did my bodyguard try to kill me?" Her voice trembled so badly that it would be a miracle if Kara understood her.

"Long story," Kara replied.

"Why are you helping me?"

"Longer story."

Grace didn't try saying anything else until Kara led her into a storage closet.

"Take a moment to catch your breath," Kara told her as she set to work removing a ventilation grate from the wall.

Grace rested a hand on a shelf of cleaning supplies and realized how badly she was shaking. Hoping to distract herself from her shock, she asked, "Why did he use a gun and not a blaster? I've never seen a gun on anyone in the palace."

"It would divert suspicion from the staff when news got out," Kara replied as she leaned the grate against the wall. She reached into the bag at her side. "Everyone on Starr's security team uses blasters. With a gun as the murder weapon, they could blame gangs. It would also give them an excuse to increase police patrols."

Grace's brow furrowed. Kara removed a large metal hook and fastened it to the top of the vent shaft.

"Wait," she said, a new wave of fear snaking its way in. "Wait, wait, where are we going?"

"I'm getting you somewhere safe."

"But—I live here—I—"

"Grace," Kara said, her voice sympathetic but firm. "Do you realize what's happening?"

"My bodyguard tried to kill me."

"The *governor* tried to kill you." Kara glanced up at Grace.

Grace's heart stopped in her chest. "But—but he took me in. He let me stay here, gave me tutors—"

"I'm sorry, Grace, it's complicated." Kara removed a coil of rope from the bag and began tying it to the hook. Once it was secure, she rose to her feet. "I promise I'll explain more when we're out of here."

After that, Kara explained how they would be taking the rope down the shaft to the bottom of the palace, where they'd be able to exit and drop into the city below.

Ordinarily, a height like this wouldn't bother Grace, but she couldn't stop herself from thinking about how if she slipped, she wouldn't be able to get her wings out in such a tight space. There was no point in taking off her jacket to free them.

Kara hooked them to the rope via belts, and they went in, Kara first. The elaborate hooks on the belts were set up in a way that allowed the two to drop in a freefall at a pace just slow enough to prevent injury when they stopped at the bottom.

Despite claiming she'd wait until they were safe to elaborate on what was happening, Kara did offer Grace one more tidbit of information on the way down, explaining why the section of the palace around Grace's room had been so empty.

"Things have been rearranged over the past few months to empty that entire floor without raising suspicion. No one knows that everyone else has been rerouted or scheduled elsewhere. It would have been chalked up to an unfortunate accident."

Grace tried to focus on the facts Kara was laying out, hoping to distract herself from her growing nausea. All that trouble just to kill her. She was grateful to be rescued, but... "Why were you watching me in the first place?"

"When you first made the news, we matched your name and face to a girl who was abducted from Puerto Rico—that's a place on Earth. Though, there's a bit of a...timeline issue with that. But we can sort it out later."

At the bottom of the shaft, Kara blew open the grate leading outside with her blaster. The two descended farther on the ropes, into the air beneath the palace. Four steel pillars held the palace in the air far above

Kronos's tallest skyscraper, and one of those four stood only a few feet away, offering a small amount of cover.

"We have to get to the subtrains," Kara said. "We'll take them to my safehouse, and I'll call for pick up."

"Pick up?" Where were they going afterward? Were they...leaving Kronos?

More pressing than that question was the mention of the subsurface trains. Grace had never been on the subtrains. In fact, since being taken by the governor, she hadn't even been to the city's lower streets. But she'd heard about the subtrains, about how they were full of criminals, thieves, muggers waiting to harass people on their way to work. About how gang members hung out down there, trading weapons and guns...

Kara glanced up briefly before she went back to fiddling with the section of rope still coiled at the end of the line. "You look scared. Well, more than you already did."

"I haven't heard great things about the subtrains."

Kara lifted an eyebrow. "They're not as bad as the people up here make them out to be," she said. "And, well, Starr could solve the problems that do exist if he'd direct more funds to public transportation." With another glance up, she added, "You have nothing to worry about as long as you're with me."

Kara let out the last of the rope, and the two dropped onto the roof of the skyscraper below. Kara broke the lock on a service door leading inside. From there, they used a few different elevators to get down to street level. It was apparently common for a single elevator to only cover either the upper, middle, or lower districts, with maintenance and private elevators being the exception.

Once they were done with elevators, Kara led an anxious Grace down a set of stairs into a dim underground. Crowds pressed in on them from all sides. Grace lifted the hood of her jacket to hide her face.

Would anyone really recognize her, even if they did get a good look? She'd been fifteen four years ago. Her face had changed since her rescue of Governor Starr hit the news. Sure, photos of her did get out every time she left the palace, rare as those occasions were. But she wasn't *interesting*.

They navigated a maze of wide corridors and train platforms. When they stepped onto one of the trains, Grace noted that it was headed north. Her next thought was that that information didn't help her at all. She was familiar with Kronos's geography in relation to the upper districts, but the planet's surface was an entirely different beast.

As the train pulled out of the station, Grace racked her brain for questions she could ask Kara. Kara might not want to share her entire story until they got to their destination—wherever that was—but maybe Grace could at least get a few more pieces of the puzzle.

"So, you work with a group of people, then?" Grace asked. "Is it like the Interstar Council?"

"A bit. We're not a government, though, so we can act where the council can't." A bitterness crept into those last few words. Grace got the impression that Kara wasn't the council's biggest fan.

"And we're going to your...base?"

"We're going to one of our ships," Kara answered. "I doubt we'll go directly to our base, after that. It's...pretty far from Kronos."

Grace glanced around the crowd, heart skipping whenever she noticed someone looking even slightly in her direction. Logically, she knew it was unlikely anyone was actually focused on her, but it was hard not to assume otherwise.

The train jerked to an abrupt stop, sending Grace stumbling forward. Her already-racing heart skipped another beat as the neon green tunnel lights flickered outside the train windows. Murmurs spread through the crowd of passengers.

A hand grabbed Grace's arm to steady her. "You okay?" Kara asked.

"Yeah." Grace adjusted the hood of her blue jacket to better hide her face. "What's happening? Does this have to do with us?"

Kara didn't respond. The tunnel lights flickered twice more before going out entirely. The train's interior followed.

"What do we do?" Grace pressed.

"It's going to be fine." Kara sounded more like she was trying to reassure herself than Grace. Her grip on Grace's arm tightened.

The subtrain intercom clicked on. "Callisto," a deep voice said. "Kronos police have you surrounded. We know you've kidnapped Grace Alvarez. Turn yourself in now and we'll spare your life."

"Why are they saying you kidnapped me?" Grace whispered as loud as she dared.

"You're proof of Starr's secret lab experiments," Kara replied. "If I can get you to Earth, we can persuade the Interstar Council to help us stop him."

Grace's blood went cold. That was right. She'd escaped from a lab. It was easy to forget, when her memories of all but those last few steps out the door were gone. Wiped on purpose, according to the scientist who'd helped her. He hadn't made it out.

The first part of Kara's sentence finally wriggled its way into the forefront of Grace's thoughts. "Wait, *Starr's* lab?"

A thud came from the back of the train car. Its metal doors let out a terrible screech as they were forced open. Flashlight beams passed over the crowd, offering brief glimpses of the other passengers, a blend of aliens from all over the Kronos system and beyond. Light illuminated skin in every color, scales and fur, antennae, animalistic ears and eyes, and a handful of people who looked as human as Grace and Kara. Or, nearly as human, in some cases.

Regardless of what planet they were from, everyone in the train looked somewhere between confused and scared.

"Grace," Kara whispered. "If something happens to me, you have to keep going. Get off Kronos, get out of the Janus system, get to Earth."

"Earth?" Grace's chest constricted. Breathing now felt like an impossible task. How was she supposed to get anywhere near the Solar System?

"You need to find other people from Earthguard," Kara continued. "The Kronosian government has been experimenting on abductees, and we need you as proof to get the council to act." Her head turned, and she gave Grace a smile that was probably meant to be reassuring. "I'm sorry I couldn't get you farther. I knew from the start this mission would probably be my last. But we expected Starr to get rid of you soon, and I had to take the chance to save you."

A flashlight beam blinded Grace. "Found them!" a Kronosian police officer shouted. Grace squinted as his silhouette raised a blaster.

"Get ready to run," Kara whispered. Without waiting for a response from Grace, she lifted her arms and stepped forward. The simple black and white clothes she'd worn to disguise herself as a diplomat were stained with blood and grime. Stray pieces of blonde hair had fallen from her ragged ponytail. "I surrender."

A blaster's blue laser struck her chest.

Kara's body dropped to the floor of the train.

"She was turning herself in!" Grace shrieked. She barely heard her own voice over the shouting that followed Kara's collapse.

An officer's order rang out above the chaos. "Grab Alvarez!" Hands tightened around Grace's arms. Someone yanked back her hood, and her long waves of dark brown hair fell free around her face.

Grace struggled in vain against her captors. More beams of light landed on her. She looked desperately to the shadows in hopes that one of the passengers would step forward to help, but deep down she knew there was no chance. Even if someone wanted to step in, they were no match for the Kronosian officers. No match for the blasters.

The officer who'd shot Kara stepped forward. "Stun her."

Cold metal touched Grace's neck. Lights flashed in her vision, followed by darkness. The next thing she knew, she was being pulled out of the back of a hovering police cruiser, too disoriented to resist as officers led her across a skywalk and into a lobby.

Bright lights reflected off white walls and tiled floor. Grace attempted to shield her eyes and found that handcuffs had been placed on her wrists. Her jacket had been taken, too, leaving her in a long-sleeved white shirt, dark blue pants, and white boots.

Her identity would be obvious to everyone in the station. Even folded up as tightly as possible, she couldn't hide her wings without her jacket. They rested flat against the back of her shirt, emerging from the same two slits that had been cut in all of her tops.

The officers led her to a sleek black desk. A receptionist with purple, velvety skin typed away on a holographic keyboard with clawed fingers. When she opened her mouth to ask the man at her right a question, she revealed dozens of tiny, sharp teeth.

Grace didn't hear the question, but she recognized the man: Bruce Wright, the Sky District's cyborg chief of police. Pale blue skin, buzzed dark hair, one violet eye, and one silver cybernetic orb to replace the eye he'd lost. "Keep filling it out," he told the receptionist.

"What's going on?" Grace asked, finally finding her voice. It came out hoarse. "Why am I being arrested? I was kidnapped!" She winced inwardly at the guilt that came with blaming Kara, but if she wanted to fulfill the woman's dying wish, she had to keep herself out of prison.

"You can drop the act," Bruce said. "Governor Starr himself told me you went with Callisto willingly, which makes you an accessory to the damage she did during your escape." He laughed. "She was a good spy, but Starr caught on and planted bugs. He heard every word you two exchanged on your way out of the palace."

Grace's heart sank into her stomach. No, no, no, there had to be a way out of this. She drew in a shaky breath. "What are you going to tell the public?"

"You mean the people who think you're a hero because you saved Starr's life, what, a starcycle ago?" Bruce shrugged. "We'll think of something."

More than a starcycle and a half, actually. But Grace's brain was wired to put long stretches of time into Earth years, though she could make the conversions to Kronos time pretty easily.

A younger officer burst through the front doors of the station and sprinted toward Bruce. When she reached him, she skidded to an abrupt halt and whispered something to the chief between ragged breaths. Her pale pink skin had flushed bright red in her cheeks.

Bruce's eyes went wide. "You're joking."

The officer shook her head.

"Guard her," Bruce ordered, nodding toward Grace. "I'll be right back to sign the intake paperwork."

His departure left Grace with nothing to do but watch the receptionist type. Her eyes stung, but she refused to let Bruce see her cry. He'd probably laugh at her. What made her feel even more pathetic was the desperate hope she clung too that Starr would step in and fix all this. Take her back to the Governor's Palace. Another part of her thought it all might be a dream.

The station doors opened again. Shuffling papers and footsteps around the lobby quieted. The officers standing around Grace turned their heads, and she slowly followed their stunned gazes.

It had taken no less than fifteen officers to bring the girl in. The sound of her heeled boots clicking against tile broke the silence, and despite being handcuffed and chained to her captors, she wore a wicked grin.

She was human, like Grace.

Despite being a criminal, she carried herself as if she were a celebrity, flashing smiles and winking at anyone who looked her way. Which was everyone. Her expensive suit, black overcoat, and long black hair pulled in a high ponytail made her look even more out of place. It all looked sharp against her light skin. The gleam in her brown eyes suggested was fully aware of that fact.

Bruce walked at the front of the entourage, wearing a smile as wide as the prisoner's. "I can't believe this," he said when he reached the desk. "My two biggest targets, arrested on the same day."

The receptionist's large, triangular ears twitched. Almost under her breath, she asked, "Since when has Grace Alvarez been a high-profile criminal?"

"What was that?"

"Nothing, sir."

Bruce tapped the side of his head. His left eye—the cybernetic one—lit up and projected a holoscreen into the air. "You're taller than I expected," he said to his latest arrest. "Now, let's get this over with. Name?"

The girl smiled. "You know my name."

"It's protocol."

"All right." The girl leaned against the desk, earning a nervous glance from the receptionist. "I'm Jasper Van Terra, the most dangerous villain on Kronos."

Bruce responded with a cold laugh. He tapped a box on his screen. "That's a little dramatic, don't you think?"

"You said yourself that I was your biggest target." Jasper raised an eyebrow.

"Sure, your ridiculous stunts have made you a nuisance, and the governor has a higher reward by your name than most. But you're far from the most dangerous villain out there." Bruce typed something into the box. "Age?"

"Sixty-eight. I've aged well."

"Stop trying to be funny."

"You're no fun. Seventeen. Earth years, that is. You can translate that into starcycles yourself." Jasper tipped her head and surveyed the crowd around the desk. She was younger than Grace had expected.

Grace and Jasper's eyes met for the briefest of moments, and it was enough to make Grace's heart rate spike. The woman she'd heard terrifying stories about for nearly a starcycle—stories of robberies and explosions and ransoming of upper-district elites—was younger than her?

"Reason for arrest." Bruce frowned as new data scrolled across his screen. "You tried to rob a Kappa-Omega? Aren't convenience stores beneath you?"

Jasper shrugged. "I wanted a Nova Cora."

"Unbelievable." Bruce waved his hand, and the screen disappeared. He nodded to the receptionist. "I'll be back to sign off." To the rest of the officers, he barked an order to follow him.

One of the officers grabbed Grace's arm, and she was escorted along with the rest of the group away from the station lobby. They walked down a well-lit hallway into a starkly contrasted black elevator, where Bruce pressed a button marked "B1." A screen above the panel prompted him to enter a code.

Grace frowned at the size of the panel. "Why does the station have so many floors?" she asked, internally cringing at how hoarse her voice came out.

Bruce smirked. "This isn't all part of the station. But our storage is down in the basement." With a chuckle, he added, "Including prisoner storage."

"Yikes," Jasper muttered.

The elevator ride was silent after that. It was a quick ride, for such a far drop from an upper district into the building's basement. The dim lights that greeted them in the cell block were dramatically overpowered by the glow of neon signs outside, their red light seeping in through window wells. It was much colder down here than the lobby had been. Grace considered asking for her jacket back but doubted Bruce would return it.

Bruce stopped in front of a cell and produced a key. "Enjoy your brief stay, Van Terra," he said as he opened the door. "You'll be shipped off to the Shark Tank in the next couple hours."

Jasper stepped into the cell, apparently unfazed by the news that her next destination was the most secure prison on the planet.

"What are you waiting for, Alvarez?" Bruce asked. "Get in there."

"What?" Grace yelped. She shot him an alarmed glance. "With her?"

"Don't worry, she'll be chained to the wall." Bruce gestured for two officers to move in and secure Jasper.

Seeing no other choice, Grace entered the cell while the officers checked the locks on Jasper's chains. She scrambled to the wall opposite Jasper and put her back to it.

"I assume Van Terra's been searched?" Bruce asked.

"Of course," an officer replied. "We ran her through the X-rays and metal detector thrice to make sure we got everything. There is the issue of the modifications—"

"I know about that," Bruce interrupted with a dismissive wave of his hand. He waited for the officers to step out, then closed the door and locked it. "She should be fine in here for an hour or so, but triple the guards around the cell block. She's not getting away from us."

Bruce led the officers away. The thick metal door between the cells and the elevator slammed shut, leaving Grace alone with Jasper Van Terra.

Grace attempted to fold her arms, only to realize she was still in handcuffs. She sighed and leaned back into the wall, keeping her eyes on the ceiling and silently hoping Jasper wouldn't talk to her.

"It's a real surprise seeing you here," Jasper said. "I never thought I'd get to meet you."

"What? Me?" Grace lowered her gaze. Jasper looked even more villainous in the red light. And the way she towered over Grace was more than a little intimidating. She was leaner than Grace, but Grace had no doubt there was plenty of muscle hiding under those black clothes.

"Yes, you, Angel."

"Angel?" Grace repeated. Was that supposed to be an insult? A nickname?

"Can I see them?" Jasper asked.

Grace didn't have to ask what she was referring to. With a slight shrug, she turned around. The wings had been designed to fold tight enough to hide under a jacket, but stretched out, they spanned the entire cell. Whatever metal the feathers were made of was a striking white.

Without her memories of the lab, it was impossible to be certain the extent of the modifications done to Grace's body. There had to be interfacing between her muscles and the wing's cybernetics, of course. But to move the wings and hold her body straight while she flew, she assumed there had to be changes to the rest of her musculature as well.

"Wow. The feathers look so real." Chains clinked as Jasper took a few steps forward. "You don't remember who gave them to you?"

"I don't remember anything before Governor Starr took me in," Grace replied. She folded her wings back up and turned around to face Jasper again.

"Right. After you saved his life." Jasper's tone turned bitter.

Grace shrugged. It apparently hadn't meant much to him, given the morning's events.

A frown abruptly crossed Jasper's face. "Can you hear that?" she whispered.

Grace stilled. The cell block was quiet, but after a moment, she detected Bruce's voice carrying through the door down the hall, barely audible. What was he still doing down here?

"He's getting impatient," Bruce said. "Too many people have their eyes on Alvarez."

"What are we going to do?" a second man asked.

"I'm going to go check the cameras. I have a feeling they're going to malfunction for a few minutes. Enough time for someone to get shot with this."

"Plassite gun," Jasper whispered. The intent look in her dark eyes suggested she was seeing something that Grace couldn't. "It could slip through the metal detector, and even X-rays if you're careful enough. How did he get his hands on—?"

"Sir?" the other officer sounded hesitant.

"It's simple," Bruce told him. "Shoot Alvarez, frame Van Terra, and get the governor off our backs. We never had this conversation."

Grace pressed a hand over her mouth to restrain a cry of alarm. Footsteps moved away from the cell block door and faded into the distance.

"Wow," Jasper said. "Starr really wants you dead."

"I don't know why." Grace's hand dropped. Her voice cracked. "I didn't do anything!"

"I believe that," Jasper muttered. "I actually have a theory. But we have more important things to worry about right now."

"Like the fact I'm going to die?"

Jasper didn't respond to that. Instead, she held up her hand and counted down on her fingers. "Three, two, one."

The cell block lights went out.

Grace blinked in surprise. "What's happening?"

"Look, Angel," Jasper said. Her pale skin shone completely red now that there were no hallway lights to drown out the neon. "I don't usually do favors. But I would like to know why the governor suddenly wants you dead after housing you for four years. So, if you want, I'll bust you out of here."

"And then what?" Was escaping an upper district police station even possible?

"We don't have all day. I have to get what I came here for and get out." Jasper laughed. "You didn't think I got arrested for fun, did you?"

What other choice did Grace have? Stay here and die? "Okay," she said. "I'll come with you."

Chapter Two
Damned If You Do, Dead If You Don't

Footsteps approached the cell before Grace had a chance to ask how Jasper intended on getting out of the station. Grace instinctively backed away from the bars, fearing it was her death approaching, while Jasper appeared unconcerned. Grace couldn't say she found that reassuring.

A young woman stopped in front of the cell and began fiddling with the lock. It was difficult to discern much of her appearance in the soft glow, but she appeared to be wearing a police officer's uniform.

"Got the key?" Jasper asked. "And my comm device?"

"Obviously," the probably-not-an-officer muttered as she drew a key from her pocket.

Grace watched her unlock the cell with wide eyes. "Who is that?" she asked Jasper. "What's happening?"

"Shh." Jasper gestured to their rescuer. "This is Holly. Stay quiet until we get out of the building, all right? And move fast. My hacker can't keep the station's power out forever."

Holly unlocked Jasper's chains next, and then the two were hurrying out of the cell. Grace rushed to follow them down the hall.

Even though the world darkened with every step away from the windows, Jasper led the way with ease. How could she see so well? She was surprisingly quiet, too, considering her dramatic entrance earlier.

"Big group of guards at the end of the hall," Jasper whispered. "On the other side of that door. Thea, you on comms?"

In the silence that followed, Grace became painfully aware of the sound of her own breathing.

"Excellent," Jasper said. "And your heat scanning drone is working?"

They stopped in front of what must have been the door. Grace narrowly avoided bumping into Jasper.

Jasper continued in a hushed tone. "Quite a few guards between us and evidence storage. And they'll all have flashlights. Holly?"

"Ready," Holly replied. She pulled something out of her pocket. Grace could just make out the silhouette of a small sphere passing from her hand to Jasper's.

After that, Holly took out another key and set to work on the locked door in front of them. It opened with a faint creak. Jasper grabbed Grace's arm and pulled her forward into the darkness beyond. There was a click, followed by the sound of the sphere rolling across the floor. Hissing filled the air. Flashlight beams swung toward the three.

The light never reached them. Thick, black fog filled the air just in time to mask the three from view. "Smoke bomb," Jasper whispered, sounding smug.

"Stop showing off," Holly hissed.

"I'm just following the plan!"

"And narrating for your new friend."

The three slipped past the confused officers. The officers' quiet chatter helped hide Holly and Jasper's exchange, along with Grace's footsteps and heavy breathing. Jasper guided her and Holly through the basement labyrinth, and Holly occasionally dropped more smoke bombs from her pockets to keep them hidden.

A few minutes of walking brought them around a corner to a seemingly empty hallway. Jasper released Grace's arm. A moment later there was a thud, a grunt, and the sound of a body hitting the ground. Grace winced.

Holly turned on a flashlight and pointed it at the door in front of Jasper. Jasper drew two pins from her hair and set to work picking the lock. It clicked a minute later, and she eased the door open. She entered, followed by Holly, then—after an anxious glance at the unconscious guard on the floor—Grace.

Neon pink light flooded the evidence room through the blinds. Metal lockers took up most of the wall space. Jasper trailed a finger across them as she circled the room. When she found the locker she was looking for, she picked that lock, too.

"Before you ask what we're here for, this was all taken from my team during our last job," Jasper said to Grace as she opened the locker door.

"We barely got away." She pulled out a data drive, black leather gloves, a miniature drone, a smartsphere model that looked a few starcycles old, and some cords. They all went into various pockets inside her coat. The last item, a silver cylinder about half an inch in diameter, stayed in her hand.

"Seen one of these before?" Jasper pointed the device at the ground.

Grace shook her head. "What is it?"

"Laser." Jasper pressed a button on the cylinder's side. A thin red beam struck the concrete floor with a hiss. Grace stepped back as Jasper guided the laser in a rough circle.

"How much longer, Thea?" Holly asked, a hand pressed to her ear. It was light enough now that Grace could see her sharp—and human—features: her green eyes, strong jaw, pale skin, and long braid of crimson red hair. The color looked oddly natural on her, despite being unnaturally vibrant for human hair. A black bag hung at her side. The dark blue officer's uniform she wore was slightly too large. Of course, it was probably stolen.

Jasper finished the circle. The section of concrete she'd cut away fell into the dark and crashed into whatever was beneath the station. She gestured to the gaping hole. "Tunnels. Sewer pipes, maintenance access, abandoned train routes, et cetera."

Grace leaned forward to peer into the darkness. "Wait, we're just going to—?"

Jasper jumped into the hole and disappeared. With an annoyed sigh, Holly followed.

The room's lights came on, wiping away the pink glow with blinding white. Grace glanced at the door. With the cameras presumably back online as well, she didn't have long before she was found. She wiped her sweaty palms on her pants and sat down next to the hole. How far down was the drop? Her legs swung over the edge. Shouting came from the other side of the door.

Grace pushed herself into the unknown.

She hit cold concrete. The landing was awkward and left her legs aching, but she'd managed to avoid serious injury.

Jasper laughed. "You're doing great, Angel." Grace couldn't tell if that was meant to be sarcastic.

Holly turned in a circle, illuminating the tunnel they'd dropped into with her flashlight. Fading yellow letters marked dark walls. Train tracks rusted beneath them. Trash littered the ground.

"Which way?" Holly asked.

Instead of answering, Jasper slid off her heeled boots and held out a hand. Holly pulled a pair of black combat boots from the bag at her side and tossed them Jasper's way.

Once the boots were on, Jasper crouched next to a metal cover in the ground. She must have been stronger than she looked, because she lifted the circular cover without any apparent effort. "Down the ladder. Quick." She glanced at the gaping hole above them. "Officers are about to come down."

Holly went down first. Grace followed with shaky hands. The metal rungs were slick, and she lost her grip near the bottom. Her arms waved wildly as she dropped the last few feet to the ground. Holly raised an eyebrow, not making any moves to help.

Jasper pulled the cover shut, dropped from the top of the ladder, and somehow managed a graceful landing. She set off down the new, narrower tunnel they'd entered with a quick stride.

Grace jogged to catch up on Jasper's right. "Where are we going now?"

Jasper pulled on the gloves she'd taken from the evidence locker. "Now's not the best time for a lengthy explanation."

"So, I'm just supposed to follow you blindly?" Grace asked.

"You're welcome to leave," Jasper replied with a shrug. "You're not my prisoner."

Seriously? Grace had been somewhat under the impression that this was a polite kidnapping. "Where would I go?" she asked.

"Jasper, she's not our problem," Holly cut in as she fell into pace at Jasper's left. "She'll only slow us down."

"She has connections to Starr," Jasper countered.

"Exactly. She could be a spy!"

"Why would I be a spy for the man who tried to kill me?" Grace asked.

"The attempt on your life could have been staged." Holly rolled her eyes. "Duh."

"No, I really think Starr wants her dead," Jasper said. "And if Starr wants her dead, then she won't last more than a few hours on her own. He has eyes all over Kronos."

"Why would he have her killed? Why now?"

"We could theorize—and I do have theories—but that's not important right now." Jasper glanced at Holly with a raised eyebrow.

Holly huffed. "Okay, fine. But what's in it for us?"

"Information on Starr."

"I barely knew him." Grace tipped her head back to examine the pipes running overhead. It didn't do much to combat the stinging in her eyes, but she was able to keep tears from surfacing. "He gave me a room at the Governor's Palace, but I didn't see him much after I saved his life."

"I think you're more valuable than you realize." Jasper stopped and looked at Grace. Grace's head lowered to meet her gaze.

Despite the reputation, infamous villain Jasper Van Terra wasn't going to hurt her—at least, not yet—but Grace had to mask the spike of fear Jasper's intense gaze sent through her. Grace swallowed. "That still doesn't answer my question. Where are you taking me?"

"A quick detour, then back to my place." Jasper rested a hand on her hip. "If you're with me, that is."

"I don't know what I should do."

"I'm going to give you some advice I got from the side of a skybus one time: *trust your gut.* I mean, it was an ad for probiotics, but it's pretty profound if you ask me."

Grace stared. Jasper had to be messing with her.

"I'm the only person keeping you alive right now, and I'll do whatever it takes," Jasper continued. "But you need to do everything I say. Got it?"

One other person had been willing to fight for Grace's life, but Kara Callisto was dead now. The least Grace could do was keep herself alive until she found some way to carry out Kara's last request. *Get off Kronos, get out of the Janus system, get to Earth.*

"Okay," Grace said. "I'll follow you." For now. As soon as she had a chance to escape Kronos, she would take it.

Jasper grinned. "This is going to be fun."

Chapter Three
Bringing Good Vibes to a Gunfight

By the time the three came across an intersection in the tunnels, Grace's hands had finally stopped shaking. She still didn't feel anything remotely resembling calm, but her heart wasn't on the verge of exploding anymore, either.

Jasper nodded toward a smaller tunnel branching off the one they'd been walking through. "Get in position," she told Holly. "Make sure the others are ready."

A ladder waited on the opposite wall. While Holly disappeared into the darkness behind them, Jasper and Grace climbed the ladder, passed through a manhole cover, and emerged in an alleyway.

"Whoa," Grace breathed as she scrambled onto concrete. The buildings around them stretched into the upper districts, some for nearly a mile, leaving only thin slivers of the pale red sky peeking through overhead. "It's sunrise already?" All in all, she hadn't felt like they'd spent much time in the police station or the tunnels, but maybe all of the adrenaline coursing through her had warped her perception of time.

Jasper straightened up and adjusted her coat. "Yep. Follow me."

Grace was too nervous to annoy Jasper with more questions, so she trailed her silently through a maze of alleys. Her gaze darted in every direction as they walked. Dumpsters around them overflowed with garbage, and small rodents scurried into the shadows beneath as the two passed. Puddles of liquid that probably weren't water reflected neon signs and flashing billboards.

It was wildly different from the upper districts Grace had spent the past few years living in.

They finally stopped in front of a dented door in the side of a sleek black building. "You gonna ask what we're doing?" Jasper asked as she picked the lock.

"I wasn't sure you'd want to tell me," Grace replied.

"Well, we're going up."

"How?"

"Out of service elevator. My technopath—the aforementioned hacker—got it running with her—" Jasper spared a hand to make a wavy motion. "—techy mind powers." The door opened with a click. "We're going all the way to the top, so we'll have time to talk."

"About what?" Grace followed Jasper into the building.

"You, obviously." Lights flickered on, and a short walk down a hall brought Jasper and Grace to an elevator waiting with open doors. "Can you think of anything that would lead to Starr turning on you now?"

The elevator's silver—and slightly rusted—doors closed and reflected Grace's ragged reflection back at her. "It probably has to do with Kara Callisto," she answered, wiping at a dark smudge on her chin with her thumb.

"Thea, take us to the roof," Jasper said into her ear comm. The elevator jerked up. "Kara who?"

"She showed up at the palace a few pentasols ago and said she was an ambassador from Earth," Grace explained. "And then—well, a couple of hours ago, my math tutor didn't show up to my rooms for our usual lesson."

One of Jasper's eyebrows shot up. "That early?"

"My lessons have always started pretty early." Grace shrugged. "I'm always done by early afternoon, though."

"And that leaves you plenty of free time to…?"

"If I'm not invited to any events—" These days, that was usually one of Starr's public speeches or rallies. It had been a long time since Grace got to go to a party where people were allowed to mingle with her. "—I usually watch TV or read. I eat dinner in one of the dining halls and chat with palace staff." A bit awkwardly, Grace shrugged again. "My life hasn't exactly been exciting, until this morning."

"Right." Jasper rose onto her tiptoes and lifted a portion of the elevator ceiling. She pulled a black duffel bag off the roof. "And what happened when your tutor didn't show up?"

"I went looking for him and realized the halls around my room were completely deserted," Grace recounted. "Kara found me in time to save me from one of my bodyguards. He shot at me, Kara hit him with her blaster, and we ran. She didn't have time to explain much before police found us and killed her." Her chest tightened at that last bit. At the memory that resurfaced with the words.

"What *was* Kara able to tell you?" The bag dropped to the ground. Jasper knelt, unzipped it, and drew out a small knife.

Grace had to think for a moment to find the useful bits of information among frantic memories of her time with Kara. "She said she's from a group called Earthguard, and that I match the profile of a girl abducted from Earth."

Jasper pulled out bigger and bigger daggers from the bag and stashed them in various pockets. "'Bout time someone did something," she muttered. Louder, she asked, "So, you are from Earth, then?"

"I guess." Grace's brow furrowed. "Kara also said something about an issue with the timeline that she would explain later."

"Timeline issue? What's that supposed to mean?" Jasper asked. A wider variety of weapons and devices came out of the bag. A gun, a smartsphere, a tablet…

"No idea." Grace swallowed. "And I guess I'll never know, now that she's dead." Remembering Jasper's earlier question, she added, "Anyway, Earthguard also wanted me because they can use me as evidence that Starr has secret labs. They might be able to use me to make the Interstar Council take action."

Grace hesitated a moment before continuing. "I'm not sure how useful I'll be without any memory of all that, but I guess my wings are evidence enough, if they can prove they were made in Starr's labs." She turned a little so that she could glance at her folded wings in the elevator door's reflection.

"Kara's arrival must have scared Starr, then. He realized he'd run out of time to deal with you quietly." Jasper stood, leaving the empty bag on the floor of the elevator.

Grace looked Jasper up and down quickly, impressed by how much stuff had gone into the coat's pockets without any obvious bulk. Just a few slight bulges here and there. "Kara made it sound like Starr's been abducting a lot of humans for these secret experiments," Grace noted.

"Not just humans," Jasper replied. "And it's been happening since before Starr was born. Syrus Starr, I mean." Jasper's expression darkened.

Right. Syrus, the current governor, was one of many in the Starr family that had held the title of governor.

"Did Kara mention how long Earthguard's been investigating the abductions?" Jasper asked. "Or how long they've even been around?"

Grace shook her head. "Nope. Sorry."

The elevator let out a terrible creak as it slowed. Grace flinched. It had been out of service for a reason. What if it broke down? What if they got stuck? Or dropped all the way to the ground? What if—?

"You good, Angel? You look nervous." Jasper drew a knife with a hot pink handle from one of her pockets and inspected the blade. She was too smart to use a dangerous elevator, right?

Maybe Grace's fears were irrational, but she needed to distract herself from all the ways her mind was telling her she could die in the next five minutes. "You gave Bruce Wright your age in Earth years. Are you from Earth, too?"

"Yeah."

"Oh." Seeing Van Terra in the news, Grace had always assumed she was one of the many humans whose ancestors had been recruited to come to Kronos for work-related reasons. Travel between star systems was ridiculously expensive. "Why'd you come here?"

The elevator stopped. "Sorry, no time for my backstory now," Jasper said as the doors opened. She returned the knife to her pocket.

The two stepped out of the elevator and onto the roof of a skyscraper. This was the view of the city Grace was used to. Rooftops, streams of flying vehicles, and glimpses of the planet's ocean in the distance. The sky had lightened to a faint pink, but the sun Gemma rose in the east, rapidly turning it blue.

Kronos was on the far side of Gemma now, and the Janus System's other sun, Myni, wouldn't be visible in the sky for another season. Kronos's two moons were up, though, faintly visible on the horizon. Hedas reflected a gray-green light, while the larger Iros had an iridescent sheen to it.

The rest of the Janus System's planets orbited one star or the other. Kronos was the only one to move in a figure-eight around both. That entire figure-eight was a starcycle—roughly two and a half Earth years.

"Well, looks like we're running with the theory that your wings were made in Starr's secret lab." Jasper's gaze swept over the city.

"Starr's secret lab," Grace repeated, the phrase still sounding utterly unbelievable to her. "And where is that, exactly?"

"Underground. The place is called Sky Labs, ironically. The Starrs obviously didn't want their name attached to their experiments." Jasper pointed to a door on the other side of the roof. "We're going in there."

The door opened before either of them could move. Eight people emerged. The group was made up of various species from around the star system, but they all wore the same black pants, black combat boots, and red shirts.

"Are they with us?" Grace asked.

"Absolutely not. I don't do the whole matchy-matchy thing." Jasper lowered her voice. "Do you not know who these people are?"

"Am I supposed to?" Grace asked as the eight formed a loose circle around them.

"They're Red Blades."

"What are Red Blades?"

Jasper groaned. "You don't have a clue, do you? Okay, keep quiet and I'll handle this." She flashed a smile. One of her hands slid into a pocket. "Hello there! What brings you all to this...rooftop?"

A man whose skin was covered in dark green scales stepped forward and held up his empty hands, a cold smile on his serpentine face. Grace's eyes quickly went to the tattoo on his wrist: a knife dripping with blood.

"I could ask you the same thing, Van Terra," the man said. His hands dropped to his sides. "But I already know you're here to rob the jewelry store a few floors down."

Grace shot Jasper an incredulous look. "You're what?"

"What did you think we came up here to do? Enjoy the sunrise?" Jasper's focus shifted back to the man. "Don't tell me you're here to stop me. You've done far worse than robbery."

"We're not here for you, despite the reward on your head." The man nodded at Grace. "We're here for her."

"Me?" Grace yelped.

"Too bad," Jasper said. "She's mine."

"We're not letting you leave with her." The man flexed one of his hands. His associates inched forward, their own hands moving to guns at their sides. Along with the weapons, Grace spotted more bloody knife tattoos. Were they part of one of the lower district gangs? The name "Red Blades" did sound familiar, the more she rolled it around in her head.

Jasper drew a dagger.

"Bringing a knife to a gunfight?" The serpentine man laughed as he drew his gun from his side holster. "Idiot."

Jasper's head tipped to the side. "Angel, you may want to get down."

The other Red Blades lifted their guns. Heart pounding, Grace dropped to the ground.

Jasper moved with speed and grace that bordered on inhuman, deflecting every bullet with the dagger's blade as if it were a shield. With her other hand, she drew a second dagger. The gunfire continued and she danced in a circle around Grace, throwing bullets to the ground. Grace remained crouched, frozen, with her hands over her ears.

The gunfire finally stopped.

"Guns run out of bullets." Jasper smirked. "And I'm Van Terra. Idiot."

She lunged forward and stabbed the closest man in the chest. Grace flinched.

A woman to Grace's right, with the pale green skin and pointed ears of a West Kronosian, drew a dagger of her own and darted forward. Grace tried to scramble away but wound up staggering backwards and falling.

The woman was halfway to Grace when Jasper sent a knife flying into her shoulder. Clutching her arm, the Red Blade cried out and dropped to her knees. Another Blade, a blue-furred man, swung at Jasper with a pocketknife. Jasper laughed and knocked it aside.

Grace dropped her gaze to the ground beneath her and focused on getting back up. Her legs had turned to jelly, her hands had gone numb, and every frantic breath brought her closer to passing out. She squeezed her eyes shut and tried to think about anything besides the clinking of metal on metal. The tang of blood in the air.

The rooftop fell quiet. A hand grabbed Grace's shoulder. She yelped and looked up.

"Whoa, it's okay, it's me," Jasper said. "Take a deep breath. If you pass out, I'm not carrying you."

Grace risked a glance around the roof. They were the only two left standing. "Are they dead?" she asked, avoiding looking at any particular body for more than a second.

"Not yet. But some of them might get back up if we stick around too long, so..." Jasper jutted a thumb at the door.

Grace climbed to her feet, took a shaky step, and then another. "Okay. I'm okay." As they started across the roof, she asked, "What are your daggers made of?"

"A galaxium alloy," Jasper answered. "It's tough stuff, but even the best knives break after enough bullets." She lifted an eyebrow. "So, you really haven't heard of the Red Blades?"

"I guess they do sound familiar."

"They're the biggest gang on the planet." Jasper reached the door first and opened it. A light flickered on automatically to illuminate the staircase on the other side.

Grace had heard about gangs operating in the lower districts, but... "I didn't think there were any gangs up here."

"That's what the government wants you to think." Jasper laughed. "Seriously, though. The gangs—some of them, anyway—bring the elite families drugs and other illegal imports. In exchange, they get a degree of protection from the law." After a pause, she added, "Though, you are right that they don't usually make themselves *visible* up here. Today was a rare exception. You were enough of a target to make them come up."

Grace was too focused on not tripping down the steep roof-access staircase to fully grasp everything Jasper said. "Why does the biggest gang on Kronos want me dead?" she asked, still processing the new information.

"Because they work for Starr, obviously."

"What?" Despite her best efforts, Grace stumbled at the next landing. Her legs were still shaky from the confrontation on the roof. Her hands weren't any better, she noticed as she caught her balance.

"The Red Blades do all of Starr's dirty work for him," Jasper explained. "The governor has his own personal army, and the public has no idea. And that's on top of the upper district police forces that are more loyal to him than they are the law."

Grace glanced at her as they started down the next flight of stairs. "How do you know all of this? And about the lab experiments?"

"I have my ways." Jasper hopped over the last three steps.

"And I'm—" Grace swallowed. "How sure are we that the lab I escaped was one of Starr's?"

"It explains why Starr's so determined to get his hands on you again," Jasper answered with a slight shrug. "And the Sky Labs experiments mostly revolve around cyborg enhancements."

Grace frowned. "I'm not a cyborg."

"Yeah, you are. That's what your wings are. Cybernetic."

"Right. I guess I never thought about it like that." Grace paused a moment before starting down the next flight of steps after Jasper. "But a lot of people in the city are cyborgs. They aren't all experiments."

"Sure, they have basic replacements for missing limbs. If they're rich enough, with the right connections, they might have a computer chip in their brain or an illegal weapon implant." Jasper waved a hand as she leapt down to the next landing. "But Sky Labs tech is next level and has been for decades. Nothing like those wings exists anywhere else."

Jasper exited the stairwell and led Grace into a hallway bathed in the warm glow of dimmed lights. "Now," she said. "This is where it gets serious."

Grace stared at her. "And the gunfight on the roof wasn't?"

Jasper shrugged.

Chapter Four
My Five-Year Plan Involves Fighting the Government

Jasper couldn't blame Grace for having a torrent of questions, but this robbery was going to go *much* smoother if she wasn't distracted trying to infodump in a way that wouldn't scare Grace off. Ordinarily, Jasper would have stashed Grace away somewhere and picked her up later, but the Blades out and about made that a terrible idea.

"Why would Starr let me live in the palace for so many years if he wanted me dead the whole time?" Grace asked.

Jasper paused in the middle of an intersection. "This way," she said as she headed down the hallway to her left. "And Starr's public image is of the utmost importance. Offering a home to the poor, amnesic orphan who saved his life made him look good. You had no memory of the labs, so you weren't a threat until Kara showed up." She threw a glance over her shoulder to make sure Grace was following.

Grace's brow furrowed. "My earliest memory is of a man—a scientist—leading me out of...some underground facility, I guess. We were chased, and he was killed. I ran into Starr later that day." A faraway look crept into her gaze.

So, Kara wasn't the first person to die saving Grace. That couldn't be great for the whole "emotional stability" thing most people had going. *Nothing like a heaping serving of survivor's guilt first thing in the morning!*

"Huh. Surprising that one of those scientists would help you escape." Jasper led Grace around another corner. They passed offices and conference rooms, all of which were dark and empty thanks to Holly and Dax's earlier evacuation. "I bet Starr was hoping the public would forget about you, but they really tried to keep up with you. They were hoping you'd be sent out to do more heroic acts and good deeds as you got older."

"Well, I failed at that," Grace muttered. "And saving Starr turned out to be a mistake, too."

They took another turn. "You want to make things right?" Jasper asked.

Grace jogged a bit to catch up on Jasper's right. "Huh?"

"Help me help you. The reason I think you're valuable, the reason I'm keeping you alive, is because I want to take down Starr. And you want that too, right? He's corrupt and wants you dead." Jasper stopped in front of her destination: a custodial closet.

"If Starr's so terrible, why do you want him gone?" Grace asked as she paused next to Jasper. "I have a hard time believing a supervillain cares about fixing the government."

"Let's just say it's personal." Jasper opened the closet door.

Grace looked over the cleaning supplies neatly organized on the other side. "Where are we?"

"This floor is mostly offices. The jewelry store is directly below us." Jasper adjusted her gloves. "The top few floors of the building are closed today for fumigation."

"Uh, is it safe to be here?"

"Of course." Jasper entered the closet and flipped on the light. "I suppose I should mention that there's not a real pest problem, and the people who evacuated the building aren't real fumigators." She pulled out the laser they'd recovered from evidence, pointed it at the ground, and turned it on. Over the hiss of the burning floor, she added, "With the building empty, all we have to worry about are alarms."

"What about security cameras?" Grace asked.

A small section of floor broke away and fell into darkness. After turning the laser off, Jasper dropped to one knee next to the hole. "Thea has them playing empty rooms and hallways on a loop. No one can see us," she explained. "That being said, we still need to be careful in the store. Instead of putting alarms on the cases, they've rigged the whole floor with sensors that the employees activated before leaving. Even moving within a few inches of it will set it off."

Thea spoke up over the comms. "Holly, Dax, you've got incoming."

Jasper sighed. "What kind of incoming?"

"What?" Grace asked, brow furrowing in confusion.

Jasper procured a spare comm from her coat and tossed it to Grace. "Put this in your ear."

Grace nearly dropped the thing when she caught it. She hesitated a moment before sliding it in.

"Security's headed our way?" Holly asked, sounding more annoyed than concerned.

"No, no, it's not security," Thea replied. "It's Red Blades."

"The Blades aren't here for us," Jasper told them. "Technically. We just need to hurry."

"Wait, Jasper, who's with you?" Thea asked.

"I'll explain later. Holly, Dax, take care of the Blades. I'm entering the store." Jasper reached into her coat. "I finally get to use my new grappling hook."

"That won't be necessary," Holly told her. "There's a display case directly below the ceiling tile I marked, and a whole maze of them covering the store."

"Ugh. Fine." Jasper hopped into the hole she'd carved in the closet floor.

Grace followed her into the dark space between the floor above and the ceiling below. An "X" marked a ceiling tile a few feet away in red spray paint. Jasper lifted the marked tile, set it aside, and went through the opening. She landed on top of a jewelry display, dropping just low enough for the tips of her gloved fingers to graze the glass before rising. The overhead lights were off, but the display cases gave off a soft golden glow.

Jasper took a step back and looked up. Grace attempted to slide off the edge of the gap but lost her balance and fell awkwardly. She landed hard on top of the display and stumbled to the left.

Jasper grabbed her arm before she could fall. "Careful."

"Couldn't your hacker just turn the alarms off?" Grace regained her balance and shot the floor an apprehensive glance.

"Thea says—"

"Their system is super sensitive," Thea interrupted through comms. "It's constantly scanning for intrusions and adapting to keep out the best hackers, even technopaths. I could set the alarms off just trying to find a way in." After a moment, she added, "Don't get me wrong, I could do it with enough time. But it's easier to just avoid the floor."

Jasper aimed the laser at the glass below her feet. "Put the jewelry under bulletproof glass," she said in a mocking tone. "That'll stop those thieves."

Grace surveyed the store while Jasper lasered open the display. "Won't it take forever to go through every case?"

"It would, if I didn't have this." A disk of glass dropped into the case, and Jasper pulled out the last tool she needed for the job: a gun-sized electromagnet. She pointed the magnetic end at the case and turned it on. A gold necklace flew out of the hole she'd made and slammed into the device.

Jasper guided the magnet along the top of the display, pulling the rest of the jewelry up and through the opening. Once she was done, she shoved the cluster of jewelry into a pocket, hopped over a small gap to the next case, and started the process again.

"I have a question," Grace said.

Of course you do. More jewelry disappeared into Jasper's coat. "Go ahead."

"Usually, I see you on the news because you make a scene." Grace glanced toward the front of the store, where a metal sliding door spanning the store's length blocked any view the doors and windows might have offered. "But right now, you're going out of your way to avoid getting caught."

Not technically a question, but Jasper got what she meant. "I'm only noticed when I want to be," she explained. On to the next case.

"Jasper, we have a problem," Thea said.

Jasper restrained a groan. "What now?"

"Security guards are coming your way. Real guards, not Blades."

"Okay." Jasper straightened up. "I've got one more case to get through."

"Can't you just leave it? If you don't get out now—uh oh."

"Thea?" Despite Thea's protests, Jasper moved on to the last display.

"The security system's kicking me out."

"Well, get back in!"

"I can't just 'get back in.' Hurry!"

"How far is security?" Holly asked.

"I can't access those cameras anymore," Thea said. "Last I checked, though, they were a floor below you. You've got about a minute."

Jasper lifted an eyebrow. "They went past the fumigation signs we put up?" She pointed the laser at the glass beneath her and turned it on.

"They did stop in front of the warnings, but it didn't stall them for long."

Holly jumped back into the conversation. "How many?"

"Two," Thea answered.

Jasper's eyes rolled. "We can handle two security guards." Laser off. Magnet on. *Shiny jewelry come to Jasper.*

"You said you wanted stealth," Holly reminded her.

"Stall them, then. I'm almost done." Jasper brought up the last of the jewelry and turned the magnet off.

Grace spread her wings and pushed herself up to the ceiling. She hung from the edge of the opening for a moment before climbing up with a grunt, followed by a thud.

"You good?" Jasper asked. She strolled to the edge of the display case and jumped to the next.

"I'm okay," came Grace's muffled reply.

"Guards are here," Holly muttered. She cleared her throat. "Excuse me, what are you doing up here? We're about to start the fumigation, you really shouldn't be—"

Grace's head popped down from the ceiling, brown eyes wide with panic. "Are you coming?"

"Relax, I'm almost there." Jasper hopped to the next case.

"Well, that can't be right," Holly said. "They called us yesterday complaining about the roach problem, didn't they?"

"Yep," Dax added, his tone a little too cheery to be discussing an imaginary roach infestation. "Scheduled us to come in as soon as possible."

Jasper paused. Holly, Dax, and the two guards were standing directly in front of the jewelry store. The metal door hid them from view, but she could just make out the guards' voices from here.

"Who exactly scheduled this?" one of the guards asked.

"The building manager," Holly replied.

"Do you have your contract?"

"Jasper!" Grace called in a half-whisper.

Jasper leaped to the case she'd started on and looked up. "Could you scoot over?"

"Do you need help?"

"I think I can manage." Jasper shook out her hands.

"Where's your equipment?" the second guard's voice asked outside.

"It's on another floor. We just came to scout out the area," Holly told him. "Yeah, it sure is...roach infested."

Something glinted at the end of the case, catching Jasper's eye. Damn it. She'd missed a bracelet.

The first guard spoke again. "I don't see any roaches."

"Well, you're not a trained professional, are you?" Holly snapped.

"Forget the contract," the second guard said. "I'm supposed to be on my lunch break. Let's just check the store and go."

Jasper pulled the magnet back out and darted to the end of the case. "I need thirty more seconds!"

"The store?" Holly blurted at the guard. "What store? The jewelry store?"

"Yeah. We were told something weird happened with the security system and came to check it out. If we'd known there was a fumigation scheduled—"

"Jasper!" Grace was even more frantic now.

"I'm coming!" Jasper pulled the bracelet off the magnet and slid them both into her coat.

"I wouldn't worry about it," Holly said. "I mean, we've been here all morning and we haven't seen anything weird."

"Probably a false alarm," Dax added.

The second guard was insistent. "We need to check it out to be sure."

Jasper raised her arms and jumped. She grabbed onto the edge of the gap, swung, and pulled herself up and in.

"They're coming in," Holly warned under her breath.

Jasper slid the ceiling tile back into place while the metal door screeched open. Footsteps entered the store below.

"Come on," Jasper whispered to Grace. "We're going back the way we came."

"What now?" Thea asked.

"We're taking the jewelry to the meeting. Regroup on the roof," Jasper ordered. "We'll go from there."

Chapter Five
Live Fast Drive Faster

Three people waited for Grace and Jasper on the roof. The Red Blades they'd fought earlier were gone, the only sign the gang had been there at all being a few scattered bloodstains that everyone else seemed content to ignore.

"Great, everyone's here," Jasper said as she and Grace walked to meet them. "Grace, you already met Holly, but that's Thea Smith and Dax Cho. And everyone already knows who you are."

Holly and Dax were in the process of taking off fumigator jumpsuits. Underneath hers, Holly's clothes were entirely black, save for a purple stripe running down the legs of her pants. Once the jumpsuit was off, she stepped into a pair of red boots and shrugged on a matching red leather jacket.

The outfit sparked recognition. Grace shifted her attention to Thea and recognized her, too. Dark brown skin, tight curls of black hair, eyes that glinted gold in the morning sun, and the outfit: a black zip-up jacket with a yellow lightning bolt across the front, complimented by yellow pants and black sneakers.

"Wait," Grace said. "Red Holly? Jolt?"

Holly rolled her eyes. Thea's gaze remained fixed on her tablet screen.

"Oh, good, you already know them." Jasper slid her gloves off and shoved them into her coat.

"I know of them," Grace said with a glance her way. "They work for you?"

Holly appeared genuinely offended by the statement. "Work *for* her?"

"We're a team," Jasper said.

"And who's this?" Grace asked, returning her attention to Dax Cho. "I don't recognize him."

Like the rest of the team, Dax appeared to be a human in his late teens. He was pale-skinned with black hair, and he brushed one of the short pieces off his forehead as Grace glanced his way. He stood at about Thea's height—she and Dax were the shortest of the five.

Dax wore simple black pants and a blue shirt, both made of thick, sturdy material. Not a flashy outfit that stirred recognition the way Holly and Thea's had.

"Dax isn't a well-known villain like the rest of us," Jasper explained. "He has healing abilities, though. Code name Remedy."

"You're the only one who calls me that," Dax said.

Jasper waved a hand dismissively. "Well, you're a real villain in my heart."

"Thanks?"

"You're welcome."

Dax turned to Grace and offered a polite nod. "Nice to meet you, Grace." He seemed way too nice to be hanging around a bunch of villains.

"You too," Grace replied, managing a small smile despite the...everything. Her heart had yet to settle back into its resting rate, and a faint tremble still lingered in her hands. Her legs didn't feel much steadier.

Thea glanced up from her tablet just long enough to wave at Grace. As her gaze returned to the screen, though, she said, "Welcome to the party."

Jasper pulled a black smartsphere from her coat—Grace wondered just how much stuff she had in her pockets at any given time—and held it up. "Mia, summon the car."

The sphere answered with a gentle, feminine voice. "Calling the car."

"No, don't call it. Summon it."

"Summoning the car."

Jasper sighed. "Thank you."

"Mia?" Grace asked.

"It's a nickname," Jasper replied, as if that were a thorough explanation for what had just occurred. She shoved the sphere back into her coat.

"What is she?" Or should Grace have asked *who?* Was that a person on the other end of a call, or the smartsphere itself speaking? The voice sounded a bit robotic, but Grace rarely saw spheres used for anything other than accessing the net on holoscreens and making calls.

Jasper pressed a fist into her opposing hand. Knuckles cracked. "An A.I. that does everything I say." She switched hands. "At least, she's supposed to."

An engine revved nearby. Grace whirled around.

A sleek, black vehicle sailed over the edge of the building next to them and landed on the roof. Strips along the bottom of each side emitted a neon pink glow that was faint in the sun but undoubtedly striking at night. The inner rings of the tires gave off a similar light. Jasper grinned as the car screeched to a stop in front of her.

"Could we please obey traffic laws for once?" Holly asked. "If there's Blades around, the least we could do is avoid attracting their attention."

"Where's the fun in that?" Jasper replied. She pointed to the other side of the car. "Shotgun, Angel."

Grace's brow furrowed. "What?"

"She wants you in the front seat," Holly muttered.

The interior of the car was as black as the outside, illuminated only by the various neon lights of the dashboard and what little sun that made it through the deeply tinted windows. Jasper flipped a few switches and grabbed the steering wheel. "Seat belts, everyone!"

Grace clicked her belt into place. "Where are we going now?" *Somewhere safe?* All she wanted was to sit down and process the past few hours of her life.

"Bibi's," Jasper answered.

"The diner? Why?"

"The jewelry isn't for us. We're trading it in exchange for—"

"Are you just going to tell her all of our plans?" Holly demanded, leaning forward into the space between Grace and Jasper. She'd squeezed into the middle seat behind them, Thea and Dax on either side. "We don't know if we can trust her!"

"I didn't say I trusted her, but she's with us for now." Jasper pushed the car into drive.

They shot forward. Grace yelped in surprise and reached for something, anything to hold on to, but the smooth interior didn't offer any handles. She stared out through the front windshield as they neared the edge of the roof. "This is a flying car, right?"

"Duh." Jasper slammed a button on the dash with her fist. Thrusters activated, tires folded, and they joined the rest of the traffic cutting through the Sky District.

Well, joined wasn't the right word. Jasper weaved in and out of traffic streams, occasionally leaving designated airspace to swoop unnervingly low over the concrete skyways carrying non-flying vehicles, or to veer within inches of a building.

"Stop showing off!" Holly exclaimed. "Police will be after us in minutes."

"My bad. I forget how much more they care about the law up here. Don't worry, I'll take us down to the streets."

Thea sighed. "Sudden drops aren't great for the sensors—"

"Angel," Jasper interrupted. She pulled the gearshift back and lifted her hands off the wheel. "I need you to do something really important for me."

The car dropped.

Grace's stomach went somersaulting. "What?" she yelped.

"Open that compartment in front of you."

Grace could hardly think as she fumbled with shaking hands to find and open the compartment. "Now what?"

"Hand me one of the bottles."

Grace grabbed the first bottle her fingers touched and held it out to Jasper. It was soda, she realized. Nova Cora.

"Stop making this poor girl enable you," Holly said. "She doesn't know any better."

Poor girl? Grace was at least as old as everyone here, if not older.

Jasper laughed as she took the bottle. "Enable me? It's soda, not drugs."

"Yeah, 'soda' in giant quotation marks." Holly's eyes rolled. "That stuff's full of garbage."

"I'm pretty sure there's not technically enough water in there to be defined as soda," Thea added.

Holly leaned forward to take the bottle from Jasper, but Jasper yanked it out of reach. "Whoa, I'm driving! You trying to get us killed?" Jasper twisted the bottle's cap off.

"Your hands aren't even on the wheel!"

Jasper pulled the bottle away from Holly again, spilling a few drops of the fizzy black liquid.

Grace leaned forward and peered out the front windshield. Skyscraper windows and neon lights and flying vehicles passed by in a dizzying blur. "Uh..."

"Don't worry," Dax said, sounding way too reassuring for the given situation. "She does this all the time. You'll get used to it." On the other side of Holly, Thea was back on her tablet, tapping away as if they weren't in danger of crashing into a building at any moment.

Jasper slid the Nova Cora bottle into the cup holder and grabbed the wheel with her left hand. With the other, she pushed a lever on the dash up. The vehicle tipped forward in response.

There was a burst from the thrusters, slowing their descent. Wheels unfolded. Then, they slammed into a slanted roof. Jasper yanked the wheel to the right, and the car skidded toward the edge. They shot off the roof and onto a street.

Not a skyway. A real street. They were back on the planet's surface.

"Damn good shocks on this thing," Jasper commented with a grin. Grace wanted to disagree after the jolt that still lingered in her bones, but she supposed the fact that nothing was broken was a testament to the car's construction.

Cars honked and swerved as Jasper cut across traffic. One man nearly stepped into the road in front of her but jumped back when he realized she wasn't stopping.

Jasper cracked her window. "Get the hell out of the way!" she shouted.

Holly raised an eyebrow. "Would it kill you to watch the language?"

"Look, I can either swear or run this guy over, but my anger's gotta go somewhere." Jasper turned into an alleyway, sped around a few corners, then came to an abrupt stop that flung everyone forward.

"Which Bibi's are we going to?" Thea asked coolly.

"The one at the top of the Silver District. It's next to a medical center." Jasper threw open her door. "Why?"

Thea held up her tablet. "So I can get their net password."

"We're going to be there for five minutes," Jasper replied as the rest of the team climbed out of the car. Grace hurried around to the driver's side quickly, not wanting to spend too much time out of reach of Jasper. There was no telling when more Blades would show up to kill her.

"And I have to stay online to keep us out of trouble." Thea rested her free hand on her hip and raised an eyebrow. "Especially with you driving around like that. Security cameras or civilian videos could catch us—"

"Whatever," Jasper said, waving a hand dismissively. "As long as you're online, could you check the Earthnet for me? See if anyone good has dropped new music."

"I'm not going to do that."

"Cool. Thanks." Jasper set off down the alley. She carried the Nova Cora bottle she'd opened in the car.

Grace scrambled to keep pace with her. "What are we doing at Bibi's?"

"Oh, right." Jasper took a swig of the drink. "We're trading the jewels for access to Starchatter."

"Starchatter?" Grace asked. "The news site?"

Behind them, Holly let out a cold laugh. "I'd hardly call it news."

"Their quizzes are fun," Dax said. "Uh, the articles are pretty bad though."

"Whatever you want to call it doesn't matter." Jasper shrugged. "This isn't about Starchatter, it's about their location. The races. Ringmaster."

Grace had no idea what Jasper meant by races, but she did recognize that name. "Ringmaster? The supervillain?" she asked. "Wasn't he robbing banks on Sa Ren last…week?" She opted for that over pentasol, even though it wasn't a perfect exchange. Jasper seemed to prefer Earth measurements of time to Kronosian ones.

"He was, but he's back on Kronos. For now." Jasper adjusted her coat. "Thea, get me the nearest elevator to the middle districts. Preferably one that's not open to the public."

Thea tapped her screen. "On it. Follow me. And I added a few new albums to your personal playlist."

Jasper grinned. "Thanks, Jolt. Knew I could count on you."

"You can access the Earthnet yourself without even touching a—"

"Yes, yes, I know, but I'm busy. Anyway, Angel, Ringmaster's hosting a competition," Jasper explained as they followed Thea around a corner. "A series of street races. It's a chance for criminals and villains from all over the Janus System to show off."

"You being one of them," Grace guessed.

Jasper waved a hand. "I don't need anyone's help to show off," she said. "No, remember what I said about taking down Governor Starr? This is step one. Ringmaster works for Starr behind the scenes. We catch Ringmaster, we deal a huge blow to his operation."

"Ringmaster works for Starr?" The exclamation came out louder than Grace had intended, but that statement was absurd. Ringmaster was one of the major supervillains Starr called a threat.

"Sort of. Ringmaster does his own thing a lot of the time, but sometimes Starr will specifically ask for a favor," Jasper explained.

"Ringmaster blows something up as a distraction, or kills one of Starr's political opponents, or lets a few of his henchpeople get arrested to make the government look good. In return, everyone working directly for Starr leaves Ringmaster alone. Including upper district police."

"What does Starr need Ringmaster for if he has Red Blades?" Grace asked.

"Oh, Ringmaster's much more powerful," Jasper replied. "The Blades only operate on Kronos, and they have to compete with other gangs for territory."

The group took another corner, this time into a narrower alley darkened by a wide walkway above connecting the buildings.

"How do you know about all of this?" Grace shot Jasper a sideways glance. "How has no one else figured it out and told the public?"

"I've been studying Starr for years. I've gotten—" Jasper hesitated. "I've gotten close to his operations. I've seen the evidence with my own eyes, even if I don't have physical proof. Yet." Chin lifting, she added, "I'm hoping to find some when we get our hands on Ringmaster."

Up ahead, Thea paused next to an elevator whose doors opened into the alley. "Here's our ride," she said. She rested a hand on the panel next to it. "It'll take a minute to get to us. Fair warning, it's old. Doesn't seem to get much use."

"Perfect," Jasper said.

"I'm not the only one who thinks Jasper shouldn't be telling this girl all of our plans, right?" Holly asked, folding her arms as she stopped with the rest of the group. "What if she was bugged?"

"She's not," Thea said. "I'd be able to tell. No bugs, no trackers."

Holly didn't look satisfied, but she didn't make any further comments.

"Okay," Grace said slowly, still mulling over everything Jasper had told her. "What does Starchatter have to do with—?"

"Hold that thought," Jasper cut her off. "I'll fill you in on the Starchatter thing later, but right now..."

The elevator doors screeched open.

"Is this safe?" Grace assessed the inside as the five entered. Wrappers littered the floor and graffiti covered the walls. At least the elevator she and Jasper took earlier had been clean.

Jasper slammed a button. "Most of what we do isn't safe."

The elevator shuddered and creaked as it ascended. When the doors opened, Grace was the first to hurry out. Jasper chuckled as she followed.

The five crossed a skywalk to the Bibi's. Grace peered over the railing at the city below. At the walkways and skyways filled with people and cars. The flying vehicles, flashing lights and billboards. The urge to jump and spread her wings made her heart ache. She'd rarely had the opportunity to fly while living at the palace.

The end of the skywalk connected to a walkway wrapping around the skyscraper. Similar walkways clung to most public floors in the cities—the floors of buildings filled with restaurants and shopping centers. Stretches of buildings with nothing but windows and balconies on their outer wall typically signaled offices or apartments on the inside, only accessible by interior elevators requiring keycards or a code.

"Won't people recognize us?" Grace asked as they reached the diner's front door.

"Not unless we do something to get their attention," Jasper said. "And Bibi's shouldn't be busy yet."

Well, Kronos *was* home to life from all over the galaxy. There was such a diverse variety of people on the streets that it was hard to attract attention by sight alone, regardless of what you looked like. No one would pay much mind to people who were just walking. Plus, Holly and Thea had left their jackets in the car, making themselves less recognizable.

Still, Grace wished she had a jacket to hide her wings, even if they folded up tightly enough to not be blatantly obvious.

The group entered the Bibi's and found it empty. Jasper tapped the bell by the register. A moment later, a teenage girl emerged from the back, loudly chewing gum. She had dark blue scaly skin, lighter blue hair pulled up on top of her head, and an annoyed expression on her serpentine face. "You're early."

Jasper shrugged. "Things went smoother than usual for me. Statistically speaking, something terrible is bound to happen at any moment." She clapped her hands together. "So, you have the passwords for the employee database?"

The girl blew a pink bubble and reached into the front pocket of her shirt with a clawed hand. She held up a folded piece of paper. "You have my jewelry?"

Jasper emptied her pockets onto the counter. The girl picked up a necklace and examined the vibrant red jewel at the end of its chain. Apparently satisfied, she handed the paper to Jasper and began scooping the jewelry into a paper bag with the Bibi's logo on it.

"How did you get these, anyway?" Jasper asked as she tucked the paper into her coat. "We couldn't find them in any of the Starchatter databases we hacked."

"They don't keep them in the system, they keep them on paper. They've had issues with security in the past," the girl explained. "Lucky for you, I have a close connection there."

"Follow-up question," Holly said, raising an eyebrow as she looked around the diner. "What are you doing working in a place like this? We just handed you hundreds of thousands of janos worth of jewelry. You have connections with people like Van Terra." Her tone was tinged with suspicion.

The girl shrugged. "My mom would be suspicious if I didn't have a job."

As the last of the jewelry went into the bag, a gunshot echoed outside. Jasper had a gun of her own gun in hand in an instant. Holly drew a blaster from a holster at her back. Thea and Dax tensed but didn't look particularly alarmed.

Grace only had a moment to be surprised by the weapons she hadn't noticed the team carrying. She stared, frozen, as a bullet came through the door and struck the wall behind the counter.

"Oh, come on," the employee groaned. "I left the Green District to get away from this kind of thing." She stormed into the back.

A few more shots went off. Jasper took a step toward the door. "Who's there?"

The door burst open, revealing three Red Blades. Grace yelped and stumbled backward into the counter.

"What were you shooting for?" Jasper asked the Blades. "Door was unlocked."

The blue-furred Blade in the middle stepped forward, one of his large ears twitching. "Hand over Alvarez, and we'll let the rest of you go."

"Not a chance." Jasper cocked her gun. "Holly, help me. Everyone else, get to the balcony."

"You think we don't have more Blades in the area?" the Blade asked.

"This close to the upper districts? Can't have too many of you in one group. You'll scare the rich people." Jasper took aim. "And not all of the police are quite as cozy in Starr's pocket as you are."

Grace hurried after Thea and Dax to the open doorway that led to an outdoor dining area. The Bibi's was positioned in the corner of the building, allowing the diner a massive balcony jutting out the side to accommodate their lunch rushes.

More gunshots rang out behind the three as they stepped outside, joined by the sound of Holly's blaster firing. Grace dove to the side, aiming to take shelter under a table. The floor was slicker than she expected, and she found herself rolling back out into the open. She pushed herself out into a crouch and glanced back at the doorway.

Bullets whizzed by overhead. Grace scrambled forward blindly and collided with the balcony railing. Another shot. Then a second, and a third.

The fourth bullet hit Grace's right wing, bounced off, and grazed the back of her shoulder. She yelped, more from shock than pain. It took a few ragged breaths before the sensation of torn flesh hit her. It took a few more before she could crane her neck and attempt to assess the damage.

Dax and Thea were crouched under a table nearby. "Let me take a look!" Dax called, starting toward her.

Thea grabbed him and pulled him to the ground. "Look out!"

Grace ducked. Her hands tightened around the bars of the railing. This time it wasn't bullets, but red beams of energy that cut through the air. One of the Blades had a blaster of their own.

One shot struck the railing, ripping an entire section off the balcony. The section Grace was clinging too. She went down with it.

Her wings unfolded on instinct. Fresh pain coursed through the right side of her body. She was able to catch enough air to slow her descent, but every second was a battle.

Grace extended her arms, hoping to find something to catch herself on. Her hands met a railing. She swung against the bars and grimaced through the next wave of pain. Great. Now her ribs were almost as unhappy as her shoulder.

A few seconds was all she got before losing her grip. She didn't get a chance to spread her wings again, landing a moment later on a fire escape hugging the side of an office building. She tumbled down the steps and came to a stop at the next landing.

With shaking arms, she tried to push herself up but slipped and slammed face first into the metal platform. Blood trickled from her lip. Gunshots echoed above her.

Grace grabbed the railing above her head and pulled herself to her feet. A bullet ricocheted off the stairs a few stories up. Leaning out over the railing, she peered up and tried to locate her pursuers. The painfully close sound of the next shot made her jump in surprise. She tumbled off the fire escape.

The world dimmed. More and more passing windows were shattered or boarded up. Fewer flying cars moved through the air, replaced with vehicles that were confined to the pothole-riddled skyways of the lower city.

A slanted roof sped toward Grace. She gritted her teeth and forced her wings to their full length.

Her spinning head and ringing ears made it difficult to process what happened after she hit the roof. She was rolling, falling, crashing. She bounced off the lid of a dumpster and fell one last time. Concrete greeted her at the end of her final descent.

Groaning, Grace pressed a hand to her pounding head. She managed to pull herself into a sitting position, but standing was beyond her. The world blurred. Her eyes stung. She'd never been in this much pain before. Was she dying? Would someone find her before she did?

She wanted to cry, but even that seemed impossible. Her eyes closed. The passing of time became something distant, a hazy concept her mind couldn't grasp. Any coherent thoughts she had faded away.

Chapter Six
Stop, Drop, and Reevaluate Your Life Choices

"Hear that?" Jasper asked as the sound of blasters firing echoed outside the diner. "Must be some higher-ranking Blades if they've got blasters. Most only get guns."

"Which begs the question of why you use them." Holly squeezed her own blaster's trigger, firing a purple beam that knocked a Blade to the ground with a nasty burn on his arm. The team had no qualms using lethal force against the Blades, but Holly generally kept her blaster on a lower setting to reduce collateral damage. "When you're not using knives, that is."

Jasper briefly inspected her gun before taking aim again. "I use the stuff I was trained on."

"What moron trained you on knives and swords?" Holly asked.

Jasper's grip tightened. "Now's not the time." She fired off three shots and looked toward the balcony. More red beams sliced through the air. A few Blades were probably positioned on nearby skywalks.

Thea pulled Dax to the ground. Grace clung to the railing, face twisted in pain. Jasper frowned. Had she been hit?

Another blast tore apart the railing. Grace went over the edge.

"Oh. That's unfortunate." Holly fired again.

Jasper didn't have time to be annoyed by Holly's apathy. She leaped over the nearest table and sprinted onto the balcony. Thea yelled her name as she passed, but Jasper didn't respond. At the edge of the balcony, she jumped.

She landed on a skywalk with a thud. Unconcerned with how the narrow walkway trembled beneath her, she peered over the edge. A straight shot down would be difficult. Maybe Grace hadn't fallen far. Of course, the longer Grace stayed still, the better chance the Blades had of finding her.

Gunfire forced Jasper to keep moving. She dropped from the skywalk to a balcony, and from there leaped to a window ledge. A fire escape below the Bibi's looked promising. Jasper inched to the other side of the ledge and jumped.

Her hands caught the fire escape's railing, and she swung onto a landing. Fresh drops of blood were splattered across the metal. Jasper dropped her gaze to the city below. Traffic and walkways and buildings made it impossible to see far. Grace was nowhere in sight.

Jasper shifted her focus to the closest stream of air traffic. Numbers flashed in her vision, estimating the speed of approaching vehicles and the distance she would fall to reach them. She climbed up onto the railing, selected a target, and stepped off the fire escape.

She bounced off the top of the first car and landed on the next. Its driver honked at her as she paused on their hood to scan her surroundings. A heartbeat later, she jumped out of the flow of traffic and grabbed the top of a hovering billboard. Its thrusters struggled to support her weight, sinking and bringing her a few feet above a skywalk. She let go.

Jasper continued downward into the city, trying to maintain as vertical a trajectory as possible. The sunlight faded, replaced by flickering signs and dim streetlights and long shadows. Five more minutes and a few rough landings brought her into the Blue District.

Her final drop left her standing in a maze of back alleys. A skyway overhead blocked out most of the remaining sun that made it this close to the ground. Anyone she ran into back here would likely be a criminal of some variety.

Not as terrible as herself, of course.

Jasper kept her gaze upward as she walked, searching for signs of Grace's path. A flash of movement brought her attention to a staircase spiraling up the side of a building ahead. Three people raced down the stairs. Red Blades. At the rate they were moving, they had to have eyes on Grace.

The Blades were still a few stories up when Jasper sprinted around the corner and found Grace.

She was slumped over a pile of trash bags. A dumpster—Jasper winced at the dent in the lid—shielded her from view of the main street. Jasper kept moving until she was standing over her. "Angel?"

Grace's eyes fluttered open. "Where am I?" she mumbled.

"Down there!" one of the Blades shouted.

Jasper groaned. "Where are you guys?" she asked into the comms.

"Where are you?" Holly demanded in response.

"Under the interchange of skyways H and 72. Backup would be nice."

"You're on the streets? We're still in the Silver District."

The Blades were almost to the ground. "Fine," Jasper said, turning around. "Guess I'm on my own, then." She drew out the largest dagger she had and threw a quick glance back. Grace's eyes were closed again. She'd sunk back into the trash pile.

The Blades came around the corner. "You're outnumbered, Van Terra," the one in the middle said. He was bald, blue-skinned, and easily the largest of the three. There were more tattoos than just the bloody knife covering his heavily muscled arms.

Jasper twirled the blade around her fingers as she strolled toward the trio. "You're outmatched."

"Are you sure about that?" came a voice from behind her.

Jasper glanced over her shoulder. Three more Blades. She could handle them without much effort if she were alone, but she had an unconscious Grace to worry about.

The blue-skinned Blade from the first group raised his gun. "How long do you think it'll take them to find Alvarez's body?" he asked.

"In this part of town?" the man to his right asked. "Could be a few days." He smirked.

Jasper drew a smaller knife with her free hand. "You gonna shoot, or waste all day talking?"

"A high profile kill like this? I'm going to take my time." This blue guy seemed to be in charge. To his associates, he ordered, "Do what you can to keep Van Terra out of the way, but Alvarez is mine."

A gun went off behind Jasper. She spun and deflected the bullet with her larger blade. In the same instant, the smaller knife left her hand, spun end over end, and landed in the shooter's chest.

As he collapsed, Jasper asked, "What, planning on taking all the glory for yourself?" She turned in a slow circle, waiting for one of the others to shoot. They eyed each other nervously while their leader moved toward Grace.

"Everyone fire at her at once," he barked. "Are you all too stupid for basic strategy?"

Jasper raised an eyebrow. "Avoiding the question?"

Two of the four remaining Blades pulled their triggers. Damn, fights had gotten a lot easier once she earned the kind of reputation that made Red Blades hesitate to shoot at her. She jumped, snatched a couple of throwing stars out of her coat, and sent them flying into one of the men. A third star whizzed past the leader's face, delaying his approach toward Grace.

He glared at Jasper. "I was the one put in charge."

"But you aren't here alone. It kind of sounds to me like you're going to use this to boost your rank, while your teammates here don't get any credit." Jasper shrugged.

The leader raised his gun and fired three shots in Jasper's direction.

The world slowed down. Jasper's heart hammered a steady rhythm in her chest as she watched the bullets approach. At the last possible second, she ducked, moving only slightly faster than the Blades around her, despite the rapid boost to her perception.

The bullets hit a man behind Jasper. He cried out in pain and dropped. Jasper took down the last Blade on that side of the alley with another throwing knife.

"I'm sure we'll all get credit for surviving a fight with you, Van Terra." The leader shot the last two Blades still standing a warning look. "Assuming I get some help, that is."

He was ten feet from Grace now. But enough Blades were down that Jasper felt she could take her eyes off her opponents for more than a few seconds. She lunged and pointed her dagger at the leader's chest.

He fired, forcing her to jump and twist in the air to dodge. She landed between him and Grace, deflected two bullets from the remaining Blades, and attacked again.

The leader stepped aside, but Jasper's blade grazed his arm. He slammed his gun into her head. She staggered. He knocked her dagger aside with the gun and took aim again.

Jasper dropped to her knees, feigning surrender. The leader lowered his gun to follow her head. Before he could decide to pull the trigger, she sprung up and swung her fist into his jaw. Her right fist. The Red Blade slammed into the concrete, unconscious before he hit the ground.

Jasper rose to her feet slowly. Her nails dug into her palms as she fought to hide her dizziness. The last two Blades exchanged uncertain looks.

"Tell me." Jasper tipped her head to the side. "What do you think your chances are of beating me?" She drew her gun and fired a bullet into their leader's shoulder. "Be honest."

"What, you giving us an out?" the Blade on the right asked.

"We'll face a lot worse if we go back empty-handed," the other said.

"You think I'll be nice and give you a quick death?" Jasper shrugged and aimed the gun their way. "I mean, if that's what you want—"

"Whoa, whoa, whoa," the first said. "We'll take the out, thanks." He shot his colleague a glare.

They ran. Jasper's shoulders sagged and she turned around.

As her shadow moved over Grace, Grace's eyes opened again. She tipped her head back. "Jasper?"

"Can you walk?" Jasper asked.

Grace pushed herself to her feet and stumbled forward. Jasper instinctively reached out to steady her, but Grace found her balance first. She craned her neck to examine her right shoulder.

"What happened?" Jasper asked.

"Bullet grazed me." Grace winced. "I can't really move the wing on that side."

"Dax and Thea can fix it." However intricately the cybernetic wing was connected to the rest of Grace's body, those two could figure it out.

"Where are we going now?" Grace asked.

Despite the dull ache in her head, Jasper smiled. "My apartment."

Chapter Seven
Physically I'm Here, Spiritually I'm Lying Face Down in a Puddle in a Fuel Station Parking Lot

There were plenty of lower districts that made great hideouts for people like Jasper. The Blue District and the Tide District were particularly popular choices for villains, but her apartment happened to be in the Gray District. It had the highest crime rates, few police precincts, several non-Blade gangs determined to protect their territory, and a lot of people crammed into small living spaces.

The team left the car in a parking garage that charged exorbitant prices to simply keep vehicles behind a locked gate. Even that sometimes wasn't enough to keep out more daring thieves, but everyone in the area knew who Jasper's car belonged to. And they knew anyone caught near the thing on her cameras would regret it.

After that came a short walk to the apartment complex across the street. Grace's eyes darted back and forth anxiously, as if she expected any one of the people passing by to attack.

"Relax, Angel," Jasper said quietly. "Most of these people are just trying to get through the day. And anyone dangerous is nowhere near a match for me."

"Right." Grace's eyes dropped to the crack-ridden pavement. "I keep forgetting who's protecting me."

They reached the entrance to the building, the exterior of which was covered with once-shiny panels of white metal that were now grimy and graffitied. Jasper punched in the code on the keypad by the gate and led the way inside. "Any criminal in the area with half a brain cell knows I live around here. They stay away from this block. In exchange, the apartment manager doesn't rat me out to the police." They rented under a fake identity, of course, but there was bound to be one officer out there brave enough to go looking for Van Terra if he thought it would win him a promotion.

Holly caught up on Jasper's right. "Can we move faster?"

"Go ahead if you're so impatient," Jasper told her. "I've got to make sure Angel here doesn't pass out." And, truthfully, Jasper didn't want to walk any faster. She was in much more pain than she was letting on.

Holly rolled her eyes but kept pace with Jasper. "What's the plan?"

"What do you mean?"

"For tomorrow. When are we leaving for Starchatter? What disguises are we using?"

Jasper shrugged. "I thought tomorrow would be a 'go with the flow' sort of day."

"So, what are you doing at Starchatter, exactly?" Grace asked. "What does that have to do with Ringmaster and his races?"

Holly shot Jasper a glare. "Do you have a plan on how to handle her? Are we going to lock her up?"

"For starters, she's a person, not a stray animal," Jasper said. "And I hadn't thought that far ahead."

"Right. Why would you do that?"

They reached the elevator. Jasper pressed the call button. "Ringmaster gave out limited information about the races, but he made it clear he would be monitoring the courses extensively," she explained to Grace. "Which means he's going to need to spend some time setting up and scoping out the area."

The doors opened, and the five crammed into the tiny elevator.

"The first race will take place here on Kronos," Jasper continued as the elevator jerked upward. "We found out that a building on the course has a whole floor closed off, as of a few days ago. Signs mention renovation, but they're vague, and security is ridiculous. Every entrance guarded at all times by people who are probably undercover goons working for Ringmaster."

"The renovation is fake?" Grace guessed.

Jasper nodded. "Most likely. The guards won't let us get close enough to find out. And I don't want Ringmaster knowing I'm after him, so violence is unfortunately not an option. Instead, we're going to infiltrate Starchatter. Their offices are directly below the target area. We'll see what we can learn and maybe find another way in."

They stepped off the elevator at the thirteenth floor and made the short walk to the apartment. Jasper flung the door open with as much flair as she could muster through her pain. "Welcome to my home."

"Our home," Holly corrected.

"All you do is complain about the place."

"I just find the decor a bit—much." Holly's fingers brushed the gold frame of an abstract painting stolen from an upper district museum. The rest of the apartment was furnished in mostly black, balanced with some white, and accented with more gold. And hot pink. And anything that caught Jasper's eye while she was out and about.

Jasper gestured to the black couch in the living room. "Have a seat, Angel. Dax, Thea, could you take a look at her injuries? I have no idea how much is cybernetic and how much is good old-fashioned biology."

"I don't really know, either," Grace admitted as she sat down. Pain flashed across her face when she stretched out her wing for Dax and Thea to examine.

Jasper leaned against the wall nearby and carefully traced a finger along the blade of a sword hanging behind her. It was her favorite sword: a huge weapon with a wide blade that excelled at deflecting bullets. Components integrated into the metal made the blade glow pink with the flip of a tiny switch in the darker pink handle. She usually kept it on her but had left it home today to ensure the police wouldn't have a chance to confiscate it when she got arrested.

"Thea, is the extra bedroom still filled with your junk?" Jasper asked.

"It's not junk," Thea replied as she sat down next to Grace. "You wouldn't get anything done without that tech."

"Okay, whatever, is the bed clear at least? Can our guest sleep in there?"

"Yeah, she'll be fine." Thea rested a hand on Grace's shoulder and raised an eyebrow. "There's some pretty complex wiring going on here."

Dax settled in on the other side of Grace and examined the bruises forming on the side of her face. His palms glowed a faint blue, signaling the use of his healing power.

"Is my wing okay?" Grace asked.

"There's not a scratch on the wing," Thea told her. "Whatever the feathers are made of, it's tough. Probably a galaxium alloy." She leaned in and frowned. "There is some damage to some components under your skin, but I think they just need a circuit reset. I can get them working again with my powers alone."

Holly moved to Jasper's side. "I still think this is a terrible idea," she whispered.

"Noted," Jasper replied.

"Are we really going to keep her around until we take down Starr? We have no idea how long—"

Jasper cut Holly off with a sigh. "I don't know. Right now, I'm focusing on Ringmaster. Once I have a better idea of how useful she'll be when it comes to Starr, I'll start thinking long-term."

The blue glow faded from Dax's hands, and he stood up. His powers weren't a cure-all, instant fix. He could get rid of light scratches in seconds, but for anything worse, he essentially sped up the healing process through a form of biological energy manipulation.

Thea stood, too. "Go ahead and see how that feels," she said.

Grace stretched out the wing and winced. "Well, it's better than it was," she said. "Thanks."

Jasper clapped her hands together. "If you two are done, I'll show her to her room."

She led Grace down the hall and opened a door on the right. "You've got your own bathroom, and there's a closet you can go through for clothes," she said. "We keep tons of extras around for disguises. I'm sure you'll be able to find stuff that fits."

Jasper watched Grace survey the room for a long moment before continuing. "We aren't hitting Starchatter until tomorrow morning, so you have a full day to rest."

Grace turned around, surprised. "You're taking me with you?"

"I don't like the idea of leaving you unattended," Jasper said. "I mean, you *can* stay here, if you prefer. But you'd be safer with me than here alone." Holly would throw a fit if Grace did tag along, but the team would split up to do reconnaissance anyway. And once Grace got her bearings, she might actually be helpful.

"I guess that's true."

"We're just infiltrating the building and looking around," Jasper added. "Nothing exciting."

Grace swallowed. "Okay."

"I'll let you get some rest. Holler if you need anything." Jasper pulled the door shut and turned around. She found herself face-to-face with Holly.

"You're going to give me a heart attack one of these days," Jasper said.

Holly's dark expression didn't change. "I sincerely doubt the Blades would find her here."

"I'm not taking any chances," Jasper replied. "Now, could you go be creepy somewhere else?"

Holly rolled her eyes and stormed off to her room. Wondering if Holly's eyes ever got sore, Jasper walked to the kitchen. Thea sat cross-legged on the counter, typing on a laptop, while Dax searched the fridge.

"Does anyone else want to file a complaint about our guest?" Jasper asked.

Thea shrugged. "Honestly, I don't really care."

"Cool. Dax?"

Dax straightened up and closed the fridge door, an assortment of meats and cheeses and vegetables in his arms. "Uh, I guess she seems nice?"

"So, you two don't think I'm the world's biggest idiot for helping her?"

"Not for that reason, no," Thea said.

"You kind of did the same thing with us, didn't you?" Dax dumped his food onto the counter. An onion rolled until it bumped against Thea's foot.

"Yeah. You'd think Holly of all people would get that," Jasper muttered. She left the kitchen and went to her own room—across the hall from the guest room—where she shrugged off her coat and laid down on the bed. Her thoughts were too scattered for her to sleep right now, but she figured she'd at least give her aching body a chance to rest.

Chapter Eight
Alien Abductee Club

Shallow breaths. Light footsteps. Jane Clarke pressed herself against the wall and listened to her parents argue in their room.

Dad's voice filtered through the narrow gap at the bottom of the door. "—don't understand why you're so worried," he was saying.

"It's been two years, and she's still obsessed! We should take her to see someone," Mom replied. "She won't even tell us what really happened."

"She's told us a thousand times."

"Aliens, Will? You really believe she saw aliens?"

"Well, why not?" Dad sounded like he was giving Mom that half-hearted shrug of his.

"Only conspiracy nuts believe aliens are running around kidnapping children."

"I don't see why it's not possible."

Jane carefully unfolded the newspaper page she'd grabbed from the trash bin that morning, wincing at the crinkling sound it made. The crumpled headline was barely visible in the light spilling from under the bedroom door. *Are aliens kidnapping children? Conspiracy theorist says yes.*

"Okay, fine," Mom said. "Let's pretend for a moment it's true. That's all the more reason to have her talk to someone."

"We can't afford a psychologist, or therapist, or whatever you're thinking."

"Her teachers have been telling us for years that she has trouble connecting with other kids. I swear this has only made it worse."

"She does great in school," Dad pointed out, setting off a swell of pride in Jane's chest.

"Grades aren't the only thing that matters."

Mom had more to say after that, but Jane forced herself away from the conversation. She crept to the end of the hall, through the kitchen, to the front door of the apartment that William Clarke and Nancy Van Camp had lived in since they'd had Jane twelve years earlier.

The door creaked as Jane pushed it open. She froze. Her parents' voices continued, barely audible from here. She stepped into the dark hallway of the apartment complex, and the door clicked shut quietly behind her.

Although Mom had praised Jane for devouring book after book when she was younger, pride had turned to concern once Jane claimed she'd seen aliens with her own eyes and took an interest in space politics. She read everything she could find on the Star System Alliance—which, to her dismay, wasn't much.

The Solar System had officially been invited into the alliance nine years earlier, near the beginning of 1955. The Janus System, The Aquila System, and the Ra System had been allies for nearly a thousand years prior.

But Earth wasn't new to aliens, even back then. Plenty of heroes and villains over the span of human history had claimed to hail from other worlds. No one knew the extent of what was out there before the alliance made contact, though. And they still didn't. Despite agreeing to join the alliance, Earth hadn't been given much information on the other star systems.

Some felt Earth didn't have enough say or power in the alliance, while others argued the minimal communication was fine. The alliance was supposed to be for emergencies and occasionally trading resources. Travel between star systems was too difficult and expensive for any concern about aliens coming to Earth regularly and causing problems.

After what had happened to her two years earlier, Jane knew that wasn't entirely true. She reread pieces of the newspaper article while she made her way out of the apartment building. *According to theorist Dawn Teller, New York City is a prime location for these supposed intergalactic bounty hunters.*

Teller asks anyone who may have seen these aliens to come forward and share their story.

The nearest payphone was right behind the apartment building, but the walk felt much farther at night, when the world was dark and every distant sound made Jane jump. This had seemed like a better idea in the daylight.

But she had to do this. She needed answers.

Two years earlier, she'd gone out with Mom to get groceries. It should have been a mundane thing, the sort of day that would blur together with all the other supermarket trips in her memory. But they'd been separated in the crowd near the store. In the desperate search for her mother, Jane wound up in a quiet alleyway behind the building.

That was where she saw them.

The woman had leathery red skin, limbs that were a little too long, and neon green eyes with rectangular pupils that glowed in the shadows. The man was similar in appearance, but his skin was a deep blue and his red eyes held cat-like pupils. They both stood at nearly seven feet, were completely bald, and wore all black.

They spoke to each other in a language unlike anything Jane had ever heard. Then, the woman took a step forward and said, in perfect English, "Hey, kid, you lost?"

"I'm—I'm okay," Jane stammered. She took a step back toward the street.

"Where do you think you're going?" the man asked.

"She looks like an easy target." The woman studied Jane, taking in her ragged secondhand clothes. "Doubt many people will miss her either, by the looks of it."

Whatever they wanted with Jane, she was lucky enough to not find out that day. She wasn't sure if they attempted to chase her when she ran, or if they decided she wasn't worth the effort, but she made it back to the street and into the crowd of New Yorkers. Mom found her a few minutes later.

Now, two years later, Jane entered the phone booth. "Dawn Teller," she muttered as she scanned the newspaper for the phone number that had been printed after the theorist's plea for stories. "Dawn…"

She hadn't even made it halfway down the page when movement outside the booth made her heart skip. Her gaze darted to the shadows at the edge of an alleyway entrance.

A figure stood with their back to Jane. The clothing, the black hood over their head, the height and stature—Jane recognized it instantly. The figure's head turned to the left, offering the briefest glimpse of red skin.

A moment later, the alien woman disappeared into the alley.

Jane dropped the newspaper and flew out of the booth. If the woman was here, the other alien might be, too. Jane could spy on them and find out what they were up to.

When she peered around the corner into the alley, she found it empty, despite the dead end. She took a few cautious steps forward. A shadow passed by overhead. Jane spun around as the alien woman dropped from a fire escape and landed at the front of the alley, her hood down now.

"It is you!" Jane exclaimed.

The woman's head tipped to the side. "Kids like you shouldn't be out so late on their own. Right, Eriph?"

"Didn't your parents ever teach you that?" came a deeper voice from behind Jane. A rough blue hand grabbed her arm.

"Hey!" Jane shrieked, her momentary excitement washed away by terror. "Let me go!"

"Sounds like she recognized you, Ybra," Eriph said, ignoring Jane's frantic attempt to escape his grasp.

Ybra squinted at Jane. "I don't know. I guess she looks familiar. Let's just get her to the hub."

Jane fought more violently now. With his free hand, Eriph pulled a weapon from his belt. It looked vaguely like a gun, but it was too small and rounded, and it was made from a white metal.

"Someone, help—" Jane tried.

Eriph pressed the weapon to Jane's neck and pulled the trigger. An electric pulse shot through her body. The world went black and for a few moments she was entirely unconscious. Then, she was faintly aware of Ybra throwing her over her shoulder.

Through blurry vision, Jane watched Eriph lift a manhole cover and descend a ladder. Ybra followed, moving with ease despite carrying Jane.

A weight sank into Jane's stomach, growing with every passing second and squeezing her chest. She couldn't move. Couldn't protest. Could hardly breathe at all. She drifted in and out of darkness, but the fear never let up.

After traveling through a dim tunnel for what could have been anywhere from a few minutes to a few hours, Eriph paused and pressed a hand to the wall. A section of stone popped out and swung open, revealing a hole for the key Eriph drew from his pocket. The three passed through a hidden door and entered another tunnel.

This was followed by more walking.

Eriph finally stopped next to a large steel door in the tunnel wall. This one slid open to reveal a space the size of Jane's closet at home. A circle of shiny black material covered most of the floor. Eriph tapped a seemingly random spot on the wall, and a semi-transparent glowing rectangle appeared in the air.

"Get her a translator while I set the warp coordinates," Eriph said. A flick of his wrist caused a keyboard covered in strange markings to slide onto the screen. At least, Jane was pretty sure it was a kind of keyboard. She'd only seen pictures of computers.

Maybe she had been unconscious this entire time and everything happening was a strange dream.

Ybra slid Jane off her shoulder and onto the floor with surprising gentleness, leaving Jane sitting, dazed, with her back to the wall.

"You can drop her," Eriph muttered. "She's human, not glass."

"I don't want to lose money over bruises or scratches." Ybra crouched and held up a black sphere the size of a grain of rice in front of Jane's face. "You can swallow this, or I can find a more painful way to get it into your skull."

Jane mustered the strength to glare at her. "How is swallowing that going to get it into my skull?"

"It knows its way around. If you don't have it, you won't understand a thing that's going on."

"I already don't understand." Jane tried to stand, but her limbs refused to cooperate. "I want to go."

"That's not an option," Ybra hissed. "Do I need to get out my knife?"

Jane held out a shaking hand and let Ybra drop the sphere into her palm. "What does it do?"

"You ask a lot of questions, kid."

Jane responded with another glare.

Ybra rolled her eyes. "It's a universal translator. Programmed with every known language. Works for reading and speaking."

Jane would need that if she wanted a chance of escaping and getting home. She put the thing in her mouth and swallowed, grimacing at the metallic taste it left on her tongue. "How long does it last?"

"It's permanent, unless you have it removed or upgraded." Ybra straightened up. "Make sure you're all the way on the warp circle."

Jane tried again to climb to her feet. She nearly collapsed, but Ybra grabbed her arm and kept her upright.

"If she can stand now, the pulse will finish wearing off by the time we get her checked in," Eriph said. "Maybe I should give her another one."

"The port has guards. She won't stand a chance of escaping." Ybra shot Jane a warning look.

Eriph tapped the center of the floating screen, and it disappeared. A deep, monotone voice spoke. "Prepare to warp."

Jane understood the meaning of the words, but she could tell they weren't English.

There was a blinding white light, and the sensation of being flung through space while suspended in the air at the same time. Jane's ribs squeezed her chest, air abandoned her lungs, her stomach twisted. She tried to scream, but she couldn't hear anything except wind rushing past her ears.

Then they were standing on the warp circle again, only it was a different circle, red instead of black and in the middle of a large open space. And Ybra and Eriph were the ones standing. Jane smacked into the ground face first.

White. Pristine. Blinding. Jane struggled to adjust to the bright lights after so long in the dim tunnels. More warp circles in bright colors lined the floor along the wall behind her. A light shot out of one nearby, and a woman with blue skin like Eriph's appeared. She stepped out of the circle as the light faded.

Eriph and Ybra forced Jane to her feet and off the warp. Her head swiveled back and forth as they led her through the place they'd called a port. She couldn't watch the people passing long enough to fully process what she was looking at. There was skin in a wide variety of colors and textures, scales and feathers and tails, people that were too tall or too short. Sharp teeth. Clothing of strange materials. Too many limbs. Things that should have been limbs but were tentacles instead.

Aliens.

Aliens.

Many of the aliens had smaller ones with them. Other kids. Judging by the fear on their faces, they were prisoners, too.

Jane nearly walked into a wall and was only saved by Ybra yanking her back. They'd stopped in front of a large window set into the wall. A man sat at a desk on the other side. He could have passed for human when Jane glimpsed him out of the corner of her eye, but his pale skin was slightly transparent, he had four completely silver eyes, and his proportions were just a little off.

"You two in the system already?" he asked, his voice raspy.

Eriph nodded. "We just need a form and a chip."

"Great." The man reached through the hole at the bottom of the window, a small metal square pinched between two fingers. "Payment will be sent to your account once she's assigned."

"Arm on the counter, kid," Eriph said. "Let him put the chip in."

Before Jane could protest, Ybra grabbed her arm and positioned it where the man could reach. The chip touched the skin of her upper arm.

It burned. Jane cried out as the metal sank beneath her skin. She couldn't think through the pain. All she could do was act on instinct and try to yank her arm free, but Ybra's steel grip didn't give her an inch.

When the man's hand finally moved away, Jane's skin resealed itself over the chip. The only thing left behind was a mild throbbing sensation. Jane gasped for air. Ybra released her.

"Go ahead and take her to the transport craft," the man said.

Her captors pushed her forward again, this time escorting her toward a crowd. Jane's eyes widened. The waiting spacecraft was so shiny it was practically a mirror reflecting the port around it. It vaguely resembled an airplane, but sharper and smaller and sleeker. Guards dressed in black and red led kids up a ramp into the craft.

The guards all had tattoos of bloody knives on their arms. Or necks. Or wrists.

"We'll take her from here," one of them said, nodding toward Jane.

Ybra and Eriph left without another word. Jane found herself scanning the crowd for them as she was led into the spacecraft. That was it? They'd taken her off the streets, dragged her here, and now they were dumping her into the hands of—

"This one seems pretty agitated," a woman said. "Give her a pulse."

Cold metal touched Jane's neck. Another shockwave ran through her. This time, it took longer for her to come to. She was sitting down when her eyes opened. A very human-looking woman sat next to her, the tattoo on her upper arm marking her as one of the guards.

Jane tried and failed to speak a few times before finding her voice. "You look human," she finally croaked.

The woman gave her an annoyed look. "And?"

Jane swallowed. "How did you end up here? Were you taken?"

"My family's been out here for generations."

Jane almost wished she could go back to the disorienting semi-conscious state the pulse put her in. Her heart beat so hard she thought it might explode. Every breath hurt. Her own voice sounded strange to her when she asked, "Where are we going?"

"You nosy kids are the worst." The woman blew out a breath of air. "And we're too close for me to give you another pulse—If I answer this, will you shut up?"

Jane nodded.

"We're going to the city-planet Kronos. Capital of the Janus System. It's a mix of people and cultures and tech from all over, Earth included." The woman glanced at the watch on her wrist. When she tapped the top, it projected a screen into the air, casting a pale glow in the dim spacecraft. "Now, leave me alone."

There were no windows inside the craft, so Jane turned her gaze to the ceiling. Was anyone going to find her? Rescue her? Maybe she could find her own way back.

Then the woman was standing, pulling Jane to her feet with her. They joined the crowd pouring out of the ship. Jane became one of many kids standing in a line.

It didn't take long after that for Jane to realize what was happening. They were getting assignments. Some kids were sent to 'the palace,' others to what sounded like factories or warehouses. The rest were going to a lab.

The assignments were issued by a man who towered over the children and most of the guards, easily standing over six and a half feet tall. His pale skin shimmered slightly in the light, and the opal eyes he swept over the kids were cold. The sharp, hard features set into his face were a little oddly proportioned. They gave Jane the impression that the man had been carved from stone.

He wore clothing that could almost have passed for a business suit, but the blue and black material was strangely slick. It made him look important, regardless. Bits and pieces of conversation around Jane allowed her to piece together the man's identity. It was the governor of Kronos himself, a man named Tyrso Starr.

When he reached Jane, he studied her with a raised eyebrow. "Human. From Earth?"

"Uh…" What did it matter to him? What answer would save her? Jane didn't dare meet his eyes. Her gaze slid up to his cropped black hair before darting to the floor. "Yes."

"Put her in the palace."

Then he was gone, strolling away to determine the next child's fate.

I. STARCHATTER

64

Chapter Nine
Flight or Flight Response

Grace woke up feeling heavy. She groaned as she turned over, wanting nothing more than to sink into the bed beneath her and never come out.

A knock at the door flipped a switch somewhere in her brain. She jolted upright.

"You awake yet?" Jasper called.

Grace rubbed her eyes. "Yeah, I'm awake. What time is it?"

"Uh, you were out almost a full day. Come out when you're ready. I'm making pancakes."

Grace barely caught that last part. She'd been out for a day? She dragged herself out of bed and followed the sound of voices to the kitchen.

She'd caught a glimpse of the kitchen on the way in yesterday—it was just to the left of the front door, and the apartment's open concept made it visible from the living room—but now she had a chance to fully take it in. The space was mostly sleek black surfaces, illuminated by strips of neon lights and the glow of the city outside the window.

Jasper was already dressed in a similar all-black outfit to what she'd worn the day before, and her hair was in its usual high ponytail. Everyone else appeared to have crawled out of bed not much earlier than Grace had. Dax wore simple blue pajama pants and a shirt, and Thea had similar clothes in yellow that were covered in tiny black lightning bolts.

Holly's sweatpants and oversized purple sweater made Grace look twice. It was strange seeing her in clothes that weren't menacing. Or a disguise. She was in the process of running a brush through her red hair.

"Told you she wasn't dead," Jasper said.

"Hurray," Holly replied sarcastically.

The other two were much more polite. Thea offered a wave, anyway. Dax actually said, "Good morning."

Grace returned the greeting as she slid onto a stool at the counter next to him. Jasper slid a plate of pancakes in front of her. "Once we get to Starchatter, the passwords will let Thea add us to the employee database and print fake badges with some names I made up. We'll just need to snap some photos before we leave."

"How do we avoid getting recognized?" Grace asked.

"People know us the way we present ourselves to them," Jasper replied as she crossed the kitchen to the fridge. "With civilian clothing, a bit of makeup and some acting, they rarely give us a second look."

Jasper pulled out a large bottle of Nova Cora and unscrewed the cap. "Once we're in, we just have to avoid drawing attention while we look for a way to access the floor above," she continued. "And keep an eye out for any signs of Ringmaster."

Grace picked up a fork and began cutting into the pancakes Jasper had given her. "When's the race?"

"We'll have three full days to poke around Starchatter. Race is at the end of the last night. After that, we'll follow Ringmaster to the next race location."

"Which is?"

"We don't know yet. He's only announcing locations after the previous race ends. But it'll be somewhere in the Janus System." Jasper took a sip of the Nova Cora and walked to the coffee maker.

"If it's off Kronos, we won't have to deal with Red Blades, right?" Grace asked, unable to sound nonchalant despite her efforts. She doubted she'd be able to go anywhere in Kronos without looking over her shoulder for the gang members, even if she had Jasper at her side.

"Correct." Jasper poured some coffee into a bedazzled mug, then held the pot out to Grace. "Fruit coffee? It's good stuff. Imported from Hatu."

"Uh, I'm good. Thanks." Grace's mind was far from the coffee, or the food on her plate. If she went with Jasper to another planet in the Janus System, she might be able to find a way from there to Earth without worrying about Red Blades or police catching her.

Jasper took another sip from the Nova Cora bottle before adding it to her mug.

"You're going to stop your heart if you keep drinking that garbage," Holly said.

Jasper shrugged as she opened an overhead cupboard and picked out a yellow can labeled 'extreme energy.' The highlighter-yellow liquid inside joined the mix. "Big day today."

"You say that every day."

"And you lecture me every day." Jasper sipped the mixture without batting an eye. "If you're done eating, go get clothes for everyone."

Holly slid off her stool and disappeared into the hallway. Grace put a bite of pancake in her mouth and chewed contemplatively. It wasn't bad, maybe a little bland. But she certainly wasn't going to complain. She'd been given free room and board. And protection from the people who wanted to kill her. She could handle food that wasn't prepared by the palace chefs.

Holly returned a minute later with a pile of clothes and dumped them on the counter. Jasper reached for a shimmery silver top. "Everyone get dressed. Dax, help Holly out with makeup." When she saw Holly's glare, she sighed and added, "Please and thank you."

Grace sifted through the pile. As compact as her wings were, she didn't want to wander around without a jacket to hide them. She settled for a sturdy black one, along with black pants and shoes, and a pale blue shirt that would be easy to cut slits in the back of.

Before Grace left to change, Jasper handed her one of the comm devices the team used and said it was hers to keep. She pointed out the small button that would allow Grace to mute herself when having a conversation the team didn't need to hear.

"Are you sure no one will recognize me?" Grace asked when she returned to the kitchen after changing. The jacket gave her some confidence, but it wasn't enough to shake the fear that anyone who saw her face wouldn't hesitate to report her to the police.

"Starr had you presented a certain way to the public, when you made appearances at all," Jasper said. "We just have to change up your look. Keep a low profile and no one will recognize you." Her gaze moved to where Holly had started on Thea's makeup. "Trust me. I've been doing this for a long time, and I'm one of the most wanted people in the galaxy."

"Don't flatter yourself," Holly said. "You've only been in the public eye for a starcycle."

"Two years is plenty of time to establish my reputation." Jasper sounded indignant, but there was the barest hint of a smirk at the corner of her mouth.

"But you've been doing this kind of stuff before people knew you as Van Terra?" Grace asked her. "How long?"

"Yeah, Jasper, good question," Holly chimed in. "How long have you been a criminal?" Her tone was heavy with suspicion. Grace's brow furrowed. What was that about?

"We don't have time for this. Starchatter employees are going to start showing up to work soon." Jasper grabbed a black coat off a chair at the nearby dining table.

Holly stepped back from Thea and glanced at Dax, who was working on his own makeup in a mirror. "When you're done, could you finish up Thea's eyes for me?"

"Sure thing," Dax said.

Holly turned around and faced Grace. "Hold still," she ordered as she grabbed a new makeup brush off the counter.

Grace's mind wandered while Holly worked, taking her through memories of her lonely days at the Governor's Palace, running through all the ways she could have died yesterday, and reminding her that she was working with criminals now. Villains.

Maybe if Grace were stronger, smarter, tougher, she could find some other way out. She wouldn't need to work with Van Terra. Guilt tightened her hands into fists. Was her survival worth whatever terrible things she was about to get involved in?

Jasper left the room, prompting Grace to swallow her fear of Holly and ask, "You guys have been with Jasper since she became…famous, haven't you?"

"Famous," Holly muttered. "That's one way to put it." She leaned back and assessed her work. "Yeah, she found us well before that. Over a starcycle and a half ago. We did some jobs in secret, trying to take down Starr directly, but they all failed. He's got too many people on his side."

"That's almost four years," Grace realized. "You're all around my age, aren't you?" They would have barely been teens when Jasper found them, wouldn't they?

"Just about," Holly said. "I'm…eighteen, if you want to use Earth years. Thea's seventeen. Dax is sixteen."

Grace had guessed correctly. They were all younger than her, if only by a little. Jasper too, then, must have only been…

"Jasper should have been thirteen when she rescued us from—well, that's not important." Holly's expression darkened as she brushed up the area around Grace's nose.

"Only thirteen. Wow."

"Note that I said, 'should have.'" Holly added a few final touches with her makeup brush before tossing it back on the counter. "Jasper looks the same today as she did four years ago."

"Is she lying about her age now? Maybe she's older than seventeen." It was a bit of a stretch, but Jasper could pass for early twenties.

"I don't know, but she's lying about something. Or, at the very least, hiding information from us."

Jasper returned, putting a halt to the conversation. She'd turned her ponytail into a simple updo and finished the look with a pair of fake glasses. But even with the businesswoman look, it was hard to believe she could be much older than she claimed.

Thea snapped pictures for the team's ID badges, and then they were off. Grace was a little less jumpy on the walk back to the parking garage, but she still found herself nervously eyeing strangers who passed by a little too close for comfort.

"Mia, get me the fastest route to Starchatter offices," Jasper said as the team climbed into the car. Grace once again found herself in the passenger seat.

"Head north toward Skyway G," Mia said.

"That can't be right." Jasper tapped the top of the sphere she'd nestled into the car's console. A holoscreen map popped up. "Mia, I meant the closest office. Why would I want to go to a building on the other side of the planet?"

"Head north toward Skyway G."

Jasper rolled her eyes. "Whatever. I know a way." She slammed her foot on the gas, and they shot through a short tunnel onto the road, where they narrowly missed another car. The driver honked.

"Rerouting," Mia said.

"No, Mia, end the route."

"Make a U-turn."

"Thea, could you turn Mia off for me?" Jasper asked. "Pretty please?"

"Me?" Thea replied, glancing up. "The sphere's right next to you. End the navigation with that."

"While I'm driving? That seems a little dangerous." Another car honked as Jasper made a less-than-legal left turn onto a skyway on-ramp.

"So, you want me to hack into your smartsphere from three feet away and turn the program off?"

"Yes."

Thea sighed but typed something on her tablet. Grinning, Jasper pushed the gearshift forward. The car cut across five lanes of traffic and crashed through a flimsy construction barrier. The accompanying thud wasn't nearly as loud as Grace had expected.

She could only assume the vehicle was, like most that flew around the upper districts, paneled with galaxium that could take a much harder hit before denting. It was expensive to make cars and aircraft that didn't dent while simultaneously keeping them safe for passengers. When you wanted to make something cheap safe, you made it crumple.

As the car soared off the edge of the unfinished skyway, Jasper flipped a switch to activate the thrusters. "How close do we have to be for you to get into Starchatter's system?" she asked Thea. "I'd like our badges to be ready when we arrive."

"Already on it," Thea replied. "We do need to figure out parking. We can't access their garage without the badges. I'm not sure how long it would take me to fool the system without setting off any alarms."

"That's fine," Jasper said. "We'll just have to walk. And by walk, I mean do some light parkour."

"How do you expect Grace to do that?" Holly asked. "She has no training."

Jasper shrugged. "She has wings."

"So?"

Grace lifted her chin. "I can do it."

"It's not as simple as sneaking in through a window," Thea warned. "Avoiding people and cameras usually requires quite a lot of jumping and climbing."

"I'm more than just my wings," Grace replied. "I've got super strength and endurance, too." Not that she had much experience testing her abilities, but she had to start somewhere.

"That's the spirit," Jasper said cheerfully. After a moment, she added, "Of course, a couple of us could go in ahead, grab the badges, and come back. Then we could all go in the main entrance."

That did sound easier, but Grace felt too awkward to back down now. Besides, if she couldn't do something as simple as following the team into an office building, how was she supposed to survive the next few—days? Pentasols? Seasons? Oof. Hopefully, she wouldn't be stuck with these people longer than that.

Grace caught Holly's annoyed expression in the rear-view mirror, solidifying her decision. "No, we can all go together," she said. "I don't want to waste time."

"Great." Jasper pulled back the gearshift. They jerked to a stop, then dropped a solid ten feet. The car thudded against the ground, bouncing slightly.

Grace tried not to look apprehensive as she climbed out of the car. They'd landed on a rooftop near the city's upper limits. It took a moment of scanning to spot the dark blue dome of the Governor's Palace in the distance. Her and Jasper's team were too far west of it to be in the Sky District. They were probably in the Prism District, now.

Jasper walked to the edge of the roof and pointed at the bronze building next to them. "That's the one. Thea, which window do we want?"

"We'll have to go through a few rooms." Thea examined her screen. "Best route starts there." She pointed. "Three over from the right side of the building, two up from the walkway."

Jasper looked at Grace. "You sure you can do this?"

Grace pulled off her jacket and let her wings out. The breeze felt incredible, and it was a pleasant distraction from her from her nerves. "I think I can manage getting to a window." It came out snarkier than she'd intended, and she immediately regretted it.

To her surprise, Jasper laughed. "Great. Follow me." She backed away from the edge of the roof, rolled her shoulders, and tipped her head to each side to crack her neck.

Jasper broke into a sprint. The others followed. One by one, they disappeared over the side of the building.

Grace scrambled to the edge and peered over. Jasper, Holly, Thea, and Dax were balanced on the railing of a balcony below. Mind blank, heart pumping, Grace stepped off the roof to follow. Her wings expanded and slowed her descent. Her right side ached a bit, but besides that, everything worked fine.

She landed harder than she'd intended and had to wave her arms to keep her balance on the railing. Thankfully, no one else seemed to notice.

Jasper assessed the gap between them and the next building. She leaped and grabbed a metal beam supporting one of the overhead walking bridges. Her body swung forward. She let go.

Grace's stomach lurched as Jasper fell ten feet, only to grab hold of a hovering billboard that drifted back and forth between the two buildings. Jasper let it carry her toward Starchatter. The other three followed her path, using other thruster-powered billboards to make their way over the gap.

Wings at the ready, Grace hopped off the railing and glided down to a billboard advertising new flavors of Nova Cora. Once she'd steadied herself on top, she looked to Jasper.

Jasper reached up as the billboard she clung to slowed and prepared to move back the other way. At the last possible second, she jumped to a walkway support beam. She pulled herself up and moved from beam to beam until she could climb over the railing.

Grace waited until her own billboard was as close to the building as it was going to get. Then, forgoing the complicated climb up the interlocking metal beams, she soared over the other three and landed on the skywalk next to Jasper.

Grace glanced around at distant pedestrians while she folded her wings up and pulled her jacket back on. No one appeared to have noticed her quick flight.

A thought struck her. "Has Starr said anything about me in the news?" she asked.

"He's kept his statements vague, but he has asked anyone who sees you to call the police. Just don't let anyone get a super close look at your face." Jasper abruptly leaned toward Grace and stared with an intensity that made her heart skip. "Then again, Holly did pretty good on your makeup. I wouldn't worry too much."

The others came over the railing. Jasper led the way toward their target window. "Finally, a chance to use my grappling hook," she said, a hand moving into her coat.

"Actually, the windows are connected to the building's computer system," Thea said. "They've got some stupid app that people can use to open their office window from their smartsphere. Anyway, I can open the one we want remotely, and it's low enough for us to get up without help. Screen should be easy to pop out, too."

"Ugh. Fine." Jasper's hand dropped as the group came to a stop beneath the window Thea had pointed out earlier. It was close enough to the skywalk that Grace doubted even she would struggle to climb through it.

Thea fiddled with her tablet for a moment, and the window slid open. "Move quick. If I don't close it fast enough, the security system might flag it."

Jasper jumped and grabbed the bottom of the windowsill. With a grunt, she pulled herself up, kicked the screen in, and disappeared into the building. Holly went next, followed by Dax, then Thea. Grace flew the short distance up to the window and followed them inside.

Chapter Ten
Let's Split Up, Gang!

While the window closed behind Grace—the screen already placed back in its frame by Dax—she surveyed the small room the team had entered. It was packed with metal filing cabinets and illuminated only by a red exit sign.

Jasper leaned over Thea's shoulder to study the floor plan she'd pulled up on her tablet. "I don't think we'll run into anyone," Jasper said. "But keep it quiet just in case. Thea, lead the way."

The five crossed a narrow hallway and passed through a few more rooms. Thea guided them to the back of an empty office, where she pointed to the ceiling. "Room above us. Map says there's a vent we can access."

"Sweet." Jasper hopped onto a desk and lifted one of the ceiling tiles.

The team climbed into the space between floors, through a metal grate and a few feet of ventilation shaft, then emerged in a dark room filled with humming electronics and the soft glow of lights on machines. Thea led the way to the corner where a large printer waited. Five badges sat in a tray sticking out from the side.

"Learn your fake names," Jasper said as she grabbed the badges, slipped them into plastic sleeves with clips, and handed them out. "In case anyone talks to you."

The idea of interacting with anyone was nerve-racking. Still, Grace accepted her badge and examined it. Next to her photo was the name Wren Starwright. Jasper pinned her own badge to her shirt, displaying the name Seth Galax.

"Seth?" Thea questioned, raising an eyebrow.

"It's short for Sethany." Jasper started toward the door. "My backstory is that I—"

"Do we really need backstories?" Holly interrupted. "We aren't going to be here that long."

"What are you going to do if someone corners you by the water cooler and asks about your childhood pets, huh?"

"I'll make something up."

"Not all of us are good at coming up with lies on the spot." Jasper opened the door and led the way into the hall. "Dax, where did you grow up?"

"Huh?" Dax asked. "Oh, um, Blue District. No, wait, Gold."

"Dax does fine when he's actually under cover," Holly said. "And no one's going to interrogate us about our lives."

Jasper shrugged. "I'm just saying everyone should keep some ideas in the back of their mind."

The conversation only served to make Grace more nervous. While they walked, she started mentally listing middle districts she could name if asked where she grew up. Or would an upper district be better?

"Now, keep your eyes peeled when we get into the Starchatter offices," Jasper ordered. "Look for anything that could be a way up. Our analysis—"

"My analysis," Thea corrected.

"—showed no direct vent routes. And there are galaxium panels surrounding the area. They'd take a week to get through with brute force, but Ringmaster must have some way of getting in and out."

Distant chatter reached their ears. Jasper's voice lowered. "We're almost to the main office," she said. "We should split up. Five new faces walking in at once might draw attention."

Thea lifted a hand. "I'll go in alone first and see if I can sense anything interesting on the computers."

"Dax and I can scope out the offices," Holly added. "Get a feel for who hangs around what parts."

"Great," Jasper said. "Angel, you're with me."

Grace nodded.

Jasper clapped her hands together. "All right, criminals and gentlethieves. It's showtime."

Thea headed toward the Starchatter offices, followed a minute later by Holly and Dax. Jasper gave them a few minutes more before gesturing for Grace to follow her down the hall.

The office was like a dream: surreal and strange, despite its ordinary appearance, and accompanied by a nagging sense that something bad was about to happen. Grace tried to reason her way out of her apprehension as she walked with Jasper through a lobby. They entered a maze of desks, a huge space filled with people and conversation and glowing screens and stacks of files and ringing communicators and—

"You good?" Jasper asked. "It's a little chaotic."

"Understatement," Grace muttered. She sucked in a deep breath. "I'm okay."

She had no idea what to look for but pretended to carefully examine desks as they passed. She didn't notice the man approaching her and Jasper until she almost crashed into him. Jasper grabbed her arm and pulled her out of his path.

"Sorry about that," Jasper said. "If we could just squeeze past you—"

The man—a pale green, amphibious guy—looked them up and down. "You two are with the intern wave?"

Jasper didn't miss a beat. "Yes, Mr.—" Her gaze moved to his badge. "Omic Attom?"

"Attom will do just fine." Attom reached out a webbed hand to shake one of Jasper's. "You are?"

"Sethany Galax. My dog died when I was seven."

"I—what?"

In a panic, Grace stuck her hand out to distract him. "Wren Starwright."

Attom shook her hand. "You two should get to the conference room. I'm about to start the intro meeting."

"We were just on our way," Jasper said.

"Perfect. Why don't you follow me, then?"

Grace shot Jasper a nervous look as they walked. "What about the plan?" she whispered.

Jasper shrugged. "Conference room's as good a place to look as any," she replied. After tapping her comm's unmute button, she added, "Hey Thea, could you look up Omic Attom for me?" She spelled the name out.

After a few seconds, Thea answered over comms. "He's the head editor of Starchatter."

Grace and Jasper followed Attom into a room occupied by a long black table. The rest of the space was packed with people, none of whom looked much older than Grace and Jasper.

Attom moved to the front of the room. "I'll keep this brief," he said as the chatter died down. "Welcome to Starchatter. You'll mostly be observing. Staff will be available to answer your questions or help you with whatever assignments you have from your professors. If you're lucky, you might get asked to help out and even go into the field."

"And," he continued. "If you're really lucky, and make a good impression on me, you'll get invited to the staff party in a few days."

A few days? As in the day of Ringmaster's race? Grace threw Jasper a sideways glance.

Jasper raised her hand. "Excuse me, where is the staff party being held?"

"Here in one of the back offices," Attom replied. "Room 72-7A. That might not mean much to you now, but those offices are usually off-limits to everyone but management, so this is a very exciting opportunity."

"About as exciting as watching paint dry," a boy to Grace's left muttered. Her gaze flickered to him. He looked human, with a mess of blonde curls and the most bored expression Grace had ever seen.

"If any of you write something good, I'll consider publishing it on our site," Attom continued. "Now get going! You're not getting paid to sit around."

"Actually, we aren't getting paid at all," a girl near the door said.

"All the more reason to get moving! Experience is all you're getting out of this."

Grace and Jasper were swept up in the crowd rushing to get out of the room.

"We should try to get invited to that party," Jasper told Grace as the interns around them dispersed. "If those rooms aren't used much, they'd be the perfect entry point for Ringmaster."

Grace glanced toward the work floor. Toward the chaos. "How are we going to do that?"

"All we have to do is impress Attom." Jasper made it sound easy. "Thea, tell me about room 72-7A."

"Let me pull up the readings I took earlier." After a brief pause, Thea said, "There's strong electrical signals coming from that spot. It could be an access point."

"How difficult would it be for Ringmaster to get back there?" Jasper asked.

"He's probably built his own entrance into the galaxium panels he set up, maybe with simple lock and key. To get to that point on this floor, he would need a Starchatter employee badge with access, or a way to bypass the locks. Not to mention dealing with building security." Thea considered for a moment. "But there might be another way into that room, through vents or the ceiling. From there, he could enter the floor above."

Jasper laughed. "I hope so. The mental image of Ringmaster crawling through a vent is hilarious."

"The party starts about an hour before the first race," Thea pointed out. "I'm not sure why Ringmaster would do that intentionally, or if he even knows about the party."

"I'm going to work on getting an invite," Jasper said. "Keep poking around in the meantime."

"Excuse me, are you two interns?" a woman asked.

Grace and Jasper turned around. "Yes. Interns. Us." Jasper folded her arms. "Can we help you?"

"I'm Karren Kassioson. You've probably heard of me—"

"We haven't," Jasper said.

"Oh." A frown crossed Karren's lavender face. "Well, one of my colleagues was going to help me with an article today, but he's sick."

"What, you want us to help?"

"Don't worry, I only need one of you." Karren's gaze shifted to Grace, making her heart skip. "Oh, you'd be perfect."

A flash of alarm crossed Jasper's face. "We were actually going to—"

"It won't take long." Karren grabbed Grace's arm. Before Grace could protest, she was dragged away from Jasper.

Jasper moved to follow but was cut off by a man carrying a stack of boxes. By the time he was out of the way, Karren had pulled Grace through a doorway, and Jasper was nowhere to be seen.

Chapter Eleven
Mediocre Theft Auto

"Hello?" Jasper weaved through the office, throwing glances at monitors and loose papers as if they might tell her what way to go. Which door did Karren take Grace through? And why did this hallway have so many doors? "What happened to everyone?"

"I got dragged into a tour of the offices," Holly said.

"Is Dax still with you?"

"No. I lost track of him."

Ugh. Great. Jasper paused next to a door and peered through the window. No Grace.

"I'm good," Dax said. "I think. I don't know what's happening. I'm outside now."

Jasper frowned. "Outside the building?"

"Yeah. I guess I'm with a group going to interview a celebrity. Sarena Trench?"

"Great." Jasper moved on to peer into the next room. Still nothing. "Maybe they're finally going to ask her if she's South Siren." Grace's lack of response was making Jasper more anxious by the second.

"Sarena's not South Siren." Holly cut into the conversation with more aggression than Jasper thought necessary. "Your theory makes no sense. Why would a pop star run around at night as a supervillain?"

"And no offense to Sarena," Thea added. "I love her music. But she comes off as, uh…"

"An idiot?" Jasper turned around and stalked down the hallway. "It's an act. The shallow controversies she gets involved in make great distractions."

Grace probably couldn't talk right now without drawing attention to herself. There was no reason to worry. The nerds working here couldn't possibly pose a threat to her, right?

"You sound like a conspiracy theorist," Holly muttered.

"Hang on," Dax said. After a moment, he returned with new information. "We're asking Sarena about the guest list for her pet hekten's birthday party."

"Is that all the people in this city care about?" Jasper tightened her hands at her sides to stop herself from flinging them out in frustration. "Some stupid party for a space octopus?"

"Hekten," Holly corrected. "And everyone's very concerned about his neoworm infection."

Jasper wished Holly could see her rolling her eyes. As far as she was concerned, a hekten was basically a six-legged neon octopus covered in spikes.

Thea chimed in again. "I do have to admit, it's cool that Sarena worked her way up from where she was born in the Tide District."

"Yeah, using her powers—ugh, never mind." Jasper was fighting a pointless battle. Even though Sarena spoke in a higher pitch than the voice she used as South Siren, she was surprised more people didn't notice the similarity. "Thea, what are you doing right now?"

"Some dude asked me to kill an arachnid in the break room for him."

"He couldn't do it himself?" Jasper asked. One of the many trains of thought running in the back of her mind offered up an idea. "Wait, what's his name?"

"Uh, Avior Roiva," Thea answered. "And no, he's terrified of them. He was seriously freaking out."

"Cool. Angel? Can you talk?" Numbers in the corner of Jasper's vision indicated that her heart rate was creeping higher.

"I'm okay," Grace said quietly. "I guess we're doing taste testing? To put together a personality quiz? Do they do any news at all here?"

Jasper hadn't realized how tense she was until the relief sank in. "It used to be more reputable," she told Grace, shoulders sagging. "Now they're just trying to get attention. The more clicks on their site, the more ads they can display, the more money they make. That's going to be the key to impressing Attom."

"What do you need us to do?" Thea asked.

"Keep gathering information. I'm working on a few different ideas. Grace, what room are you in?"

"No idea," Grace answered.

Jasper circled back to the main floor and paused next to a monitor displaying virtual memos. She swiped through them. "Okay, new question: what are you taste testing?"

"Whatever it is, it has solnuts in it," Grace answered. "Karren's slightly allergic, so she can't do it herself."

"'I need help trying weird foods for a quiz,'" Jasper read off one of the memos. "Signed by Karren. Date and time match. Does solnut gum sound right?"

"That sounds disgusting, actually," Holly said.

"Not talking to you. Angel?"

"That sounds right," Grace confirmed.

Jasper found the room number at the bottom of the message. "I'm on my way to you." She returned to the hallway wrapping around the main office.

"Why?"

"I need your help," Jasper told her. And Grace had been out of her sight long enough. "We're going to make Attom some money."

Jasper found the correct door and threw it open. She scanned the room's small crowd for a moment before spotting Grace standing awkwardly in the back corner. With a wave of her hand, she gestured for Grace to follow her out.

"Should I tell Karren I have to go?" Grace glanced back as she reached Jasper.

"Looks like she's got enough help as it is," Jasper said. "If she needs it, she'll just grab another intern. I doubt she even remembers your face." She set off down the hallway, forcing Grace to half-walk, half-jog to keep up.

"The good news," Jasper continued. "Is that we don't have to climb back into the building. We can use our badges when we come back."

"We're leaving the building?" Grace asked. "Where are we going?"

"To make some news."

Grace's eyes widened in alarm. "That sounds—"

"Dangerous? Illegal? Fun?" Jasper didn't wait for a response to her suggestions. "It will be. For me. Don't worry, I'll keep you out of danger. But you'll still be close enough for me to reach if Blades show up."

"Why not leave me here?" Grace asked.

"If Blades catch wind you're at Starchatter and get in, I won't be able to get back fast enough to protect you." There were risks either way. Any decision Jasper made could lead to Blades. But in any case, she wanted Grace near her at all times.

"What about the others?"

"Great fighters, but against a bunch of Blades? I'm your best bet."

"Hey," Holly snapped.

"I hate to admit it, Holly, but she has a point," Thea said.

"Fine. But I don't like the sound of whatever she's up to now."

"It's none of your business," Jasper said. "Thea, I need you to get into Starchatter's netsite. I'm going to send you an article soon, and I want it on the front page."

"What if it backfires and Attom gets pissed at you?" Thea asked.

"Then we'll go from there." Jasper tapped her mute button. Grace did the same.

The two left the main office, took a short hallway to a building exit, and stepped out onto a skywalk. Jasper pulled her smartsphere from her coat and set it on the railing. While she adjusted her hair, pulling it from the updo back into its usual high ponytail, she said, "Mia, show me the top Starchatter articles by Attom."

"Which screen?" Mia asked.

"Mine." Jasper ignored Grace's confused expression as articles popped up in her vision, visible only to her. "All right, Attom, what kind of chaos are you interested in?"

Grace took a step closer to Jasper's side. "What are you planning?"

Jasper scanned the headlines. "I was thinking something involving theft. Probably a car chase. A sword fight would be ideal, but I can never find someone else with a sword." She blinked away the articles and returned the sphere to her pocket. "Quick question: how do feel about riding in the passenger seat of a stolen car?"

Grace sighed. "Sure. Why not? I've already been part of a jailbreak and a robbery."

"You sure?" Jasper lifted an eyebrow.

"Everyone in the city's against me anyway, right?"

Oof. "I wouldn't say that," Jasper told her. "Starr's trying to get you arrested, but people still think you're a hero." At the very least, they were confused about what was going down between the governor and the girl who'd saved him.

"I don't even deserve that. Look, I know you'll do whatever it takes to keep me safe, however good or bad your reasons may be." Grace lifted her chin and met Jasper's gaze with a surprising intensity. "Promise me you won't hurt any civilians, and I'll stick with you."

At least Grace hadn't given up entirely. That was oddly relieving. "Deal," Jasper said. She turned and pointed down. "We're going to hit Skyway 74. I'll make my way down, and then you can follow."

"Why don't I just carry you?" Grace asked.

"You can do that?"

"Uh, yes?" Grace folded her arms. "I'm not weak. It takes a lot of strength just to move my wings. I've carried heavier things than you."

Jasper held back a laugh at Grace's attempt to be intimidating. "I'm heavier than I look," she warned. "And not just because of all the weapons strapped to my body."

"Why's that?"

"I don't have time to get into it now." Jasper jumped onto the railing. "And while I appreciate the offer, I can move faster alone." She stepped forward, off the skywalk and into a free fall. She grabbed a passing banner with her right hand and drew a dagger with her left. The blade sliced through the rope with ease, sending her swinging with the banner.

Setting her sights on a massive red carrier vehicle barreling down the skyway, Jasper braced herself for the drop. The timing had to be perfect. She risked a quick glance back at Grace, who stood on the skywalk railing, pulling off her jacket.

Jasper let go of the banner. Traffic raced toward her. She slammed into the roof of the carrier with a grunt and rolled. As she rose to her feet, Grace took to the air high above.

Grace nearly missed the vehicle when she landed. She hit a few inches from the edge and lost her balance. Jasper grabbed her arm to keep her from tumbling off.

"Thanks," Grace gasped. She tucked her wings in and pulled her jacket back on with shaking hands. "I could use some more flight practice. Starr didn't let me out much."

"We'll find time to squeeze some in." Jasper kept her hand on Grace's arm. With the other, she pointed to a sleek yellow vehicle flying overhead. Her heat vision showed only one person inside. "That's our target."

"How are we getting to it?" Grace asked.

Jasper grinned. *Finally.* She'd stolen the grappling hook nearly a week ago and had yet to find an opportunity to use it. Until now. She pulled it from the belt hidden under her coat and took aim.

"Hold on tight," she told Grace.

Grace reluctantly grabbed Jasper's left arm. Jasper pulled the trigger, and the hook latched on to the bottom of the vehicle. She tightened her hand around Grace's arm for good measure, and then they were speeding through the air.

Jasper swung Grace onto the vehicle's roof before getting to work. Punching in the window with her right fist, tossing the driver onto a nearby skywalk, pulling Grace into the passenger seat—it all happened in a matter of seconds.

"Mia, I need you to make some notes for me," Jasper said as she settled into the driver's seat. "Track my route and record the time."

"Would you like me to give your note a title?" Mia asked.

"That won't be necessary."

"Got it. Your note will be titled, 'That Won't Be Necessary.'"

"I—okay, fine." Jasper wrapped her hands around the wheel. "Let's make this interesting." She jerked the flying car to the right, taking them out of the flow of traffic and drawing a sharp gasp from Grace.

The plan forming in Jasper's mind solidified. "Can you do me a small favor?" she asked. "I need you to hit me as hard as you can."

"What?" Grace yelped.

"Not yet. I'll tell you when. You can throw a punch, right?"

"Yes." Grace sounded indignant.

Jasper's gaze moved to the cupholder between them, to the half empty bottle of Nova Cora. She grabbed it. "Nice."

Grace made a face as Jasper took a sip. "What if they were sick?"

"My immune system's seen much worse." Jasper took another swig and yanked back the steering wheel. The vehicle veered up. She scanned the dashboard. "Doesn't look like this thing has wheels. Hold on tight."

"Hold on to what?" Grace squeaked. "There aren't any handles—"

They crashed into a rooftop plaza. Metal screeched as they skidded across pavement. People darted away from the vehicle—not that any were in their path to begin with. Jasper had noted where all of the civilians were before choosing her landing angle.

Her gaze fixed on her target: a money transaction machine at the edge of the plaza, sitting against the wall of a taller section of the building. There was a security camera pointed right at it. Perfect.

The friction between the vehicle and the pavement slowed them enough to make the collision with the machine relatively painless. Once they'd come to a complete stop, Jasper threw open her door. "Wait a minute before following me," she told Grace. "And play along."

Outside the car, she lifted the hood, drew a gun, and scanned the engine. A few well aimed shots, and the whole thing was smoking in seconds. No real threat, no real danger, just something for show.

Jasper stalked through the smoke and around the car to the smashed transaction machine. The crash had torn it clean open, allowing the wind to pluck free stray jano bills. She smiled and waved at the security camera before she began shoving stray the bills into her pockets.

Around her, people yelled at each other to call the police while pulling out their own devices to record the scene. Jasper flashed them a grin.

A figure moved in the smoke. Grace coughed a few times as she stepped toward Jasper. She'd left her jacket in the car, exposing her wings. "What are you doing?" Her voice was quiet. Shaky. She didn't look scared, though, just unsure of herself.

Jasper waved one of the bills in Grace's face. "I'm taking this money," she said loudly. "I'd like to see you try to stop me."

After a moment's hesitation, Grace lifted her fists. Her hands trembled, but determination had found its way into her gaze. "Hand it over."

Jasper gave her the slightest nod.

Grace swung.

Even though she'd braced herself for it, the hit sent Jasper stumbling backward. She laughed as she rubbed her jaw. Grace was stronger than she'd expected.

People cheered. This was going well. Jasper smirked as she straightened up. "All right, Alvarez, I don't have time for this. Don't bother chasing me." She winked at Grace before turning and sprinting into a narrow walkway between two buildings towering over the plaza. The abundance of pipes snaking around overhead suggested pedestrians weren't actually supposed to come through here. Well, that, and the small gate she'd had to jump over.

Jasper emerged on the other side of the gap at the edge of a narrow, low-speed skyway that was clear at the moment. She stopped and rested her hands on her hips, wondering what the best route back to Starchatter would be. If they crossed here and then went north—

Grace came out of the gap behind her, breathing hard and clutching her jacket. She pulled it back on as she reached Jasper. "What was all that for?"

"My article." Jasper turned to fully face her.

"I mean, why did you have me pretend to fight you?"

"To piss off Starr." Jasper laughed and took a step back into the street. Then another, and another.

A car slammed into her.

Chapter Twelve
This Crime is a Group Project

The car sent Jasper flying into the air.

Grace screamed. She fumbled to press the unmute button on her comm. "Hello? Hello? Can anyone hear me?"

"Is something wrong?" Thea asked.

"Jasper got hit by a car!"

Holly groaned. "Again?"

"Again?" Grace frowned, her alarm put on pause by Holly's response.

Jasper climbed to her feet, smoothed out her coat, and flipped off the car that hit her. The driver honked angrily. Jasper ignored them as she stalked back toward Grace.

The driver's window slid down, and a man leaned out. "Hey lady, you wanna call an ambulance or something?"

"I'm fine!" Jasper snapped.

"Watch where you're going next time!"

"No, you!"

The car sped off. Grace stared at Jasper. "How are you walking?"

"It's no big deal. Just a few bruises and scrapes. Nothing Dax can't handle." As Jasper adjusted her coat, Grace caught a glimpse of torn skin where her sleeve had ripped.

"What's that?" Grace leaned in. Blood trickled from the wound. Yet, underneath the skin, circuitry and wires glinted in the light. Part of her was disturbed by just how much she could see inside, but the rush of adrenaline from seeing Jasper get hit still lingered, overriding most other feelings. "Is that—are you—?"

Jasper held up her hands. "All right, yeah. I'm a cyborg."

"How much?"

Jasper adjusted her sleeve to hide the wound and gestured for Grace to follow her. They set off down the sidewalk in the general direction of Starchatter. "My right arm and left leg were entirely replaced with cybernetic limbs," Jasper explained.

"Really?" Grace asked. "Your arm looks pretty real, other than the wires."

Jasper's pace was much slower than it had been earlier, and she occasionally winced in pain, but Grace decided against saying anything. Any response would undoubtedly be snarky.

"They did a great job of covering it up. It even bleeds, like you saw," Jasper said. "And feels pain. I think they just wanted to see if that was possible. Lucky me."

"Who—?"

"Some of my organs were replaced with artificial ones, too. And there's-basically a computer in my brain. Not super advanced, but it's there." Jasper appeared oblivious to Grace's attempt to ask a question, but Grace had a feeling she just didn't want to answer it. "I've got heat vision, X-ray vision, night vision, a low-quality camera, and I can connect to Mia and transfer files."

"But brain modifications are illegal," Grace pointed out.

"Yeah, weird, it's almost as if people break the law."

"I meant—" Grace sighed. "Who did it for you?"

"Not for me. To me."

"Huh?"

"Never mind."

Grace pressed her mouth into a thin line. If Jasper didn't want to talk about it, she wasn't going to push it. She'd made it this long without getting on the villain's bad side. No sense in starting now.

It took twenty minutes for them to return to Starchatter. It would have been closer to ten, but Jasper took them by a shop to change into clothes that weren't smoky and torn. As they walked the last stretch to the offices, Grace fidgeted with her new jacket, while Jasper dictated an article about their fake altercation to her smartsphere.

Holly waited for them in the lobby, arms crossed. "Seriously?" she hissed. "You couldn't have found an easier way to get Attom's attention?"

"Hey, it worked, didn't it?" Jasper walked past Holly into the cluttered main office. "Wait, did it? I don't know if he's seen it yet."

Holly followed. "Oh, he saw it all right," she said. "He's—"

"Is Sethany Galax here?" Attom's voice carried across the office floor, silencing scattered conversations. Grace's heart quickened.

"Mm, sounds like someone's in trouble," Thea said over comms.

"Dream on." Jasper strolled up to Attom, waving a hand. "I'm here."

"Galax here wrote me an article on a Van Terra incident minutes after it occurred." Attom gestured to Jasper. "The rest of you should demonstrate that level of initiative."

"How is that even possible?" a woman at a nearby desk asked.

"It's called being good at my job," Jasper told her. When the woman's eyes narrowed, Jasper stuck her tongue out at her.

"Van Terra and Grace Alvarez are hot topics, everyone," Attom continued. "The public wants to know what happened after they broke out of jail. Put out headlines on them that will make people click." He turned around and started toward his private office. "Now, get back to work!"

Grace leaned toward Holly. "Did you see the article?" she whispered.

"Yeah," Holly answered. "You?"

Grace shook her head. Holly pulled out a red smartsphere and tapped the top. The Starchatter netsite opened on the holoscreen.

"You won't believe what crazy stunt Van Terra pulled ten minutes ago," Grace read.

Jasper appeared at Grace's right. "Pretty good, right?"

A Nova Cora ad popped up in the center of the screen as Holly scrolled, blocking the text. She groaned. "Look at this. They post garbage headlines like, 'Did Sarena Trench really go on a date with so-and-so?' And then they take five ad-littered pages to tell me that no, no she didn't, and I just wasted my time."

"Holly, that's brilliant," Jasper said. "I'm going to start a rumor that Sarena Trench went on a date with Van Terra."

"You're Van Terra, idiot!"

Jasper put her hands on her hips. "Well, the hospital just called with the results of your IQ test. They were negative."

"Why would I go to a hospital to take an IQ test?"

"I hate to interrupt. Really," Thea chimed in over comms. "But I took new readings and found some hardware above us that's been sending and receiving messages. I tried intercepting them, but the signal's too heavily encrypted. I'll need physical access to get anything useful."

"What's the plan, then?" Holly asked. "If we don't have a solid—"

"You worry too much," Jasper told her. "I'm putting together a plan. Now, someone turn on the news. I want to see if Starr has anything to say yet about our little skirmish."

"Governor's channel," Thea said. "If he says anything, it'll air there first."

Jasper held up her smartsphere. "Mia. Channel zero."

While an ad for some sitcom broadcast played on the holoscreen, Grace's comm crackled slightly in her ear. Quietly, she heard Dax say, "IQ tests can't even *be* negative."

The ad ended and the screen cut to Starr, who was in the middle of addressing a crowd of reporters. "Rewind to the start of the broadcast," Jasper commanded. The footage jumped back to Starr stepping up to his podium. Jasper laughed. "Oh yeah. He's upset."

Grace's brow furrowed. "He doesn't look upset to me."

"Trust me. He's good at hiding his emotions, but I know—well, if you pay close attention to his facial expressions, his movements, it's obvious." Jasper grinned. "And the fact that he's addressing it so quickly means he's concerned."

The Starr on the holoscreen began to speak. "As many of you already know, an incident involving Grace Alvarez and the villain Van Terra occurred less than an hour ago," he said. "While many have found it upsetting that Alvarez was taken into police custody in the first place, I must remind you that she did escape her cell of her own free will, with the assistance of Van Terra. Her motivations and plans are still unknown."

"Has he said publicly why I was arrested?" Grace asked quietly.

"He's kept it vague," Jasper replied. "Said that the authorities can't disclose why you were arrested, but that you are a threat and should be treated as such."

Grace wanted to believe that no one would listen to Starr, but why shouldn't they? He'd kept her hidden away for years. The fourteen-year-old girl they'd seen save his life was long gone.

"Ha. He really thinks he can turn everyone against you." Jasper turned the broadcast off and slid the sphere back into her pocket. "You're not his puppet anymore. He has no control over your actions, or what people think of them."

Puppet. Was that all Grace had been? A puppet being called a hero?

"Hey, you should come up with a name," Jasper said.

Grace blinked. "What?"

"A hero name."

"Why?" Grace asked. "I'm not a hero. Besides, everyone knows my identity already. What would be the point?"

Jasper shrugged. "It sounds cool. We could throw together an outfit, too."

"Thanks, but I'll pass."

"Okay, soft maybe. Sounds good." Jasper wandered over to the nearest cluster of desks and started poking around. "All right, everyone get back to work."

Holly leaned toward Grace. "She's a criminal mastermind, but she's also a dumbass teenager," Holly muttered. "She likes to see how far she can take jokes without getting caught, she wings everything because she can't be bothered to plan ahead, and she's impulsive. And god knows what kind of damage she's done to her brain over the years."

Grace frowned. "Why do you still work for—with her, then?"

"I ask myself that every day."

Chapter Thirteen
How To Shoplift At Mota Mart And Not Get Caught

It wasn't Jasper talking loudly in the kitchen that woke Grace, nor was it the pots banging together. Despite crashing hard her first day in the apartment, she'd struggled to sleep through her second night and found herself lying awake long before Jasper's team began to move around the apartment.

Still, by the time she mustered the energy to get dressed and enter the kitchen, the others had already made good progress on preparing for their second day at Starchatter. Thea had two smartspheres and a tablet on the counter in front of her, and she alternated between typing on the tablet, reading text on the first smartsphere, and watching a video on the second. Holly had some over-ear headphones on, blasting technopunk music loud enough for everyone else to hear. Dax sifted through a pile of clothes while taking occasional bites of a nutrient bar.

"—and that's why I'm banned from the diner on Quartz Way," Jasper was saying. "And I still haven't figured out their secret sauce recipe."

Grace slid onto the stool next to Thea. "What's she talking about?"

Thea shrugged. Dax glanced up from the clothes. "Sorry," he said. "I was listening for a minute, but I got distracted trying to find a work shirt."

Holly slid off her headphones. "Probably drank too much Nova Cora. She's running purely on sugar and caffeine and whatever other garbage she's managed to cram into her body since waking up."

Jasper paused and leaned toward them. Grace froze, wondering if she'd be upset at Holly's comment.

"Coffee, Angel?" Jasper asked.

"I'll just have water, thanks," Grace told her. "Were you saying something?"

"Was I? I think I was just going through the plan for today." Jasper chugged the rest of her drink and slammed the mug down on the counter. "All right, I want everyone in the car in ten minutes!"

"She'll level out in about five," Dax assured Grace.

Chaos followed, a hurried mix of cleaning and throwing on shoes and tossing things into bags. Grace somehow wound up with a piece of toast in her hand. Dax put makeup on her face before darting off to the back of the apartment. Someone's smartsphere blasted a news station that was repeating Governor Starr's statement from the day before. Thea juggled more devices every time Grace glanced her way.

Finally, Jasper gave Grace a push toward the door, and then they were all leaving. Today's drive to Starchatter was less terrifying, though at this point Grace was starting to think she'd become desensitized to near death experiences.

"I'll try to scan Attom's messages and put together a list of everyone who's invited to the party," Thea said as they walked into the office.

"Great," Jasper told her. "Holly, Dax, keep an eye out for anyone suspicious."

"Besides us, you mean?" Holly asked.

"Duh. Angel, stick with me. We're going to—"

"Galax!" Attom shouted from the other side of the office. "Come here! I want to talk to you."

"Ha, someone's in trouble," Jasper sang.

Holly rolled her eyes. "Jasper, you're Galax."

"I know that!" With an indignant huff, Jasper left to meet Attom at the edge of the room.

Holly sighed. "Either she's in trouble, which means the whole job is in trouble, or Attom has taken a legitimate interest in her work."

"That would be good, right?" Grace asked. "He might give her an invitation to the party."

"Anyone who likes Jasper has something seriously wrong with them," Holly muttered. She headed for an aisle of cubicles. Dax and Thea dispersed as well, leaving Grace to stand awkwardly by herself. In a panic, she ran to catch up to Jasper.

Before she could get Jasper's attention, Jasper disappeared into Attom's office, and the door clicked shut. Grace paused outside. Should she go in? She settled for waiting. Hoping to appear casual, she leaned against the wall by the door.

The conversation on the other side was just loud enough to reach her through the door. "Your article got us more views than everything else published yesterday combined," Attom said.

Thea had helped with that. She'd spent the prior afternoon pushing the article on as many social media pages and netsites as she could manage. But the article was enticing enough that it had gained a fair bit of momentum on its own, too.

Attom continued. "I have a new project I want to test, and I think you could make it work. And if it doesn't, you're just an intern, so I don't have to take any responsibility."

"Gladly," Jasper replied. "What is it?"

"People today don't want to read long articles. They're scrolling through their feeds waiting for something to catch their eye, and they want to see videos. Something they can watch mindlessly. We already have videos on our site—hacks, tips, product reviews—but I'd like to branch into more video journalism."

"And what do you want me to report on?"

"Whatever. Just make it informative. And entertaining. And concise. By journalism, I mean anything that people will spread around."

Jasper agreed to the task, and that seemed to be the end of the conversation. Grace took a step back from the door.

It swung open a heartbeat later. "I've been promoted," Jasper bragged. "I need you to be my camera person. We're making a video for Starchatter, and I'm going to use it as a cover to get supplies for the party."

"Supplies?"

"Yep." Jasper set off toward the exit.

No sense in asking for an explanation. Grace jogged to Jasper's side. "I don't have any filming experience though."

"All you have to do is hold the camera." Jasper grabbed a coat off the rack by the entrance. One she definitely hadn't been wearing when they arrived. Seeing Grace's look, she said, "Hey, it's not like they'll need it until the end of the day."

Shaking her head, Grace backtracked to the main conversation. "I think there's more to camera work than just holding the thing."

"We aren't trying to win any awards here. Don't worry about the cinematography." As they stepped onto the skywalk outside, Jasper added, "We're not going far. If I remember right, the Mota Mart is about a three-minute walk from here. We'll grab a camera there."

"Steal one, you mean?" Grace asked.

"You catch on quick."

They reached a set of stairs at the corner of the building and headed down. Every few seconds, Jasper cast Grace an unreadable glance. Was she concerned? Suspicious? Whatever it was, it wasn't helping Grace's nerves.

Finally, Jasper said, "If it makes you feel any better, I've robbed this Mota Mart before. A legitimate break-in-in-the-middle-of-the-night-and-take-expensive-stuff robbery."

Grace's brow furrowed. "Why would that make me feel better?"

"I learned something," Jasper explained. "The manager is using the store as a front. His incoming shipments are used to smuggle illegal weapons into the city. Like the high tech blasters you might see some of the gangs using."

"Are you trying to justify shoplifting?"

Jasper shrugged. "Is it such a bad thing if we take some from a guy like that? I doubt he'll even notice. It's pretty small compared to his other income sources."

They left the staircase and headed down a slanted skywalk. Grace considered for a moment. "I guess I don't really care about that. It's not going to fix the problem, though. He'll keep selling weapons," she pointed out as the walkway leveled beneath them.

"I'd love to shut his operation down at some point. But there are countless more just like him all over Kronos. I only have so much time on my hands."

Ahead of them, the walkway widened. An open-air parking lot jutted out to their right. To their left, the wide entrance to the Mota Mart let faint music and chatter spill out into the city. People moved in and out with shopping carts.

By the time it occurred to Grace to ask why Jasper cared about shutting down illegal smuggling operations in the first place, they were walking into the Mota Mart, and the colors and sounds quickly distracted her. Crammed shelves and towering displays formed a colorful maze of products that looked worryingly easy to get lost in. There were miniature flashing billboards over some of the aisles advertising specific products, while screens built into the sides of shelves played commercials that were hard to hear over the music. Grace didn't recognize the song that was playing, but she caught Jasper mouthing a few words.

Jasper grabbed a box off an electronics display and popped it open. She handed the camera to Grace and set the empty box on a shelf as they passed.

"What if someone—?" Grace started.

Jasper cut her off. "Cameras aren't monitored. We're dressed nice. Security's focused on the exits," she said. "Can you figure that thing out?"

Grace fumbled with the camera and found the power button. The battery was charged to halfway. "I got it. What are you doing, exactly?"

"Top seven secrets you didn't know your local Mota Mart was hiding," Jasper said. "We need to hit the pet department, electronics—oh, and here's the snack aisle." She veered to the right and stopped in front of a wall of packaged foods, all covered in bright labels written in various Janus System languages. The universal translator that had been given to Grace at some point before her memory began gave her access to an overwhelming amount of information.

Grace tore her gaze from the shelves and pressed the camera's record button. "Ready when you are."

Jasper launched into an explanation of how the store was changing dates on packaging instead of replacing expired products. Grace thought she was making it up at first, but Jasper pointed out that the wrapper colors were slightly off around the numbers and demonstrated that the right chemicals—Grace wasn't sure why she happened to be carrying vials of them in her pockets—could take off the fake dates.

Jasper examined the label on a bag of candies. While Grace momentarily had the camera pointed away from her, she shoved them into her coat.

Next was electronics. Jasper gave a brief overview of the store's scammy credit program—secret number two—followed by a demonstration of their poor quality "better value" electronics—secret number four. Yes, four. The demonstration resulted in smoke pouring out the side of a gaming console.

Jasper also picked up a smartsphere box. Only the box. She abandoned the device on a random shelf. Then, she swiped a candle and some matches.

This was followed by a trip to the pet department.

"Number seven, your local Mota Mart manager doesn't keep track of their fish," Jasper said to the camera as the entered the dim aisle, illuminated only by the neon lights in the aquariums. She gestured for Grace to film the fish tanks.

Grace focused on the floating bodies of fish that were dead or close to it, internally grimacing. Maybe instead of shutting down the smuggling operation, she could persuade Jasper to help her rescue the poor things.

Jasper, meanwhile, moved to the other side of the aisle, to the cages that contained a variety of crawlers. "It's cheaper not to worry about health problems unless someone points them out." She lifted a cage lid and reached her hand in. Grace's eyes widened in horror. She was pretty sure some of those were venomous.

When Jasper pulled her arm back out, a fluorescent green armored tarantula was perched on the back of her hand. "What's this guy a fan of?" she murmured. She examined the tag next to the cage. "Ooh, meat-eater."

She held up the empty smartsphere box and nudged the arachnid inside. The box went into her coat. Jasper straightened up. "Next stop, the back rooms."

Grace lowered the camera and turned away from the fish tanks. "What if they catch us?"

Jasper laughed. "I can handle them. All we need is footage of the weapons and then we'll get out."

"Also, you skipped some numbers."

"Doesn't matter. The whole point of the video is exposing the manager's smuggling operation. Everything else is a bonus."

Grace eyed Jasper's coat as she followed her out of the aisle. The only sign of the stolen merchandise was a couple of slight bulges, and Grace didn't think she would have noticed if she weren't looking for them. "I don't suppose you're going to tell me what the spider or the candy is for?"

"You'll see."

Grace and Jasper walked to the back of the store, through a door marked "Employees Only," and into the back rooms. Jasper grabbed a clipboard off a table they passed. Holding it up, she waved and smiled to a group of employees standing near the entrance to the break room. A few returned the gesture. None appeared alarmed by her and Grace's intrusion.

"What was that for?" Grace whispered.

"Act like you belong. Makes people think you do," Jasper answered under her breath.

The two entered a stockroom filled with shelves that reached the ceiling far above, all packed tight with unopened boxes. Jasper tipped her head back to scan them. "Now we just have to figure out what's real product, and what's illegal inventory." Her gaze stopped on a box to her left, about fifteen feet up. "Here we are."

"How can you tell?" Grace asked as she lifted the camera.

Jasper tapped the side of her head and started toward a rolling ladder that sat farther down the aisle. "X-ray vision," she said as she pulled the ladder into position. Once up the ladder, she pulled the box off the shelf, drew a pocketknife from her coat, and sliced the top open in one swift motion. "You filming?"

Grace nodded.

Jasper removed a sleek black blaster from the box and held it up. "Oh, this one's nice. Lotta firepower. Probably made in a factory on Hatu. See, this would ordinarily never get through a spaceport checkpoint. Illegal all over the star system."

The barrel on the weapon was longer than on any other blaster Grace had seen. Granted, she hadn't seen very many in real life—yet—but all the ones she'd seen in broadcasts hadn't looked like this illegal one, either.

Footsteps sounded in the aisle on the other side of the shelf. Grace struggled to keep the camera steady in her shaking hands. "Are we going now?"

The blaster dropped back into the box with a thud. "Hang on, I want to see if I can find drugs."

"What if we get caught?"

"Relax." Jasper pushed the box back onto the shelf and hopped off the ladder. "We may need to go down a few rows."

Grace followed Jasper to another shelf, where she showed off a box filled with bags of glittering blue powder to the camera. Grace had no idea what it was, but Jasper made it sound like serious stuff.

More footsteps sounded nearby, louder this time, as Jasper closed the box. Seeing the panic on Grace's face, she said, "Okay, we're going now. I'll put the camera in my coat if it'll make you feel better."

Grace handed her the camera, but she didn't feel any sort of relief until they were out of the back rooms.

"See, we're home free," Jasper said. "We got everything we needed, and—oh, wait."

Grace's heart sank as Jasper grabbed a giant bottle of Nova Cora off a display and shoved it under her arm. "There's no way someone won't notice that," Grace said.

“I’ve done this millions of times. Trust me, no one’s going to stop us from strolling out—”

“Excuse me, miss?” An employee in the store’s red shirt and dark blue pants approached, waving his hand. “Could you come with me?”

Chapter Fourteen
How I Got Caught Shoplifting At Mota Mart (Gone Wrong) (Storytime) (Not Clickbait) (Police Called)

Would it be best for Jasper to fight her way out of this? Or to find some way to deal with the employee without causing a scene? Was he a low-level worker who didn't get paid enough to care if she got away, or would he chase her?

"I'll meet you by the entrance," Jasper muttered to Grace.

"No, she needs to come too," the employee said. He was short, but heavily muscled. Orange skin. Bald head.

Jasper shook her head. "Listen, she didn't do anything. I—"

The guy folded his arms, and Jasper caught the briefest glimpse of the Blade tattoo under his short sleeve as the fabric shifted. Uh oh. She'd assumed the store manager was working with whatever small gangs hung out in the area, not Starr's personal army.

"Fine, she can go," the Blade said.

"No," Jasper replied. "Never mind. You're right. She should come too."

Grace's brow furrowed. "What?"

"I mean, you're an accomplice this point." Jasper tried to give Grace a look that said, "trust me."

"Suit yourself. Things are going to go the same for you either way," the Blade warned. Jasper's eyes narrowed. What was the plan? Take them to a back room where more Red Blades were waiting to kill two of Starr's biggest targets?

The Blade stepped toward Jasper and held out a hand. "Oh, and we've got metal detectors hidden at the entrance," he said, voice low so that only Jasper could hear. "A gun, three daggers, a couple of throwing stars...you weren't expecting a fight, were you? Go ahead and hand those over now."

Jasper's gaze flickered to Grace. "Or what?"

"You don't have to die today, Van Terra. Make things easy for us, and you could walk away."

With a sigh, Jasper pulled out her weapons and slammed them into his hand one by one. He tucked them into his jacket as he received them. Jasper tried to avoid meeting Grace's gaze, but their eyes locked for a heartbeat. Had Grace picked up on the fact that this had nothing to do with shoplifting? The confusion in her eyes was shifting to fear.

"How long did it take you to recognize us?" Jasper asked.

"You have more important things to worry about." The Blade gestured for Jasper and Grace to follow him.

Once they were away from civilian witnesses, they were as good as dead. Jasper wouldn't be worried about fighting the Blades if she were alone—there were plenty of potential weapons in a supermarket, if you knew what you were doing—but she had to account for Grace, who was the real target here. Starr may have wanted Jasper dead for years, but he clearly considered Grace's elimination to be a more urgent matter.

They needed to get out before the Blades could trap them.

They were almost to the back rooms. Now or never. Jasper was fast, but they were expecting that. She needed something better than fast.

She needed a distraction.

"I'm sorry I took the soda," Jasper said loudly. "I'll put it back, if you like."

The Blade gave her a weird look. "The Nova Cora? You do realize we don't care—"

Jasper held the bottle up in the air. "See? I'll put it on that shelf." She pointed to her right.

"If you insist, I guess," the Blade muttered. "Makes inventory easier. But no funny business." He leaned toward Jasper "There are more of us around than you think."

"I'm just putting it back. Don't even want it." Jasper did want the Nova Cora actually. She'd been looking forward to a little treat after all her hard work. Ugh. She slowly set the bottle on the shelf, keeping both hands visible. "See?" She rested an elbow on the shelf and leaned into it slightly. "No problem."

"Dragging this out won't help you—"

It was easy for Jasper to put more of her hidden strength into the shelf without letting on, bracing her cybernetic leg against the floor while her corresponding arm pressed against it. She gave the Blade a casual eyebrow lift as she leaned. One moment, everything was calm.

The next, the shelf was toppling.

"Hey!" The Blade shouted.

"Oops." Jasper grabbed Grace's arm. "Sorry 'bout that." She delivered a swift kick to the shelf in front of her, sending it falling in the opposite direction. "Let's go, Angel!"

Jasper flipped through her vision modes as they ran. Heat. X-ray. Shouts of alarm warned people to get out of the aisles in the path of destruction. Still, Jasper was prepared to race in and grab anyone not scrambling to safety fast enough, if she needed to.

The rest of her focus was on their pursuers. Her arm shot out to the right. She knocked a display to the ground, sending fruits rolling across the floor toward a snack aisle.

"What was that for?" Grace asked, eyes wild, chest heaving, hands shaking.

"Don't worry about it!" Grace didn't need to know about the squad of Blades approaching from that direction, just out of view. She was scared enough as it was.

The machinery and computer chips they'd jammed into Jasper's brain all those years ago hummed as they kicked into overdrive. The world slowed down, and Jasper's limbs slowed with it. The sound of shelves crashing to her left became distant. She focused on other sounds: a glass bottle dropping and shattering on the floor, a smartsphere buzzing, a gun going off.

Jasper's hand tightened around Grace's arm as her head turned in the direction of the gunshot. The timing had to be perfect. Three, two, one— she shoved Grace forward. The bullet zipped between them. She pulled Grace back. The world sped up.

They caught up with the wave of toppling shelves. Two security guards—more undercover Blades, undoubtedly—emerged from an aisle on their right to block their path.

Jasper pulled Grace to the left, into a toy aisle. "Faster!" she shouted. The shelf next to them began its fall. The patch of light on the other end, their exit, shrank. Jasper blindly grabbed at the items tumbling from the falling shelf, hoping for something that could do damage.

The shelf was mere inches from the top of her head when she and Grace burst out on the other side of the aisle. They were greeted by three Blades.

"Stay back," Jasper warned. "Or face my—" She held up her hand and found she'd grabbed a yo-yo.

The Blades laughed and lifted their blasters. Jasper pushed Grace down as they fired. The yo-yo string looped around her finger. She swung.

The closest Blade yelped in pain as the toy smacked into his fingers with surprising speed. His blaster clattered to the ground. Grace started to get back up.

The other two Blades fired again, each taking a different target. In a panic, Jasper shoved a dazed Grace back to the floor. The blast meant for her grazed Jasper's arm. She staggered back and sucked in a sharp breath. Her skin burned.

Jasper smacked the first Blade in the head with the yo-yo before he could pick his weapon back up. Then she hit a second Blade, sending the woman staggering backward and knocking her blaster out of her hands.

The third Blade fired at Jasper. While she dodged, he aimed at Grace, who was making another attempt at pushing herself up off the floor. The yo-yo wrapped around his wrist. Jasper yanked hard, and he stumbled toward her. One punch to the jaw sent him to the ground. Jasper kicked his blaster away from him, tossed the yo-yo aside, and pulled Grace up into another sprint.

An exit sign glowed up ahead. Jasper slammed into the metal door beneath it with more force than she'd intended. "Mia, summon the car!" she yelled as she flung it open.

"I'm sorry, could you repeat that?" Mia responded through the smartsphere in Jasper's pocket.

"Summon! The! Car!" Jasper pushed Grace through the doorway.

"I'm sorry, could you repeat that?"

"Ugh! Never mind!" Jasper pulled the door shut in time to shield herself from two bullets. The dents they left told Jasper the door wouldn't hold up against a third.

Red and yellow lights lit up the fire escape Jasper and Grace stood on, accompanied by sirens. Jasper glanced over the railing. Police cruisers were coming their way, fast. Jasper reached into her coat.

"Why would the Red Blades call the police?" Grace asked.

"They've got their cover as store employees," Jasper reminded her. She pulled out the camera. "But if we could get footage of them with their weapons—"

"Jasper!" Grace yelped. "We have to go!"

Jasper turned the camera on and pointed it at the door. "Back up, they're going to come through fast—"

"Police are coming up!"

Jasper glanced down. Officers were sprinting up the fire escape. Damn. "All right, up we go then." Still clutching the camera, she ran. Grace kept pace at her side.

Jasper turned the camera on her face. "I'm being chased by the police right now! But before I make my escape, be sure to subscribe to Starchatter so you never miss an update!"

Grace stumbled to a halt. "They're coming down, too." Footsteps thundered above, warning that another wave of officers were coming to meet them.

Jasper stuffed the camera into her coat and peered over the railing. Only one way out. "Jump!" she told Grace.

"What?"

"You have wings! Jump!"

"What about you?"

Jasper picked Grace up and tossed her over the side of the fire escape. "I'm right behind you!" As she climbed up onto the railing, the door a level down opened. A gun fired. Jasper dropped from the fire escape, and the bullet whizzed over her head.

Grace pulled off her jacket as she fell and stretched out her wings. Her descent slowed, allowing Jasper to catch up. Jasper grabbed one of her arms and pointed to an open window below. "Can you get us into that building?"

Grace nodded. She managed a surprisingly clean shot. They flew in through the window, crashed into the ground, and tumbled awkwardly across the floor. The lady whose office they'd invaded shrieked.

"Sorry about that," Jasper told her as she stood up. "We'll just, uh, show ourselves out."

While Jasper and Grace made their way out of the office building, Jasper sent the footage to Thea to edit and upload. After that, she led Grace on a longer route back to Starchatter to avoid trouble. Neither of them spoke during the walk. Jasper had too much on her mind to try for conversation, and keeping quiet would be safer, anyway.

When they entered the building, Jasper finally said, "Obviously, if I had known Blades were running the place, we wouldn't have gone there."

"How did you not know?" Grace blurted. "You knew about the secret weapons, and drugs—"

"I thought they were selling to smaller gangs!"

"You—"

"Galax!" Attom's interruption drew a small sigh of relief from Jasper. "Nice job on the video. The footage was enough for the police to go back and seize the drugs and guns. You've been cleared, and those blasted Red Blades have been dealt a nice blow."

"That fast?" Grace muttered.

Jasper was too distracted to reply. She folded her arms. "I'm just glad I was able to help take the guy down." Starr would be upset by the loss of one of the Blades' operations, but with viral video evidence, he couldn't intervene in the arrests without looking suspicious.

"You don't have to pretend to care about that stuff," Attom replied with a dismissive wave of his hand. "But the dead fish was a nice touch for our bleeding-heart viewers. I'm sure that helped our view count."

Jasper restrained an annoyed expression. "Of course. I'm glad my contributions to Starchatter are valuable."

"They sure are. In fact, I want you at the staff party tomorrow night. You've earned it."

"Thank you."

"I'll get you your invite," Attom told her. "It comes with a special keycard to access room 72-7A, and it lets you into the offices after hours. Keep up the good work."

Once Attom was gone, Jasper turned to Grace. "See?" she said, a grin on her face. "Mission accomplished."

"So, how long until I can go outside without people trying to kill me?" The spite in Grace's tone took Jasper by surprise.

"We've got access to Ringmaster's hideout." Jasper paused. "Well, access to the room below it. We'll gather information, and from there, make a plan to catch him."

"Sounds like you're pretty far out from taking Starr down." Grace's hands were still trembling as she folded her arms. "Which is the whole reason I'm with you."

"You're with me because I'm the only person keeping you alive," Jasper replied, sharper than she meant to. She immediately regretted it. With a wince, she added, "Angel, I want Starr gone even more than you do, trust me. But he's powerful. We have to take away his support system before we can take him down."

"You keep saying you'll catch Ringmaster and take down Starr and handle all these other guys, but I'm going to need more than vague statements."

"Or what?" Jasper asked. "You're welcome to leave whenever you want. But I don't need to tell you anything." It frustrated everyone around her, but she'd always made up her plans as she went along. And it had always worked out. For the most part, anyway. Besides, there were some things you just couldn't plan for.

And Grace wasn't leaving any time soon. She had strength, but no street smarts, and she had to know by now she wouldn't last long on her own.

Still, Jasper felt a twinge of guilt as she and Grace returned to the offices to meet back up with the rest of the team.

Chapter Fifteen
Embrace Destruction

Keeping track of Earth time with limited access to the world outside of the Governor's Palace wasn't easy, but Jane had always been pretty good at math. If her numbers were right, it was January 9th, 1968—a week after her sixteenth birthday—when she finally snapped.

She'd worked so hard during her time as a servant to make her superiors trust her, to persuade them she wouldn't beg for help or run away at the first chance she got. There was no solid escape plan, just a few vague ideas and the certainty that there had to be some way out. So, she took her time, forced herself to smile and nod and dig her fingernails into her skin so hard they drew blood. Whatever it took to keep even a hint of irritation or frustration or pure anger from showing.

Then, she would return to her room and snap stolen tablet pens in half. Rip up any paper she got her hands on. Scream in the shower.

When it was really bad, when the list of commands and criticisms of her completed tasks and lectures about moving too slow became too much to take, Jane stopped listening. She did try, but her mind refused to cooperate. It was somewhere else. Unaware. Unfeeling.

And that's where it all went wrong.

"Jane! Are you listening to me?" Her supervisor, a North Kronosian relative of the Starrs themselves snapped his fingers in front of her face. "Maybe if you stopped daydreaming, you could get dishes washed in a decent amount of time."

Jane couldn't stop her response from spilling out. "Maybe if you paid me, I'd give a damn!"

Other servants working on food prep nearby—they were slaves, really, but Starr preferred the first term—looked on in horror. A few gasps cut through the thick tension in the kitchen.

"What was that?" the supervisor hissed. What was his name again? Jane was supposed to know. She'd tried to learn. But she couldn't seem to keep much in her brain these days.

"I don't care anymore," Jane told him. "Do your worst." She'd been here four years. Maybe a change of scenery would be good. Maybe she could find some way to escape while she was transported to wherever servants were sent when they were no longer wanted at the palace.

The supervisor barked out a cold laugh. "You're going to regret that. I almost feel sorry for you." He nodded to a couple of guards nearby and pointed at Jane. "This one. Labs."

Jane expected the guards to escort her out of the kitchen, maybe with some forceful dragging if she refused to move her feet. But one moment she was standing, the next a pulse gun touched her neck, and then she was out cold.

This time there was no in-between, no vague sense of moving from place to place, no floating in darkness. Jane woke up lying on the concrete floor of a cell. She sat up and pulled herself to the bars.

"Hello?" she yelled. "Where am I?"

"Shut up!" a raspy voice called back from somewhere else in the cell block.

Jane's hands tightened around the bars. "Not until I get an answer!"

"You're in Sky Labs," another voice said. "Now shut up. Some of us are trying to rest."

"We're all as good as dead, anyway," someone else added.

Jane regretted saying anything at all as arguments broke out in the cells around her. She laid down on her back and stared at the ceiling until the voices faded and eventually, the world turned from near black to a dull gray.

Guards in plain gray uniforms came. They brought her food and water and refused to answer her questions. All she was able to gather was that she was waiting for her turn to be experimented on.

She used the meal schedule and the changing light to keep track of both Kronos time and Earth time. Days passed. Weeks passed. Months passed. On what Jane was pretty sure was Christmas morning, she was finally pulled from her cell.

The assortment of aliens in lab coats barely acknowledged her presence as guards strapped her to a table. To them, she was nothing more than a number.

"ID?" a woman's voice asked.

"Seven-dash-sixty-dash-alpha-mu," another replied.

A man set a smartsphere on a nearby table. "Begin recording," he commanded. "This is test number one of serum version twenty-eight for the Advanced Cybernetics Integration Project. Human trials." He tapped the sphere and scrolled through the text it projected. "This time, we will administer the serum three days before replacing limbs with the ones we've manufactured."

A four-armed scientist with shiny black skin and long antennae extending from his face moved to stand over Jane. He held a tablet in one hand, a pen in another, and a smartsphere in the third. With his fourth, he picked up a mask connected to a machine through a tube and placed it on Jane's face. She tried to pull away, but it was no use.

"Trust me, you're going to want to be unconscious for this," he said as he fastened it to her face.

"What is this?" Jane asked. "Anesthesia?"

No one answered. Something pricked her left arm, and she glanced down to find a needle in her skin. A dark blue liquid raced through a tube into her blood. She grimaced. It was freezing, and oddly heavy in her veins.

Her breathing quickened. "What is that? What's in my blood?" A fruity scent filled the mask. Her eyes locked onto the monitor on the opposite wall. The date and time blurred. Was this real? Was she still in her cell dreaming?

Jane woke up screaming. In excruciating pain. Her blood was ice and her skin was on fire and her heart hammered against her ribs. A monitor beeped, faster and faster, and then it flatlined.

She woke up again. Now, everything was cold. Something under her skin was cold. Her right arm was gone. The monitor on the wall hummed so loudly her skull trembled. There was an unbearable ringing in her ears.

The next time she woke up, her arm was back, but it was wrong. It felt frozen, and when she tried to lift it, it was heavier than it should have been.

"Beginning test of limb functions," someone said.

A hand took Jane's right wrist, and a blade pressed against her arm. Blood welled on her skin. Another voice spoke. "Blood vessels are functioning."

"Prepare her for the second round of brain operations," a man said as someone bandaged the cut. "If that's successful, we'll move on to limb reinforcements and artificial organs."

The next wave of darkness was longer and colder. Jane came out of it slower, with blackness receding from her vision gradually while lights danced and fuzzy people moved around her.

The date on the monitor—and some quick math—told her it was January 2nd. Her seventeenth birthday.

"Heart rate and breathing are steady. Activate the brain system."

Sharp pain fired through Jane's skull. Her vision flashed white before fading back to normal, save for the jumbled numbers and text and symbols scrolling along the right side of her vision.

"System online. Transferring time data."

The text disappeared. The current Kronos time appeared in the bottom right, semi-transparent.

"Okay, we're going to have you try a few things for us," a green-skinned woman said, not lifting her gaze from the tablet she held in webbed hands. Was she talking to Jane? "See if you can make the time disappear and reappear in the corner of your vision."

"What—?" Jane struggled for air. "Where—?"

"Just make the clock disappear—"

Jane's hands tightened around the edge of the table. "Back away!" she gasped at the scientists crowding around her. "I can't breathe."

"Heart rate's spiking," someone warned.

Jane tried to pull away from the crowd pressing in, but there was nowhere to go. She yanked a hand back and found metal cuffs around her wrists. The chain connected to them clinked against the table. "Please. I can't—"

"The subject needs to calm down before we attempt mental and physical tests," a deep voice ordered. "Put her back in her cell. We'll give her sedatives before bringing her back out."

Jane wasn't quite sure what happened after that. Did they give her more anesthesia? A pulse? Did she black out the memory of being dragged back to her cell? The next thing she knew was on the frigid concrete floor in the fetal position, every inch of her body screaming in pain.

The pain was too much for her to even think for the first few hours. After that, it either lessened, or she adjusted. Either way, she was finally able to process her surroundings. Someone had chained her to the cot in the corner of the cell. Metal shackles hung around her wrists.

Jane sat up, gasping and shivering, and held up her hands. She couldn't point out any visible difference between them, but something about her right hand was...wrong.

She turned her attention to the clock in the corner of her vision and tried to mentally command it to disappear. Nothing happened. She tried harder. It flickered.

What else did they put in her head? They couldn't have gone through all that trouble for a clock. Jane climbed to her feet. The dull ache that had settled into her body sharpened. She hissed in pain but kept herself upright.

Footsteps and voices signaled that people were coming. Jane tugged on her chains. The cot moved a few inches with surprising ease. Hadn't that thing been heavier before?

Jane moved her gaze to her right arm, desperately searching for some imperfection that would prove it wasn't her own. She frowned. There were faint scars near her shoulder. They'd cut above her tracking chip. If it hadn't been a dream and they'd really replaced her arm—she shuddered at the thought—then that thing had to be gone.

Two scientists, accompanied by six guards—a bit excessive, Jane thought—stopped in front of her cell. "Be ready to pulse her," the scientist on the right warned as one of the guards unlocked the door.

The other scientist—a man with tan scaled skin and thin white hair sprouting from his head—spoke to Jane. "It would be in your best interest to cooperate with us," he said. His deep voice was the one that had ordered a break so Jane could calm down the last time she was in the lab. "Help us with our tests, and we'll get you some better living conditions. You have the opportunity to be our equal, not our prisoner."

Jane eyed the guards. The cell door easing open. The chains that bound her to the cot. What was the worst they would do if she tried to escape and failed? She was valuable. They put time and money into her. What did she have to lose?

The first guard entered the cell.

Jane lunged, yanking her arms forward. The cot flew off the floor and slammed into the guard, knocking him to the ground.

Her skull hummed.

The next guard started toward her in slow motion. Jane moved to attack again and found herself moving slow, too, though not quite as slow as the guard. She picked the cot up off the floor and threw it at him, marveling at how easy the metal bed was to lift. The guard and the cot tumbled to the ground. The chain broke free of the leg it had been attached to and snapped somewhere in the middle.

Now Jane had a chain dangling from each wrist. The clock in her vision disappeared, replaced by numbers flashing on top of the approaching guards. Heights? Weights? She didn't have time to decipher them. She swung.

The chains worked as whips, easily knocking aside the guards. The two scientists scrambled out of Jane's path. The deep-voiced one pulled out a communicator. "Code rogue seven—" he began.

Jane knocked the device out of his hand, shattering it on the concrete floor, before turning and sprinting out of the cell block.

She collided with walls a few times as she sped around corners. She had never run this fast before in her life, and she wasn't entirely sure whether it was adrenaline or whatever they'd done to her. Though, the more she moved, the more she suspected it was the latter.

Faces of guards came and went. Jane was left with a vague recollection of throwing them into walls or striking them with her shackled wrists or simply racing around them. Whatever metal they'd used to chain her up was weak, cheap stuff that was already heavily dented and bent by the time she found what she hoped was an exit.

Twenty guards had gathered around the door to block her. Definitely an exit. The only weapons any of them had were pulse guns. Were the scientists really that insistent that they not damage her?

Jane stumbled and slammed into the wall at her left. She glanced at her right wrist. The shackle was nearly broken. She hit it against the wall once more, and it fell to the floor in two pieces, along with the chain. Jane picked up the chain and spun it around a few times, testing it as she moved toward the guards.

The world slowed again. Jane worked her way through the guards on instinct. Had the scientists intended her to have this much power? Or was some of her new strength an unexpected side effect of whatever they'd done to her body? Her brain?

Jane reached the thick, metal doors and found them locked. Of course. Her gaze flickered to the box to the right of the doors. She turned and knelt by the nearest collapsed guard. "Key card," she demanded.

He laughed and pointed his pulse gun at her. "As if I'd—"

Jane slammed her left wrist shackle into his head and ripped his badge off his shirt. Guards stirred around her. One reached for her ankle. Jane kicked the woman's hand aside, darted to the door, and swiped the key.

As she pushed open the doors, an intercom overhead announced, "We are entering lockdown. Please remain where you are."

Jane tossed aside the key card. Too little, too late. The doors slammed shut behind her.

The exit spat her out in a dark tunnel. She ran as hard as she could, blindly taking twists and turns and ladders until she spotted light coming down up ahead. For a time, she could hear distant shouts and footsteps, but they'd faded by the time she came to a stumbling halt in the faint neon glow.

The light came through a grate, and it was accompanied by sounds of traffic. Jane examined the ceiling more than ten feet above her. While she assessed the best way to get up, she slammed her left wrist against the wall until the other shackle broke off.

The clock returned to her vision. This time, when Jane willed it to disappear, it did.

She positioned herself under the grate and jumped. To her surprise, her fingers grazed the metal. Her excitement at her unexpected strength was cut short by the pain that shot through her body when she landed and tumbled to the ground.

Jane curled up and forced herself to breathe through the pain. Once it had faded to a dull ache, she stood up and tried again. This time, she was able to wrap her hands around the bars of the grate.

Now that she was here, she wasn't sure what to do next. She swung forward, and the grate lifted an inch before dropping back into place. She swung again, harder. When the grate lifted this time, she pushed her legs through.

Jane wound up lying on top of the grate beside the opening, groaning in pain. She untangled herself and slid it back into place. When she stood, a few people walking by gave her strange looks, but most didn't even bat an eye at the ragged girl who'd pulled herself out of the sewers.

She'd made it.

She was on the streets of Kronos.

Chapter Sixteen
According to an Online Quiz,
I Have the Same Personality Type as God

The race was scheduled for early morning. Very early morning. Suns-not-up-yet early morning. Well, sun, technically. Kronos was on the far side of the star Gemma now, so Myni wouldn't be visible for a couple more months. Or a season. Or whatever time system this stupid planet used.

Even after all these years, Jasper still ran through everything in Earth time. Keeping the Earth clock and calendar in the corner of her vision certainly wasn't going to help her break that habit anytime soon. What good did it do her to know that Earth was entering August of 2020?

She rubbed her forehead and took another sip from the sweet blend of coffee and Nova Cora in her mug. *Focus. Get it together.* After her Mota Mart video took off, Attom had piled more and more tasks onto her plate, and he'd even requested that she stay late the night before to finish them.

Jasper had done harder things in worse condition, but she would have preferred to get some more rest before the big day. She'd been forced to settle for the brief evening nap she'd just woken up from an hour earlier.

The race was essentially in the middle of the night, and the Starchatter party started late. Hence, the necessity of Jasper's plan to clear out the office so that the team could get into Ringmaster's hideout.

Plus, she had her other plan to worry about.

Jasper leaned against the wall of the living room while the others made their preparations for the final night at Starchatter. Holly stood in front of the mirror that hung on the wall, making minor adjustments to her facial features so that no one at the office would recognize her.

Grace frowned as she watched Holly. "Your shapeshifting," she realized.

"You thought I was human?" Holly asked, lifting an eyebrow as it changed from red to dark brown. She'd also narrowed her nose and shortened herself by a couple of inches.

"You're not? I mean, Jasper and Thea and Dax are." Grace's gaze flickered to the couch where Dax and Thea sat. "They are, right?"

"They are," Holly said. "I'm West Kronosian."

Many members of the species had shapeshifting abilities, to varying degrees. Holly was far better than most. Probably one of the few that could not only take on a form that appeared entirely human, but also maintain that form long-term.

"West Kronosian?" Grace asked. "Like the Fayes?"

Holly's gaze darkened. Before she could respond, Jasper stepped forward. "Everyone ready?"

"Ready to get crammed into a tight space with Dax and Grace?" Thea asked.

"Aw, it won't be that bad." Jasper pulled her fake glasses from her pocket and slid them on. "Good team bonding."

"Why is Grace coming with us, again?" Holly asked. "You've had her by your side this whole time."

"I'm the only one with a party invite."

"Attom likes you. You could have persuaded him to let you bring her."

"He likes my work," Jasper muttered. She took another sip of her drink. "Look, after the run-in with the Blades at Mota Mart, I think it's best we keep her out of sight. Once we head to the next race location, we won't have to worry, but I need you three to protect her in the meantime."

"Maybe she should learn to protect herself." Holly folded her arms.

Jasper sighed. "Great idea. Think we can train her up in the next five minutes?"

Holly's eyes narrowed.

Point made, Jasper continued, "We don't have time for this right now. Now, come on. Time to go."

Holly grabbed a tie, the last piece of the suit that made up her catering uniform, as she and the others headed for the door. Jasper followed them out.

They parked in the same roof lot they'd been using the past few days. It was emptier now than it was in the mornings before the workday.

With the last rays of Gemma still kissing the atmosphere—though the sun itself had dipped beneath the horizon—the sky above was a vibrant purple dusted with stars that shone bright enough to be visible, despite all the city lights. The lights below were a shifting blend of neon colors, reflecting off nearby skyscrapers and flying vehicles to make a sort of artificial aurora.

"Let's stand up here for a minute," Jasper said as the team climbed out of the car. "We're a little early."

Thea and Dax moved to sit at the edge of the roof with their legs hanging over the edge. Grace watched them, looking a little apprehensive, but the expression faded as she settled down next to Thea. Holly stood behind the three, and Jasper moved into position at her left.

Grace glanced toward Thea, hesitation on her face. Finally, she asked, "So, Thea, do you need tablets and stuff to be able to access your power?"

Thea shook her head. "If I'm close to a device, I can almost always manipulate it using my mind. I'm not the only technopath in the Janus System, though, and programmers are always coming up with new ways to keep us out." She reached into the pocket of her jacket and pulled out a shiny gold smartsphere.

"They usually use complicated strings of code meant to delay us," she continued, tossing the sphere up into the air and catching it. Her gold eyes glinted in the ambient neon. "Anyway, computers and smartspheres help me work faster and let me do multiple things at once. And they let me access systems that are farther away." The sphere went up again. "Even when it looks like I'm just typing, I'm usually interfacing with the code mentally, to some degree." She caught it.

Dax leaned forward and waved a hand. "My turn? Are we explaining our powers to the new girl?"

Grace shrugged, a small smile crossing her face. "I wouldn't mind. Do you do anything other than healing?"

"I have a form of bio-energy manipulation," Dax explained. "I'm not exactly healing; I'm speeding up the body's own healing process."

"Oh," Grace said. After a moment, she added, "The blue glow is pretty neat."

Dax beamed. "Thanks!"

Grace glanced over her shoulder at Holly, but her gaze didn't linger, and she didn't ask any questions.

"Your wings are pretty amazing," Thea said. "There's no code for me to interface with, but I can sense all the wiring and circuits that make them work with your body. I've never seen anything like it."

"Thanks." Grace kicked her feet idly. "I just wish I was better at using them. Starr never gave me any time to practice flying." A wistfulness overtook her expression, and Jasper pursed her lips. It would be hard to get Grace some flying practice in a city full of people that wanted to kill her, but maybe once they were off Kronos they could make time.

Holly folded her arms and glanced away from the three, her usual annoyed expression sliding into place.

Jasper elbowed her. "Come on," she said quietly. "She's pretty likeable."

Holly huffed. "I guess."

Holly had warmed up to Thea and Dax pretty quickly, though it might not have looked that way to outsiders. Jasper hoped that even if the walking embodiment of teenage angst continued to fight her at every turn, she'd at least start showing some kindness to Grace. In her own Holly-esque way.

Jasper looked up one last time at the glittering violet-blue sky. Then, with a glance at the time and a heavy sigh, she cracked her neck. "All right, crew. It's about time we headed in."

Grace, Dax, and Thea climbed to their feet, and the team set off. Skywalks and narrow metal stairways led them to the office building.

As they approached the exterior doors, Jasper glanced at Holly. "Where'd you leave the food cart you and Dax stole this morning?"

"A storage closet down the hall from Starchatter's entrance," Holly replied.

"Great. You guys grab that. I'll head in to the party and look for the gap."

They split up after entering the building. Jasper headed to the back offices alone, to room 72-7A, where the badge Attom had given her let her join the crowd filling the room. She found a spot near the wall that gave her a good view of the ceiling.

Thea's scans—Jasper wasn't sure what exactly she'd been scanning. Something about local signals? X-rays maybe?—had picked up an anomaly in this vicinity, but Thea hadn't been able to get close enough to this room to be precise. All she'd been able to discern was that there was a gap in the galaxium wide enough to let an average-sized person squeeze into the ceiling, and that it was somewhere in this room.

"You all right, Galax?" Attom walked up to Jasper, a drink in hand. "You look like you're thinking."

"You could say that." Jasper switched to X-ray vision. Her eyes swept the ceiling, taking in the thick layer of what had to be galaxium panels. They'd been nailed into place, preventing them from simply being slid aside by someone with unusual strength.

"Have you thought about your future here at Starchatter?" Attom asked.

"I'm a bit busy having a midlife crisis."

Attom laughed. "I don't think you're the right age for that."

"Good point." Jasper sighed. "I'm too old."

"Jasper, you got a location on that gap yet?" Holly asked over comms. "I need to know where to park the cart when I come in."

It was hard to read Attom's expression in X-ray mode. Ignoring whatever look he was giving her, Jasper leaned to the right to scan the far end of the room.

"The food being brought in looks good," she said. "Especially the fruit platter."

"The gap's above the fruit?" Holly asked.

"You a fan of fruit?" Attom asked.

"Yes," Jasper said.

"Help yourself to some." Attom waved a hand toward the food table. "You should see the genetic engineering they're doing with citroids these days."

"Sounds exciting." Jasper switched back to her regular vision, gave Attom a lie about going to look at drinks, and headed across the room.

"How long until you evacuate?" Holly asked.

"Half an hour," Jasper replied.

"I'm sorry, did I hear that right? Why do we have to wait so long?"

"You're not the one who has to sit in a cramped space," Thea added under her breath.

"I have some other plans to lay out," Jasper said. "I might be able to do twenty minutes."

"So, you're going to overcomplicate things as usual?"

Jasper heard Holly's voice twice this time. Once in her ear, and an echo somewhere behind her. She turned around as Holly pushed the food cart into the room.

"I need that fruit table out of the way," Holly said. "Thea needs to be as close as possible to get a preliminary look at Ringmaster's tech."

"Got it." Jasper made a beeline for the fruit table, noting that one of the ceiling tiles above it was slightly out of place. "Before you start those, Thea, I need you to send me a photo of—what was his name? Avior Roiva?"

"Why do you need—?" Thea started.

"Just do it." Jasper stopped short and rested her hands on her hips. If she moved the table herself, someone was bound to ask what she was doing.

"Excuse me, Miss Galax?"

Perfect. Jasper smiled as she turned. "Karren, right? Karren Kassioson?"

"That's me!" Karren smiled. "I was wondering if you would be interested in co-writing an article with me—"

"I would love to talk business with you. But could you help me with something first?" Jasper gestured to the fruit table. "I'm doing an article on the effect of a room's layout on, uh, the energy level of the different...brain types."

"Oh, I'm an expert on brain types!" Karren exclaimed.

"Of course that's a thing," Jasper said. "I mean, that's why I'd love your help. I thought we could put the fruit table in front of the drinks."

Karren nodded as if that made complete and total sense and picked up one end of the table. While Jasper grabbed the other, Karren asked, "What brain type are you? I have a quiz on the Starchatter website you can take. It's the most accurate."

"I'll have to try it," Jasper said. The table lifted into the air. "Say, I heard you have a mild solnut allergy."

"I do," Karren said as she began taking steps backward.

"'Mild' meaning you wouldn't die if you ate one, right?"

"No, I just get a rash. I can take medicine, but lunberries help, too."

"Oh, good," Jasper said under her breath.

"What was that?" Karren asked.

"I heard the Electroswinger has a new lunberry drink! That would work, wouldn't it?"

"Yeah, I guess so."

Seeing Karren's odd look, Jasper quickly added, "My cousin recently found out she has a solnut allergy, too. We've been trying to figure out what remedies actually work."

Karren and Jasper set the table down in its new position. "How are we going to do the article, then?" Karren asked.

"Oh, huh. Well, how about you stand here and take notes on people we can use later?" Jasper suggested. "Since you're an expert, I'm sure you already know everyone's…brain type."

Karren beamed. "I do."

"Great. Do that, then. Say, would you like a drink? I can bring you one."

"Sure!"

Jasper made her way to the drink table, greeting other employees here and there and ignoring periodic glares from Holly, who guarded the cart to make sure no one found the rest of the team hiding inside. After careful consideration, Jasper picked a warm glass filled with dark liquid and reached into her coat.

The solnut candy quickly melted into the hot drink. Jasper handed it over to Karren before searching the crowd for the guy who matched the photo Thea sent. She spotted Avior standing with a large group, holding a sandwich.

Her next stop was the table with the sandwich platters. The tarantula eagerly left its box to sample the various meats laid out. While it began its feast, Jasper drew a match from her pocket, swiped it on the wall, and used it to light the candle she pulled out with her other hand.

"How do you know this is going to work?" Holly asked.

"I don't," Jasper replied as she set the candle on the table. "But statistically speaking—"

"Never mind. Just get everyone out of here."

Jasper bumped into Avior with enough force to knock the sandwich to the floor. "I'm so sorry!" she exclaimed. "I would get you another one, but I'm in a hurry." She moved past him and continued through the crowd. To her comm, she said, "Holly, could you keep me updated on Avior?"

"He's just staring sadly at his sandwich on the floor—oh, wait, he's moving. He's headed for the table."

"Great. And Karren?" Jasper circled around to the drink table, dropped to the ground, and crawled underneath the tablecloth.

"People are starting to gather around her. She looks mildly distressed. Wait, what did you do?"

"What's happening?" Dax asked. "Is everyone okay?"

"Don't worry about it," Jasper replied. "Thea, do what I told you to do with the sprinklers. Holly, make sure the fire stays away from the cart when that table flips." She crossed the gap between the drink table and the dessert table.

"The what?" Grace yelped.

"Don't worry about it." Jasper was under the sandwich table now. Her hand slipped out from under the tablecloth and reached for Avior's approaching shoes.

Moments later, Avior shrieked in fear and jumped back from the table. Well, he tried to. His right shoe had mysteriously wound up tied to the table's leg, causing the whole thing—flaming candle included—to crash to the floor.

Before the flames could touch Avior, Jasper sliced through the shoestring with a knife and gave him a push away from the table. She popped up on the other side. Smoke detectors triggered the alarms, which blared over the sounds of shouting and people stampeding toward the door.

The sprinkler system also suffered a strange malfunction, which only encouraged people to move faster when Jasper casually pointed it out.

Jasper paused next to Holly. "Put out the fire, then follow us outside."

"I really appreciate you giving us these very important instructions along the way, rather than explaining the entire plan in advance," Holly said sarcastically.

"You're welcome." Jasper followed the crowd out of the offices.

The party regrouped outside the building. Jasper lingered at the edge of the crowd to make sure no one was stupid enough to stay behind or reenter. It only took a minute for Holly to appear at her side.

"Stand guard and make sure no one tries to go back in," Jasper told her quietly.

"Where are you going?" Holly asked.

"I'm following them."

"You think they'll go somewhere else?"

"Why not?" Jasper shrugged. "Party's still in full swing. We'll regroup. And I'll make sure no one leaves to come back here," she lied.

Holly folded her arms. "You sound confident."

"When do I not?" Jasper jogged over to where the party crowd was shaping into a loose circle, leaving Holly behind to keep watch. "Are the rest of you good?" she asked into the comms.

"Besides a few cramps, we're good," Thea replied. "Are you ready for me to disable the fire alarm?"

"Let me get everyone away from the building first."

"Be fast. I stopped the alarm from alerting the fire department, but someone else might call."

Jasper moved to Attom's side. "Looks like everyone made it out. What's the plan?"

"Someone should be here when the fire department arrives—" Attom began.

Jasper pointed to where Holly was standing. "She said she would handle it."

"One of the caterers?"

"I mean, we're paying them to take care of things while we have fun, right?"

Attom laughed. "I like the way you think. A few people were talking about walking to the Electroswinger. I think it was Karren's idea." He leaned forward. "Maybe once we're there, we can discuss appointing you to a more permanent position at Starchatter. There's been a lot of controversy around your journalism style, so I'd love to have you stick around. Keeps eyes on us. Which keeps revenue up."

"Great." Jasper smiled, but as soon as Attom turned his back, her expression fell. At least she wouldn't have to put up with him much longer. Which reminded her...

"Thea, could you do me a favor when you get a sec?" Jasper asked.

"Besides the dozen favors I'm already doing for you?" Thea replied.

"All I need is for you to get me backdoor access to the Starchatter netsite so that I can post whatever I want from my smartsphere."

"Oh, is that all?" Thea sighed. "I'll see what I can do. *If* I have time."

"Great. Keep me posted."

Chapter Seventeen
Life and Death of the Party

Every party guest was accounted for when they entered the Electroswinger. Karren took Jasper's advice and headed to the bar to order a lunberry drink. Attom continued trying to recruit Jasper, but the busy dance floor made it easy for her to slip away.

"Jasper, could you mute yourself?" Holly asked. "I can hear the club music from here."

"Sure thing," Jasper muttered as she tapped her comm. She picked out a few other Starchatter employees on the dance floor as she pushed forward through the crowd, but it would be impossible to keep tabs on everyone. That wasn't an issue. Despite what she'd told Holly, monitoring the party wasn't what she'd come here for. Why would any of these morons try to go back to the office, anyway?

Jasper kept her eyes on the approaching exit that would put her in the alley next door. She could hardly believe how smoothly everything was going—

A hand grabbed her arm. In a heartbeat, Jasper was thrown to the ground. She rolled to the right to avoid getting stepped on and sat up.

The man staring her down held a gun. One low-ranking Blade in front of her, and there were bound to be more around. Jasper jumped to her feet. The last thing she wanted was to get fired at in the middle of a crowd.

Jasper ran for the bar. When she reached the counter, she grabbed an empty stool and spun. The Blade emerging from the crowd behind her didn't have a chance to dodge before the stool collided with his face.

Jasper jumped onto the countertop.

"Galax?" Attom asked incredulously. He sat a few feet away, bathed in the neon green glow of the bar with a drink in hand.

"Try again." Jasper tossed aside her glasses, pulled her hair from its updo into a high ponytail, and drew out her largest dagger.

"Van Terra!" a woman shouted. Another Blade. She approached the counter and pointed her gun at Jasper. "Hand over Alvarez, and we'll let you go. For now."

"She's not with me." Jasper eyed the other two Blades stepping off the dance floor on either side of the woman. It was all but impossible for dancers in the crowd to realize what was happening with the loud music and strobe lights, but people at the bar scrambled to get away. Attom had already vanished.

"We've got twenty more Blades in here alone," the woman said. "And more waiting outside the building. All Electroswinger exits are covered. Tell us where Alvarez is."

"No."

The three Blades fired at once. Jasper deflected the bullets with ease, one after the other, sending them into the shiny black countertop and causing the whole thing to fracture beneath her feet. She sent the dagger spinning toward the woman and jumped down into the bar.

The weapon buried itself in the woman's shoulder. She cried out in pain and dropped her gun. The other two Blades flew over the counter to retaliate. Jasper grabbed a bottle off the shelf behind her and swung at the first to reach her. While he went down, she dodged a bullet from the second and brought the bottle down on his head. He collapsed.

She needed a new way out. There was an apartment complex above the Electroswinger, and a restaurant below. Which would be easier to access?

Jasper's gaze flickered to a nearby ventilation shaft sitting a few inches off the floor.

Shouting, screaming, more Blades approaching. She let loose a few throwing stars before pulling out a smoke bomb and one of the small explosives she saved for emergencies. Another Blade made it over the counter and swung at Jasper. She took the blow to the side of her head and staggered to the right. The smoke bomb and explosive slipped from her hand.

Jasper dodged the next swing but stumbled into the fists of a second Blade. He shoved Jasper into the shelf behind her, sending bottles and glasses crashing to the floor. Liquid pooled at her feet. The light illuminating the case flickered.

"Alvarez. Now." The Blade pressed a gun to her shoulder. "Or we find out how much pain you can really handle."

"Alvarez is right behind you," Jasper said.

The Blade glanced over his shoulder.

Jasper shoved her foot into his chest. He flew back into the counter. "Wow, you really fell for that." She reached behind her, grabbed the shelf, and pulled it down to block the path of more Blades coming her way.

She dove to the floor to dodge more gunshots, and to grab the explosive and smoke bomb. She peered over the edge of the counter to scan the ceiling. She had once chance. The push of a button turned on the explosive's timer.

Ten, nine, eight...

Footsteps came from Jasper's left. She threw a punch that knocked the man to the ground, scooped up his gun, and whirled around to fire at the Blade coming from the other direction.

Seven, six, five...

Jasper emptied the gun and fired blanks at the dance floor to disperse the crowd beneath her target.

Four, three, two...

Jasper jumped onto the counter and threw the explosive.

One.

It hit the ceiling and exploded, raining debris down on the floor. Jasper activated the smoke bomb and tossed it up. As dark smoke filled the air around her, she slid to the floor, crawled to the ventilation grate, and pried it off the wall.

"She's going up!" a woman shouted. "Move everyone up a level. Block all exits."

Jasper squeezed into the vent shaft and went down.

She pressed her hands and feet against the walls and worked her way to where the vent branched off to the right. She climbed in and crawled to the next grate. But before she could get it open, the shaft buckled beneath her. A moment later, it broke open, depositing her into the restaurant.

The table she landed on collapsed. The family whose dinner she'd just ruined shouted in surprise and jumped out of their seats. Jasper brushed pieces of food and shards of glass off her coat as she climbed to her feet.

"Sorry about that," she said. "Eh, I've heard this place overcooks everything, anyway."

She stepped out of the wreckage and ran for the nearest window. Bracing herself for the inevitable pain, she jumped. The window shattered and she joined a torrent of glass raining down on a balcony a couple stories down.

Ouch. She'd been hoping for a skywalk beneath the window. Suppressing a groan of pain, she stood up. The empty apartment she needed to get to was one level up. And on the other side of a sizeable gap.

Jasper's gaze moved down to the roof five stories below. That would be the quickest path to her destination. She sighed, stretched her arms, and got ready to half-climb, half-fall down the side of a building.

Chapter Eighteen
BTW

It was a huge relief to finally climb out of the food cart. Grace stretched her legs, arms, and wings while Thea climbed on top of the cart to move the loose ceiling tile.

"What if Ringmaster's in there?" Dax whispered.

"I did a heat scan. No one's up there yet." Thea climbed in.

Dax followed. Grace went last, and despite Thea's assurance it was safe, apprehension made her tense as she pulled herself up.

A workspace had been thrown together in the space above the ceiling. An elaborate computer system was piled onto a desk, with machines hooked up to several keyboards and multiple monitors. A rolling chair sat nearby. Tarps hung all around the makeshift office, isolating it.

"Awful lot of work for such a small space," Thea said, turning in a slow circle. "He blocked off any part of the building that had direct ventilation access." She stepped toward the desk and ran a finger along the top of one of the monitors. "And most of this equipment is purely security. Prevents people like me from getting into the messages or camera feeds remotely."

The screens lit up at her touch, and the computers hummed in a chorus of overworked electronics. Thea plopped into the chair.

Dax sat down nearby and made himself comfortable. Grace, after some hesitation, did the same. Anxiety faded to a sense of relative comfort, which quickly turned to boredom. Thea typed endlessly at keys, occasionally cursing and smacking the equipment.

Holly tuned in over comms from time to time to check Thea's status, and to note that she had yet to see anyone approach the offices.

Grace's mind wandered back to the comment Holly had made earlier. If she was West Kronosian, why did she make herself look human? What was the point in staying in a shapeshifted form all the time?

A West Kronosian might draw more attention than they wanted in the lower districts, Grace supposed. But what was stopping Holly from using her true form at home?

"How are things going?" Holly asked, for the…fifth time? Sixth? Grace had lost track.

"I'm doing okay," Thea replied. "I've got a program running to download the stored messages I detected to my sphere. They'll probably need decoding, too. And I'm working on camera feed access right now."

Grace wrapped her arms around her knees and pulled them to her chest so that she could rest her chin on top. "How is Ringmaster getting race instructions out to the villains? Is that what the messages are?"

Thea shook her head. "I'm not sure what the text messages are. They could be communication with the governor, though, which would be a huge help to us."

"Ringmaster announced the races last season on a hijacked broadcast and told any interested villains to send out a signal that would put them on his list," Dax added. "After that, Jasper was sent a responding signal with a code to access an encrypted audio channel. He's been sending information that way."

Jasper joined the conversation. "Yeah, there's just one complication."

"Oh, look who's back," Holly responded with a huff. "What do you mean 'complication?'"

"Sorry to interrupt," Thea said before Jasper could answer. "But I've got camera access." Various feeds popped up on the rightmost monitor. "Looks like these were set up to follow the race. Pretty much what we expected."

"That's great," Jasper said. Her breathing was labored. "Let me know when you can read the messages."

Dax frowned. "Are you okay, Jasper?"

"I'm fine."

"The decoding process is just starting," Thea replied. "I'll let you know if I get anything interesting."

"I get that the party was the easiest way to access Ringmaster's setup," Holly said. "But I'm not the only one who thinks we could have just pulled the fire alarm, right?"

"I had to get everyone away from the building," Jasper told her. "Plant the idea of going somewhere else. Otherwise, they would have waited around for the fire department."

"Still," Holly muttered.

Dax shrugged. "It did seem a little excessive."

"Jasper's always been dramatic," Thea said. Frowning, she leaned forward and squinted at the camera feeds.

"What can I say? I'm a supervillain." Jasper's statement was followed by a grunt of pain that made Grace wince.

"It's clear you have other plans," Holly said. "What are you doing, anyway? You sound like you're—"

"Running across a rooftop?" Thea tried.

"Oddly specific guess, but yeah."

"That's because she is." Thea pointed at one of the screens, though Holly wouldn't be able to see whatever she was looking at.

"Wait," Holly said. "Someone's coming."

Grace tensed. She found herself exchanging an apprehensive glance with Dax.

"Yeah, I recognize this guy," Holly continued. "He's an intern. Maybe he was at the party and left something behind." She sighed. "Should I knock him out?"

"Not yet," Thea told her. "The messages are downloading faster than I expected. Keep an eye on him, and delay him if you can. We just need to get out before he gets in and sees the hole in the ceiling." She frowned. "Jasper, what are you doing? Why are you climbing that building?"

"Hey, yeah!" Sudden realization laced Holly's annoyed tone. "Jasper, you were supposed to hang out at the Electroswinger and make sure no one came back. You clearly failed at that."

Grace climbed to her feet and peered at the monitor over Thea's shoulder. Jasper was scaling a building, using ledges and skywalks and balconies to make her way up with impressive speed.

"Wait," Grace said. "What was Jasper saying about a complication earlier?"

Jasper managed a weak laugh. "Let's just say that with the danger involved in the races, Ringmaster is anticipating a lot of elimination."

"So?" Holly asked. "We're following Ringmaster, not the races."

"Yes, well, Ringmaster wanted to reduce the chances of race locations being leaked in advance to people who could cause problems. The police, for example."

Grace folded her arms. "If Ringmaster's working for Starr, couldn't Starr just—?"

"Stop the police?" Jasper asked. "No, no, Starr doesn't control every precinct to that degree. He's never that obvious about it, either. Plus, other villains might try to interrupt the races for their own reasons." On the screen, she pulled herself onto a balcony and disappeared into a gap between two buildings. "So, as I was saying, Ringmaster is only handing out locations to villains who qualify for the next race."

Thea raised an eyebrow. Dax's eyes widened. Holly cursed over comms.

"You mean if we want to follow Ringmaster…" Grace began.

"I have to run the race," Jasper finished.

Chapter Nineteen
This Woman Could Be Inside Your Home Right Now

The chaos over the comms made Jasper roll her eyes. She'd known this was coming, but she'd hoped she could put off explaining until after the race.

She dodged pipes stretching overhead and stepped over awkward gaps in the walkway that hadn't seen use in years. The entrance to the apartment was an unfortunately placed window that faced the wall of the next building. Jasper knelt down and opened it. The family who owned the place was on vacation, making it the perfect location to stash her ride.

Technically, she could have used the car. It fit into the wide range of vehicles allowed in the races. But if she was going to do this, she was going to do it her way. Her ride had to be fast enough to give her a shot at winning. She would be sacrificing protection for agility, but she could handle any attacks that came her way. Hopefully.

She peeled off her coat as she entered the apartment and tossed aside some of her extra weapons. Waiting for her in a kitchen cupboard was her change of clothes. Her motorcycle suit.

"Jasper, where are you?" Thea asked. "Did you enter the building you were climbing?"

"Yeah, I'll be out in a minute," Jasper replied as she started changing. "I have to make a quick stop in the parking garage."

She only half-listened to the others talking over each other, asking questions she didn't bother answering. She strapped as many weapons to herself as she could without compromising maneuverability. Then, she twisted her ponytail into a tight bun.

"Thea, please tell me when you have a visual on her," Holly said.

"I'm in the lower end of the Prism District." Jasper stretched one of her arms across her chest. "There's a parking garage that exits onto Skyway F. I'll be there in three minutes." She switched arms.

"Hang on," Thea said. "I'm getting into the security system for the building you just entered. Are you in the apartments?"

Before Jasper could respond, Holly cut in. "Jasper, why didn't you tell us only qualifying racers get the next location?"

Jasper left the apartment and headed for the garage, using her night vision to navigate the dark halls. "Because I knew you'd say something like—"

"This doesn't have to be a big deal. Don't draw attention to yourself and keep a low profile until we take care of Ringmaster. No need for your—"

"Theatrics?" Jasper asked. "You know me too well."

"Unfortunately," Holly muttered.

"Heads up, Jasper," Thea said. "Five Blades are coming up a fire exit near you."

Jasper paused. "Which direction?" She could take five, but it would put her behind.

"North. They're just around the corner."

Blocking the path to the garage. Of course. Jasper sighed and drew a dagger. "Fine."

"How long until the race starts?" Dax asked. "I don't think we'll want to be here when Ringmaster shows up."

"You guys getting out depends on when Thea gets done." Jasper kept her voice low as she crept down the hall. "So maybe she should stop watching me and get back to downloading."

"The download's running," Thea said. "It's almost done. Holly's keeping lookout. And I'm trying to help you!"

Jasper hoped her mind's computer had finished syncing with the electronics in the motorcycle suit. She mentally commanded the lights to come on.

The hot pink lines running along the sides of the black suit lit up, casting a faint glow on the Blades' faces as they came around the corner. She stretched out her arm and pressed the hidden button on the dagger, lighting up the matching line on the blade.

"What are you wear—?"

Thea's voice was lost in the torrent of gunshots. Jasper strolled toward the Blades, dodging and deflecting bullets. Once she was halfway to them, they started backing up. She broke into a run, jumped, and used the wall to propel herself higher into the air.

As she sailed over their heads, she slashed at the nearest Blade. He dropped to the ground with a gash running down his face. Two others fired. One bullet missed by a few feet, but the other grazed Jasper's left arm.

She landed, sprang back up, and jumped again. Her feet crashed into the next Blade's chest. As she came back down, she slashed again at another, snatched his gun from him as he stumbled, and fired at the Blade coming from behind.

Two more shots, and the Blades were all on the floor. Jasper glanced at her left arm as she sprinted down the hall. It was sore, but the bullet hadn't even broken the fabric of the suit. "This is good stuff," she muttered as she ran a hand along the material.

"Messages are all downloaded," Thea said. "We're leaving."

"Good," Holly replied. "Because the intern's almost to you."

Thea groaned. "I thought you were keeping an eye on him!"

"I am! If he gets too close before you guys are out, I'll intervene. But I want to see what he's here for."

Jasper flung open the door to the stairs and flew down them four at a time. "Thea, could you start reading me the messages?"

"Yeah, we'll camp out in a nearby office so I can take a look."

Jasper entered the garage and jogged past an array of vehicles. Her black and pink motorcycle waited at the end of a row. She picked up the matching helmet and gave it a quick inspection to make sure there were no scratches on the visor. Or the pointed cat ears.

"Where'd you get the motorcycle?" Thea asked.

"You're still watching me?" Jasper slid the helmet on. The motorcycle suit, the helmet, and the vehicle itself had all been custom-made as various favors she'd earned over the years in Kronos's criminal underworld.

"Yeah, I—oh, that's strange."

Jasper mounted the motorcycle and did one last check: weapons, explosives, everything secured. Favorite sword strapped to the vehicle's side. "What's strange?"

"The messages addressed to Ringmaster aren't incoming. They're outgoing," Thea explained. "This isn't a conversation between Ringmaster and Starr, although Starr is mentioned."

"Ringmaster wasn't actually there?" Jasper's hands tightened around the handles.

"No, it looks like he has someone else keeping an eye on things for him. They're referred to as the 'Apprentice.' I can show you the rest after the race."

"No, keep going," Jasper told her. "Tell me everything interesting you find."

"But the race is starting soon."

"I can listen and drive." The engine roared to life. Jasper grinned.

Her excitement was cut short by the sound of shouting. Some of the Blades must have gotten back up. Jasper pulled out the sphere hosting Mia's A.I. and slid it into the dock in front of her. "Mia, send the race map to my screen."

While the overlay loaded in Jasper's vision, voices and footsteps came closer. She hit the gas and shot forward. "Holly, any sign of—?"

"I left the building," Holly cut her off. "There was a commotion outside, and I figured since the others were safe—"

"We need to find this Apprentice person." Jasper shot past the Blades entering the garage from the stairwell and waved at them. "They might show up to monitor the race."

"Jasper, the streets are crawling with Blades. I think they're looking for you. They're following the race map, and your involvement with Grace probably has you at the top of Starr's wanted list right now." Holly paused. "Well, almost at the top."

How did the Blades know what the course was going to be? "I'm on a motorcycle. I can handle them," Jasper told Holly. "Go find the Apprentice. He could make tracking Ringmaster easier."

"Ringmaster's doing a job for Starr and doesn't want people wondering why he's running all over the star system," Thea said. "The races are a cover."

"Seems excessive," Jasper replied. "There has to be more to it."

"If there is, he hasn't told the Apprentice."

Jasper reached the parking garage's exit and opted to jump over the concrete wall rather than following the street that curved down.

"Ringmaster's in Kronos right now because he has a meeting with a Red Blades leader," Thea continued. "He's picking up sensitive information they'll need for their mission. 'They' being him and the Apprentice."

Jasper landed on a roof and cut across it, slowing as she approached the edge. She was almost to the race's starting point. "Mission?"

"Again, Ringmaster has kept things very vague here."

Jasper turned the motorcycle and came to a halt at the edge of the roof. The next building over was a couple stories shorter, allowing Jasper to peer down at the villains gathering on top. On the other side was the Prism Spire, one of the tallest structures in Kronos. It glittered iridescent in the night and reflected an array of colors onto the crowd.

"Wow, Ringmaster pulled in villains from all over the Janus System," Jasper said. There had to be at least a hundred people waiting on the roof below. She picked out a few of the more recognizable ones. Cutthroat, the infamous space pirate. Grim Machine. And South Siren, of course.

Jasper stretched out her arms. Maybe she should keep a low profile after all. Only do well enough to learn the next location. The better she did, the more people would target her, and she had worn herself out more than intended over the past few days.

"Holly," Jasper said. "You find the Apprentice yet?"

"I got locked out," Holly replied. "Finding another way in."

"Have one of the others help you."

"No, I can get back in before the race is over," Holly insisted.

A few golden birds flitted past Jasper. Something buzzed in the air overhead. She tipped her head back as a golden orb, not much bigger than the average smartsphere, soared over the starting point.

"May I have your attention please. The race will be starting shortly." The announcement came from the orb. The shrill voice wasn't particularly loud, but the orb's amplification carried Ringmaster's words through the crowd of villains.

Chapter Twenty
And It Keeps Getting Better

Deep breath. Jasper stretched her arms, stretched her hands, adjusted her posture. Her fingers wrapped around the motorcycle's handlebars. The engine revved, and she shot forward.

Jasper sailed over the edge of the roof. "Coming through!" she shouted. As she dropped, she scanned the crowd of villains waiting below and aimed the motorcycle at a space just large enough for her to land, between Cutthroat's racing cart that resembled his black starship, and—

"I knew Van Terra would show up." Grim Machine laughed as Jasper thudded against the roof next to him. Well, he made a screeching, metallic sound that vaguely resembled laughter.

Jasper looked the bulky white robot up and down. He was more than twice the size of her and her motorcycle combined. His inner components gave off a pale blue-green glow that spilled through the gaps in his outer shell.

"Where's your vehicle?" Jasper asked, raising an eyebrow.

"Let's just say I've gotten some upgrades recently."

Intriguing as the mystery behind Grim Machine's creation was, Jasper didn't have time to probe him for information today.

"It's time," Ringmaster spoke again through the hovering orb. "You all know the course. I have an extensive network of cameras and equipment set up along the way. Don't bother trying to take shortcuts. And of course—"

A spotlight turned on over a nearby roof, casting a beam on the golden platform hovering in the air over the villains, as well as the man standing on it. "—I will be watching," Ringmaster finished.

"Ringmaster's here," Jasper hissed.

Ringmaster was dressed in his usual attire: black, red, and gold clothes—and a black top hat—that made him look as if he'd walked right out of a circus. The only thing setting him apart from an ordinary human was his unique form of energy manipulation.

"I've got eyes on him," Thea said. "He's got a tablet and is probably connected to live feeds. Plus, he can review the footage later if needed. He might have only needed the hidden room to set up."

"So, the Apprentice might not show up at all?" Jasper replied with a groan. "Ugh. Okay." One thing at a time.

"Don't cry to me if you get arrested," Ringmaster continued. "Police, competitors, any other unsavory characters who show up—it's all part of the race. All weapons and powers are fair game." He raised an arm. Golden energy shimmered in the air, materializing into a flag in his grasp. "Racers, on your marks."

Engines roared to life across the roof.

"Get set."

Grim Machine's parts and components shifted around, transforming the robot into a tank with startling speed.

"Go!"

Jasper shot forward and immediately swerved to the right to go around a vehicle equipped with massive guns. She'd braced herself for an onslaught of attacks right off the bat, but most racers seemed to be waiting for things to thin out before attempting to eliminate their competition.

The first couple minutes of the course ran entirely over rooftops. A few drops, a few jumps, and a few places where Jasper activated the motorcycle's anti-gravity and drove up the sides of buildings.

Jasper picked up speed as she landed on a domed roof. She skidded around the edge and shot off, aiming for the skyway below where other racers had already joined regular traffic. The motorcycle couldn't fly, but it did have small thrusters that slowed her descent enough to soften the landing. Ignoring the blaring of horns around her, she took advantage of her small vehicle to weave through traffic.

As Jasper emerged ahead of a cargo carrier, another motorcyclist rammed into her. The collision nearly sent her into the railing. She steadied herself and looked to the left. "Hey, watch it!"

The humanoid man on the red motorcycle grinned at her, his crimson eyes shining in the traffic lights. He lifted one of his tanned, unnaturally long arms to wave. And show off the tattoo on his forearm.

Jasper's eyes narrowed in recognition. "You really should be wearing a helmet!"

Red Boss laughed. "Unlike you, I can handle a little pain."

You have no idea what I can handle. Jasper bit back her response. She wanted to ask what a high-ranking Red Blade was doing in Ringmaster's race, but speeding down a skyway wasn't the best environment for conversation.

Jasper swerved around a few cars. To her dismay, Red Boss followed. What was he doing?

Was this about Grace?

Red Boss caught up on Jasper's left and rammed into her. Before she could get her bearings, he hit her again.

She careened into the railing and flew over the edge. Her right hand managed to keep hold of the handlebar. Which was great for not losing the motorcycle, but not so great when it landed on top of her.

The roof she'd landed on wasn't empty. Blades—ten of them— approached on all sides.

"Ten?" Jasper asked as she climbed to her feet. "Now we're talking. Who's first?"

The closest man lifted his gun—no, blaster. These guys had some experience. "Last chance to lead us to Alvarez," he said. "But we'll gladly go find her once you're not around to protect her."

Jasper picked her motorcycle up off the ground. "Do your worst."

Blasters fired. Jasper lunged forward. She swung her motorcycle at the closest Blade. After knocking the man aside, she kept going, using the momentum to take down two more. She let go and the motorcycle went down with a fourth.

Jasper jumped to dodge the next round of blasts, pulling throwing knives from her side as she flipped. Three knives, three more Blades down.

The last four fired within heartbeats of each other. One of the blasts struck Jasper's shoulder, knocking her to the ground. Her suit fared well against the blast, but she'd definitely have a nasty bruise. And one more shot could be enough to tear open the suit's material.

Jasper pushed herself up and attacked the man closest to her. The others moved to fire again but quickly realized they risked hitting their fellow Blade. Jasper attempted to wrestle the blaster from the man's hands for a moment to distract him before elbowing him in the face. He went down, and Jasper fired at the other three Blades in rapid succession with his weapon. They dropped. She tossed the blaster aside and walked to her motorcycle.

Note to self: steer clear of Red Boss.

By the time the first of the Blades were back up, Jasper was already speeding toward the skyway. She used a slanted portion of the next roof over as a ramp to launch herself back into traffic.

The throbbing pain in her shoulder was worse than she'd anticipated. If she avoided any more delays, she could pull off a decent spot in the race, but she was beginning to question whether it was worth it. She hopped off the skyway pavement and onto the concrete barrier beside it to speed things up a bit. It required a lot more effort to stay balanced, but the lack of traffic was a plus.

The course moved lower into the city, forcing racers to make use of walkways and rooftops and anything else they could find in order to move forward within the course boundaries. Every drop was hell on Jasper's shoulder.

"You slowing down, Jasper?" Thea asked. "I thought you had a shot at top ten for a minute there."

Holly was quick to express annoyance at the comment. "Don't encourage her."

"Is she okay?" Dax asked. "She looks injured."

"Geez, why are you all so obsessed with me? I'm fine." An explosion went off somewhere behind Jasper, making her wince. She veered off the edge of the under-construction skywalk she'd been travelling and dropped back into skyway traffic.

Grace was next to chime in with a question. "Did those Blades you fought say anything about me?"

"Now's not the time—"

A huge white motorbike up ahead slowed, falling into place next to Jasper. South Siren laughed. "Shame to see the great Van Terra isn't doing so hot! I honestly thought you'd be farther ahead."

"Don't tell me you guys don't see the resemblance," Jasper muttered. "She's Sarena!"

South Siren had Sarena Trench's dark teal skin, curvy build, and gills in the same place on her neck. The only obvious differences were South Siren's glowing eyes and straight bob of hair, both as bright a white as her motorcycle suit and boots. Even the orange hekten perched on her shoulder resembled Sarena's pet, though with South Siren it manifested rings of darker orange around its scattered spikes.

"Stop joking around," Holly said sternly.

South Siren didn't give Jasper a chance to respond to her jab before speeding off. Eyes narrowing, Jasper upped her own speed. Navigating traffic was taking too long, and this section of the skyway had no side barriers; it simply ran right up to the edges of buildings.

Over the top, then.

Jasper located an empty carrier vehicle built for transporting smaller cars. A small hop brought her onto its back, where she was able to use it as a ramp to launch herself onto the top of a skybus.

Thea sighed. "I hope you know what you're doing, Jasper."

"What's she doing now?" Holly demanded.

Jasper hopped from vehicle to vehicle. The skyway entered a tunnel up ahead, where the increase in traffic was causing congestion around the entrance. Even some of the other racers had been forced to near standstill. You could only plow through so many vehicles when there was no more space to shove them aside.

Jasper sped off the front of a transport vehicle and hit the street, eyeing a small gap at the edge of the tunnel entrance.

It was all she needed.

She turned the anti-gravity back on, jumped, and pushed the wheels into the tunnel wall. She veered up, narrowly missing a massive cargo transport. Within seconds, she was hanging upside down from the ceiling of the tunnel. The pink lights on her suit and motorcycle glowed bright in the darkness, outshining the dull tunnel lights.

Jasper expected that most of the other racers—the smart ones, anyway—had included anti-gravity systems. It was allowed, through flying vehicles weren't—her thrusters were the most powerful accepted under Ringmaster's guidelines. Basic gliding mechanisms were okay, too.

Sure enough, a few other vehicles also clung to the tunnel walls. Jasper laughed as she passed them, pushing her motorcycle to its maximum speed. The gap between her and South Siren shortened.

South Siren glanced back. Her hekten, still clinging to her shoulder, opened its beak and fired a blast of white energy at Jasper. Jasper yelped in surprise and yanked her motorcycle to the right. She dodged the blast but slammed into Grim Machine, who was barreling through traffic at the bottom of the tunnel in his tank form.

"Ow!" Jasper rubbed her arm as she pulled away from Grim Machine. The robot was completely unfazed by the collision. "Come on, how do you explain South Siren having the same pet as Sarena?"

"Sarena's hekten doesn't have laser powers," Thea pointed out.

"It's not like she's going to show them off!" Jasper approached South Siren again, this time with more caution.

South Siren shot Jasper a glare over her shoulder. "Back off, Van Terra!" Her power magnified her voice, turning it into a shockwave that pushed Jasper and her motorcycle back a few feet. Jasper gritted her teeth. The race was almost over. She was ahead of the majority now, and if she could just get past South Siren, she had a shot at the top ten. Maybe even top five.

Jasper reached the end of the tunnel. As she flew off the ceiling, she twisted herself right side up and switched off the anti-gravity. Her gaze moved to an empty skywalk running parallel to the skyway. She jumped the barrier.

"Hey, I found out what Ringmaster's helping Starr with," Thea said. "Sort of. He mentions it briefly. They're tracking down research on something called...spacetime warps?"

No.

No, no, no.

Jasper collided with the skyway at an awkward angle, sending her motorcycle end over end and launching her off. She skidded across the walkway and grunted in pain as her vehicle crashed into her.

"Jasper?" Dax's concerned yelp made grimace. "Is something wrong?"

"I'm switching back to cameras—" Thea started.

"I'm fine," Jasper hissed, grateful they hadn't watched the landing. She staggered to her feet and grabbed the motorcycle. "I think I misheard you."

An onslaught of flashing lights and sirens—loud and bright enough to break through the usual chaos of city traffic—came from the direction of the skyway. Police cruisers swooped down from the air to target any villains in the race they stood a chance against with simple blasters and ordinary strength. Though, any cyborgs on duty would have definitely been sent out to the frontlines.

There was a hint of unease in Thea's voice. "About the spacetime warps?"

Jasper's fingers twitched. She was going to kill Ringmaster. And Starr. Did they have any idea what they were messing with? "What else did he say?" She climbed back on the motorcycle. Racers on the skyway shot past her. She was too overwhelmed with anger and memories to care.

"It's only mentioned once," Thea replied.

"What's a spacetime warp?" Grace asked. "Isn't that what they use at the spaceports?"

Grace's voice was reassuring. There was no immediate danger, Jasper reminded herself. The team was safe. She took a deep breath and pushed herself to full speed. "No," she said. "Those are space warps. They're basically wormholes, manipulations in space used for transportation. Space*time* warps are different. And they're dangerous."

"I've never heard of them," Thea said.

"Me neither," Holly added. "How do you know about them?"

"That's—" *Focus.* Jasper's hands tightened. "That's not important right now. Just get back to—whatever you're doing."

A golden banner hung over the skyway. Above it, Ringmaster stood on his pedestal, watching racers approach the finish line. Villains who'd passed Jasper crossed. Cutthroat. Grim Machine. South Siren.

Jasper managed to pass a few racers before crossing the finish line herself. She expected relief but instead found herself pulling into the first alleyway she found, climbing off the motorcycle, tossing it aside. Within seconds, her helmet was on the ground, and she was pacing back and forth like a caged animal.

"Jasper, where should we meet?" Thea asked. "Are you coming back here? Jasper?"

"I—" Jasper rubbed her forehead. "Give me a minute to think."

"You don't have a minute," Holly said. "Twenty Red Blades are approaching Starchatter."

"Oh, come on!" Jasper's hands clenched into painful fists. She gave her helmet a restrained kick, her frustration outweighed by her desire to not break the thing. "Are you inside yet, Holly? Any sign of the Apprentice?"

"Haven't seen him, but I'm nowhere near the party room. I'm currently straddling a window. What do you want me to do?"

"Get to the rest of the team. Get them out. Preferably without being seen. And Thea, get me logged in to Starchatter's site." Jasper sucked in a sharp breath. "I'm on my way."

Chapter Twenty-One
Ugh, Not This Guy Again

Jasper reached Starchatter in five minutes, an accomplishment only obtained by taking a lot of painful drops, driving up the sides of buildings, and screaming at people on skywalks to get out of the way. Fortunately, she'd already written the article she'd wanted published, so hopping onto the site and posting it was easy enough to do while driving.

When she arrived, she didn't bother dismounting. She fired at the building's exterior doors with a blaster she'd nabbed off a stray Blade and drove right through the shards of glass raining down.

"Do we have a visual on the Blades?" Jasper asked as she raced through the halls toward Starchatter's offices.

"They just left the west cubicles. I think they're headed for the lobby," Holly said. "I'm on my way. I left the rest of the team in a security office."

"No, stay with them!"

"Even you can't fight twenty Blades alone."

"I have a motorcycle!" Jasper exclaimed. "I can run them over!"

"Not if they shoot you first!" Holly shot back.

"Fine." Jasper slowed down. "Where are you?"

"I'm right behind the Blades. They just walked onto the main floor in the office."

"Great. I'm coming from the other side. We'll trap them." Jasper stopped in the middle of the lobby, slid off the motorcycle, and raised her blaster. She used her other hand to pull off her helmet and toss it aside.

"Sethany Galax! Or should I say Van Terra?"

Jasper whirled around as Attom entered the lobby. He was accompanied by ten people dressed in matching white leather.

"Attom? What are you doing back here?" Jasper kept the blaster pointed toward the office behind her and reached for a dagger with her free hand.

"The real question is why you're here," Attom replied. He stopped and folded his arms. "Why are you trying to destroy my career?"

Jasper lifted an eyebrow. "You saw that already?"

"Of course! My sphere's been buzzing nonstop with notifications."

"Is that Attom?" Thea asked. "What's he going on about?"

"Oh, nothing much. I just dropped an article trashing the beloved Sarena Trench. Under Attom's name." Jasper surveyed the people who'd formed lines on either side of Attom. Louder, she asked, "Who are your friends?"

Attom's arms unfolded and spread out wide, a gesture that encompassed the people gathered around him. "I couldn't let Red Blades march into my office like they own the place. So, I brought some of my *other* employees."

"Ah," Jasper said. "You're involved with gangs, too. Now I feel even better about making you look like an idiot."

"What, you ruined my career to make the city a better place?"

Jasper rolled her eyes. "No. I just don't like you." She gestured at Attom with her dagger. "Plus, I did all that work for you and didn't even get paid! You took my ideas for your own gain!"

"You think you outsmarted me, but you won't be laughing when my Slicers defeat you." Attom sighed. "It's a shame. Your vlog that got the Blades' smuggling operation shut down was very beneficial to me. If we worked together—"

Jasper laughed. Hard. "Me? Work with you? I'm Van Terra, idiot." She fired the blaster, and the first Blade to come around the corner collapsed to the ground with a scream. "I don't work nine-to-five jobs for mediocre villains."

Confusion flickered across Attom's gaze at the suggestion of a standard work schedule that didn't quite make sense under Kronos's twenty-two-hour days. It was quickly replaced with annoyance. "Fine. Slicers, take care of the Blades and Van Terra."

More Blades poured into the lobby, drawing blasters. One at the back of the group soared over the rest and crashed to the floor in front of Jasper, thrown by the newest arrival.

Jasper grinned. "Nice one, Holly!"

Holly still wore her catering uniform, but she'd ditched the tie and thrown on her favored red leather jacket. She'd also shapeshifted back to her usual form, and the hair that had been down when she'd infiltrated the party had been hastily thrown into a wild red braid.

Jasper fired again and strolled toward the approaching Blades, ears straining for the sound of triggers being pulled—the Slicers behind her had blasters, too. But before anyone else could shoot, the lights flickered overhead, and the weapons in the lobby ceased functioning.

Thea came around the corner behind Holly. "Shame no one brought guns," she said, waving a hand. "Blasters are so easy to disable."

Jasper tensed. "You're supposed to be with—"

"They can handle themselves."

"We don't need blasters," a Red Blade shouted. She lifted her fists. "Take care of Red Holly and Jolt, then go find Alvarez."

"Don't let the Blades go any farther!" Attom ordered.

"Oh good. An old-fashioned three-way fight." Jasper tossed her blaster aside and grinned. "Let's do this."

The lobby descended into chaos. Jasper tossed Blades and Slicers alike aside as she fought her way to Holly and Thea. The two moved back-to-back, exchanging blows with everyone around them.

"I'm at nine," Jasper announced when she reached them.

Holly rolled her eyes. "Now is not the time to brag about how many people you've taken down."

"Yeah, we can't all be cyborgs," Thea added.

"Technically, we could." Jasper swung her left leg to knock a Blade off his feet. She glanced toward the edge of the room, where Attom was creeping around the fight toward a door tucked away in the corner of the lobby. "I'm going to take care of Attom."

"Do we really need to worry about him?" Holly asked.

Jasper ignored her and escaped the fray. She sprinted toward Attom as he neared the exit. "Not so fast!"

Attom turned around. "What, you're not done with me?"

"You've got money and connections. You might lose your job here to satisfy the public, but they'll forget about this in a few days, and you'll keep on keeping on behind the scenes somewhere else."

"You're not wrong," Attom said. "But you don't have time to deal with me right now." His gaze moved to the fight behind Jasper, and he raised his voice. "Alvarez is in the security office, down the hall behind the offices and to the right!"

Jasper hissed. "How did you—?"

"I'm paying closer attention than you think." Attom tapped the watch on his wrist. A holoscreen popped up to display several camera feeds. "And I've got some tech experts of my own. Now, you should get going. Three Blades just slipped past your friends." He smiled. "But I'm sure this won't be the last we see of each other."

Jasper rolled her eyes and turned around. "Whatever."

"You should be more careful," Attom called as she stormed away. "Your recklessness is going to be your downfall some day!"

"I'm going to expose your affiliations with the Slicers!" Jasper yelled back. It was at the bottom of a very long to-do list, but it was there. "Which is a stupid name, by the way!"

"Whatever you say!"

Jasper jumped and used a wall to propel herself over the fighters still standing, Holly and Thea included. On the other side, she raced through the Starchatter main office and around the corner in time to watch one of three Blades kick down the door to the security room. She grabbed a painting off the wall and sent it spinning through the air. It hit the first Blade and knocked him out cold.

The other two darted into the room.

Jasper ran in behind them, assessing the room in a heartbeat: Dax stood in front of Grace, one arm out in front of her. Grace had backed into the desk behind her. Her hands were wrapped so tightly around the edge that her knuckles had gone white. The Blades stalked toward her, daggers in hand.

Jasper went for the one on the right. He turned and slashed at her, his blade piercing the motorcycle suit enough to leave a scratch across her chest. Her right hand snatched his wrist. The man grimaced as her superhuman grip tightened. He released his dagger, and it clattered to the ground. Jasper tossed him into the wall.

Grace cried out, making Jasper's head snap toward her. Dax had been thrown to the floor. He was getting back up, but he wasn't moving fast enough. Jasper lunged at the last Blade.

She was too slow. Before she could get her hands on him, a monitor smacked into the side of his face so hard the screen shattered. He staggered a few steps before dropping. The monitor slipped from Grace's shaking hands.

Jasper relaxed, releasing a small sigh of relief. "Nice one, Angel. Let's go."

The three left the security room and found Holly and Thea waiting in the lobby, surrounded by the incapacitated bodies of gang members.

"So, no one saw the Apprentice?" Jasper asked.

Holly's eyes narrowed. "We were a bit busy with the three-way fight."

Jasper crossed the lobby to where her motorcycle waited. "Send me the message logs," she told Thea as she picked it up off the floor.

"There's a lot," Thea warned.

"That's fine." Jasper double-checked that her comm was muted before sliding on her helmet. "Congrats, Holly. You get to drive the car home."

As she sped off into the night, Mia responded through the sphere in the motorcycle dock. "Incoming data packet detected on channel labeled 'R1.'"

"Send a summary to my screen," Jasper ordered.

The message was from Ringmaster. He'd previously sent voice recordings on this channel, but this time the signal carried a text file containing rankings from the race, along with the next location. Jasper skimmed the list. Eight-seven had successfully crossed the finish line. Red Boss wasn't among them, thankfully.

Jasper had placed twenty-first.

She was halfway through an empty alley when a blinding gold light swallowed her. The motorcycle screeched to a halt. Jasper flipped through her vision settings, trying to find one that would let her see, but the light was too overwhelming.

"Van Terra," a familiar voice said. The light faded, and the orb emitting it dissipated. Jasper glanced back as Ringmaster walked toward her.

"To what do I owe the pleasure?" Jasper asked. She was grateful her helmet hid her face, because she was struggling to maintain a neutral expression.

"I have a question for you." Ringmaster paused at her side. "About your involvement with Alvarez. Purely curiosity."

No, you're working with Starr. But Ringmaster wasn't going to tell her that, and Jasper couldn't let him know she knew. He was close enough for her to see the golden rings around his brown irises and the lines on his face that put him in his mid-to-late forties. With his hat nowhere to be seen, she also spotted a few gray hairs that had sprouted among the dark brown he kept neatly combed.

Putting as much cool as she could muster into her voice, Jasper asked, "Alvarez?"

"Grace Alvarez."

"Oh, the girl I broke out of jail." Jasper stretched her arms. "Yeah, I helped her and then she ran off to play superhero. Some thank you."

"So, you aren't helping her?" Ringmaster asked, one of his brows lifting ever-so-slightly. "Because the Red Blades seem to think otherwise."

"They're following out-of-date orders. Alvarez pops up in the same places I do, though, so I can't blame them for thinking we're working together." Jasper shrugged. "But really, I've barely even thought about her. I've been busy with other things. Like preparing for the races."

"Really?" Ringmaster asked. "Well, maybe you should put a little more effort into preparing for the next one."

There was another flash of gold light. When it faded, he was gone.

"Rude," Jasper muttered. She took a moment to regain her composure. It was concerning how easy it had been for Ringmaster to catch her off guard. *Something to keep in mind.*

"Mia," Jasper said as she started moving again. "Bring up the message logs Thea sent over."

On the drive back to the apartment, Jasper found two interesting pieces of text. The first was from Ringmaster to the Apprentice, informing him that at the next location, his job would be to locate a target in addition to setting up monitoring systems for the course.

The second—also from Ringmaster—was a single line: *I asked for the records from Sky Labs. Starr said they didn't have any data that would be useful to us. I'm looking for another way to access them.*

Ringmaster had an interest in Sky Labs. Enough of an interest to go behind Starr's back for information. Why?

Jasper reached the apartment before the others and waited for them in the kitchen. "I've got the next race time and location," she told them as they entered.

Grace perked up. "Where are we going?" She was undoubtedly hoping they'd be headed somewhere less populated with Red Blades. And she was in luck.

"Sagev."

II. SAGEV

Chapter Twenty-Two
Good Graces (Reprise)

The girl didn't know why she was running. She didn't know who the man in the lab coat leading her was. And she had absolutely no idea why people were chasing and shooting at the two of them.

All she knew was that her name was Grace Alvarez, and she was fifteen years old.

Out of place memories tumbled through her mind, but they may as well have been a dream she'd just awoken from. The fragments of her past were confusing, foggy, and rapidly fading.

"We're almost out," the man ahead of her said as they reached a set of double doors. He slammed his badge against a box on the wall. The box's red light turned green, and the doors unlocked with a click. The man led Grace from clean white halls to a dark, dirty tunnel. When the doors closed behind them, they blended in perfectly with the tunnel wall.

The man who was apparently—hopefully—saving Grace had scaley green skin, and a thin reptilian tail poked out from under his lab coat, swaying as he ran. His head was human-shaped, but when he briefly glanced back at her, she saw that there was a serpentine curve to his mouth and that his pupils were narrow slits in his oddly reflective emerald irises. His hands ended in clawed fingers.

Something in what lingered of Grace's memory told her she could trust him.

Grace and the man powered through several twists and turns and even a few flights of spiraling metal stairs. The burning in Grace's legs grew steadily more intense, but it was easy to ignore in favor of the fear that kept her in motion.

They didn't slow until they reached a rusted ladder. "You go up first," the man told Grace.

"Why?" Grace's mind was starting to catch up and override the instinct that had told her to run. To follow him. "Who are you? Where are we going?"

"I'm sorry," the man said. "We couldn't get to you before they started the memory wipe procedure. I'll explain everything as soon as I can, but right now we have to—"

A gunshot echoed through the tunnel. The man clutched his chest and staggered into the wall. A dark violet liquid splattered across the front of his white lab coat. Grace could only assume it was his blood.

"Go!" he gasped.

The violent shaking in Grace's hands made the climb up the ladder difficult. She feared she wouldn't make it to the top. Guards in gray uniforms approached below, guns up. Grace's rescuer drew a weapon of his own, a blaster, and pointed it at them. The guards slowed.

"Go!" the man repeated. His trembling hand squeezed the trigger, and the ensuing blue beam sent the closest guard to the ground with a hole in his shoulder. More blood spread across the front of the man's lab coat. "Now!"

Grace reached the top of the ladder and lifted the cover. She pulled herself onto cold concrete and collapsed onto her back.

She couldn't stay here. They would find her.

The ladder had brought her into an alleyway. Buildings on all sides stretched impossibly high into the sky, and more beyond blocked out most of the sunlight. Grace rose to her feet and ran toward the sound of traffic.

She burst out of the alley onto a sidewalk. Vehicles raced by. People walked past her, not giving her so much as a second glance. Grace didn't linger in the spot long, but she did take a moment to study the various alien races walking the street ahead of her. Then, the pothole-ridden street and the broken windows in the building on the other side.

She wandered aimlessly from there, not daring to stop, constantly throwing glances over her shoulder. Her body gradually stopped trembling, and her thoughts calmed. Who could help her? Police? That sounded like a good idea, finding the nearest police station.

Grace took the next staircase she saw and started moving up. She saw no signs of police on her way up, but the city did appear to be getting cleaner the farther she went, so she continued her ascent.

After nearly an hour, when she finally seemed to be nearing the city's upper limits, screeching and blaring horns shook Grace from the daze she'd slipped into. She froze and looked up in time to watch a vehicle flip over a barrier and off one of the overhead streets. It fell toward a walkway stretching between buildings.

The shadow of the falling vehicle passed over a man.

No one was around to help him. Even if he moved out of the way, the walkway he stood on wouldn't hold up when the vehicle collided with it. Grace started toward the man, but she wasn't moving fast enough—

Wings.

She had *wings.*

They came out of slits in the back of her shirt—she noted, for the first time, that she was dressed entirely in plain gray clothes—and extended to their full length. Grace jumped and embraced the open air, relieved to find the wings easy enough to move. Controlling her flight path was another story entirely, but her trajectory to the man was a straight shot, and she made it to him before the vehicle did.

Grabbing him, dodging the falling car, carrying him to safety—it all passed in a blur. Moments after she'd grabbed him, they were tumbling safely onto the balcony wrapped around the nearest skyscraper.

Grace got the impression that the man was trying to hide his identity. He wore sunglasses and dressed in casual clothes, complete with a hood that hid his face in shadow. But the disguise didn't last. Police and reporters and nosy citizens descended on the balcony, and the man was forced to reveal himself as Governor Syrus Starr.

The name rang a bell somewhere in the back of her mind, but when Grace tried to figure out where exactly she'd heard it before, she realized she hadn't. Not that she could remember, anyway.

Grace watched as Governor Starr dismissed everyone but the medics and a handful of officers, who worked to keep the growing crowd and reporters away. And then the governor was talking to Grace, asking who she was, apprehension in his gaze.

Grace admitted she had no idea. She told him all she knew, explained how she'd wound up in this part of the city after her escape. The governor appeared to relax after that.

He offered her a place to stay while the authorities investigated the tunnels and tried to determine what had happened to her. He would provide shelter. Education. A life. It sounded like a good option.

Not that Grace had any other choice.

Chapter Twenty-Three
Due to personal reasons, I will be living in a shack in the middle of the desert.

Si Hera was one of two planets orbiting the star Gemma. Its surface held wide expanses of desert, only broken up by long ranges of snowy mountains. In the summer, when people moved to the mountains to keep cool, the desert cities were practically ghost towns.

But now, with the northern hemisphere deep in its winter, the city of Sagev was one of the most bustling places in the star system. A bright spot in the middle of the otherwise empty Great Eastern Desert.

Under less time-constrictive circumstances, Jasper and the others could have secured a ship to make the flight to Si Hera from Kronos. Today, they had to lie their way through a spaceport and warp to Sagev without getting attacked or arrested.

Oh, and they had to bring the motorcycle.

"So, where are we staying when we get there?" Dax asked as they entered the spaceport. "And how are we going to get around without the car? And how—?"

"Relax, Dax." Jasper glared at a couple that came a little too close to her freshly washed motorcycle for comfort. "Sagev's got extensive public transportation. And I already have a place we can stay. I just need to clean up a bit before anyone's allowed in."

"Of course you have a place in Sagev," Holly muttered.

"It's technically outside the city limits, but it should still be there. I hope. It's been a while." A very long while.

"Wow, sounds great." Holly's voice was thick with its usual sarcasm.

The team strolled past the long lines at the ticketing desks and luggage drop-offs. Conveyor belts crisscrossed through the air above them, carrying the bags that people couldn't be bothered to carry to the warp pads themselves. Above all that was a glass dome that let the colors of the late evening sky wash over the shiny steel and polished white marble that had been used to build just about everything else in the spaceport.

"Look, we're almost to the security checkpoint, so how about we all shut up and let Thea do her thing." Jasper slid her fake ID out of the front pocket on her neon pink floral-patterned shirt. The shirt had short sleeves, but she wore a long-sleeved black one underneath to cover her arms. She'd pulled up her hair with a pink scrunchy that complemented the floral shirt nicely.

Thea stepped into line first. She handed her ID and printed ticket—which was about as real as the ID—to the security officer with her left hand and let her right graze his computer. The monitor flashed green as he scanned her ticket.

"You're good to go." The man nodded to Grace. She stepped forward, handed over her stuff with shaking hands, and took a deep breath. The officer raised an eyebrow.

Jasper rested a hand on Grace's shoulder. "First time taking the family off planet," she told him with an easy smile. "Money, you know?"

"I hear that." Another green flash. The officer handed Grace her ticket and ID back. "You're good. Next!"

Jasper went through, followed by Dax, then Holly. They tossed their bags onto the conveyor belt, and Jasper reluctantly handed her motorcycle to an officer for inspection.

Thea went through the metal detectors first, then hung around close enough to the machines to use her power on them while the others passed through. The most important part was altering how their bags—particularly the one with Jasper's extensive collection of weapons—showed up on the X-ray screens.

Thea also had to prevent Jasper from setting off the metal detector. Cyborg limbs were fine, but they warranted closer inspection, and that would lead to the discovery of the illegal components in Jasper's brain.

Despite her trust in Thea, Jasper tensed in the split second it took for the machine to clear her.

The five grabbed their bags off the belt, Jasper took back her motorcycle, and they were good to go. As they walked, Jasper's gaze darted to Grace, who looked like a deer caught in the lights of a UFO.

"I'm guessing you've never been to a spaceport," Jasper said.

"No," Grace admitted. "I rarely even left the Sky District when I lived at the palace."

"The port is divided up by location. This side houses warps that lead to places around Gemma. We'll head to the wing for Si Hera and hop in line at a warp to Sagev." Jasper tapped the shirt pocket where she'd stashed her ticket. "They'll check our tickets one more time, but we won't have to deal with any more security."

Grace lowered her voice. "I feel like everyone's looking at me. Like they know who I am."

"You're imagining it," Jasper said. "If people look this way, it's probably because they're checking me out."

"Oh, please," Holly said. "We all look ridiculous."

"We look like tourists!" Jasper swept her gaze over the team's colorful, tropical clothing, accompanied by oversized hats and sunglasses. Okay, Holly had managed to pick out floral patterns that were entirely black and gray, but everyone else looked colorful. "We're ready for a nice family vacation."

"This is not how tourists—ugh, never mind."

They reached the Si Heran warps and stepped into one of several Sagev lines.

"If you've never been to a spaceport, I'm guessing you've never used a warp, either," Jasper said to Grace once it was almost their turn.

"No, but I've seen them on broadcasts," Grace replied.

"It'll feel weird, but since you already know what's happening, you'll be fine." Jasper absentmindedly traced a finger along the motorcycle's handlebar. "My first warp was terrifying."

"How old were you?" Grace asked.

Jasper froze. "Hm?"

"You said your first warp was—"

"How many in your party?" a warp technician asked.

"Five," Jasper told them, grateful for the interruption.

"Show me your tickets."

One by one, the team flashed their tickets so that the technician could confirm the destination they'd allegedly paid for was Sagev. After that, the tech said, "Go ahead and step onto the platform."

Jasper pushed the motorcycle up the ramp onto the pale blue warp pad. The others followed. The technician punched a few buttons into the keypad in front of them, and the floor glowed.

There was a flash of white light, and the team was in Sagev.

The air was noticeably hotter and drier. Bright early afternoon sunlight poured in from the massive windows around the Sagev spaceport. Warp techs ushered the team off the platform to make way for the next group.

"You good?" Jasper asked Grace as they descended the ramp. "Because if you're going to be sick—"

"I'm fine," Grace said, lifting her chin. "Now what?"

Huh. Okay then. Jasper brushed off her surprise. "Our first order of business is to locate where Ringmaster and his Apprentice are setting up shop this time."

"Actually," Holly said. "Our first order of business is to dump our stuff and change."

"I'll drop our stuff off and meet back up with you once I'm done," Jasper countered. She glanced up and was relieved to see the warp they'd stepped off of was close to an exit. "You guys go see if you can find anything useful."

Jasper took Grace's bag as the team stepped outside and fastened it to the back of the motorcycle. Security guards glanced at them as they walked out, but they were there to keep people out, not in.

Holly rolled her eyes and tossed Jasper her own bag. "Fine."

Once everything was secure, Jasper climbed onto the motorcycle. She waved as the four walked away. "Stay together, kids! Look both ways before you cross the road."

Holly didn't bother looking back as she flipped Jasper off.

Jasper had managed to keep her thoughts elsewhere until now, but as she sped off, all she could focus on was her destination.

It could barely be called a shack. The place was all metal sheets and wood and tarps, held together by nothing more than ropes, nails, and sheer willpower. It was surprising to see it still standing.

And painful.

Jasper rolled to a stop and dismounted. It wasn't much by way of shelter, though it had been better than being crammed into the barracks by far. But those days were long gone, she reminded herself. Today she had five minutes. Five minutes to let the pain and memories drown her. Then, she'd pull herself out and put the feelings in a box and not think about them for the rest of the mission.

Chapter Twenty-Four
Winging It, As Usual

"Good news," Jasper said over the comms. "The place is still standing."

"That's reassuring," Holly said, sarcastic as ever.

"Is the net connection good?" Thea asked.

"How far is it?" Dax added.

Grace barely processed what the others were saying, transfixed by the city ahead. The spaceport was just outside the city proper, with a walking path connecting them and the occasional shop or restaurant along the way. A road ran parallel to the path, and both buses and personal vehicles zoomed by. Despite being at ground-level, many of the cars were propelled by thrusters rather than driving on wheels.

Thea had said she would work on finding them a bus. Grace hoped that would be happening sooner rather than later. Otherwise, it was going to be a long walk before they were anywhere worth poking around.

Although Sagev's streets were as populated with pedestrians as any in Kronos, the skyscrapers in the city were nowhere near as tall. Or densely packed together. Endless blue sky was visible in every direction during their trek from the spaceport, interrupted only at the horizon ahead by metal and glass buildings shimmering in the heat.

God, the heat. It was nearly unbearable. The light jacket Grace had on to hide her wings made it even worse. For a moment, she wondered why she was out here, sweating and running around helping Jasper Van Terra. The more she saw behind the scenes, the more she forgot about the reputation of the ruthless villain who stalked Kronos's streets. She didn't think she could even say she was afraid of Jasper anymore.

That villain was still there, though, underneath the loud and impulsive teenage girl ordering them around. She had been Grace's only hope on

Kronos, but here, far from the Blades, maybe Grace could find a way to Earth.

But there wasn't time to dwell on that at the moment.

"Have you guys found anything?" Jasper asked. "And where are you? I'm on my way back."

"We're still walking toward the city," Thea told her. "We're headed for a mall called Silvium Center. I scanned some local news reports, and it turns out Ringmaster's made his presence known."

"Oh?"

"He publicly attacked Silvium Center. The damage forced three stores to shut down for repairs. People are speculating his motivation was robbery, but—"

"He could be using one of the closed stores as his base," Jasper finished. "Great. Oh hey, I see you guys!"

Grace, Thea, Holly, and Dax all turned around as Jasper sped toward them on her motorcycle, waving.

"You gonna give us a ride?" Holly asked.

"I'd love to, really, but—" Jasper flew past them. "I don't exactly have room. But hey, I saw a bus coming this way you can take!"

"She's right," Thea said, swiping at the holoscreen projected from her watch. "Bus bravo-28 will drop us off right in front of the shopping center. We just have to make it to that stop up ahead."

"Thea, could you check and see if there's a Bibi's in at Silvium Center?" Jasper asked as the team gathered around the signpost for the bus stop.

"There's three."

"I hate public transportation," Holly muttered.

Grace watched the approaching bus begin to slow. It had three levels of seating, and its rounded metal exterior was plastered with ads. "What's so terrible about it?" she asked. "I've never been in a public vehicle before."

"They're super unhygienic," Dax said.

"They never run on time," Thea added.

Holly folded her arms. "And there's always all kinds of weirdos."

"Ooh, yeah," Jasper said. "Be careful. You wouldn't want to run into some kind of criminal!"

"Jasper, I'm going to throw you into traffic," Holly threatened.

"Oh, come on, you can do better than that. Tell me you're going to, I don't know, set my spleen on fire."

"You're atrocious."

The bus came to a screeching halt by the sidewalk. Thea handed cash to the driver as the team entered, and the four made their way through the crowded bus.

"If the government actually put money into the bus system, it could be pretty nice," Thea said under her breath. "But they'd rather give themselves raises."

Dax's gaze moved to a woman who was coughing violently into her arm. "Can I—?"

Holly grabbed Dax's arm. "Not right now, Dax," she said, her voice surprisingly gentle. "You cure one person, and everyone else will come begging..."

The bus jerked forward. Grace stumbled and bumped into Thea. "Sorry!" she exclaimed.

Thea grabbed a pole in the center of the aisle. "Hold on tight. This is going to be a rough ride."

Grace leaned over to peer around her. "Are there no more empty seats?"

"There's two. Your options are to squeeze in by that group of kids who've been playing in mud, or next to the woman who looks like she's going to throw up any moment."

Grace's hand wrapped around the pole. "I can stand." Where had the kids even managed to find mud in a desert?

"On the bright side, the Silvium Center will probably be dead after the attacks," Holly said. "People will be too scared to shop there."

Grace may not have known Holly long, but by the time the bus let the team off at the mall, she was pretty sure Holly had never been more wrong about anything in her entire life.

The team stepped off the bus—Dax "accidentally" brushed a glowing hand against the sick woman on the way out, leaving her looking startled at the sudden ceasing of her cough—and found themselves in a massive crowd, worsened by lines so long they poured out of stores and wrapped around corners.

"Yikes," was all Thea had to say.

"What the hell?" Holly exclaimed. "What are you morons doing here? Didn't you hear about the Ringmaster attack?"

"Duh," a girl said as she walked by. Her uniform marked her as an employee of one of the stores, and she was struggling to keep a stack of boxes balanced in her arms. "Nothing draws in tourists like a big villain. Or hero, but you know, people will take what they can get."

Someone tapped Grace on the shoulder. She jumped and yelped in surprise.

"Whoa, it's just me," Jasper said. She took a sip from the smoothie in her hand, the Bibi's logo prominently displayed on the cup.

Holly raised an eyebrow. "I'm surprised you aren't chugging Nova Cora."

"Oh, this?" Jasper held up the smoothie. "It actually has Nova Cora in it! Amazing what they can do with food these days." She took another sip. "So, what stores did Ringmaster hit?"

Thea tapped her watch. A map of the mall popped up, and three red X's appeared over different stores. "He was all over the place."

"We'll have to split up, then." Jasper pointed to a spot on the map. "Angel and I will infiltrate that clothing store next to one of the attack sites and see if we can learn anything."

"Great. I'll take the electronics place here," Thea said. One of the stores on the map glowed yellow in response to her statement.

"Dax and I will look around that big furniture store at the south end." Holly folded her arms. "How do you propose we get in?"

"Easy. This place is a mess," Jasper said. "Employees will be so desperate for help they won't think twice about letting us work. Once we're in, we can poke around back rooms and ask workers if they've seen anything unusual. Oh, and keep an eye out for anyone going in or out of the closed stores." She finished her smoothie and tossed the cup in a perfect arc into a nearby trash can. "Then we'll regroup. Any questions? No? Great, let's go. Yay teamwork!"

The others dispersed into the crowd, leaving Grace to follow Jasper to the clothing store. The store spanned three floors next to the boarded-up jewelry shop Ringmaster had all but destroyed.

"You ever had a job before, Angel?" Jasper asked.

"No," Grace replied.

"Follow my lead."

Jasper elbowed her way through the crowded store. Grace apologized as she awkwardly followed Jasper's path to the "Employees Only" door at the back.

"Stand here and keep watch," Jasper told Grace.

"What am I supposed to do if—?"

Grace didn't get to finish her question. Jasper disappeared into the corridor on the other side and pulled the door shut behind her. Grace turned around and eyed the crowd gathered around the clearance racks. Was it really worth all of this just to say they bought something at the shopping center Ringmaster attacked?

The door reopened a minute later, and Jasper emerged holding lanyards marked with the store's logo. "Here, throw this on so other employees think we work here," she said. "Your name's Robin. Now we can walk around the back rooms without anyone bothering us. There's a hallway back there connected to the jewelry store, but there were employees hanging around—"

"Excuse me," a woman with lime green skin said as she appeared in front of them. Her skin's texture wasn't far off from a lime's, either. "Could one of you grab me this jacket in a size 99 from the back?" She looked the two up and down. "Oh, are you new?"

Jasper didn't hesitate. "Yes."

"I'm Dyana. Sorry you have to train when things are so hectic. We have a great system, but with the crowd..." She shook her head, making her sandy curls bounce. "It's organized chaos out there."

"The worst kind of chaos." Jasper took the jacket from Dyana. "Well, I think I can find this."

"Great. While you do that, I could train you—" Dyana turned to Grace. "—on how the dressing rooms are run."

Grace glanced at Jasper. "Uh..."

"That's a great idea," Jasper said. "Wink, wink."

"Okay?"

Dyana ignored Grace's confusion. "Follow me."

"This is perfect," Jasper said over comms once she was out of sight. "You can ask her about the Ringmaster stuff."

"How?" Grace asked.

"Great question!" Dyana exclaimed. "We track items with the computer system."

Grace followed her into the dressing rooms. "Huh? Oh. Cool."

"Ask her if she was here the day Ringmaster attacked," Jasper said.

"Were you here when Ringmaster attacked?" Grace asked.

"I was, but I was on break." Dyana stopped in front of a monitor and tapped the screen. "Here's a map of the fitting rooms. Red boxes are occupied, green are available."

"Okay," Grace said. Seemed simple enough. Not that she needed to know—

"When you check someone in or out, tap the room on the map to change its status."

"Ow!" Jasper exclaimed.

Grace feigned a cough. "You okay?" she whispered.

"Fine. I found the entrance to the jewelry store. Door's locked, but I think I can bust it down—*ow!*"

"This menu here is for tracking items," Dyana said. "You scan them with that device, which you turn on from this sub-menu. Make sure you turn it off when you're not using it, otherwise it glitches out—"

"Ask her if she's seen anything weird since the attack." A loud thud came from Jasper's end, followed by a string of curses.

"—and that's how you contact security—"

Grace's head spun.

"Ask if she ever works in the back rooms." Jasper grunted. A loud crash followed.

"—that button's only if a code tango-red-seven is announced, which I mentioned earlier—"

"See if she's been on any closing shifts."

"Do you think you've got it?"

"Uh—" Grace cleared her throat. "Yeah, I got it. I just have a couple of questions—"

"Great! I'm taking my break. Good luck!" Dyana walked away.

"Wait, what?"

An old woman walked up to Grace with a stack of clothes in hand. "Excuse me, I need a room."

Grace stared at the screen in front of her. "Um, go ahead and try room five?"

"You don't sound like you know what you're doing," the woman said sternly.

"Thanks. I don't."

Chapter Twenty-Five
Work Harder Not Smarter

Jasper finally broke the lock on the door, momentarily distracting her from whatever Grace was dealing with. On the other side was a gold sheet of metal. "Holly. Dax. Thea. Status updates."

"I got in," Thea said. "Nothing here but some equipment for the renovations."

"Same here," Holly added. "Nothing."

"Great. My location's boarded up tight. This must be Ringmaster's base." Jasper ran a hand along the metal. It seemed tough, but it wasn't galaxium. "We'll have to figure out a way in."

"What do you want us to do now?" Thea asked.

"We'll regroup in the food court," Jasper replied. "Angel, hold tight. I'm on my way to you."

"Great. I'll just keep pretending I know how to help these people." Grace didn't bother trying to mask her exasperation. "Excuse me, I need to scan that!"

Jasper closed the door and returned to the sales floor. As she worked her way to the fitting rooms, she said, "Angel, you could just walk away."

"I'm pretty sure these people would start an actual riot."

"Not our circus, not our fire-breathing reptiles."

"Okay, but—yes, sir, the dressing rooms are full. If you could just wait in line—"

Jasper paused to let a child run by in front of her. She gave the crowd a quick scan, curious if the kid had a parent anywhere nearby. Instead, her gaze found an older teen boy standing with a backpack slung over his shoulder, eyes darting around suspiciously. Pale-skinned and sporting curly blond hair, he could pass for human. From where she stood, anyway.

"Hang on," Jasper said. "I think this kid's shoplifting. I'm going to follow him." She started toward him.

"What? Why?" Grace asked.

"You think I'm gonna let some punk steal on my watch?" Jasper followed the kid to the wall shared with the next store. The one hit by Ringmaster.

"What do you care if some kid shoplifts?" Holly asked.

"They've got a sign posted in the back saying the employee who catches the most shoplifters gets a bonus." Jasper's eyes narrowed as the kid slipped behind a rack. She paused next to it and activated her heat vision.

The kid pushed a bunch of coats aside and pressed a hand to the wall. A rectangular section heated up, and he stepped through.

Jasper switched back to normal vision and moved around the corner. When she inspected the wall behind the rack, she found that a section seemed to have been cut out and replaced with metal. A silver metal, not gold like in the back hall.

"Thea," Jasper said. "If I send you a picture, could you get me an ID?"

Thea sounded skeptical. "You want me to run facial recognition on a shoplifter?"

"No, I want you to run facial recognition on a kid who just walked through a wall." Jasper backed away from the rack.

"Jasper, where are you?" Grace asked.

"Waiting for this kid to come back. I think he's—" Jasper's gaze darted to her right. "Ooh, these coats are nice." She picked up a long black overcoat and tried it on.

"Don't you have a dozen other coats just like that?" Thea asked.

"Are you spying on me?" Jasper glanced up at the nearest security camera.

"I got into the cameras to see what you're doing. What happened to regrouping in the food court?"

"That's still happening, but I'm pretty sure I just found the Apprentice. We need to ID him." Jasper found a mirror and adjusted the coat.

"Well, I tried getting into the cameras in the store next door, and they're all shut off," Thea said. "What if he takes a while to come back out?"

"Then we wait." Jasper grabbed a wide brimmed hat off a nearby shelf and set it on her head. "If you're going to spy on me, then tell me what you think of this."

"I don't think it really works with the neon floral shirt."

"Whatever. I'm taking it."

"Hey, I just got promoted," Grace said. "At least, I think that's what happened. The manager I just spoke to was very hungover."

"Congratulations." Jasper glanced at the wall and switched back to heat vision.

"Wait, he's sending people over to me. Oh, god, he wants me to train them."

The metal was heating up again. "Kid's coming back. Thea, get ready for a photo." Heat vision off. Jasper opened her camera.

"I can't promise he'll be in any of the databases my program checks," Thea warned.

"Well, let's find out."

The boy stepped out from behind the rack, glancing around to check if anyone had noticed him. Jasper snapped a photo before turning away. She slid her sphere out of her pocket. Under her breath, she said, "Mia, send image 1228 to Thea's tablet."

"No results found for 'These Apples.'"

"Thea's. Tablet," Jasper hissed.

"What would you like to do with Thea's tablet?"

Jasper groaned. "Send image 1228." Artificial Intelligence was rapidly becoming her most detested misnomer.

"Sending."

"You got that, Thea?"

"Yeah, I got it. Could take anywhere from a few minutes to an hour for the program to find a match. *If* it finds a match."

"Great. I'll meet you all at the food court." Jasper walked to the fitting rooms. "Angel, you still over here?"

Grace emerged from behind a line of people, carrying a stack of clothes. "These need to go back out to the floor." She dumped them into Jasper's arms.

"We can go now," Jasper told her.

"Look, Yrag said I'm the best employee they've had all year. I don't know if I'm actually that good or if the bar is incredibly low, but I want to enjoy this while it lasts."

"Who's Yrag?"

"He's either a supervisor, a manager, or a fear-induced hallucination." Grace shook her head. "Sorry. I've never been in a situation like this before.

It's weirdly rewarding. But we should get out of here before I lose my mind."

"Really?" Jasper dumped the stack of clothes onto a random shelf, and she and Grace headed toward the exit. "You were enjoying this?"

"Oh, I hate it. I had no idea people could be so rude over something so unimportant. But accomplishing things on my own is nice," Grace said. "I always had everything I needed handed to me. Until my bodyguard tried to murder me, I mean."

A man tapped on Grace's shoulder, bringing her to a halt. "Excuse me," he said. "I asked you to bring me this jacket in red."

"We don't make that jacket in red," Grace told him.

"Well, why not?"

"I don't know, I just work here! Do you want to call the designer and ask them why they didn't make it in red?" Grace ripped off her badge and tossed into a nearby trash can. "I quit."

Jasper tossed hers too, unable to hide a smirk. "Not bad, Angel. You're starting to get the hang of this."

They headed for the exit. Grace frowned. "I wouldn't put being a fake employee and a master criminal on the same level."

Jasper chuckled. "Okay, okay. Whatever you say."

Chapter Twenty-Six
Silvium Drift

Grace and Jasper exited the clothing store. "Anyone at the food court yet?" Jasper asked.

"Dax and I have been here for ten minutes," Holly replied sharply.

"I'm almost there," Thea said. "I got turned around looking for a tablet shop. This side of the mall is a maze and the map on their website is out of date, for some reason."

Jasper lifted an eyebrow. "What store are you in front of now?"

"Twin Sunrise Books."

Jasper spotted Thea in the crowd before Grace did and pointed at her. "Found you."

Thea turned around as the two approached. "Oh, great. Let's go." She had a new tablet box tucked under one arm.

"Whoa, hold on," Jasper said, pausing by the display in front of the bookstore. She picked up one of the books. "I never see bookstores anymore."

"Well, they're a bit outdated," Thea told her. "It sounds like Holly and Dax are ready to go. Let's get back to that place you were going on about and figure out how we're getting into Ringmaster's base."

"'Breaking Skies,'" Jasper read off the book's cover. "D. S. Teller. Interesting." She put it back and picked up another one.

Grace frowned. Sure, Jasper occasionally took pleasure in being extra obnoxious, but this felt different. It was almost as if she were—

Thea rested a hand on her hip. "Are you stalling?"

Jasper slammed the book back down on the shelf. "Of course not. Why would I be doing that? Let's go. We don't have all day." She hurried off toward the food court, leaving Thea and Grace to exchange confused looks before catching up.

They caught up to Jasper as she entered the food court, and the three quickly found Holly and Dax sitting at a table sipping drinks. A basket of fried somethings sat on the table between them.

"Aw, you guys got food without us?" Jasper asked.

"You were taking forever." Holly stood up. "Are we going now?"

"Yeah, yeah, we're going. The place we're staying is outside the city limits, so you won't be able to get there by bus."

"Thank god," Holly muttered.

"You'll all have to walk."

"Jasper, we'll all get heatstroke if we—" Dax started.

"I'm kidding, I'm kidding," Jasper cut in with a laugh. "I'm going to get us a car."

"Steal us a car?" Thea guessed.

"Duh." Jasper jutted a thumb over her shoulder behind her. "I saw one back there that looked nice. What do you guys think?"

"Oh, the display car?" Holly asked in a mocking tone. "Yeah, sure, wonderful idea. Steal that. I'm sure you'll have no problem getting it out of the mall."

"Just so you know, I was joking until you said that, but now I'm going to do it."

"You know what?" Holly barked out a cold laugh and sat back down. "Go ahead. I'm going to sit right here and watch you get your ass arrested by mall cops." She picked up a drink and took a sip. "Have fun."

"Okay, Holly's out. Dax?"

"I'll stay here with Holly," Dax said, fiddling with the straw of his own drink.

"Lame. Thea?"

"I'm starving. I'm gonna go hit up the Bibi's," Thea said.

"Okay, as long as you grab me some fries."

"You can buy your own fries."

"Cool." Jasper turned to Grace. "What about you, Angel. You in?"

"Uh…" Grace glanced at Holly and Dax. Holly slid in earbuds to listen to music. Dax started a video game on his smartsphere's holoscreen. Thea was already walking away. "I guess?"

"Great! Let's go."

Grace and Jasper walked to the intersection of two main corridors of the Silvium Center, where a cube-shaped car in an obnoxious shade of neon orange waited. The handles and other metal accents were gold, which made the paint color look even worse, and the yellow-green tires were the cherry on top.

"I think this is the worst car I've ever seen." Jasper put her hands on her hips. "I need it." She walked around to the back. "And it should fit the motorcycle just fine."

"How are we going to…?" Grace trailed off and looked around, wondering if anyone was listening.

"Well, if Thea had kindly offered to help, she could do her technopath thing and it'd be a piece of cake. But we'll have to do this the old-fashioned way." Jasper slid a knife from her pocket and stuck it into the crack between the door and the rest of the car.

Grace strolled to the other side of the car, hoping that if someone noticed Jasper fiddling with the door lock, she could pretend she was innocent. "Who buys these things, anyway?" She hadn't really meant to ask the question out loud, but she did, and Jasper laughed.

"Maybe some people really like squares. And construction zone orange."

Now Grace laughed. "Honestly, I doubt anyone was ever going to buy this. I think we'd be doing the mall a favor by stealing it."

She caught Jasper's grin through the windows. Then there was a clicking sound, and the driver's door popped open.

"Thea, could you do me a favor?" Jasper asked, pressing a finger to her comm.

"Do I have a choice?" Thea replied.

"I just need you to grab my motorcycle from where I left it outside before meeting back up with Dax and Holly."

"Fine."

"Be careful."

"I will."

"I mean it! I don't want a scratch on that thing, or you're grounded."

Grace's hand hesitated over the handle a moment before pulling it open. What did she have to worry about? Mall security didn't stand a chance against Jasper. Especially Jasper behind the wheel of a vehicle.

Jasper settled into the driver's seat and popped a panel off under the steering wheel. After watching her work for a couple of minutes, Grace said, "I'm guessing you've done this before."

"Yep."

"A lot."

"Yep."

Grace rubbed her arm. "Why?"

"Well, sometimes I needed transportation and didn't have money."

"I mean, how'd you end up in that situation in the first place? Didn't you say you used to live on Earth?"

The dashboard lit up as the engine came to life. "It's a long story." Jasper slid her hands along the wheel. "Buckle your seat belt."

Grace quickly obliged. The belt had barely clicked into place when Jasper hit the horn. People jumped out of the way, and the car inched forward.

"This might be a little less thrilling than I was hoping for," Jasper said. She checked the rear-view mirror. "Oh, wait, security's here! Aw, they have hover scooters. That's cute."

Grace twisted around in her seat to get a look. "How are they planning to catch us?"

"I don't know. It would be hilarious to watch them try to pull us over, but I'd rather not give the real police time to show up." Jasper blared the horn again. "My path's almost clear. Brace yourself."

They shot forward and flew toward the food court. When they entered the dining area, Jasper yanked the wheel to the right, and they slid past the table Holly, Dax, and Thea were waiting at. Jasper's motorcycle leaned against the table next to them.

Jasper waved at the three through the front windshield. Dax gave a half-hearted wave back, Thea raised an eyebrow and sipped her drink, and Holly rolled her eyes.

They came to such a hard stop that the right side of the car lifted off the ground.

"Oh, wow, this thing's terrible." Jasper laughed as they slammed back down onto all four wheels. She rolled her window down. "Okay, everyone in! Put the motorcycle in the back."

While the team piled in, security drew closer. "How are we getting the car out of here?" Holly asked.

"My plan goes something like this: Central staircase. Upper level. West balcony. Roof."

"That's not a plan, that's a bunch of random words strung together."

"All right, it's more of a vibe. I'll throw together a mood board if that'll make you happy." Jasper glanced back. "Everybody in? Seat belts buckled? Great."

By then, shoppers had realized there was a rogue car on the loose and were packing themselves into the stores or along the walls, leaving the corridor open for Jasper to speed down. The security guards raced out of her path when she came flying toward them, nearly falling off their hover scooters in the process. Jasper waved at them as she passed.

They took corners a little too fast for comfort. Jasper knew how to walk—well, drive—the fine line between looking cool and pushing things too far, but Grace held on tight to the first handle she found, fearing they would fully tip over at any moment.

The ride up the central staircase was bumpy. Navigating the upper level involved a lot of swerving around fountains and kiosks. They were nearly to the west balcony when a second engine joined the sound of the car's.

"Security's got a motorcycle," Thea warned.

"At least someone's putting in effort." Jasper's gaze flickered to the mirror. "That guy's fast. He might actually catch us."

"What's he going to do?" Holly asked, arms folding. "Ask us nicely to pull over?"

Dax twisted to look out the back window. "Uh, actually, he's got a blaster. It's pretty big—"

Jasper swerved to the left, and a green blast of energy shot past them. "Okay, that's unexpected for a mall cop, but it's nothing we can't handle." She swerved again. "Think we can make it through that archway to the balcony?"

"Looks pretty tight," Thea said.

The guard fired again, blasting off the right-side mirror.

"How about now?" Jasper leaned forward and squinted at the rapidly approaching exit. "Looks like we'll get an inch on either side, if I line us up right."

"And if you don't?" Grace asked.

"Just hold on to something."

They made it out onto the balcony without anything breaking, although there was an alarming scraping sound on Grace's side. Jasper barreled through chairs and tables on her way to the edge of the balcony. There, the car crashed through the glass railing and landed on the roof below, sending a solid jolt through Grace's bones.

"He's right behind us!" Holly warned.

Jasper zig-zagged to dodge more blasts. "Don't worry, we'll lose him in a second here."

"Jasper, we're headed to the edge of the roof," Thea said.

"Yep!"

"This isn't a flying car."

"Yep!"

They reached the edge and soared over. "You all put your seat belts on, right?" Jasper asked.

"You're asking us this now?" Holly shrieked.

The awning over the restaurant entrance below broke their fall, becoming completely shredded in the process. Still, they hit the ground hard enough to knock the air out of Grace's lungs.

"This thing may be hideous, but they went all out on the shock absorbers." Jasper hit the gas, and they shot through the parking lot.

"The security guard's stuck at the edge of the roof," Thea said. "Guess he's not as insane as you are."

"Yay us." Jasper tapped a finger against the steering wheel. "Next stop: home sweet home."

Chapter Twenty-Seven
Open Seas / Closed Eyes

Stealing was easy. Jane learned how to move around stores without being noticed. And on the rare occasion she did get caught, she could outrun just about anyone.

The ground level streets of Kronos weren't nearly as well-regulated in terms of temperature as the palace was, so she got her hands on a lot of layers. Even so, even on the warmest days of summer, there was a chill in her blood that never left.

Sometimes, people recognized her. People sent to hunt her down. The attacks didn't come often enough for Jane to think her pursuers had a way to track her, but they kept her on edge.

She hardly remembered most of her fights. What she did remember was standing over people she'd left on the ground, badly injured. Sometimes dead.

Kronos finished circling the far side of Myni and moved away from the star. Gemma returned to the sky, a distant second sunrise. The world grew colder. Jane couldn't take the streets anymore.

She found a carrier ship that made runs across Kronos's oceans. It was a lot of work, a lot of time on the sea, and very dangerous. They would take nearly anyone willing to sign up, with no questions asked.

So, she gave them the name Juliet Stark and took to the seas.

When the icy water sprayed her face, when ropes burned her hands, when strange things in the water rocked the ship, she closed her eyes and reminded herself she just needed to save enough money to get off Kronos. She just needed passage to Earth.

If it all went according to plan, it wouldn't take more than a few years. And hopefully, as more time passed, less people would be looking for her.

Another human showed up on the ship in what would have been early January of 1972. Her name was Naomi. She had long pale hair, freckles scattered across her tan skin, and she came from a long line of humans who'd been born and raised on Kronos. She followed Juliet around even after Juliet had finished training her.

Juliet was twenty, but she didn't feel like it.

Throughout February, they worked on most of their tasks together. Juliet couldn't remember the last time she'd had a genuine conversation with someone before Naomi showed up.

In March, Juliet nervously told Naomi that she had a cybernetic leg. Naomi didn't care. Juliet mentioned the arm. When Naomi still didn't care, she told her about the stuff in her brain and that she had no idea what any of it did.

Naomi didn't ask Juliet for the full story. Instead, she got out her tablet.

"If they could transfer data to you remotely, I'm sure there's a way for me to—oh, I think this is you." Naomi pointed at the screen. "See? You're showing up as a printer."

"I don't want to be a printer," Juliet replied with a frown.

"Aw, being a printer's not so bad. I hear the job market's booming."

Juliet laughed and adjusted her position on Naomi's bed. "Okay, okay. Are you sure that's me?"

"Yes, because this device only shows up in my menu when you're nearby."

"Why didn't you ask me about it sooner?"

"My first thought wasn't exactly, 'hey, maybe my friend has a computer in her brain.'"

"Fair enough." Juliet took a sip from the Nova Cora can she'd liberated from Naomi's cooler.

"I'm going to see if I can open you up as a file folder—ah, here we go. Oh, yikes, it's a mess in here."

"Well, I already knew my brain was a mess."

"Ha, ha." Naomi scrolled through the list of programs and files and documents. "Would it have killed whoever did this to give things names other than random strings of numbers and letters?"

"Can you tell me what any of it does?" Juliet asked.

"I'm afraid not. Most of the files are locked, anyway. Which might be a good thing, because trying to mess with them could screw up your brain."

Naomi continued scrolling. "Wait, you said there was a clock in your vision?"

"Yeah, with the Kronos time and date. I can make it disappear and reappear, but I have no idea what else I'm supposed to be able to do."

"Hmm." Naomi tapped on something and brought up a box filled with code. "I'm going to try something. Tell me if anything happens."

Juliet raised an eyebrow. "Promise you won't screw up my brain?"

"Pinky promise," Naomi replied. She held up her hand. "That is how it goes, right?"

"Yeah. That's right." Juliet locked her pinky with Naomi's. "What are you doing?"

"Hang on." Naomi pasted a bunch of code in at the bottom of the box, added a few more lines, and closed it out.

Juliet blinked, and the numbers and names in the corner of her vision changed. "Whoa, what did—is that the Earth date?"

"Yep. I know you like to keep track."

Juliet willed the time to disappear and reappear. She grinned. "Well, I'm glad I befriended a tech genius."

"I'm literally not. I just know how to use a search engine."

Juliet flipped the clock on and off again. Earth time. No math needed. Despite the strange mix of emotions in her chest, she couldn't help but start laughing. After a moment, Naomi joined in.

In early April, the captain announced his retirement. He assured the crew that his replacement would be great.

He was wrong.

Shifts became longer. Work became more brutal. The ship's routes changed entirely, only adding to the confusion. Juliet tried not to let it get to her. As long as she was getting paid, she couldn't care less.

Naomi had a different view.

"The people running the ship now are up to something. I'm pretty sure they're involved with one of the gangs," she told Juliet one afternoon on their too-short break.

Juliet didn't move her gaze from the sun setting over the ocean. "Maybe. But what are we supposed to do if they are?"

"If we could get proof that they're smuggling drugs and weapons—"

"Sounds like a great way to get killed." Juliet leaned against the railing in front of them. "If I can just make it a few more months, I can afford to go home." She finally looked at Naomi. "What are you doing here? Where are you going after this?"

"I want to go to school, eventually." Naomi sighed. "But that doesn't matter right now. I grew up in the Tide District. I've seen the kinds of things these imports—and the gangs bringing them—do to the lower districts."

Juliet grimaced. "I understand. I just don't see what we're supposed to do about it."

"I guess."

A long moment passed. Juliet held up her right hand and studied it. "Do I look twenty to you?"

"Huh?"

"Never mind."

A few nights after that, Juliet went to Naomi's room to find her gone. Her first thought was that maybe Naomi had been given an extra shift and simply forgot to mention it.

But no, she'd told Juliet she would be in her room just an hour earlier. She'd have at least stopped by to give Juliet a heads-up if she had an unexpected shift, right? Juliet turned away and began to wander the hallways. Where else would Naomi have gone?

Something felt off.

Numbers flashed in Juliet's vision, numbers she wasn't controlling. One warned her heart rate was speeding up. She broke into a run toward the deck. "Naomi?" She'd meant to call louder, but her voice came out as a whisper.

A new message popped up. *Distant audio detected. Increase audio input?*

Juliet still didn't understand how she was meant to control the screen, but the clock thing seemed to be tied to her mental commands. *Yes*, she tried.

Nothing happened.

Juliet paused next to a door to the deck, hands trembling. *Yes*, she tried again.

Distant voices became audible. "—should we do with her?" a man was asking.

A second man answered. "We can't have people thinking they can snoop around and get away with it."

Juliet rested a hand on the door handle. Maybe they were talking about someone else. Maybe this had nothing to do with Naomi.

"You won't get away with this forever," Naomi said. "What gang are you involved with, anyway? Coasters? Red Blades?"

No. *No, no, no.* How could someone so smart do something so stupid? More numbers flashed in Juliet's vision. The next thing she knew, she was watching the heat patterns of six people on the other side of the door. She had heat vision?

A woman laughed. "We aren't involved with the gang. We *are* the gang. Ever heard of the Thunder Serpents?"

One of the figures was being held by two others. Naomi. Juliet's mind raced. She could take down the five gang members, but what would they do to Naomi before she could get to them?

"Just kill her and throw her overboard," the second man who'd spoken said. "She's not worth any more effort."

Juliet turned the door handle. Her heat vision switched off, and the world moved slow. She ran onto the deck, aware of everything around her, soaring with each step. She set her sights on the Thunder Serpent holding Naomi's right arm.

No sooner had Juliet struck the man in the face than two more were on her, grabbing her arms. She kicked the one to her right. Pain reverberated through her leg. She ripped herself free and punched the guy at her left.

Behind her, Naomi screamed.

Juliet whirled around as the fourth Serpent pulled the trigger on his gun.

The fifth Serpent crashed into Juliet, taking her by surprise, knocking her to the ground.

Juliet clawed and kicked until she forced the woman off her. When she climbed to her feet, the shooter was throwing Naomi's body over the railing.

In her blind rage, all Juliet could think to do was push him over after.

"Everyone on patrol, get to the lower starboard deck," the woman behind her said into a communicator. "We have a situation."

Juliet lunged, but the woman was backing away and the other Serpents were getting up and footsteps and voices signaled more were coming. How many could Juliet to fend off before she joined Naomi in the ocean?

She ran. Serpents charged her, but she jumped and pulled herself up the wall onto the upper deck. From there, her getaway became a blur of leaping over equipment and sliding down ropes and poles and sprinting as fast as she could.

At the front of the ship, the colorful Kronos skyline glittered in the night. Juliet slammed into the railing and paused to catch her breath. She stared out at the dark ocean, at the port they were supposed to dock at within the hour. How far to shore? Could she swim? Did she have any other choice if she wanted to live?

People were coming. She kept running, headed for the side of the ship. She could steal one of the motorized lifeboats. She'd be an easy target, but she could at least get a head start.

Juliet pushed crew members aside, not caring if they were Serpents or not. She stole a knife from one of their belts and went over the railing. Her stomach dropped. Wind whipped past her. She slammed into a lifeboat and landed on her side.

With a groan, she climbed to her feet and started slashing at the ropes around her. As she cut the last one, Serpents appeared at the edge of the deck.

"Too late!" Juliet screamed into the wind as she fell. The boat hit the sea. A spray of frigid water washed over her, making her shriek. Shivering, she slid into the driver's seat and started the engine.

They had another boat in the water behind her within minutes. As soon as guns started firing, Juliet scrambled to the side of her boat and jumped.

She stayed under the water as long as she could manage, swimming in what she hoped was away from her pursuers and toward the shore. When she finally broke the surface for air, she heard an approaching engine.

Her head snapped to the right. The Serpents' boat was coming her way, but if they didn't see her, they were going to miss by about ten feet. Instead of waiting around to find out if they'd noticed her, she went back under.

The next time she came up for air, the boat was far ahead of her, moving in circles. Treading water, she lowered herself as far as she could manage while keeping her nose up.

The boat turned and drove back toward the ship.

Juliet breathed a sigh of relief and sank under to keep swimming. After coming up a few more times, she dared to stay at the surface.

The city approached at a painfully slow rate. Juliet swore every stroke, every kick, every breath would be her last before her aching body succumbed to the darkness. But then she told herself she could manage one more, and then another, and then another, and then a lady with tentacles in place of arms passed by in a small boat and honked at her and asked if she needed a ride.

Juliet didn't trust her, but she could always jump back into the ocean.

The woman gave her a blanket and a ride to the docks. When they arrived, Juliet thanked her and jumped out and ran off before the woman had a chance to fully stop.

She'd barely left the pier when trouble caught up with her. A passing man grabbed her and tossed her to the ground with unexpected force. Pavement scraped Juliet's skin. The taste of blood hit her mouth. She rolled onto her back.

A woman appeared at the man's side and stepped on her chest. "What, did you think our friends on the ship wouldn't send a warning ahead to shore?"

"Serpents?" Juliet gasped.

The man smirked. "You're strong. And fast. And since you won't do us any good on the ship anymore, we're sending you off to the Lion's Den. I'm sure they'll pay us a decent amount for you."

Juliet braced herself for a fight, but more people gathered around. Two, four, six—she counted ten in total. If she could get her hands on something she could hit them with, maybe she could—

A pulse gun was jammed into her forehead, and she was out.

Chapter Twenty-Eight
This shack would cost five thousand janos
to rent in Kronos!

The setting sun bathed the desert landscape in shades of violet red. A few particularly bold stars had begun to twinkle in the sky, and both of Si Hera's moons accompanied them as pale slivers. Beneath all of that cosmic wonder, Grace shielded her eyes and took in the tiny pile of garbage Jasper had called a shack.

It didn't seem very…Jasper.

"I pulled out some blankets and pillows and whatnot," Jasper said as she led the team inside. The place had one main room connected to a makeshift kitchen, and a doorway filled by a tarp leading to rooms that couldn't be much larger than the one they were in.

"No beds?" Thea asked.

"There's one bed, and there's no way it's fitting all of us. Thing's falling apart anyway." Jasper clapped her hands together. "Which is fine! We can all sleep on the floor. It'll be like a sleepover. We can play truth or dare."

Holly ran a finger along a shelf and eyed the dust it left on her skin. "Is there dinner here?"

"There's unopened boxes of pasta somewhere," Jasper said. She began trying cupboards.

"How old is it?" Thea asked skeptically.

Jasper pulled a box from a shelf. "Older than you." She shrugged. "It's probably fine. Maybe. I've eaten worse."

"We aren't you," Holly muttered.

"I saw some plants growing outside in the shade of the shack," Dax said. "I've seen them before in recipes, and they're pretty healthy. For desert plants, anyway." After a pause, he added, "Well, they won't kill us, at least."

"Thank you, Dax," Holly said as Dax moved toward the door. "We'll have plants. You can keep your gross pasta, Jasper."

"Great! More for me, then." Jasper slammed the box down on the table sitting in the middle of the room. One of the legs snapped, and the table crashed to the ground.

Grace winced. Once the dust settled, she asked, "What is this place, anyway?"

"There was a war out here almost forty years ago," Jasper explained. "About sixteen starcycles, I guess. Some of the soldiers set up shacks like this one."

"How'd you find it?" Holly asked.

Jasper opened a different cupboard and pulled out a rusty pot. It took her a few moments to respond. "I did a job out here. Robbed a casino. Found this place by luck."

Luck didn't seem like the best word to describe it.

Grace found an overturned chair, set it up, and sat down, eager to rest her aching legs. She peeled off her jacket. After a moment's hesitation, she let her wings stretch out as much as she could in the small space.

Jasper picked up a jug of water from the corner, poured some into her pot, and set it on a metal rack. In the space beneath the rack, she started a fire with a lighter from one of her coat pockets. Thea settled onto the floor nearby and turned on her tablet. Holly seemed determined to inspect every inch of the shack.

It wasn't long before Dax came back in with an armful of waxy leaves and scrub brush roots, which he set on the small stretch of counter space beneath the cupboards. He poked around until he found a plate to put them on, then laid out a few on the rack next to Jasper's pot.

"Oh, hey!" Thea jumped to her feet and nearly hit her head on a rusted pipe. "I got a result on the facial scan!"

"Really?" Jasper poured the box of pasta into the pot and made a face when mostly crumbs came out.

Thea swiped a hand across her tablet screen. The image she'd had pulled up jumped to the holoscreen projected from a smartsphere she'd left on the counter. "His name is Aymes Bell."

Grace frowned as she studied the picture that came up. "Wait, I recognize him! He was an intern at Starchatter."

"Must be the Apprentice then. He was using the internship as a cover, like us." Jasper glanced at Thea. "Got any other info?"

"He attends a school on Sa Ren called East Marina High," Thea said. "He's...eighteen in Earth years."

"This is great! Ringmaster's careful, but we might have an easier time getting info from this kid. He probably has a sphere or tablet or something we can hack, right?"

Thea nodded. "I'm sure he'll be easier to hack than Ringmaster."

"I still want to find a way into Ringmaster's base at the mall before the race. Which is in a few Si Heran days. Which are roughly twenty-two hours each, for the uninformed," Jasper said. "We should find out what exactly the kid was doing there earlier. I'll have a more detailed plan tomorrow morning, but I think if we blow a hole in the roof—"

"I'm not discussing explosions until I've had a good night's sleep," Holly told her.

"Fair enough." Jasper grabbed her pasta pot and tipped the excess water into the sink. "Okay kids, dinner time. Gather around the table."

"The one you broke?" Holly asked.

"Don't smart mouth me, young lady. We'll just break the other two legs and sit on the floor."

Grace thought it was a joke, but Jasper walked over and snapped the table's legs off with surprising ease. Once the top was lying flat, she grabbed her pot and the plate of vegetables Dax had assembled and brought them over.

"You're really going to eat that?" Holly peered into the pasta pot with disgust.

"Yes. Thea, put your tablet away." Jasper returned to the counter and opened a few drawers. "I know there are forks here somewhere—"

Grace settled onto the floor between Thea and Dax. Jasper returned with a fork and a bottle of Nova Cora and sat on the other side of Thea, next to Holly.

Holly eyed the bottle. "That label looks weird."

"It's vintage," Jasper said.

"Sounds like a fancy way of saying expired."

Jasper shoved a bite of pasta in her mouth, popped the cap off the bottle, and took a swig. She swallowed. "That's disgusting."

"The soda or the pasta?" Thea asked.

"Yes."

Dax pointed to the plate. "You're welcome to the vegetables."

"I'm fine, thanks." Jasper shoved more pasta in her mouth. "I lied. The pasta's great. I'm going to quit my life of crime and become a chef."

Thea laughed. "I'd love to see that."

"I would pay money to see that," Holly added before popping a leaf in her mouth.

"I'd go," Grace said, surprised to find herself getting caught up in the hypothetical Chef Jasper scenario.

Jasper raised an eyebrow. "Really?"

"Sure. I could start a food review blog." Grace shrugged.

After a moment, Jasper grinned. "That's the spirit."

They finished the food. Jasper, despite making faces every time she took a sip, downed the bottle of Nova Cora. "We'll get groceries while we're in the city tomorrow. No more...this."

The team shuffled into what Jasper referred to as the bedroom. Technically, there was a bed, but it was the only furnishing and looked to be one wrong move away from collapsing. The five selected various places across the floor to set up bedding and took turns going into the next room—the designated bathroom—to change.

The full weight of the day sank into Grace's tired muscles during her turn in the bathroom. While she poured water from a jug onto an old towel to wash her face, she noticed something sticking out from behind the mirror. A piece of paper? She grabbed it.

It had been folded and unfolded countless times. Grace set it on the edge of the nonfunctional sink and spread it out. In the middle of the page was a single printed photo. A pale girl and a brown-skinned boy, standing next to each other, dressed in light military clothing that matched the desert sands and holding long-distance blasters.

Wait. Grace squinted and took a closer look at the girl. Her straight black hair only reached her chin, and the top half was pulled back in a short ponytail, but her face was one Grace had seen countless times before.

Jasper?

Someone knocked on the wooden door frame. "You almost done, Angel?" Jasper asked.

Grace quickly folded the picture back up and shoved it into her bag. "Yeah, I'm coming."

Back in the bedroom, she set her bag down next to her pile of bedding and settled in. Exhaustion pulled her under even before the lamps were turned off.

She awoke sometime later and found herself in complete darkness. As her eyes adjusted, she became aware of a figure moving nearby. She slowly turned her head and watched Jasper tiptoe into the front room.

Just pretend to be asleep, Grace told herself. Yes, she was curious as to what Jasper was up to, but following probably wasn't a good idea.

Ten seconds passed. Grace sighed and sat up. Waiting around wasn't getting her anywhere. For better or for worse, her life was dependent on Jasper right now. If everything else was out of reach—safety, her memories, passage to Earth—maybe Grace could at least get some answers about Jasper Van Terra.

Grace quickly changed from her sweats into sturdy pants, pulled on boots, and crept to the front of the shack. Outside, Jasper stood next to the motorcycle she'd pulled out of the car, putting on her helmet. She wore the black overcoat she'd stolen from the mall over her racing suit.

Grace watched Jasper climb onto the motorcycle and speed off toward the city. Once she'd shrunk to a speck in the distance, Grace stretched out her wings, sucked in a deep breath, and took to the air.

Now *this* was flying. No buildings or traffic to dodge, no enemies trying to knock her out of the sky. Just Grace and the night air. She flew straight for a minute before daring to try a few spins and wide loops. It was harder to keep her balance than expected, and she dropped a few times before figuring out how to angle her wings correctly.

Once the initial thrill of flight wore off, Grace switched her focus back to Jasper. It was easy to follow the faint pink glow of the motorcycle as it moved far below. Grace wondered if Jasper noticed her following. She wondered if she cared.

Finally, Jasper pulled into a parking spot next to a fuel station and slid off her motorcycle. Grace landed on the roof of the station's convenience store, debating whether she should say something.

Jasper took off her helmet and shook out her ponytail, leading Grace to briefly wonder how often—if ever—she let others see her with her hair down.

"Yes, Angel," Jasper called. "I see you up there."

Grace glided to the ground, landing directly in front of Jasper. "What are you doing?"

"Just getting some air. You should head back."

"Well, maybe I want some air too."

Jasper tensed. "What are you really doing?"

"What do you mean?"

Jasper set the helmet on the motorcycle, adjusted her coat, and started walking. "Why do you care what I do in the middle of the night?"

"You're kind of my only hope of getting back to a normal life," Grace replied as she hurried to follow. "I mean, I know I can't go back to my old one at the palace, but—"

"Right, right." Jasper rubbed her forehead.

"You've been acting weird at the shack," Grace continued. Frowning, she added, "Well, you always act kind of weird, but this is a different weird."

"You're not the only one to notice." The two crossed a street. The sidewalks became busier.

"Do the others know something I don't?" Grace asked.

"Nope," Jasper replied. "They know about as much as you do. They've just been around me long enough to know what I'm like. I don't think they care to know the reasons why."

"I'm sure they do." When Jasper didn't reply, Grace glanced around the crowded streets. "What time is it?"

"About one in the a.m. Listen, if you really want to follow me around, I won't stop you. But I don't think you'll want to be out here."

Grace bristled at the statement. "I can handle myself. I know you all think that losing my memory and living in the Governor's Palace made me weak, but I can do more than just be proof of Starr's experiments."

Jasper glanced at her. Raised an eyebrow. After a long moment, she said, "Alrighty then. Let's do this."

Chapter Twenty-Nine
Supervillain Weekend Getaway

Jasper had left the shack with no plan. All she knew was that she needed to go somewhere, to do something, and maybe that would allow her to outrun the weight in her chest.

Despite Grace's protests, part of Jasper still wanted to steer clear of anything that might scare her. But Grace knew by now what she was signing up for. And, Jasper had to admit, she wanted to believe that Grace was right about herself. That she was strong. More than just a sheltered girl who'd lived half a life.

Someone who really could be a hero.

"You're going to keep following me even if I steal? Even if I go weird places?" Jasper asked. "Because I'm not changing my plans for you."

"Good," Grace replied. "I can handle it."

"Great!"

"Why are you doing this, though?"

Jasper shrugged. "It's called self-care." The two reached the Humming Casino and walked through the front doors.

"Aren't you hot in that coat?" Grace asked. "I'm dying in just a shirt." Her wings rested flat against her back on top of the dark blue t-shirt she wore—Jasper was pretty sure it was the sleep shirt she'd dozed off in—but it was unlikely anyone who did notice them would give them much thought. Not here in Sagev.

"Nah." Jasper scanned the crowd. "Maybe if we pick enough pockets, we can afford to hit up Atzy's."

"Atzy's?" Grace asked. "Wait, we?"

"It's a restaurant-slash-bar-slash-dance floor. Think Electroswinger. And are you with me or not? These people are too rich to notice some missing cash, anyway."

"Whatever." Grace rubbed her eyes.

"You tired?" Jasper asked as they crossed the casino floor.

"No, I'm fine—"

Jasper grabbed a glass of fizzy black liquid resting on a slot machine and held it out to her. "Nova Cora. Full of caffeine."

Grace made a face. "No thanks."

"Come on. Have you even tried it?"

"No. They don't have it at the palace."

"Of course. Rich people only put expensive drugs in their bodies. Not peasant drinks." Jasper took a sip.

"I'm less concerned about the fact that it's Nova Cora and more concerned about the fact you took it from some random person," Grace said. "What if they're sick?"

"Oh no, guess I'll die. What a tragedy." Jasper offered Grace the glass again. "Pretty sure I already mentioned that my immune system has seen worse. Are you saying your body isn't tough enough to handle a couple of germs from a stranger?"

Grace's eyes narrowed. She grabbed the glass and downed the rest of it.

"Great!" Jasper exclaimed. Her head turned. "Oh my god, it's South Siren!"

Grace whirled around. "Where?"

Jasper laughed. "She's playing twin suns. In costume and everything. They really don't give a damn out here. The villains are all probably trying to have some fun before the race."

"Should we avoid them?" Grace asked.

"Hell no. I'm Van Terra." Jasper turned her head in the other direction as a group walked by. "Oh, hey, easy targets."

One man paused and knelt to tie his shoe, and Jasper plucked a wallet from his back pocket. She grabbed a purse hanging off a chair as she passed and slung it over her shoulder.

"Jasper!" Grace hissed as she caught up.

Jasper wasn't sure if that was about the theft, the villains, or something else entirely. Instead of responding to Grace, she opened the wallet and pulled out a stack of jano bills. "You ever played twin suns?"

"I don't know what that is."

"Oh, this'll be fun." They stopped in front of the game table where South Siren was playing, and Jasper tossed the bills into the pile in the middle. "It's a card game."

"I don't know what I'm doing!" Grace protested.

"Don't worry about it. Just have fun."

The dealer held out cards to them. Grace reluctantly accepted her hand.

"Well, well, well, if it isn't Van Terra," South Siren said from across the table. She tossed two of her cards face down in front of her. "Who's your friend?"

"This is my associate, uh, Superangel. One word." Jasper threw down one card. Grace's gaze flickered between them. She put down one as well.

South Siren was dressed as she had been during the first race, in a sleeveless and very low-cut white bodysuit that had dark gray panels running down each side. There was no white glow in her eyes at the moment, leaving her with the same dark brown irises as Sarena Trench the popstar. But instead of Sarena's matching long waves of hair—which Jasper assumed was a wig—her white hair fell straight, stopping just above her shoulders.

"Rumor has it Ringmaster's up to something big," South Siren said, lifting a dark teal hand to pat her hekten's head. "You wouldn't know anything about that, would you?"

"Nope. Just here for the fame and glory." Jasper assessed her hand and pursed her lips.

Other players around the table either threw down cards or drew from the deck as their turn came. Grace leaned toward Jasper. "What do the symbols on the cards mean? Are they related to the numbers?" she whispered.

"Don't worry about it." Jasper drew from the deck. "You're doing fine."

"I genuinely thought you would do better in the first race." South Siren raised a white eyebrow. "A lot of people discredit you because you're young and new, but you've pulled off some impressive stunts."

"Well, I would have done better, but some Red Blades attacked me over an...unrelated issue."

Grace threw down three cards without even looking at them.

"Still." South Siren shrugged. "If I were with the betting crowd, I might have even put money on you."

People were betting on the races? Jasper should have expected as much. "We've only had one race," she said. "I'll have plenty of chances to—"

"Drink, miss?" a server asked, holding out a tray of glasses. Jasper accepted. To her surprise, Grace took one too.

"You're not even going to ask what it is?" Jasper asked as she drew again. Another awful card. Ugh.

Grace took a sip. "Nope. Am I playing this right at all?"

Maybe that Nova Cora had been spiked with something. Or maybe Grace had simply never had much caffeine or sugar before. That wouldn't surprise Jasper. Still, bringing Grace had been a terrible idea.

Jasper swallowed her guilt. Grace had insisted, after all.

South Siren drew a card, and annoyance crossed her face for a split second before she masked it.

"You hear anything else about Ringmaster, or just that he's up to something?" Jasper asked.

"I heard he's working for someone, but he never struck me as the type. His name is Ringmaster, after all," South Siren replied. "You could try talking to Cutthroat. He's the one I heard it from."

The man to Jasper's left tossed down his hand. "I'm setting," he announced. Everyone else around the table threw their cards down, some groaning and others cursing.

Grace put her cards down, and the attention turned to her.

Jasper whistled. "Wow, nice hand."

"Impressive," South Siren added, her tone walking a fine line between admiration and annoyance.

"What just happened?" Grace asked.

"You won all that money is what happened." Jasper grabbed jano bills from the center pile and held them out to Grace, who stared in confusion. Sighing, Jasper shoved the bills into her own pockets. "Let's go find Cutthroat."

Cutthroat stood on a balcony overlooking the casino floor. He was dressed in his usual layers of black and purple leather, accented with silver buckles here and there. There were silver rings on his hands, and a couple in his ears, too.

Jasper had no idea where he was from, or what species he was. His skin was a pretty neutral shade of light brown, his hair and short beard were dark, and his only visible feature that couldn't pass for human was his silver eyes that practically glowed in the low light. Maybe he was some kind of half-breed.

Jasper climbed the winding stairs leading up to the balcony and strolled toward him, Grace trailing behind her. "Cutthroat," Jasper greeted him as she leaned against the railing to his left. "Space pirate. How is space?"

"What do you want, Van Terra?" The gruff response didn't exactly suggest he was in the mood for conversation.

"Ouch." Jasper tapped the railing. "I heard that you might have new information on Ringmaster."

"And why would I tell you that?" Cutthroat asked. "You're a teenage girl who thinks she can keep up with real villains."

Teenage girl. Jasper's fingers twitched. Now wasn't the time for fighting. She could kick Cutthroat's ass later, if she really wanted.

"You don't have much by way of employees, do you?" Cutthroat continued. His gaze flickered to a spot farther down the balcony, where a few members of his pirate crew were chatting quietly. Was that supposed to be a threat?

"I have a crew. They're better than mindless henchgoons." Jasper jutted a thumb at Grace behind her. "In fact, this is my latest recruit."

"Another child." Cutthroat rolled his eyes. "Look, I don't know much about what Ringmaster's up to. I noticed him earlier in a back alley while I was robbing some tourists."

"Isn't a big shot villain like you above mugging?"

"I wanted food and it was the fastest way to get money. I wouldn't rob a bank just to buy a sandwich."

"I would," Jasper said.

"That would be wildly impractical."

"And hilarious."

Cutthroat shook his head. "Do you want to know what I heard or not? Ringmaster was on a call. I didn't catch much of the conversation, but I got the feeling he's working for someone."

"Aw, cute, you finally figured it out." Jasper laughed. "I've known who he was helping for some time now."

"Really?" Cutthroat's eyes narrowed. "And who would that be?"

Jasper stepped away from the railing. "Why should I tell you?"

She and Grace walked a few feet before Cutthroat stopped her. "Van Terra," he called. "If you really think you're as good as the rest of us—"

"I think I'm better, actually," Jasper said as she turned around.

"Prove it. Come to Atzy's. Most big names are gathering there soon. I doubt you can play our games with us."

On another night, Jasper would have been tempted. But her other plans had her too distracted to worry about proving herself to the other Janus System villains right now. "Thanks," she told Cutthroat. "But I don't need to arm wrestle a couple of losers to prove myself."

"Suit yourself."

A thought struck Jasper. "One last thing."

"I wouldn't be above injuring you to make you shut up," Cutthroat warned.

"It's just a quick question. You hang out in space a lot. Have you heard of spacetime warps?"

Cutthroat's reaction surprised Jasper. His eyes briefly widened, and his expression darkened in a way that sent a chill down her spine. "Where did you hear that?"

Jasper lifted her hands. "What if I told you I've seen one?"

"We're not discussing them. Period. Go bother someone else."

Alrighty then. Jasper led Grace back down the steps. "All right, Angel, I think I got what I needed to out of my system. Let's head back."

"Are you sure?" Grace asked, frowning. "It sounded like Cutthroat knows something about the spacetime warp thingies."

"He's not going to tell us anything. And I shouldn't have brought you here in the first place."

"Are you forgetting I have super strength?" Grace shot Jasper an exasperated look. "You can't shelter me forever."

"There's a difference between sheltering you and keeping you from getting killed by villains." Jasper liked that Grace was showing some fight, but in Sagev of all places? Jasper had expected her to shut down at the first sight of a villain.

"Why would anyone here want to kill me?" Grace asked.

Jasper lowered her voice. "Look, they probably don't. I'm the only person who knows why Starr's after you, and the only villain who wants to take him down, as far as I know. But it's still dangerous out here."

"It's dangerous everywhere! You're dangerous!" Grace flung up her arms. "We drove off a roof today!"

"Technically yesterday, since it's past midnight—"

"And we've risked our lives a dozen other times. Because we're doing what it takes to get to Ringmaster and Starr. And we know they're after research on the warps," Grace pointed out. "Whatever Cutthroat knows could help us figure out why Starr's interested."

She had a good point. A really good point.

Jasper paused and glanced back up at the balcony railing. Cutthroat was gone, probably on his way out to Atzy's.

"Okay. We'll follow him. If I keep pestering him, maybe I can get him to talk more about the warps." The more likely scenario was him punching Jasper in the face, but whatever. Worth a shot. "We can walk, or we can go by rooftop. Rooftop would be faster, but—"

"Let's do that!" Grace said. "I never get to fly!"

"Holly's going to kill me if she finds out about this," Jasper muttered. "Dax would be mildly disappointed. Thea would do that thing where she lifts an eyebrow and—whatever, let's go."

They found a stairwell in a dark corner of the casino and went up. Jasper gave the locked door to the roof a hard kick, and it responded with a shuddering crack.

As she finished forcing the door open, someone spoke behind her. "Excuse me, you can't be up here—"

"Security guard!" Grace warned.

Jasper held open the door. "Run!"

Grace ran through first, and Jasper followed before throwing the door shut behind her. The two sprinted across the roof.

Jasper pointed to an emerald tower a few buildings over. "Atzy's is the bottom floor of that building."

Grace picked up speed and spread her wings and caught the air, letting it carry her over to the next roof. Jasper leaped and landed on top of a wall between the two buildings. She jumped, grabbed on to a fire escape, and pulled herself up. From there, she climbed to the roof where Grace waited.

"And you were worried about me? You're the one who can't keep up." Grace laughed. A real, genuine, loud laugh, and Jasper realized it was the first time she'd heard it.

"You okay?" Jasper asked, laughing herself. "I thought you were the sane one."

"My old life is gone for good." Grace shrugged. "I think I have to change a few things if I want to survive this new one."

Jasper froze. For a heartbeat, she was in a spaceport, a young child ripped away from her home. Her old life gone for good.

"Look, a swimming pool!" Grace pointed, oblivious to Jasper's internal battle. There was a motel roof far below them, and beyond that, the pool.

Jasper snapped back to the present. "Huh?"

"I'm dying. It's so hot out here." Grace dropped to the lower roof, using her wings to slow her fall.

"Wait up!" Jasper hopped over the edge and used pipes running up the building to scale the wall.

"I bet you can jump into the pool from here," Grace said as Jasper reached her side.

Jasper assessed the distance. Numbers flashed in her vision, telling her how far the water was and how high she'd need to jump, but she could hardly process the math with how fast her head was spinning. "I don't know."

"I've seen you jump farther!"

Jasper laughed. "Okay, okay." She backed up. Took a deep breath. Ran. Soared over the fence below.

Crashed into the pool.

Everything slowed down. As Jasper sank to the bottom of the pool, the water muffled the sounds of people screaming and shouting. Gold glitter danced in the water. She sank farther. A figure stood over the pool, staring down at her.

Something plunged into the water above. Grace.

The world resumed when Jasper hit the bottom. She pushed off and broke the surface. Grace came up next to her.

"I called security!" a woman shouted. "They're on their way!"

Uh oh. Jasper grabbed Grace and dragged her out of the pool. "Let's go!"

Jasper vaulted the fence with ease. Grace awkwardly flew over and almost fell when she landed on the other side. Jasper helped her regain her balance, and they ran.

It didn't take long to reach their destination from there. "There's Atzy's!" Jasper pointed to the entrance as she and Grace raced around a street corner. The two sprinted up the steps to the open doorway, soaking wet. The bouncers gave them weird looks. Jasper glared back. She and Grace entered without a problem.

They stopped just inside, both breathing hard as they took in the music and flashing lights and moving crowd. Jasper scanned the scene quickly. "Cutthroat's at the bar," she told Grace, nodding toward the far end of the main floor.

Jasper drew a dagger, strolled up to the pirate, and drove the blade into the counter next to him. The black surface fractured, distorting the neon lights it reflected. "You're going to tell me everything you know about the spacetime warps."

Cutthroat didn't even look her way as he reached for the dagger's handle. "I told you not to—"

Jasper grabbed his wrist and slammed it into the table. "How strong do you think I am? I'm not just some girl."

Cutthroat finally looked at her, rage burning in his silver eyes. He tried to free his arm. Jasper smirked when she managed to keep it pinned. He pulled again, harder, and she nearly lost her hold this time.

"Listen here—" Cutthroat started.

A new voice cut through the chatter around the bar. "I'll have a citrine tea."

Jasper froze. Whatever Cutthroat said next went in one ear and out the other. "Tyrso?" she asked hoarsely, the name slipping from her lips before she could stop it.

"Yeah, Tyrso Starr's here. The senile old man who keeps to himself and wanders the city at night." Cutthroat raised an eyebrow. "I'm sorry, weren't you in the middle of threatening me?"

Jasper wasn't sure if she responded or not. She didn't remember pulling her blade from the counter. She didn't remember seeing Grace as she stepped away from the bar. All she remembered was pushing her way through the crowd with the weapon in her shaking hand.

Chapter Thirty
Now That's What I Call Unresolved Trauma!

Grace had to fight to avoid losing Jasper in the crowd. She followed her into the bathroom and found her standing in front of the mirror, hands on the sink.

"Jasper?" Grace waved her hand next to Jasper's face. "Are you okay?"

"We should go," Jasper said. Her eyes were fixed on her reflection in a blank stare. "Cutthroat's not giving us anything." White-knuckled hands tightened around the edge of the sink. Cracks appeared.

"Is—" Grace's head was finally clearing. Freeing itself from the chaotic buzz it had picked up during their run through the streets. "Do you—know Tyrso?"

"How would I know him?"

"I don't know!" Grace exclaimed. "How would you know about a shack in the middle of the desert? Or about spacetime warps that freak out Cutthroat? Maybe you don't want to tell me about your past, but—"

"You're fine," Jasper muttered to herself. The cracks in the sink lengthened. "You can handle an old man. You can handle him. All of them." She sucked in a deep breath and grabbed the dagger she'd dropped into the sink. She flipped it once. "Let's make Cutthroat talk."

Grace grimaced. "Do you want to go? Maybe we should go." Why had she insisted on following the pirate when Jasper suggested they head back to the shack?

"Nah. Let's do this." Jasper cracked her neck, rolled her shoulders, and took another deep breath. The pink lines on the motorcycle suit lit up under her coat, and the press of a button on the dagger's handle made it do the same. She stormed out of the bathroom.

Grace caught up as Jasper reentered the dance floor. Jasper twirled the dagger in one hand and drew a gun from her coat with the other. She pointed the gun at the ceiling. Fired twice. "Everyone out of my way!"

People screamed and scattered. The bar cleared out quickly, leaving Cutthroat alone to laugh. He sipped from his glass and set it down. "Back so soon, Van Terra?"

Jasper tossed the gun aside. With one hand, she grabbed Cutthroat's arm and threw him onto the counter. With the other, she pointed the dagger at his face. "Third time's the charm."

"You are stronger than you look," he admitted.

"What do you know about the spacetime warps?"

"You'll have to do better than that. I've seen my share of violent threats."

"Okay." Jasper stuck the dagger through his coat, pinning him to the counter and putting a new fracture in its surface. She waved to the bartender cowering on the other side. "Two splash and Coras, please."

"I don't want one," Grace said. She'd stopped a few feet from where Jasper now had Cutthroat in her gasp, and she wasn't sure what to do with herself.

"They're both for me." Jasper cracked her knuckles. "You heard of the Lion's Den, Cutthroat?"

"Of course I have," Cutthroat answered. He shot the dagger in his coat an annoyed glance.

Grace slid onto the nearest stool, the energy she'd gained earlier rapidly draining away.

"I was in it. For years." Jasper's smile was cold, her eyes were dark, and even Cutthroat was starting to look unnerved. "How old are you, again?"

Cutthroat huffed. "How is this relevant?"

"I'm guessing early forties? Late thirties?" Jasper drew another knife, a smaller one, and pressed it to his neck. "You've seen war? Violence?"

"Yes."

"The depths of space?"

"You can push that blade in all you want. I'm used to pain."

"I'm not torturing you for information. I know that won't work." Jasper's head tipped to the left. "I've been out in the cold heart of space, too. I know what's it like to be alone in the darkness, just you and your ship and an infinite fabric of stars in front of you."

Grace shifted uncomfortably in her seat.

"So much of that space is nothingness. Really makes you think." Jasper leaned in. "Especially when you see things they didn't warn you about. Rips in that fabric. A place where there's nothing and something all at once. And you can feel it, right? That you shouldn't be near it? You shouldn't even be looking at it?"

"You have seen one," Cutthroat breathed.

"It shouldn't be alive." The light was entirely gone from Jasper's eyes. "It's just an anomaly. A hole. But it pulls you in like it's hungry."

"You should stay away from them," Cutthroat said. "I've seen strange things come out of them."

Jasper paused. "Now we're getting somewhere. You saw something come *out*?"

"All kinds of things. Blasts of energy. Strange particles. Dead things, not from any planet I've been to." Cutthroat shook his head. "I've learned what readings mean they're around. I used to be curious, but I keep my distance now, even if it means taking a longer route."

Jasper pulled away from him. "You ever have anyone go in?"

"To a warp? Once."

"You ever see them again?"

Cutthroat laughed. A cold, bitter laugh. "Pretty sure that's impossible."

"Don't be so sure. Things go in, things come out..."

"Yeah, dead things," Cutthroat said bluntly. "Whatever's on the other side, I don't think it's survivable." He sat up and rubbed the front of his neck, where Jasper's blade had touched his skin. "No one should be going anywhere near those warps, if they can help it."

"I agree," Jasper told him. "Unfortunately, other people don't feel the same."

"Uh, two splash and Coras?" The bartender set the drinks on the counter with shaking hands.

"Great." Jasper pointed her dagger at him. "Now hand me all the money in the cash box." With her other hand, she downed the first glass.

"What's happening over here?" South Siren asked as she approached. "Van Terra, what—?"

"Is there a problem?" Jasper snapped. "Can't a villain rob a place in peace?"

South Siren held up her hands. "We usually don't touch Atzy's."

"Well, I felt like it." Jasper downed the second drink. "Now unless anyone wants to fight, I'm going."

"You're just going to show up, attack Cutthroat, and leave?"

"You a cop or something? Mind your business." Jasper snatched the cash box from the bartender. "Is Tyrso still here?"

"He left," South Siren replied, frowning.

"Well, if anyone sees him, tell him I'm ready to throw down."

"You want to fight an old man?"

Jasper jumped up onto the counter. "I could take you all down. You're lucky I don't." She tossed aside her glass and fished around in her pocket for something. The glass shattered against the floor. "You ready, Angel?"

"Ready to go?" Grace asked, eager to finally get back to the peace of the shack.

"Yeah. Screw this place." Jasper held up a black sphere and pushed a button. She chucked it at the wall.

The wall exploded into a cloud of dust and debris. Grace flinched. Jasper stormed through the opening without hesitation.

Grace hurried after her into an alleyway. "What's the money for?"

"I don't know." Jasper headed for the street.

"Are you okay?" Grace fell into step at Jasper's right.

"Of course I'm okay! Why would you ask?" Jasper tossed the cash box on top of a dumpster. "Are you okay?"

"I'm fine," Grace told her. "A little surprised by the explosion, but I'm good." It really was exhaustion weighing down on her now, not terror. Even after being so close to agitated supervillains. The realization came with a small swell of pride, but Grace was too concerned with Jasper's erratic behavior to dwell on it long.

"Sorry." Jasper shook her head. "I wasn't planning on doing any of that, but..." She glanced at Grace as she trailed off.

"As far as I can tell, you're an invincible, unstoppable force," Grace told her. "Except when it comes to spacetime warps and Tyrso Starr."

"Well, I'm not really in the mood to tell you—"

"I'm not asking you to explain. I'm just...realizing there's a lot more to you than I saw in the news." Grace folded her arms and lowered her eyes to the pavement as she and Jasper reached the sidewalk. "I think there's a lot less to me than what I was built up to be."

Jasper laughed weakly. "Oh, that's definitely not true."

"What makes you say that?" Grace asked, eyes darting back up.

"Did you see yourself tonight?"

Grace felt a small smile touch her lips. "You know, parts of that were kind of fun."

"Really?" Jasper asked. "I thought your idea of fun was much less illegal and dangerous."

"I thought that too," Grace said. "Before the governor tried to kill me."

Jasper grinned. She seemed less shaky now, less pale, but still not quite back to her usual self. "Great. Maybe don't mention it to the others. I'm sure they'll blame me for making you more irresponsible."

"I'm not saying it's *not* your fault."

"Oh, so you are going to blame me for your spiral into a life of crime?" Jasper asked, lifting an eyebrow.

"Maybe just a little."

Jasper tipped her head back to look at the sky. The city lights glinted off her eyes, and for a moment all Grace could think of was her and Cutthroat talking about the warps with that faraway look in their eyes. The dagger in Jasper's shaking hands. The way the sink cracked in her grasp.

Grace was starting to wonder less about the terrible things Jasper had done, and more about the terrible things she'd seen.

Chapter Thirty-One
The One Where She Learns To Fight With Swords

Juliet awoke to the sensation of her feet dragging on concrete in a dim hallway. Harsh white lights flickered overhead.

Well, there wasn't really a point using that name anymore, was there? She was Jane. She'd always been Jane. Oh god, she'd never told Naomi her real name, had she? And now Naomi would never know. It would have been nice to hear her say it, even just once—

"Good, she's awake," someone said.

"Stand up," another ordered.

Guards released Jane's arms, leaving her to stumble into the nearest wall. She was led through a door into a room of other people who looked as confused as she was. Confused and terrified.

Was she scared? Was she supposed to be scared? All she could focus on was her pounding headache.

"Line up!" someone barked.

The prisoners obeyed, Jane included. Guards in black uniforms paced back and forth. Studying them. Assessing them. Occasionally, someone would be selected and taken off.

Jane struggled to breathe as she caught up with her surroundings only to be promptly dragged back under by memories. She was in the spaceport. Then standing in a line of children. Tyrso Starr was sending kids to the palace. Sending kids to the lab.

A man stopped in front of Jane and towered over her. Dark red skin, buzzed white hair, and completely black eyes marked him as East Kronosian. "You," he barked. "Come with me."

Jane followed, desperate to escape the suffocating crowd. She only hoped her next destination wouldn't be worse. "Where am I?" she asked.

"The Lion's Den."

"What's that?"

"You'll learn." The man led her down a hallway. "I'm going to be your handler."

"Handler?"

"I'll train you. I'm responsible for you and your schedule. If you screw up, I'm the one who deals with you. So don't screw up." He stopped in front of a door. "This is the room that houses one of my units. You're replacing someone."

"What happened to them?" Jane asked, a terrible feeling stirring in the pit of her stomach.

"You'll be able to make a pretty good guess soon." The man opened the door. "I'm Mars, by the way."

It took Jane a moment to process the introduction. She blinked. "Oh, uh, Jane."

"Not anymore."

"What?"

"I'll assign you a name, after I see what we're working with." Mars gestured for Jane to enter the room.

It was hardly more than a large cell packed with bunk beds. Nineteen people watched her enter, their gazes ranging from suspicious to bored to tired to scared.

"That bunk will be yours." Mars pointed to the back corner. "You'll come back after your physical. Come on."

The door, a good six inches of solid metal, clicked shut and locked behind them as they left.

Mars led Jane to a small room. Inside, a woman covered in a thin layer of gray fur and wearing a lab coat motioned for her to sit down on a table. Jane shuddered.

"Scared of needles?" Mars asked. "Don't worry, we're not going to hurt you. Not today." A slight, cold smile followed the words. "We just want to find out what you're made of."

The woman started with a simple physical examination, then moved on to scanning Jane with a metal wand and pricking her finger for blood. The blood went onto a disk that slid into a machine.

"Human. Earth," The woman read off a monitor. She rubbed a clawed hand across her foxlike snout, ruffling her whiskers. "No other species in her genes. Were you born there?"

Jane frowned. "What?"

Mars huffed. "Were you born on Earth?"

Oh. "Yes."

Mars raised an eyebrow. "You know, my name comes from a planet in your star system."

It was all Jane could do to keep from rolling her eyes. Was this an attempt to get her to trust him?

The woman spoke again. "X-rays are far more interesting. Your cybernetics are extensive." She pointed at her screen. "Who did this for you? No legal operation would put this in your brain."

"I don't know," Jane mumbled.

"You don't know who cut you open and put all this in your body?" Mars asked skeptically.

"No."

"Well, do you know what any of the computers do?"

Clock. Heat vision. Calculations. Jane shook her head. "No idea."

"That's fine. Your strength alone gives us a lot to work with." A cold grin crossed Mars's face. "You should rest. Your training starts tomorrow morning."

"Morning" was pushing it. Jane was taken back to her shared room for a few sleepless hours before being dragged back out at roughly five a.m. Training began with a brutal routine of running and push-ups and lifting weights, with other exercises thrown in at random.

Three days passed. Mars still had yet to tell Jane what she was doing all of this for. He did give her a name, though.

"You said you're from Earth?" Mars stared at a tablet while Jane scaled a rock wall. "You'll be Jaguar."

"Huh?" Jane slipped, and the next thing she knew, she was lying flat on her back, struggling for air.

"Your name is Jaguar now. And today we're starting you on weapons."

She followed Mars to a room in the training wing she hadn't seen yet. Other prisoners, many of whom Jane—Jaguar—recognized now, were engaged in practice fights across the room. The far wall was filled with quite the assortment of weapons. Swords and daggers. Throwing stars. Maces and axes and whips and spears.

"I'm sorry, what century is this?" Jaguar asked.

Mars laughed. "Funny. You think we're going to hand our fighters guns and let them shoot each other? Where's the fun in that? The rounds would only last a few seconds."

"Rounds?"

"The Lion's Den is all about entertainment." Mars waved at someone nearby. "Wolfoid, grab a staff. You'll be fighting Jaguar."

"I've never used a staff before," Jaguar told Mars.

"You have to start somewhere."

Jaguar had barely selected a staff from the wall when something struck her in the side. She flew a few feet and slammed into the concrete floor.

The boy, Wolfoid, stalked toward her, spinning the staff in his hand. His skin was a light gray, he'd pulled back his long mess of darker gray hair, and when he smiled, his sharp teeth shone white.

"Better start learning!" Mars called.

Jaguar adjusted her grip on the staff as she rose to her feet. Wolfoid hit her again. She staggered back. The world slowed and she swung at his face. She missed.

Another blow to her side. Something cracked.

She didn't win that fight. Or the next. Or the one after that. In fact, she hardly remembered them. All she could recall in the weeks after were the bruises they left all over and the taste of blood in her mouth.

First, she focused on dodging. Then she started hitting back. As soon as she was decent with the staff, Mars threw her into her first sword fight.

The slashes on her arms healed surprisingly well, considering Mars didn't give her anything beyond bandages to wrap them up before throwing her back into the fray. They did leave some nasty scars, though. But once Mars decided she'd been beaten enough, he actually showed her the technique behind the weapons and had her practice more carefully with other new arrivals.

One night, as training ended, Jaguar stood in front of one of the room's large mirrors, clutching a dagger. Her scratched and bruised face stared back. Her hair was a mess, and she was sick of it.

She sliced through it in chunks as fast as possible. The cut was messy, but it would make fighting easier.

A few mornings later, Mars woke her and informed her that she would be having her first real fight that day.

"What do you mean?" Jaguar asked groggily.

"Jaguar's listed as an opening act. All newcomers get the same treatment. They'll pit you against a big dumb monster. Do well, and you'll move on to real fights."

"Real fights?"

Mars left without further explanation. Jaguar dressed and ate her breakfast like she would any other day. When she was done, a squad of guards entered the cafeteria to take her away.

She was escorted to a room by a grate that stretched to the ceiling twenty feet above. Mars was in the room, too, talking to a girl Jaguar had fought a few times in training. The girl was chained to the wall by a shackle on her wrist. A similar shackle was put on Jaguar.

"This is only until it's your turn to fight," Mars told her as he approached, noticing the annoyed look she gave the chain. He handed her a sword. "After that, you'll be returned to your room. Assuming you survive, that is." He laughed.

Jaguar stared past him at a group of people standing in a circle in the corner of the room, all shackle-free. "Are they fighters? They're not chained up."

"They're free agents," Mars replied. "Some people choose to come to the Den and compete. Villains looking to show off, assassins looking to find clients, et cetera."

"So, they're not prisoners like me?"

Mars responded to the question with more laughter. Jaguar was getting real sick of the sound. "You'll do great."

As he walked away, the grate at the end of the room creaked and inched up. The same guard who'd shackled Jaguar procured a key and freed her.

"Really?" she muttered. What a waste of time.

The guard nodded toward the opening gate. An announcer's voice boomed on the other side. "Tonight will be the debut of Earthling Jaguar, facing an alkura from Hatu."

Jaguar tested the sword with a few slow swings as she walked under the rising gate into an arena. The stadium seating around it had to hold upwards of a thousand people. All watching her. Massive screens hung on every side, magnifying her for them to see.

Two massive wooden poles stood in the middle of the arena. Dozens of weapons stuck out of them, and they were both heavily scratched and damaged. They were probably more for show than structural support, despite connecting to the ceiling far above.

Another gate opened on the opposite side of the arena. It had hardly creaked past the halfway point when a creature burst out from underneath it.

The alkura was built like a bear on steroids. Dark green fur covered its body, and shiny white antlers protruded from its head. It spotted Jaguar and immediately charged, not giving her much time to think before she had to move.

Jaguar darted out of the alkura's path. As it passed, she swung at its leg with the sword. It roared in anger, turned, and slashed at her with a paw.

The blow flung her into the air. The sword slipped from her grasp. Her back collided with dirt and she slid several feet, throwing up a cloud of dust that sent her into a coughing fit.

Despite the massive gash she'd left in its leg, the alkura stalked toward her at a steady pace. Jaguar needed to find a weaker spot to strike. Its neck muscles were thick, but if she could get just under the jaw—

She rolled aside, grabbed the sword, jumped to her feet, and ran. The alkura's claws missed her by inches. She risked a glance back as it chased her.

One shot. If she went for the neck and missed, she'd be in the path of claws and teeth.

Jaguar reached one of the poles. She jumped, pushed off, and twisted in the air. Her brain finally decided to slow things down for her. Well, better late than never. She aimed the sword and tightened her grip. The alkura reached her.

The blade sank deep into its neck. The sudden stop sent Jaguar flying over the beast's back and into the dirt. A shriek pierced the air behind her. She staggered to her feet, ready to run, and looked back.

The alkura collapsed, the light gone from its eyes. Blood stained the blade and rapidly spilled into the dirt. A few people in the audience clapped. Cheered.

Poor thing, was all Jaguar could think once her heart started to slow. The alkura had been a prisoner just like her, hadn't it? Ripped from its home and brought here to fight?

At least she'd given it a quick death.

"Not bad," Mars said as she exited the arena. "Once you move on to real fights, they'll cheer much louder."

"Do I have to kill them?" Jaguar asked.

Mars frowned. "What?"

"My opponents. Do I have to kill them to win?"

"Technically, once they're unconscious, they've lost. Whether or not they die from injuries later—"

He kept talking, but Jaguar barely heard the rest.

For now, all she could do was survive.

Chapter Thirty-Two
Panic! At The MoonCo

Grace yawned as the team piled into the stolen mall display car. She was trying to follow Thea's explanation of how her pattern-recognition software could use the mall cameras to find Aymes Bell the moment he walked in, but some of the techier words were tripping her up.

"I can't promise the facial recognition will be perfect," Thea said as the last door slammed shut. "But our chances of catching him fast are pretty good."

"Great," Jasper said. She started up the engine. "We just need to make a quick stop for supplies."

"A quick stop?" Holly asked skeptically.

"I need materials for the explosives I'm going to blast through the ceiling with."

"Don't you have explosives?" Grace asked, thinking of the hole Jasper had blown in the wall at Atzy's the night before.

"Mine aren't strong enough. They're for distractions and minor damage." Jasper set Mia on the car's dashboard. "Mia, get directions to the MoonCo on Silvium Drive."

"MoonCo?" Dax asked. "How are we getting in?"

Grace glanced at the back seat. "What do you mean? Isn't MoonCo just a store?"

"You have to have a membership to shop there," Jasper explained. "It's fine. I know a trick or two."

They arrived ten minutes later and climbed out of the car. As the team approached the front doors, a woman ahead of them showed a card to the employee sitting out front. He nodded for her to go in.

"Excuse me," Jasper said to the employee. "Our mom's waiting for us inside."

The employee's gaze moved from Jasper Van Terra, dressed more for a high-class function than shopping; to Dax, who hadn't bothered to change out of the wrinkled shirt he'd slept in; to Thea, who typed away on a tablet with second tucked under her arm; to Grace, too hot to wear a jacket to hide her wings; and finally to Holly, dressed in all black, arms folded, headphones in her ears, rolling her eyes.

"Yeah, okay, go ahead," the employee said.

Jasper grabbed a cart on the way in. Grace's gaze darted from employee to employee as they walked. "What if someone catches us?" she asked.

"It's a supermarket, not the Pentagon," Jasper replied.

"Pentagon?"

"Let's try that again. It's a supermarket, not the Governor's Palace. No one cares." Jasper grabbed a jug of drain cleaner off a shelf. "Thea, I need you to grab powdered Y-engine coolant. Make sure it contains polyplassites."

"Got it." Thea broke off from the group.

"Dax, I need a sealable container. Jar, bottle, whatever."

Dax nodded and walked away.

"Holly, I need you to get some Nova Cora."

"I'm not getting you that stupid soda!" Holly exclaimed.

Jasper lifted a hand. "I swear I need it for the explosive."

"You know what? I'm not surprised you can make explosives with that garbage," Holly said as she stormed off.

"Angel, could you head down that aisle and grab me some ruby vinegar?" Jasper gestured to the right. "It needs to be MoonCo brand."

"Sure," Grace replied with a nod.

She scanned the shelves carefully as she walked the aisle, a little overwhelmed by the selection. At least it wasn't as chaotic as the Mota Mart had been. "Vinegar, vinegar, vinegar—oh, sorry!" Grace turned to see who she'd bumped into.

"It's fine," the woman said coolly, not looking up from her wristwatch. "Just watch where you're going next time."

She had nearly a foot on Grace in height. The white bodysuit she wore looked like it was made from the same fabric as Jasper's motorcycle suit.

Her scaly skin was a pale green, and her black hair had been cropped close to her head. And in her other hand, she held a long white metal spear.

As the woman strolled past Grace, she held the watch up to her mouth. "I've cleared aisles one through ten. She's not here."

"Uh, Jasper?" Grace whispered into her comm once the woman was out of earshot. "I think someone's looking for you."

"Could you be more specific?" Jasper asked.

"She kind of looks like South Siren. She's wearing similar clothes. And she's got a giant spear."

"She's probably a siren. One of South Siren's henchwomen—oh, oops."

"Oops?" Holly pressed.

"I've been spotted," Jasper said. "Yeah, they're sirens. I'm leaving our cart by the dairy cooler. Everyone, meet here."

Grace went back to scanning the shelves with more urgency. Once she spotted the bottles of ruby vinegar, she grabbed one and hurried back to the cart.

Thea appeared a moment later with a black jug that she tossed in. "Do we know where Jasper went?"

A crash came from a nearby aisle.

"Over there?" Grace turned toward the sound. "Should we help her?"

Thea shrugged. "She said to meet here, didn't she?"

Holly and Dax came around the corner and added their items to the cart. "Yeah," Holly said. "I'm sure this'll blow over and we'll be out of here in a few minutes—"

Jasper came flying over nearby shelving unit and crashed into a nutrient bar display. Three sirens emerged from the aisle on the other side and strolled toward the team, all wielding spears.

"At least they have short range weapons," Thea said. "We can run—"

One of the sirens pointed her spear at Holly and fired a blast of blue-green energy from the tip. Holly yelped and dove out of the way. Dax and Thea ducked behind the cart. Grace took a few quick steps back.

"Why are they attacking us?" Holly exclaimed.

Jasper rose to her feet, shoving a few of the bars into her pockets. "I must have really pissed her off last night."

"What do you mean last night?"

"Mm, on second thought, I probably pissed off everyone. We might have to fend off a lot of henchpeople over the next few days."

"You couldn't just keep your head down and blend in, could you?" With a swing of her arm, Holly emptied a nearby shelf of boxes. She snapped the metal shelf off the display and held it up.

Jasper grabbed a shopping basket off the top of a nearby stack. "I swear there was an attempt." She chucked the basket at the same time Holly sent the shelf spinning through the air. They each knocked down a siren, leaving the third to lunge forward and fire another spear blast at Jasper.

Jasper ducked. "Someone put the groceries in the car. I'll be out in a minute."

Thea grabbed the cart and headed for the exit. Grace and Dax joined her. While Jasper and Holly were able to distract most of the sirens that came crawling out of the woodwork—Grace thought she counted eight— two decided to pursue Grace, Thea, and Dax instead.

"They're faster than us!" Dax warned.

"I can see that." Thea's hands tightened around the cart.

As they emerged from an aisle, Grace grabbed the shelf to her right and pulled. For a moment she feared she didn't have enough strength, but then the other side lifted off the ground a few inches. The shelf tipped just enough to send dozens of huge crates tumbling to the floor, blocking the path of the pursuing sirens.

Grace let the shelf fall back into place caught up to the others. A smaller display toppled to the ground nearby and Jasper leaped over it, laughing, Holly behind her. The two caught up with Grace and the others.

They shot out the front of the store, into the parking lot, to the car. "Holly, you're driving," Jasper said as doors began opening. "I have a bomb to make."

Holly eagerly took the driver's seat. Dax took passenger, and Grace found herself crammed between Jasper and Thea in the back.

"Next stop, Silvium Center," Jasper announced.

"Please try not to blow us up," Holly said.

"Don't worry, I won't. I'd rather not be caught dead in such an ugly car."

Chapter Thirty-Three
Save The Birds!

"I'm running all of the mall's camera feeds through my facial recognition program," Thea said as the team pulled into the Silvium Center's parking lot. "I'll also put a few drones in the air with my own cameras. If he shows up, we should get a match."

Grace stared out the window. The crowds weren't as bad as they'd been the day before, but there were still a lot of people milling around.

"Great," Jasper replied. "Thea and I will head to the roof and access the closed store from there. She'll look for any new messages between Aymes and Ringmaster."

"Can't we bug their equipment so that we can see any messages they send in the future?" Holly asked.

Thea shook her head. "I tried at Starchatter, but Ringmaster must have good techs working for him. I couldn't get any of my own code to stick," she explained. "But, if we find out Aymes is using his own personal devices to communicate with Ringmaster, I could hack them."

"While Thea and I are breaking in, I need you three nearby," Jasper told the others. "If Aymes shows up, you'll need to distract him so he doesn't catch us."

"Distract him how?" Grace asked. "Fight him?"

"Don't worry, violence won't be necessary. Just, I don't know, tell one of those kiosk dudes that Aymes wants free lotion samples. That'll take a while for him to get out of." Jasper threw open her door.

A few people gave the vehicle weird looks as the team climbed out, and Grace realized just how beat up it was. Not to mention all the dirt and sand it had picked up on the drive out to the shack. "Uh, is it a good idea to bring the car back to the place we stole it from?" she asked.

"Eh, it's fine," Jasper said. "I turned the F's on the license plate into E's with a permanent marker."

"That's stupid," Holly told her. "But it is so dirty and banged up at this point, I'd be surprised if anyone recognized it."

The five entered the mall and split up. Grace wandered down a random corridor and realized she was on her own in public for the first time...ever? Aside from the few seconds she'd spent alone in an aisle at MoonCo, anyway. She carefully eyed everyone who passed by, suddenly fearing she'd be attacked at any moment.

There are no Blades here, she reminded herself. After a few minutes of walking the first floor and willing herself to relax, Grace moved up to the second level to get a better view.

"Aymes is here," Thea announced over the comms. "North entrance. First floor. He's walking pretty fast."

"I can intercept," Holly said. "Do you have any information I can use?"

"He's indicated interest in attending some pretty prestigious universities around the star system," Thea said. "He also plays volleyball—"

"Volleyball?" Jasper asked. "Like, some kind of space volleyball?"

"Uh, just regular volleyball. The Janus System does pick up the occasional sport from other systems."

"Huh."

Grace's gaze swept across the crowd below. Across the corridor was a travel agency. *Get away today!* the banner out front read. *Transportation across three star systems.*

Maybe it wouldn't be hard for Grace to get to Earth on her own. Would Jasper come after her if she did? She felt a strange twinge of guilt at the thought.

Kara had asked her to find a way to Earth. But that had all been part of her organization's plan to take down Starr, hadn't it? Wouldn't helping Jasper handle the governor instead be more effective?

Still, it was hard not to feel more guilt at the thought of disregarding the woman's last request. She'd died to protect Grace. Grace rested her hands on the railing in front of her and squeezed until her knuckles paled.

After a long moment, Grace took a deep breath, quashed the internal debate, and turned her focus to the north end of the main corridor, where she spotted Aymes walking at an impressive pace. He had on a backpack and stared intently at the screen of the tablet he was holding. He didn't notice Holly until she was waving a hand in front of his face.

"Excuse me!" Holly's voice echoed through the comm, and it sounded like she'd managed to plaster on a fake smile. "Would you be interested in a program that will help you get into university?"

Aymes looked up at her with a distressed expression. He spoke loud enough for Grace to hear him through the comm, too. "Sorry, I'm in a hurry." He stepped forward.

Holly took a step back to keep herself in front of him. "It'll only take a few seconds to sign up."

"Sign up for what?"

"Uh, the email list."

"I don't have time for this." Aymes ducked under her arm. "Maybe later."

"First ten people to sign up get, uh, free textbooks? You need textbooks, right? Damn, lost him." Holly's face dropped as Aymes walked away. "Dax?"

"Headed toward him," Dax responded. His voice rose. "Excuse me, I'm part of a program looking to recruit—"

"Bit busy." Aymes dodged Dax.

"Ouch," Jasper said. "He looked kind of anxious in the school pictures Thea found. I was hoping he'd be too polite to say no."

"I could catch up to him and shapeshift." Down below, Holly folded her arms. "But I don't know what would get him to stop."

"Just keep stalling as much as possible," Jasper replied. A boom came through the comms, followed by a burst of static. "We're in."

"I'll try," Grace said. She climbed over the railing and glided to the ground in front of Aymes, stopping him in his tracks. "Excuse me, do you have a moment to talk about, uh—"

"I'm in a hurry—" Aymes started.

"The birds are dying!" Grace blurted. "At an alarming rate. If you could spare a few janos—"

Aymes pulled a bill from his pocket and tossed at her. "That's all I've got."

Grace snatched the bill from the air and turned to watch him leave. "Uh, I didn't stop him, but he threw five janos at me."

Then, to her surprise, Aymes did stop. And turn around. "Wait a minute," he said. "Have I seen you somewhere before?"

Grace shoved the bill into her pocket, cursing inwardly. She shouldn't have brought out her wings. "I don't think so."

"Yeah, you were an intern at Starchatter. Wren Starwright. What are you doing on Si Hera?"

Grace breathed a small sigh of relief. He recognized her as a fellow intern, not wanted criminal Grace Alvarez. "I'm...writing an article about the birds. That are dying."

"Which birds?"

"Red ones?" Grace tried.

"The only red-colored birds on Si Hera are an invasive species, and they're doing pretty well," Aymes said.

"What a nerd," Jasper muttered.

Aymes shook his head. "I'm sorry, I don't have time to talk right now." He turned and disappeared into the crowd.

Grace sighed. "He's getting away."

"Thea?" Jasper asked.

"No, I'm not done," Thea replied. "You can see me typing, Jasper!"

"Could we get a time estimate?"

"Five minutes. And before you ask, I'd say Aymes is three minutes away."

"Great." Jasper sighed. "Then I guess it's my turn."

Chapter Thirty-Four
We Are All Idiots On This Blessed Day

The Apprentice's race monitoring headquarters had been set up among a maze of plastic sheets hanging from support beams overhead, and that was all enclosed by floor-to-ceiling panels of gold and silver metal. Jasper dropped into the middle of the maze from the brand-new hole in the ceiling and made her way toward the section of wall Aymes had passed through the day before. She tossed aside her coat, slid on a pair of sunglasses, and picked up a hard hat left on the floor.

The rectangular patch of wall shimmered silver, and Aymes stepped through. He froze. "Who are you?"

"I'm here to make sure repairs are going smoothly," Jasper said.

Aymes frowned. "Repairs have been delayed."

"What I meant was that I'm here to make sure everything's ready for when they do happen." Jasper folded her arms. "And what are you doing here?"

"I'm, uh, from the mall. To check in. No one else is supposed to be here for a few more days."

"Right, of course. Except for the surprise inspection. To make sure no one is coming in. Which is what I'm here for."

"Why are you wearing sunglasses?" Aymes's eyes narrowed. "It's dark in here."

"I have an eye disorder. My eyes are...radioactive. If I took my glasses off, you'd die. Instantly. Why do you have a backpack if you work for the mall?"

"It has all of my...mall employee...supplies."

"Jasper, I'm out," Thea said. "You can leave."

Jasper clapped her hands together. "Well, everything looks to be in order," she said. "So, I'm going now."

"Wait, how'd you even get in?" Aymes asked. "I locked—um, we mall staff locked it up to keep nosy civilians out."

"My team was ordered to put a hole in the roof. To knock out an old pipe. I'll throw a tarp over it on the way out."

Aymes didn't have anything further comments, to Jasper's relief. After leaving him by the entrance, she found a ladder just tall enough to let her climb out of the store. As promised, she threw a tarp over the hole, then walked to the other end of the roof, where Thea worked on her laptop.

"Well?" Jasper asked.

Thea pointed to the screen. "Here. Ringmaster sent a message to the Apprentice, telling him he knows the target is in Sagev. Last night, the Apprentice replied saying that he found the target and asked what to do next. Aymes is probably here now to see Ringmaster's reply. The last message came in this morning, saying he has a task for Aymes to do during the race."

"Target, eh?" Jasper sat down next to Thea. "Is the target named anywhere?"

"Nope."

Of course not. It was never that easy.

Chapter Thirty-Five
I Think We're Done Here

A twenty-three-year-old Jaguar stared at her face in the cracked training room mirror. She was growing more certain with each passing day that those features hadn't changed since she'd left Sky Labs. Sure, there were more bruises, more scratches, more scars, but—

"Jaguar. It's time." The approaching guard held up a pair of wrist cuffs.

Jaguar accepted her fate.

When they arrived at the arena gate, Mars held out her assigned weapon: a tiny ass dagger. "This?" Jaguar exclaimed as she took it. "Really?"

"It'll make things more interesting," Mars told her. "Good luck."

"Make things interesting," she muttered as the gate went up. "Those assholes." She stormed into the arena, the blade twirling in her fingers.

Well, she wouldn't be here much longer. Not if everything went according to plan.

Her opponent stepped out from under the opposite gate: a bulky orange alien from the planet Reo, triple her size. He wielded a mace that he swung in wide circles as he stalked toward her. As usual, her speed would be her best hope of winning. The dagger in her hand was all but useless.

"Our next match is Jaguar versus Blaze," the announcer told the crowd.

Blaze charged and swung. Jumping out of the way was easy enough, but Jaguar had to carefully time her duck to avoid the next blow, and then he was only feet away. She sprang up and drove the dagger into the shoulder of the arm wielding the weapon. Blaze hissed, tossed the mace's handle to his other hand, and swung again.

Great. Ambidextrous. Jaguar yanked the blade free, dodged another swing, and backed up. The mace would be perfect for her escape plan. She needed to keep it in the arena for her next fight.

Jaguar kept moving backward, veering toward the nearest wooden pole. She threw a few slashes at Blaze's arms and legs, both to distract him and keep him close. She feigned a look of alarm when her back hit the pole.

Blaze swung. Jaguar ducked. The metal spikes dug into the pole above her, and she lunged up to drive her dagger into the alien's neck. Quick. Clean. She yanked the weapon free. Yellow blood splattered across the dirt.

Jaguar could have dragged the battle out longer, earning more praise from the crowd and Mars, but she was saving her energy. She had one more fight, and it was going to be quite the show.

Still, Jaguar had done well enough to earn a "Not bad" from Mars when she returned through the gate. "Though, Blaze has been losing his edge lately," he added. "I wonder if they'll bother trying to heal him."

Years ago, Jaguar would have thought that knife to the throat fatal. It probably still would be, even if the Den's medical staff made an effort to save Blaze, but she'd been surprised by some of the wounds she'd seen healed during her time here.

She didn't let her thoughts dwell on Blaze for long. While the guards chained her to the wall, she ran once again through the plan that had been her every waking thought for months. Her biggest obstacles were the guards, the heavy doors around the facility, and the fact that she was always in her cell, in chains, or in the training rooms.

The training rooms had seemed to be the best place to begin her escape at first, but Jaguar had heard stories over the years of failed escape attempts, and even witnessed a few herself. Sure, the prisoners had access to weapons in the training rooms. But so did the overwhelming number of guards and handlers.

And then Jaguar realized there was a place where she had no chains, no guards in her immediate vicinity, and access to weapons.

The arena.

The location also came with the added advantage of spectators. Above all else, Lion's Den personnel were going to protect the people who made them money. Of Jaguar's two matches today, the second one would be far more crowded for a variety of reasons: time of day, the placement of well-liked fighters in the time block, and the fact that Jaguar was not fighting another prisoner, but a free agent. The only one scheduled this pentasol.

There were still unknown variables she'd have to deal with along the way. But a failed attempt would be better than another day in the Lion's Den. Anything would be better.

Jaguar was handed a whip for her second match. While the gate lifted, she focused. Focused on the way air filled her lungs, the way her boots thudded against the dirt when she started forward, the way dust floated in the light spilling into the waiting room from the arena. *Now or never.*

She stepped into the arena and cracked the whip, earning cheers from the crowd that she didn't give a damn about. Her opponent, known only as Nightfall, entered on the other side. He was tall, toned, dressed in all black, and wearing a belt with two large daggers and an array of throwing stars.

Nightfall surveyed Jaguar. She let the whip fall limp, not wanting to give him insight into her movements.

In a heartbeat, he unleashed three throwing stars. One came directly at her, and two others would pass on each side, blocking her escape. They were too low for her to duck.

She jumped and flipped. Something else whizzed toward her mid-flip, and she twisted to see a fourth star. She snatched it out of the air with her whip. Her fingers wrapped around the star, and she sent it back at Nightfall. He dodged easily.

Time to see if he was as good with his daggers as he was with the stars. Jaguar ran at him, zig-zagging erratically to avoid giving him a straight shot. Still, a few stars nicked her arms. Blood trickled down her skin.

Nightfall's hands moved from his stars to his daggers. Jaguar ripped one away with the whip, sending it flying, and then the other blade was slashing at her chest. She grabbed Nightfall's wrist before he could land a good hit. His free hand struck the side of her face. She staggered.

Jaguar flicked her wrist, and the whip wrapped around Nightfall's arm. He pulled, making her stumble forward, but she stayed on her feet. She landed a kick to his stomach and reached for the dagger's handle. He twisted his hand. The blade sliced her palm.

Pain shot through the hand as Jaguar tightened it into a fist and threw a punch. Nightfall moved his arm to block, and she ripped the dagger from his grasp. She tossed the dagger aside before turning and running toward the center of the arena. Toward the pole. Toward Blaze's mace.

More stars cut through the air, whistling a quiet warning. Jaguar dropped to her stomach and let them pass. Then she was back up, almost to the pole. The mace was just out of reach. She jumped. Grabbed the handle.

Her weight wasn't enough to dislodge the mace, leaving her dangling a few feet above the ground. More stars came her way. She let go. *Duck. Dodge. Jump. Try again.*

This time, the mace came free when Jaguar grabbed it. She whirled around and swung, knocking a star out of the air before it could strike. Murmurs rippled through the crowd above. She stalked toward Nightfall, but she only kept her focus on him long enough to avoid his last few stars. Then, while he was running to retrieve his daggers, she veered toward the wall. Her eyes moved to the metal mesh fence separating the crowd from the arena.

Briefly, her gaze darted to Tyrso Starr and his teenaged son, Ryse, sitting on one of the balconies above the rest of the audience. The first time they'd shown up, it had completely thrown her off. She'd nearly been killed by her opponent.

Jaguar had no chance of getting anywhere near them today. And as much as her blood boiled at the sight of Tyrso, she wasn't ready for a confrontation.

She flung the mace with as much momentum as she could muster. It sailed through the air and ripped open the fence.

Now people were screaming.

Something raced through the air behind Jaguar. She glanced back and spotted one of Nightfall's daggers coming her way. She dove to the left. The dagger sank into the wall, about a third of the way up to the fence.

Jaguar's hand tightened around her whip. She ran. Leaped. Her foot hit the handle of the dagger, and she pushed off. The whip wrapped around one of the metal posts supporting the fence. She pulled herself up.

Her hands found the fencepost next. There was no dodging Nightfall now. She moved on to the mesh and inched higher, listening for the sound of weapons coming her way. She was nearly to the hole the mace had made when a throwing star grazed her left arm.

She gritted her teeth and kept moving. The top of the fence wasn't much higher than the hole, but every second she saved herself could mean the difference between escape and death.

As she pulled herself through the hole, another star sank into her left leg. She tumbled forward and smacked into the ground in front of the first row of spectator seating.

There was nobody in the seats. Everyone was on their feet, scrambling to get to the exits, not realizing that the chaos would make it easier for Jaguar to escape. She pushed herself up and staggered into the crowd.

Her main fear now was that the facility would go into lockdown before she could get out. Guards might usher the crowd somewhere secure while they searched for her. She needed something that would give them no option but to evacuate.

Fire sounded like a pretty good idea.

Jaguar picked up abandoned bags as she walked, fishing through them for anything useful. The fifth one she checked yielded a lighter. On her way up the stadium steps, she also grabbed a long coat, a hat, sunglasses, and a sanitary wipe to clean the dirt and blood off her face.

Guards were fighting to get to her, so she started with the lighter. The various bags and articles of clothing lying around burst into flames quickly. She also kicked over any bottles of alcohol she came across. Not all of the spilled liquid caught fire, but enough did.

As it turned out, Nova Cora was flammable too. Jaguar resisted the temptation to drink from the cans and bottles she found and instead dumped them out, adding to the flames.

Alarms blared and evacuation orders came over the loudspeakers. Jaguar threw on the coat and accessories she'd grabbed and ducked her head low as she merged with the crowd. The disguise kept eyes off of her for now, but it wouldn't be enough to get her out of the building. Guards were bound to catch her on the way out. She needed to blend in long enough to get her hands on something better.

When Jaguar glanced back, Nightfall was pulling himself up over the fence. She quickly looked forward. Sharp pains shot through her body. She tugged down on her coat, making sure it covered the star in the back of her leg. She couldn't pull it out until she had some way to stop the bleeding. In the meantime, she did her best not to limp.

Guards yelled up ahead, warning that they needed to check everyone leaving the Den, ushering people into lines, asking them to please be patient for their own safety. Jaguar located a guard about her size. She hurried toward them and raised her voice. "Excuse me, where's the nearest restroom?"

The guard's face was hidden under a helmet—marking her as one of the facility's exterior guards—but her tone made it clear she thought Jaguar was crazy. "We're evacuating, ma'am."

"It's an emergency!"

"Okay, okay, follow me. Be quick."

The guard led Jaguar away from the frenzy and down a hall. Jaguar waited until they were at the restroom entrance to strike. She slammed the woman into the wall.

The guard immediately began fighting back. As they exchanged and dodged blows, Jaguar pulled her into the restroom, out of sight of security cameras. She yanked the guard's helmet off, knocked her into the sink, and let her drop to the floor unconscious.

Jagur changed into the guard's uniform and ran. Hopefully, by the time security realized it was Jaguar and not the guard that had left the bathroom, it would be too late. If she was *really* lucky, security would be too busy checking the faces of the evacuating crowd to have anyone on cameras at all.

Rather than going out the main exit, Jaguar cut down a hallway toward the training rooms. She'd take a shortcut there and go through the guard's quarters, to the back exit they came and left through.

She flung the door open, thinking no one would be around to hear.

Mars stood in the middle of the room, staring at the wall of weapons. He looked toward her as she entered. "What are you doing?" He sounded more curious than suspicious, but that didn't stop Jaguar's racing heart from dropping to her stomach.

Jaguar hesitated. If she could deepen her voice enough and keep the helmet on, maybe she could get past him without any trouble. "I was told to check the guard's quarters for stragglers."

"Good idea." Mars's gaze returned to the wall.

Walk past him. Just walk past him. Jaguar tried not to think about all the hours he'd spent watching her get stabbed and thrown and hit. About all the scars that covered her arms and chest…

Curiosity nagged at her. She paused. "Why are you still here?"

"They'll put the fire out long before it gets this far."

Jaguar's mind replayed the time he broke her right foot so that she'd learn to fight with her cybernetic leg. When he'd warned her to hide her limp so others wouldn't spot her weakness.

All she could think to say was, "Right. Of course." *Keep walking. Keep going.* She was almost free.

The silver galaxium sword hanging in the center of the wall reflected Mars's black eyes. That hungry look that came out when fresh blood turned up in the Den.

Jaguar stopped again, two-thirds of the way to the exit.

"Is something wrong?" Mars asked.

She couldn't stop the Lion's Den, not right now. Mars was just a tiny part of a huge machine, a bigger system feeding on people like Jaguar. A system that found new victims every day. Him being dead wouldn't make a difference.

But it would be better than nothing.

Jaguar turned around to find his blaster pointed at her.

"Take the helmet off," Mars ordered.

Jaguar slowly lifted her hands, slowly lifted the helmet, and then threw it with as much strength as she could muster. The split second that Mars was caught off guard was enough for her to dart past him and grab the sword. The helmet clattered to the ground. She turned and slashed at the air in time to deflect the blast. The sword trembled but didn't break.

"I underestimated you, Jaguar," Mars said. "I suppose that's what you were hoping for. But part of me hoped you would be the kind of fighter to enjoy the glory. Some learn to like it in the arena." He lifted the blaster again.

"How did you get here?" Jaguar asked.

The question took Mars by surprise. "What?"

"In this place. Hurting kids like me. You didn't just spring into existence a monster, did you?"

"You're calling me a monster?" Mars asked. "I'm not the one who goes out there and kills day after day."

"Don't even try that. You know you're not better than us. You *made* us." Jaguar calculated how long it would take for him to fire the blaster, how long for her to reach him, how long to swing the sword.

"Hate to break it to you, kid, but some people are born down here in the shadows," Mars said. He raised an eyebrow. "Let me guess, you were born into an ordinary life on Earth? Picked up by bounty hunters? You were dragged here into the underworld. I've been here my whole life. You can't make me feel bad for you."

Jaguar sidestepped the blast just in time. She swung, aiming for Mars's neck but missing when he stepped back. The blade sliced his hand and the blaster slipped from his grasp. Good enough. She stepped forward and swung again.

Mars lunged forward and grabbed the handle, squeezing Jaguar's hand so hard she thought it might break. "I taught you everything you know. You really think you can beat me?"

"I'm the one fighting for my life every day," Jaguar hissed. "I think I've put in more hours." She swung her fist. He caught her arm. She kicked. He faltered long enough for her to yank her hands free. The sword clattered to the ground.

Jaguar pushed Mars into the wall. Weapons fell around them. "I'm stronger than you. You know it, deep down. You're scared of me." She leaned forward. Her voice dropped to a whisper when she added, "I think they made me stronger than they meant to."

Despite the frantic look creeping into his gaze, Mars doubled down. "You know it's not about strength, it's about outsmarting your opponent. You've fought things much bigger than yourself."

"Because I'm faster than them. Are you faster than me?" Jaguar braced herself for the pain from her wounds and threw Mars to the ground. Hard. Something cracked and Mars made a sound somewhere between a grunt and a wheeze. Jaguar picked up the sword.

Blood spilled from her handler's nose and mouth. He coughed as her shadow moved over him. She lowered the tip of the blade to his neck.

"Killing me won't fix you," Mars spat.

"I know."

"You think it will make you feel better?"

Jaguar tightened her grip on the sword. "I'll feel better knowing you aren't breaking anyone else."

She pushed the blade down.

Chapter Thirty-Six
Still Having Fun?

Jasper stood at the edge of the roof while the team talked quietly behind her. The setting sun bathed the city around them in shades of red, but no matter which way she turned her gaze, it was hard to focus on anything but the impending race.

Tonight's course was a straight shot across Sagev, through the Silvium Center, followed by a loop in the desert around the city. She was determined to do well this time. Holly had a point about not drawing attention, but Jasper couldn't stand all those smug villains thinking they were better than her.

So, she had a few tricks up her sleeve for this race.

"I'm going," Jasper finally announced.

"Good luck," Grace said.

"Thanks." Jasper lifted her helmet and inspected the visor for smudges. "But I don't need luck." She'd learned to make do without it a long time ago.

"Quit being dramatic," Holly said. "I'd tell you to keep a low profile, but I feel like that's out the window at this point."

"It's not just out the window, it's in a whole different neighborhood." Jasper slid on the helmet and gave the team a thumbs up. "But thank you all for the words of encouragement."

Thea raised an eyebrow without looking up from her tablet. "Grace is the only one who said anything remotely encouraging, and you dismissed it."

"I'd say good luck too," Dax began. "But—"

"All I hear is praise and admiration." Jasper laughed. "See you nerds later."

She jumped off the roof and landed on an apartment balcony. From there it was a few short drops to the ground where her motorcycle waited. The roar of engines in the distance grew louder as the racers converged on the starting point nearby: an abandoned construction site waiting for demolition.

Jasper rolled up to an empty spot at the edge of the pack. When the race countdown she'd added to her screen reached zero, Ringmaster emerged from the shadows above, stepping into a shaft of red sunlight on a metal rafter.

"On your marks, racers." His voice echoed around the skeleton of a building. A golden platform appeared in the air in front of him. He jumped onto it.

Jasper performed one last quick check of the tools she'd added to her belt: a few of her stronger smoke bombs, extra explosives, and a container holding a deep sea neoworm she'd nabbed from a pet store. She'd also strapped her longest sword to the side of her motorcycle. It wasn't strong—she doubted it could handle more than a few bullets, if any—but it would work for her purposes tonight.

"Get set." The platform carried Ringmaster upward. "Go!"

Jasper accelerated faster than most of the bigger vehicles, quickly shooting from somewhere in the middle of the rankings to near the front. As she approached the edge of the building, Ringmaster's platform carried him even higher, out of the construction site entirely. Why was he getting out so fast?

Jasper passed through the opening and glanced back as Ringmaster, now high above the construction site, lifted his hands. A golden orb appeared in the air in front of him and dropped down into the building. A detonator formed from his energy. It was one of his signature moves.

Jasper was forced to slow as the course merged with traffic on Oasis Street. Without her consciously thinking about it, a countdown had popped up in the corner of her screen. The amount of time it typically took for one of Ringmaster's energy bombs to go off.

She pulled onto the median between the two opposing directions of traffic and zig-zagged around the palm trees lining the center of the road. The ground shuddered. She threw another glance back.

The bottom sections of the building groaned as they collapsed. The upper levels quickly followed.

"Leave it to Ringmaster to blow up a building for the drama," Jasper muttered, though some part of her wondered if he was trying to get people killed. Maybe he didn't want any winners at the end of this.

"That's rich, coming from you," Holly replied.

"I wouldn't blow up a building!"

"You blew a hole in the roof of the Silvium Center just yesterday," Thea pointed out.

"And Atzy's," Grace added, quieter.

"Wait, when were you at Atzy's?" Holly asked.

Jasper ignored the question. The course shot under an overpass, and she veered up onto the ramped concrete side, using the higher ground to survey the other racers. She spotted South Siren near the front, hekten wrapped around her upper arm.

Perfect. Jasper eased back down into the flow of traffic. The Silvium Center's dome glowed up ahead against the darkening sky. The first racers left the road and headed up the long set of stairs leading to the mall's north entrance. When Jasper reached the stairs, she hopped onto the railing instead. She wobbled but managed to keep her balance as she shot past the vehicles climbing the steps.

She flew off the railing at the top and landed right behind South Siren. As they passed through the front entrance, South Siren extended the arm her hekten was perched on.

Jasper's hand darted to the neoworm in her pocket. She popped the lid off its container and swerved to avoid the first blast from the hekten. The fluorescent green worm inched onto Jasper's gloved hand. She held it up.

The hekten hissed and scrambled up to South Siren's shoulder.

"That's right, you spiky monster!" Jasper flung the worm onto the hekten's head. It latched on tight the moment it landed. Even if South Siren was able to rip the thing off immediately, it was already laying its eggs. That should put the hekten out of commission for a week or so. South Siren yelled a string of curses as Jasper passed her.

Jasper navigated the tables in the food court—and the people running around them—with relative ease. Larger vehicles were forced to take the long way around. They would also be forced to take the central staircase up to the second floor.

With her motorcycle, Jasper was able to instead aim for the nearest up escalator. "Outta the way!" she shouted at the last few people scrambling off.

From there, the course ran along the same path Jasper and the others had used during their little joy ride they day they'd arrived. Jasper tipped her head back and laughed as she flew off the roof and sailed through the air.

She whizzed through the parking lot and onto Silvium Drive. The sky was all purples and pinks and blues now. Jasper lifted her gaze to take it in.

Storefronts and restaurants and casinos and dance clubs flew by, a blur of flashing lights and glowing signs. As traffic lessened and buildings became shorter and father apart, a bang went off in a passing alleyway.

"Was that a gunshot?" Jasper asked. She glanced back, but there was no sign of anyone behind her.

"Where?" Thea asked.

"Right by the intersection of Silvium Drive and Sunshine Boulevard."

Grim Machine's tank form was coming up on Jasper's right. She frowned when a long pipe emerged from his side. That had to be some kind of weapon, right?

More racers broke free of the city traffic and turned onto the older road leading out into the desert. Grim Machine summoned a surprising burst of speed and passed Jasper. As he did, a dark cloud shot out of the pipe.

The racers that drove through the cloud didn't show any immediate adverse reaction. Still, Jasper steered clear. "I don't suppose anyone could tell me what this weird cloud is."

"Hold on, I'll bring up a camera feed," Thea replied. "Make sure your smartsphere is pointed forward."

After a moment, Dax said, "Looks kind of like bird seed."

"What? How do you know what bird seed looks like?" Jasper asked.

"I go bird watching sometimes."

"There aren't any birds in Kronos."

"There are in the Tide District," Thea said.

"Don't those birds eat people?" Holly asked.

Grace chimed in. "I thought that was a myth."

"This debate is completely pointless, because there is absolutely no reason for Grim Machine to put bird seed in the air during a race." Jasper opened her own camera as the robot fired off another cloud. "I'm going to send Thea a close picture so someone with more than half a brain cell can tell me what it is." She zoomed in, snapped a photo, and sent it to Thea's tablet.

"Oh, yeah, that's definitely bird seed," Thea said.

"Yep," Dax confirmed.

Jasper's brow furrowed. "Really?"

"Specifically, it's the seed of a plant that produces a rotting meat smell," Thea explained. "This particular brand adds a bunch of chemicals to increase its potency. It's meant to lure in carnivorous birds from over a mile away." After a brief pause, she added, "It's pretty disgusting that he's using it, actually. Those chemicals are awful for the environment—"

Something shrieked in the distance, and a long-forgotten memory stirred in Jasper's mind. A memory of desperately seeking cover. Of watching people get snatched up like mice. Her heart dropped. "No, no, no, no, no—"

"Jasper? What's wrong?" Dax asked.

"This is bad."

"Jasper?" Grace pressed.

Focus. She needed to focus if she was going to get out of this alive. "Snatchawks." Jasper fought to keep her eyes on the road and not the sky. "Invasive species. Brought in during the Waste Wars to destroy armies."

"Oh?" Holly's tone was more intrigued than concerned. "I've always wanted to see one of those in person."

"No, you don't," Jasper told her sharply. "They're monsters. And Grim Machine's summoning them to pick off racers." He had nothing to worry about, being a massive hunk of metal. Even if the birds were strong enough to lift him, they had no interest in something they couldn't eat.

The shrieks sounded again, closer now.

"You sound like you've seen one before," Holly said.

Jasper didn't answer Holly. She barely heard the statement. She squeezed her handlebar with painful force as she watched the first of the red, helicopter-sized birds of prey appear on the horizon.

Chapter Thirty-Seven
Fight and Flight Response

The panic in Jasper's voice should have been enough to paralyze Grace. If Jasper was afraid, things were bad.

Instead, she rose to her feet. "We have to do something."

The rest of the team exchanged apprehensive glances.

"Can we shoot them down?" Grace asked.

"Not from the ground," Thea said. "They fly too high and move too fast when they dive for prey."

Grace spread her wings. "Good thing I'm not confined to the ground."

Jasper was even more distressed now. "Angel! Don't you dare come out here—" She cut herself off with a yelp.

"Jasper? Are you okay?" Grace frantically glanced around. She needed something to fight with. Her eyes found the bag of tools and weapons Jasper had left with them.

"I'm fine! They grabbed someone in front of me."

"I'm coming to help." Grace grabbed a blaster.

"No, you're not!"

"Grace, don't," Thea said. "She can handle herself. She's faced worse enemies. Alone. Dozens of times."

"Please," Dax added.

Holly watched with narrowed eyes.

"Sorry," Grace told them. "But I'm going to try."

She raced to the edge of the roof. Her wings spread out as she ran, her metal feathers caught the desert air, and then she was flying. She sucked in a deep breath and pushed herself higher, high enough that she could see seven terrifyingly large birds circling in the sky beyond the glittering city.

While Grace flew toward them, she looked over the blaster. She'd never used one, but all she had to do was pull the trigger, right?

The closest snatchawk took an interest in her. She lifted the blaster as it soared her way. How close did she need to be for the blast to do any good? How close was too close? Too late?

Grace squeezed the trigger. A blue laser fired and missed the bird by ten feet. She tried again. And again. Her fourth shot struck the middle of the bird's head.

It silently dropped from the sky.

"I did it!" Grace cheered. She halted and beat her wings against the air to hover in place. Three more birds looked her way. *Uh oh.*

"Get down here!" Jasper yelled into the comms.

A fourth bird dove toward the racers. Toward Jasper.

Grace folded in her wings and dove. "Jasper, look out!" She caught herself as close to traffic as she dared and soared over the heads of the racers.

Jasper yanked her motorcycle to the right, barely dodging the bird's talons.

Grace lifted the blaster and fired. The bird shrieked, but the hole in its stomach wasn't enough to stop it. Grace fired again. It swooped toward her.

It was almost on top of her when her third shot sent it crashing into the road, causing a few vehicles to either collide or fly off the course.

"Okay, that was cool," Jasper admitted. "But you've got three more coming your way."

"They're faster than me," Grace realized, panic overriding her determination. She flew as low to the ground as she dared in hopes that the racers would distract the birds from her. "Jasper!"

"It's going to be okay." Jasper sounded only slightly more confident than she had before. "Catch up to me. I have something that'll help."

Jasper slowed. Grace shot past a few racers, including Cutthroat, who watched her pass with a curious expression.

"Here!" Jasper removed a smoke bomb from her belt and held it out as Grace caught up. Grace's fingers grazed the sphere. Her hand wrapped around it, and she slid it into her pocket.

Jasper passed her three more. "Please don't die!"

"I know, I know, you need me to take down Starr. Don't worry, I won't ruin your plans."

"It's not—" Jasper stopped herself. "Good luck!"

Grace managed a small smile as she ascended. "I don't need luck!"

Jasper laughed. That was good. Maybe they weren't totally screwed. Grace drew out the first smoke bomb. Two snatchawks changed paths to pursue her. She pushed the button on the bomb and threw it their way.

The smoke swallowed them. Grace fired blindly into the cloud, not stopping until both birds had fallen. "Where are the other—?"

Sharp talons dug into Grace's shoulder, drawing blood and a cry of pain from her lips. The blaster slipped from her fingers.

"Grace!" Jasper screamed.

Grace grabbed at the bird's leg and clawed blindly. A gunshot—no, something louder—went off below. The bird let out a deafening shriek. Its claws released their hold on Grace. As Grace fell, the sound echoed again. She looked down.

Cutthroat was firing from the miniature cannon on his vehicle. His next shot sent the bird that had grabbed Grace crashing into the desert sand.

Grace forced her wings to move through the pain. That probably wasn't helping the whole bleeding out situation, but she could deal with that on the ground. She located the blaster lying in the sand, adjusted her wings, and glided toward it.

The landing was rough, and more pain shot through her legs as she stumbled and fell to her knees. She grabbed the blaster and looked up.

Two snatchawks left. "What happened to the racers they grabbed?" Grace asked.

"They drop them off somewhere to eat later. Of course, we're tougher than their usual prey. Most of the racers will probably survive and get away."

Grace swallowed and pulled out another smoke bomb. This was going to hurt like hell. She thought about all the times she'd seen Jasper get hit or wounded or fall a little too far and still get back up to keep fighting. Her wings unfolded. She jumped.

The snatchawks swooped down to meet her. Grace activated the smoke bomb and tossed it up as hard as she could. She aimed and fired off shots, one after another.

"You know blasters have a limit before they have to be recharged, right?" Jasper asked.

Grace paused. "Wait, what?"

One bird fell. The other emerged from the smoke shrieking, talons out, red wings spread wide. Grace was close enough to see the rows of razor-sharp teeth filling its beak. She tucked in her own wings to drop out of range, then flew behind and up. As the bird turned itself around, she rose above it. "How do I know how many shots I have left?"

"There's a screen on the back with a number," Jasper said.

"You mean the tiny blue square?"

"Yes, that!"

Grace's heart skipped a beat. "It says one."

"Oh. Well, better make it count!"

The snatchawk was close. Grace needed more time to take aim. While she fought to rise higher and stay out of the bird's grasp, she readied another smoke bomb. Activated it. Let go. The bird shrieked as the smoke surrounded it and obscured its sight. Grace took aim at the cloud, waiting for the bird's shadow to appear. One shot.

Movement at the edge of the cloud. *Not yet. Almost.*

The snatchawk's head broke free of the smoke. Grace pulled the trigger. The blue laser cut clean through the bird's neck.

"I got it!" Grace twisted in the air and searched for Jasper among the racers.

"I knew you could, Angel." Jasper reached for the sword strapped to the side of her motorcycle and, as she passed Grim Machine, jammed it into a gap in the tank's side. "Take that, you dumb idiot robot!" she yelled as he flipped over and tumbled off the road.

"You couldn't string together a more intelligent insult?" Holly asked.

"I'm too angry for that right now!" Jasper had almost made it to the front of the pack, and Ringmaster's finish line was less than a minute away. Grace followed from above, trying to focus on the feeling of wind on her skin and not the way she was still shaking from her fight with the snatchawks.

Jasper moved into fifth. Fourth. Third. Grace veered away from the road and moved to hover above the sand a few hundred feet off. She wasn't sure if the final stretch of the race would be dangerous, but if anyone had any last-minute tricks up their sleeve, she wanted to be far out of range.

Cutthroat came up on Jasper's right. He pushed a lever, and his exterior weaponry, cannon included, detached from his cart, rolling along the road behind him and crashing into racers before they could get out of the way. Flames exploded out of the back of the vehicle, pushing Cutthroat into third and across the finish line seconds before Jasper.

Grace expected complaining or cursing from Jasper, but the comms stayed silent. Jasper swerved off the road and cut across the sand, toward where Grace was hovering. Grace lowered herself to the ground. The sky had faded to a dark violet now, turning to fire at the horizon.

Jasper hopped off the motorcycle and pulled off her helmet. "Are you okay?" she asked, wide eyes darting over Grace.

"I'm going to have some pretty bad scars on my shoulder, but other than that I'm good." Grace's entire body still trembled. She pressed a hand to her aching shoulder where the talons had found her flesh. Her shirt was damp with blood, but the pain had faded enough that the wound didn't feel urgent anymore. "Why hasn't anyone gotten rid of those things?"

Jasper leaned against the motorcycle and tipped her head back to watch the stars appearing overhead. "No particular government wants to take responsibility for them. And they usually keep away from civilization, so they're not a threat to people unless you go out into the desert unprepared."

Grace sank into the sand. "I just need to sit down for a minute, and I'll be okay," she said when Jasper shot her a concerned look.

"We should get you to Dax," Jasper said. The concern in her expression didn't let up in the slightest. Did she really think Grace was worth worrying about, now? Maybe the fight with the snatchawks had proved she wasn't as useless as she seemed.

"I don't think I can fly again tonight." Grace looked back at the city. "Looks like a pretty far walk."

Jasper sighed. "All right, take a few minutes to rest. You'll have to ride back with me on the motorcycle."

"Okay." Grace scooped up a handful of white sand and watched it pour through her fingers. "So, have you seen them before?"

"Seen what?"

"The snatchawks. It sounded like you did."

Jasper stared at her for a moment before sliding up a finger to mute her comm. "It was a long time ago."

Grace muted hers, too. "How long?" When Jasper didn't answer, she added, "I—I saw a photo somewhere in the shack. Of you. Dressed in a military uniform, I think."

Jasper kicked at the sand. "I don't know how long Sky Labs has been running, but Syrus Starr's grandfather was the one in charge when I was taken to Kronos," she said. "And I'm not going to explain all of that to you right now. But the labs—that's where it happened. The cybernetics. The computers in my brain. They did it. And they gave me some serum." Her shoulders sagged. Her gaze lowered to the ground. "I think it was meant to be a healing thing, to make my body fix itself faster. I don't know if they intended for it to work the way it did but...I haven't...*aged* since."

Grace swallowed. "So, you're...?"

"I was born on Earth in 1952. I'm sixty-eight." Jasper eyes met Grace's for a heartbeat before moving back down. "I was here on Si Hera during the Waste Wars. I fought in them."

"Oh."

Grace couldn't begin to imagine... Sixty-eight? What else had she seen, besides war and monstrous birds? She lowered her own gaze to the sand, racking her brain for something to say. Anything.

"So, your mind's sixty-eight but your body's seventeen?" she asked after a long moment.

"Sort of? Not really. I mean, I have sixty plus years of memories, sure, but I'm pretty sure my stupid brain hasn't aged either. I still feel seventeen." Jasper rubbed her forehead. "But sometimes I feel young and old at the same time."

"Why not tell the others?" Grace asked.

"They think I'm crazy enough as is."

"You don't trust them?"

"I do. I want to. It's complicated." Jasper moved her hands into her pockets. "Maybe I'm telling you because my gut tells me I can trust you. Or maybe I'm telling you because we haven't known each other long, so it doesn't matter to me what you think."

That stung, oddly enough. Grace swallowed. "I think you should tell the others. They're your team, aren't they?"

"I guess they deserve to know. I just don't know how to talk about my past."

Grace rested her chin on her knees and stared out at where the vast expanse of sand met the dark sky. "You called me Grace."

"What?"

"Instead of Angel. When the snatchawk grabbed me."

"Oh. Did I? The whole thing's kind of a blur."

"Jasper? Grace? You guys still there?" Thea asked.

Jasper tapped her comm. "Yeah, we're good. We'll be back in a few."

"Okay, well, that gunshot you heard? It's all over the news now. Someone was killed."

"Interesting." Jasper looked at Grace. "Could be a random murder, but the fact that it took place during the race…"

"The race would make a good distraction," Grace climbed to her feet, wincing at the stabbing pains that seemed to have multiplied. "Maybe the victim is the target Ringmaster and Aymes were discussing."

A grin broke out on Jasper's face. "That's exactly what I was thinking." She tossed Grace her helmet. "Let's go."

Grace barely managed to catch it. "What about you?"

"I've got metal in my skull and the ground's made of sand. I'll be fine." Jasper swung one leg over the motorcycle. "Come on."

Grace slid on the helmet. She climbed on behind Jasper and held on tight, bracing for the high speeds and swerving she'd seen during the race. Instead, Jasper started slow and built up speed gradually.

Si Hera's silver moon Sera hung in the sky over Sagev, and its second black moon Vala peeked over the horizon. The light they reflected made small, metallic fragments in the desert sand sparkle as Grace and Jasper raced over them.

The sight made Grace want to go flying again, to see the breathtaking view from above. As awful as fighting those birds had been, realizing she could twist and turn in the air like that had been amazing. And she'd proved something to herself. To Jasper's team. She was a fighter.

Grace wished she'd seen the world outside Kronos sooner.

III. PRECINCT 421 / ARCH & ARCHER

Chapter Thirty-Eight
SHPD: Desert Detectives: Special Murders Unit

In life, Dr. Augusta Prime had been a genius. But while information on her education and degrees and early research were easy to find, her recent projects seemed to be classified. Whoever she'd been working for didn't want anyone else knowing what they were up to.

And now Dr. Prime was dead. Jasper suggested using a Ouija board to ask her about the research, which was met with either eye rolls or glares. Well, one glare. From Holly. At any rate, the team had no way of knowing what she was working on—

"Got it," Thea said from the backseat.

Jasper glanced in the mirror at where Thea was squeezed between Dax and Holly in the back seat. Her gaze then briefly flickered to Grace at her right before returning to the road. "Got what?"

"Dr. Prime's recent research. She was working for a spaceport company. They caught wind of the spacetime warps and were having her investigate their potential."

Sagev traffic was worse than usual the morning after the race. Jasper swerved to get in front of a slower car and shot across an intersection as the light changed from yellow to red. Someone honked.

"Okay, Ringmaster picked the race location so he could kill Dr. Prime, apparently for warp research reasons," Jasper said, tapping her finger against the steering wheel. "But he was watching over the race. Someone must have done it for him. Aymes?"

"Ringmaster did mention Aymes would have a role during the race, but I'm not convinced it was the murder," Thea replied. "Ringmaster has more experienced henchpeople working for him. Why would he trust a high schooler with assassination?"

"Good point." Jasper took a hard left turn across traffic. They were almost to their destination. "Maybe whoever the police arrested last night can help us figure it out."

Holly piped up in the backseat. "Hey, should we maybe reconsider driving a stolen car directly to the police station?"

Jasper shrugged. "It's been a few days. I'm sure they've forgotten about it by now."

"People don't just forget about cars stolen from malls."

"Well, I forgot we stole it, so clearly some people do." Jasper turned into a parking lot and picked a spot. She'd actually looked into the precinct and found they didn't have a great track record for finding stolen cars. Or looking very hard at all. Bringing a wanted vehicle directly to them might be pushing the team's luck, but worst-case scenario, Jasper could just steal another.

Grace leaned forward and peered out the windshield. "The sign says this spot is employees only."

Jasper raised an eyebrow. "And?"

"...Okay."

The team climbed out of the car and approached the pristine white building. "Si Hera's 421st Precinct," Jasper said, gesturing to the place with a sweep of her arm. "Fun fact, all of the Si Heran precincts are run by Sera's mayor."

"The moon? Why?" Holly asked as the team paused on the sidewalk out front. "And why do you know that?"

"It's a leftover relic from when Sera stepped in and tried to fix Si Hera's government during the Waste Wars." Jasper ignored Holly's second question.

Sera, the Si Heran moon that closely resembled Earth's lone Luna, didn't boast much in terms of civilization these days. Once things had settled on Si Hera and become relatively peaceful, a lot of people had moved from the moon to the planet's surface.

Thankfully, the spaceports that only warped between Si Hera and its two moons were far more relaxed than the ones connected to Kronos, so getting through security would be a breeze when it came time for the race on the other moon, Vala. In the meantime, Jasper and the others could keep working on Sagev.

"Ringmaster also mentioned in his messages to Aymes that Dr. Prime apparently had a hideout on Sera, though he wasn't sure where," Thea said. "We'll want to investigate that, too."

"Sure, sure." Jasper stretched her arms. "You ready, Holly?"

"I've been disguising myself as janitors to break in places for years. I'd say I'm more than ready," Holly muttered. She moved ahead of the team and entered the precinct.

A few minutes later, her voice came over comms. "Got the uniforms. Meet me on the west side of the building."

The team circled the building. Holly emerged from a first-floor window holding a stack of clothes. "I'd normally be more concerned about spending any amount of time in a police station, but I don't think we'll have any trouble here," she said as she handed them out.

Five minutes later, the team strolled into the 421st Precinct in their new disguises. No one gave them a second glance as they roamed the floor and sifted through filing cabinets.

That was, until an officer walked up to Jasper while she scanned the directory. She was a fairly plain looking Si Heran: Bald, with light blue skin that looked as rough as sandpaper. She wore the precinct's darker blue uniform, complete with a silver badge on her chest. "Excuse me, can I help you?" she asked. "You seem to be searching for something."

Jasper adjusted her dark sunglasses. "My squad and I were told to take a look at the Augusta Prime case." In addition to the glasses and uniform, she'd shifted her hair down into a low ponytail to help break up her usual look.

The officer's face lit up. "Oh, thank Vala! They told my partner and I that we would be handling it alone, but we need all the help we can get, since we have no leads."

"I thought an arrest had already been made," Jasper told her as the rest of the team gathered around. "It was on the news."

"Oh, Captain Prool told the press that so people wouldn't freak out. We actually have nothing!" The officer was strangely chipper as she stuck out a hand. "I'm Officer Alyow, by the way."

While Jasper shook her hand, another Si Heran man with brown skin and a suspicious look in his eyes appeared at her side. "Officer Alyow, who are these people?"

"We're new. Just transferred in," Jasper told him.

"Great news, Detective," Alyow said. "They assigned this whole team to help us find Dr. Prime's killer." She turned to Jasper. "This is Detective Park."

Jasper forced a smile. "Detective Park, pleasure to meet you."

Detective Park's narrowed eyes moved across the team's faces. "Why didn't Captain Prool tell us about them sooner?"

Alyow lifted onto her toes. "Why don't you ask him? He's coming this way!" She beamed at Jasper. "Captain Prool's been running this place since before I was born."

Uh oh. Jasper forced a smile as the captain reached them. Best to blame lost paperwork. That usually worked.

"Who are you?" the captain asked. Another Si Heran. In fact, he looked a bit like an older, taller, thinner version of Detective Park.

"Don't worry, Captain Prool," Jasper told him. "My team has decades of experience solving murders."

For a moment, Captain Prool's narrow gaze made Jasper fear the team would have to run. Then he smiled. "About time they gave us some help. Having some competent officers like you on the case will make people realize that the 421st Precinct isn't the joke the public makes us out to be."

"Sir, none of them look like they should even be out of training," Detective Park said. "How can they have decades of experience?"

"Combined experience," Jasper amended.

"You do look rather young to be such a skilled detective," Captain Prool agreed.

"I drink three glasses of solnut oil a day. It does wonders for the skin." Jasper clapped her hands together. "Now, let's go solve a murder!"

Detective Park sighed. "I suppose I'll join the investigation too, then. Guess my paperwork can wait."

Alyow's eyes widened. "You want to join us?"

"I think it's best a superior officer be present if a bunch of new officers are going to be jumping in." Park shot Jasper a glare.

Oblivious to the tension, Alyow waved at a heavily muscled man coming their way, whose skin was a blue a few shades lighter than hers. "This is my partner," she said. "Officer Tary, these five strangers who just showed up are going to help us with the murder."

"Great!" Officer Tary exclaimed. "Hey, do any of you watch Star Conquerors? The finale last night was crazy."

"Everything I know about that show I've learned against my will," Jasper told him. Before he could fully process the statement, she added, "Now, come on, that body's not getting any warmer!"

"Jasper!" Holly hissed as the officers started toward the front of the precinct.

"Oh, the body's already been moved from the crime scene," Alyow said. "But maybe you can find something at the scene we missed. So, your name's Jasper?"

"Uh, Detective Jasper." Jasper shot Holly a glare. "And this here is Officer Mud." She nodded to Thea, Dax, and Grace. "And they're Officers Sparks, Cure, and Starling."

Holly rolled her eyes. "Brilliant."

The real detective, the two officers, and all five members of Jasper's team stepped outside. "Were you guys assigned a patrol vehicle?" Tary asked.

"No," Jasper told him. "Not yet."

"I wonder why," Detective Park muttered.

Alyow tossed Jasper a key. "Here, take this one. Tary and I will ride with Park."

"Great. I love listening to you two to sing along to that Dragonworld Musical." Park's sarcasm rivaled Holly's.

Jasper grinned at the key in her hand. "We'll see you at the scene." She tapped the unlock button. "This is gonna be fun."

Within minutes, they were speeding down Silvium Drive, sirens blaring. "I'm pretty sure cops don't use sirens on their way to a crime scene," Holly said.

"Well, maybe they should," Jasper replied.

They arrived ten minutes before the officers. A couple of officers already waited at the scene, serving as guards to keep away curious civilians, but they were too wrapped up watching a video on the tablet in front of them to even acknowledge the Jasper's team's arrival.

Rather than waste time on the small crime scene they'd be looking at shortly anyway, Jasper had the team spread out and search the area for signs of Ringmaster.

Nothing.

"So, what have we got?" Jasper asked when the real officers finally pulled up and stepped out of their car.

"They took the body last night," Alyow said as the three joined Jasper's team. "No official cause of death yet."

"I'm guessing it was the gunshot to the head," Detective Park muttered.

"Any other evidence?" Regardless of the competence of the crime scene technicians, Jasper didn't have faith they'd found anything useful during their investigation. Not if Ringmaster had orchestrated this.

"Besides the samples of Prime's blood, nothing yet," Tary replied.

"And her apartment?"

Alyow folded her arms. "Already been searched."

"I haven't been here yet," Detective Park said, glancing at the crime scene behind Jasper. "But there could always be something more. Let's make sure the techs didn't miss anything."

Well, if he didn't have high hopes for the techs, Jasper was inclined to lower her expectations as well. She turned. "Officer Alyow, care to give my team a quick tour of the scene?"

"Of course! Follow me."

With Alyow leading the way, they all ducked under the glowing crime scene tape and moved into the alley. Alyow pointed at a dark stain on the concrete. "That's where the body was."

Thea nudged Jasper. "I'm sensing electronics up on that wall," she whispered with a glance up. "Pretty sure there's a camera."

"Any cameras?" Jasper asked aloud.

"Not that we know of," Alyow replied.

"There's a camera across the street facing the alley entrance, but it didn't see the actual murder," Tary added. "It did show a guy leaving the alley around the time of the gunshot, but that's not conclusive evidence."

Thea tipped her head back. "That ledge is perfect."

"Huh?" Alyow frowned.

Thea pointed. "It hides the camera from view. The camera can see over the ledge, but unless you were backed up against the opposite wall, you wouldn't notice it. It's small, too." Her hand dropped. "What's in that building?"

"Convenience store," Detective Park answered. He backed up to the other wall and looked up. "She's right, there's something up there." Lowering his gaze, he added, "Let's pay them a visit."

"Hang on." Jasper held up a hand as she walked to a dumpster near the bloodstain. She pointed to a cup on the ground, splattered with blood. "Is that the victim's blood?"

Detective Park moved to her side and lifted an eyebrow. "We'll have to test it to be sure, but I'd bet on yes."

"Look at the blood splatters around it." Jasper dropped to one knee. "But this doesn't match up. Looks more like the cup was close to the victim when she was shot, then tossed aside."

"Good point." Detective Park folded his arms. "But do you really think the perp was sipping on coffee in the middle of the kill?"

"I've done th—I mean, I've seen it happen," Jasper said as she straightened up. "My point is, the killer's DNA could be on the cup. We should test it."

Detective Park snapped his fingers to catch the attention of one of the officers guarding the scene. He pointed at the cup. "Bag this."

While they grabbed the cup, Jasper's team and the officers left the alley and entered the convenience store.

The cashier looked up as they walked in. "I was wondering when you'd come in!" he exclaimed. "Eight officers seems like overkill, though. Unless the murderer was a serial killer. Ooh, are you looking for a serial killer?"

"Let's take the enthusiasm down a notch," Detective Park told the kid as everyone gathered in front of the checkout counter. "Were you working during the murder last night?"

"Yep!" The cashier nodded eagerly. He was a pink-skinned Si Heran who looked young enough to be in high school.

"Can we look at the security footage from that time?"

"Sure, let me grab the key." The cashier opened a drawer in front of him.

Tary slammed a hand down on the counter. "Listen, kid, it's in your best interest to cooperate with us."

The cashier looked up, brow furrowing. "I am cooperating!"

"Oh. Well, good." Tary nodded and straightened up.

Alyow leaned in. "Nice job." She sounded completely genuine.

Jasper raised an eyebrow. Had Ringmaster chosen the location of Prime's death deliberately so that this precinct would get the case? Police officers weren't exactly known for going above and beyond, but this was incompetence on a whole other level. She exchanged a look with the rest of her team, whose faces held a mixture of confusion and concern.

"Follow me," the cashier said. Key in hand, he led the way to the back of the store.

Jasper lingered at the back of the group and grabbed a small bottle of Nova Cora off a shelf, which she shoved into an inner pocket of her uniform jacket. Grace noticed and gave Jasper a look that, surprisingly, stung a little.

The cashier led them into a back room and sat in front of a small bank of monitors. After a minute of typing, he frowned at the screen. "That's weird. The footage from about ten minutes before and after the gunshot is missing. For all the cameras." He tapped a few keys. "Someone must have deleted it."

"Maybe the computers glitched," Alyow suggested.

Detective Park sighed. "Was anyone else working with you last night?" he asked the cashier.

The cashier hesitated, all of his earlier vigor gone. "No. I was alone."

"Well, we may have some more questions for you in the future, then." Detective Park gestured for the others to follow him and headed out of the back room.

As they left the store, Detective Park said, "I think he's hiding something."

"I don't think he did it," Jasper replied.

"Who else could have deleted the footage?"

"He may have deleted it, but that doesn't make him the killer."

"It does make him an accessory, though." Detective Park let out another heavy sigh. "Maybe if we're lucky, and the techs don't screw up the analysis, there will be DNA on the coffee cop that leads us to the killer."

Jasper didn't want to get her hopes up, but Detective Park's wishful thinking wasn't far off base. When they returned to the station, an officer ran up to them holding a file. "Detective Park, I have your lab results!" She waved it around as she approached. Coffee splashed out of the cup in her other hand.

"Please be careful with that." Detective Park took the file. "Thank you," he added as he opened it.

"Anything good?" Jasper asked, leaning to peer at the file over his shoulder.

Detective Park studied the first page for a moment. He lifted an eyebrow. "The DNA matched someone in the city's employee database. Ro Mechwell." He looked up. "I think we should pay him a visit."

Chapter Thirty-Nine
Terra

No money. No connections. No identity. Jane had nothing to her name after she left the title of Jaguar behind in the Lion's Den.

But she did have her physical strength, which landed her a position on a cargo spaceship headed for Sa Ren. She was eager for the work, for the exhaustion that sank so deeply into every muscle that she was out cold every night. With most of her time spent sleeping or working, she didn't have much energy left to dwell on her thoughts. Her past. Her future.

After arriving on Sa Ren, she hung out in a coastal town for a few weeks. The planet was mostly water, its ocean only broken up by scattered islands and small landmasses. The weather was perfect. Most found it verging on uncomfortably hot in the summer months, but Jane couldn't get enough of the sun, the warm seas, the clear skies tinged with green.

She was lounging on the upper balcony of a cafe one morning, scanning the crowds below for wealthy pickpocketing targets, when she saw him.

For a moment, she couldn't believe it. It had to be someone who looked similar. A blue-skinned member of the Si Heran species wasn't an unusual sight on Sa Ren, after all. But he was wearing the same clothing he'd worn that night, and she could never forget that face for as long as she lived.

Jane slid off the balcony railing and hurried downstairs, taking a detour through the kitchen to grab a knife. Then she was outside, slipping through the crowd, not taking her eyes off the back of Eriph's head.

She followed him for five minutes before he entered an empty side street. As soon as they were out of view of people passing on the sidewalk,

"

Jane grabbed him, clapped a hand over his mouth, and slammed him into the wall. With her free hand, she pressed the knife to his throat.

"Scream, and you're dead." She removed her hand from his mouth. "Remember me?"

Eriph stared, seemingly unbothered by the blade at his neck. "Am I supposed to?"

"I can jog your memory, if you'd like. This is actually the third time we've met," she told him. "Earth. New York. 1964—about four and a half starcycles ago. Ring any bells?"

"Rings a lot of bells. I'm guessing you're one of the kids I took to Starr?"

Jane swallowed her anger, resisting the urge to let the blade sink in. "Where's Ybra?"

"Ybra?" Eriph's brow furrowed. "I haven't worked with her in a couple of starcycles. I came here to find her, actually. Starr has a growing interest in kids from the Ra System, and she's the only one I know who's been there."

"How do you know she's here?" Jane asked.

"I don't, but a pair she usually works with came here to join a squad headed to Earth. I'm hoping she's with them."

"Where can I find them?"

"Okay, enough." Eriph's hand moved toward Jane's wrist. She yanked it away and jammed the blade of the knife into his shoulder.

He gasped. Blood spurted from the wound. "You're fast."

Jane threw him to the ground. "And strong."

"How—?"

Jane crouched. The blade went back to his neck. "How do I find them?"

"They're meeting on Pier 23 at midnight. If you let me take you—"

Jane cut him off with a swipe of the blade.

She took his blaster, his dagger, and his pulse gun. The weapons waited hidden under a dumpster while she stole new clothes—mostly black, heavier material resembling the stuff Eriph and Ybra wore—and a bag from a shop. Her short, nearly chin-length hair was still a little uneven from her cuts in the Lion's Den, but she smoothed it out as best she could.

Then, she collected the weapons and headed to the piers.

Pier 23 was under construction. Jane found a secluded spot on the walkway above the beach to watch from and waited for the suns to go down.

Tourists left the boardwalk. Lights from ships glimmered in the night, far from shore. As the twentieth hour of the Sa Renian day came to a close, figures arrived on the pier, ducking under the caution tape and stepping around construction equipment. Jane descended from her lookout spot and followed them.

"—and the underground warp has been redirected to Earth station three," a man was saying as Jane approached.

"That's far from our target. What happened to stations one and two?" a second voice asked.

"They were both destroyed. By some assholes calling themselves Earthguard," the man replied. "Anyway, are we waiting on anyone else?"

Jane stepped out of the shadows, blaster drawn. "I'm looking for Ybra."

Six more blasters turned on her in an instant. "Ybra?" the first man asked.

"I know her," a woman said. "She's not here. She's taking a season or so off in Kronos." Her eyes narrowed. "Who are you?"

"Name's Clarke. I'm coming with you to Earth."

Only one of the bounty hunters attempted to fire at Jane. She dodged. Instead of firing back, she lunged forward, ducked to avoid the man's attempt to strike her, and landed a solid kick to his stomach. As he slammed into the pier, she braced herself for another attack. The others looked ready to strike, but none made a move.

"I don't want to hurt any of you," Jane lied. "Don't make me." As if they could stop her.

After a tense silence, a woman spoke. "You can come," she said. When her fellow hunters gave her weird looks, she said, "What? She has skill, clearly. She could bring in some good money."

The man Jane had struck climbed to his feet, gasping for breath. "She'd better."

The woman explained that they would take a small boat to an unregulated offshore warp. The others told Jane their names, but she didn't bother remembering them.

"Where's this station three located?" Jane asked.

"Near a city called New York," a different woman answered. "That's not our target, though. Too many do-gooder vigilantes with superpowers these days. We're heading west."

Jane didn't make conversation with the others, and she gave them vague answers to questions when they asked. For over an hour, she listened to them talk about past jobs. Share stories. Laugh.

Her hand tightened around the side of the boat. She needed to wait. She needed them to take her to Earth. Tighter. Hairline cracks appeared in the side of the boat. She forced herself to move her hand.

They docked on a tiny, rocky island. Tied the boat up. Walked to the dilapidated shack housing the warp. Jane didn't like the idea of using a warp that hadn't been approved by government inspectors. Even if it had been used safely before, there was no telling when it would break down.

The journey was rougher than Jane remembered her first warp being, but she was still in one piece at the end of it. The warp deposited her and the hunters in a room that opened into a sewer tunnel. Jane stayed at the back of the group as they walked, assessing the six hunters, running through her plan.

Go for the fastest, most agile first. Stay in the middle so they can't fire without hitting each other. Don't stop until they're all down.

She drew her dagger.

Lunge. Stab, swipe, swipe again. One down. Jane ducked to avoid the blows coming her way. A strike to the legs, the foot, and two more were down. Elbow the head, leg to the stomach. Stab. Another one down—

Someone kicked Jane in the back, sending her staggering into the wall. Her head smacked against stone. The dagger slipped from her hand. She dove to the right. A blaster fired into the wall.

The woman took aim and fired again. Jane dropped to the ground, grabbed the dagger, and threw it into the woman's chest.

The shot from the blaster grazed her arm, ripping a hole in her sleeve and burning her skin. She cried out but forced herself to stand and turn, searching for the last hunter.

The man pushed her into the wall and pressed his blaster to her head. "Why are you doing this?" he hissed.

"If you were an insect reborn as a cat, would you hunt down the bird that killed you?"

"What?"

The moment of confusion was enough. Jane dropped, pulling away from the blaster. His hand moved to aim it at her again. She shoved her foot into his stomach. Straightened up. Struck the side of his face, his stomach again, his neck. The blaster fell from his grasp. Jane snatched it from the air.

She aimed and fired.

Last one down.

Jane wandered the sewers in a haze for ten minutes—maybe longer—before finding the presence of mind to search for a way out. She emerged through a manhole cover in an alley, startling a boy throwing trash bags into a dumpster. Ignoring his surprised yelp and confused stare, she walked to the sidewalk.

Jane had picked up a limp at some point, her face was covered in grime, and there was undoubtedly blood splattered across her dark clothing. She checked her clock. August 28th. 1975. Roughly ten p.m. in the Eastern Time Zone.

It was surreal, staring up at the buildings, feeling that sense of familiarity she hadn't known in years. Everything was different, new, bigger, louder, but underneath it all was a place she knew.

Her home was nearby.

Jane had the horrible thought that she might be dreaming as she walked. This couldn't be real. Yes, she was home, but it was all wrong. There was a mismatch between her blood-covered clothes and aching limbs, and the streets she knew as a child.

Walking turned to jogging, which turned to running. Her apartment building emerged from behind taller buildings. Jane collided with the locked gate and realized she didn't have a key.

She jumped and scrambled over the top of the gate. The door to the building was in terrible condition, with peeling paint and far more scrapes than Jane remembered. More lights were burned out inside. The carpet in the main hallway had been replaced with something even uglier.

Jane climbed the stairs. Raced through the second floor. Apartment number 208 waited. She found herself frozen in front of it, her anticipation and fear and uncertainty catching up with her. *Deep breath. Knock.*

The woman who answered was not Jane's mother. She wasn't anyone Jane recognized. The dim hallway and lack of light in the apartment's entryway must have hidden Jane's monstrous appearance, because the woman didn't appear alarmed. "Can I help you?"

"I—" Jane double checked the number by the door. "Do you live here?"

"Yes."

"For how long?"

The woman pushed the door a few inches back toward the frame, nervousness creeping onto her expression. "I'm sorry, are you looking for someone?"

"The Clarkes. Will and Nancy."

"Oh. The couple that lived here before me." The woman relaxed slightly but kept the door where it was. "They caught whatever was going around and their health got bad fast. Couldn't work anymore so they had to move out. I think they're both hospitalized right now."

Oh god. Jane swallowed. "Which hospital?"

"I don't know. I'm sorry, miss, I have to go." The woman closed the door, leaving Jane to stand alone in shock.

Hospital. Which hospital would Mom and Dad be at? Not a nice one, that's for sure. Maybe the place they went when Dad broke his arm?

Jane's legs moved faster than her mind, racing to carry her back to the streets. She had no money for the subway, but if she kept her head down and didn't draw any attention to herself, she'd be fine. Maybe.

The subway station closest to the Clarkes' apartment had never been the nicest, but there was more trash littering the ground than Jane was used to. And the graffiti bordered on out of control. Everyone who looked her way seemed to be assessing whether she was a threat or a target. She avoided eye contact.

It was a ten-minute ride to what Jane hoped was the right stop. She tried to hide her shaking hands and heavy breathing, but people around her still shot concerned looks her way. As soon as the doors opened, she bolted out of the train. Out of the station. On the street, she shoved her way through the crowd and ignored honking cars as she sprinted through traffic. Into the hospital. Up to the front desk.

"Is there a William and Nancy Clarke here?" The question tumbled out of Jane's mouth as she halted in front of the desk, nearly slamming into it.

The receptionist gave her a wild look. "Are you okay, miss?"

"I'm looking for the Clarkes. Are they here?"

"I can't give you information about a patient unless you're immediate family."

"I'm their daughter!"

"Do you have identification?"

Jane's jaw clenched. "No, but—"

"I'm sorry. I don't think I can help you." The receptionist looked Jane over with nervous eyes. "There's a police precinct not far from here, if you need directions."

Jane stormed into the waiting area and began pacing. She'd have to sneak past the receptionist and check rooms until she found her parents. Her gaze darted between the double doors leading to the rest of the hospital and the front desk. Back and forth.

A family entered and walked up to the receptionist, said something to her. She turned around and opened one of the filing cabinets behind her.

Jane hurried past the desk and through the doors, entered the first bathroom she found, and stopped in front of a sink. God. The mirror reflected back a disaster. She rinsed off her face as best as she could and smoothed out her hair.

Then, it was back to the search.

She passed through an intersection, searching the walls for a directory. Two nurses walked down the hall to her right, away from her. "—next delivery will be here in a few hours, last I heard," one said. She sighed. "If people keep getting sick, we're going to run out of room in this wing."

Jane followed them. They passed through a set of double doors, and patient rooms appeared along the walls. Jane peered into windows as she passed. No, no, no—

There.

Jane froze and stared through the window at her parents' hospital beds. Her hand hovered above the door handle. Eleven years. She shook off her hesitation. She'd waited long enough.

"Is that the nurse?" Dad asked weakly as she entered. His eyes didn't open.

Mom looked up. "Hello?"

What was she supposed to say? "I'm sorry." Jane pulled the door shut behind her. "It's me. It's Jane."

Mom sat up, eyes wide. "What?" She gasped the word out, and it was accompanied by a deep cough that made Jane grimace.

"Who is it?" Dad's eyes were still shut. His voice was barely audible.

Jane rushed to Mom's side.

"How are you here?" Mom asked, voice hoarse. "What happened to you?"

"It's a long story." The words came out a whisper. Jane was choking on air.

"Is this real? Are you a ghost?"

"I'm real." Jane's heart sank as she took in the tubes and machines hooked up to her parents. "It took me too long to get back."

Dad coughed. A lot. As the fit subsided, he said, "Nancy, I hear someone talking."

"Is he okay?" Jane asked, eyes stinging. "What's wrong with him? What's wrong with you?"

Mom didn't seem to hear the questions. She reached out to grab Jane's hand. "Impossible," she murmured.

"I'm real," Jane repeated. "It was…god, I'm so stupid. The aliens got me. I went looking."

Mom only stared at her for a long moment, wide-eyed. Then the tears rushed in. "Oh, Jane," she whispered. "I'm so sorry. I wanted to get you help—"

Dad coughed again. This time, somewhere in there, Jane heard her own name. She turned around, her hand still in Mom's. Lucidity flashed in Dad's eyes as he looked at her. "Jane."

"Yeah, Dad." Jane swallowed. "It's me."

"I always hoped you'd find your way home."

One of the machines started beeping rapidly. Jane turned and squeezed Mom's hand. "Mom. Mom. What's wrong?"

No response. Mom's eyes were closed. Tears made faint trails on her deathly pale skin.

There was technology out there that could heal them. What was the point of the Star System Alliance if people on Earth were left to live like this? Why didn't they get the space warps and starships and medical advancements?

Then again, people on Kronos weren't really better off. Not in the lower districts, anyway.

There was a commotion in the hallway. Voices. Footsteps. The door opened and a nurse entered. "Who are you?" she asked as she approached the bed. "No one's supposed to be in here."

"I'm their daughter!" Jane straightened up and frantically glanced between her parents. "Mom, tell them I'm—"

More people barged in. "Get her out of here," the nurse said. She moved to the machines by Dad's bed and frowned at the heart monitor. "He's not going to make it much longer if we don't—"

"Wait!" Jane yanked her arm free of the hand that grabbed her, but more took its place. A feeling deep in her chest swelled, tightening her fists, whispering that they couldn't stop her. She was stronger. Faster. Throw them into the walls, the floor—

"No!" Jane shrieked. She pulled herself free again and knelt by Mom's bed. "Mom—"

"She's strong," a man warned. More people were grabbing her now, more people were coming in. As she was pulled back, she tried to kick at someone, but it was half-hearted. Her feet lifted off the floor and she was carried into the hall.

"Please," she sobbed.

They dragged her to another room, a small, empty one. "Stay here and we'll sort this out once they're stable," a nurse said.

And then they were gone.

Jane's body shuddered with each sob. The red, swollen part of her arm burned earlier by the blaster screamed in pain, and the rest of her body ached with it. She rose to her feet.

Fear stopped her halfway to the door. Fear of herself. The medical staff were only doing their job, and it would be so easy to hurt them. To fight her way to her parents. Her fingers twitched at the thought.

Maybe they'd let her see them after. Maybe this could all be sorted out.

Shouting carried into the hallway. Jane crept to the door as a doctor ran by. She wiped tears off her face and stepped into the hall. The door to her parents' room was open. The shouting came from inside.

The silence that followed was worse.

How long before someone looked up the Clarkes' daughter and found out she went missing a decade earlier? Would they call the police? What would they do with Jane? Her fingernails dug into the door frame.

Ybra was still out there, dragging kids into space. Starr was still paying for them. The Lion's Den still forced their prisoners to fight to the death. Gangs still killed innocent people like Naomi.

Two nurses came out of the room and walked toward Jane, moving far too slow, the solemn looks on their faces undeniable. Who had died? Dad? Mom? Both?

Jane sank to her knees.

"Miss, we have an officer here who would like to speak with you." The man the words came from was coming closer. Closer. Closer. Cold tile pressed against Jane's palms. She sucked in a deep breath.

Two nurses more nurses emerged from her parents' room and paused in the doorway, talking quietly. Jane's mind latched onto their conversation, adjusting the volume automatically.

"—have the room cleaned in a few hours."

"Miss?" A woman reached out to touch her arm. Another nurse. She was too close, too loud. When did she get here? Why were there so many people here?

Jane ripped her arm away. Staggered to her feet. Backed away.

"Please, if we could just have you sit down—" the nurse started.

Jane had nothing. Twenty-three and her only education was in weapons and violence. And she was getting older and her face was staying the same and the metal in her body wasn't going away.

She ran.

She stopped next to the too-quiet hospital room and pushed the nurses aside. "I'm sorry," she yelled into the room. Tears ran down her face in a river. "I love you. I'm going to go try to do something good."

Maybe some part of them was still lingering, some part that would hear her goodbye. Hands reached for Jane. She broke away and kept running.

As she stumbled out of the hospital, Jane's first thought was that she could warp back to Sa Ren and go from there, but she had no idea how to use the warps or even how to get back to them and only hunters knew the passcodes, anyway. Her next thought was that there was no point, right? Why go back to space? Back to the stars that had taken everything from her?

Summer wouldn't last forever. New York would freeze, and then what? She couldn't wander endlessly. If she went back to the Janus System, at least she could find Ybra and make her pay. Maybe even Starr. Everyone. All of them.

The night turned to dawn. Dawn became day after day after day. Jane lurked around the city. Stole food. Searched for a way out.

While Jane was gone, humans had gone to the Moon. They still had no warp technology. All they could do was traverse a distance that was nothing in the grand scheme of things. And if there were any humans that did have the kind of tech that could get to other systems, they weren't advertising it.

Conspiracy theorist Dawn Teller put out a book claiming there was a secret organization with advanced technology training kids to fly into space. It was probably nonsense. But she had been right about aliens kidnapping people. Jane stole the book from a grocery store and read it.

Teller claimed the organization was recruiting gifted students from schools. Jane didn't stand a chance of finding them that way. But Teller also said they picked up kids on the streets with powers.

That was something Jane could pull off.

Chapter Forty
Cops and Robbers and Robbers Pretending to be Cops

"Thea, Dax, I have a mission for you," Jasper said. The team stood in the precinct lobby, waiting for Detective Park to finish a conversation with the forensic technicians. "Instead of coming with us, snoop around here and find Dr. Prime's address. Go to her place and see if you can find anything about her hideout on Sera."

"Got it," Thea said. Dax added a thumbs up as he followed Thea away from the group.

Detective Park passed the two as he returned, a tablet in his hand and Officers Alyow and Tary trailing behind him. "Where are they going?" he asked.

"Officer Sparks left her refrigerator running and Officer Cure had to get a flu shot." Before Park could process what she'd said, Jasper added, "Now, let's go arrest the hell out of this guy!"

Detective Park stared at her for a long moment before speaking. "All right. Mechwell lives in an apartment a few blocks from here. Top floor of the Iris Complex."

"Hey, since we're down two, we can all fit in one car!" Alyow exclaimed.

"Sounds great," Jasper said. "I'll drive."

Detective Park shook his head. "Absolutely not. I'll drive."

"But—"

"Jasper, let him drive," Holly hissed.

"Back me up on this, Officer Starling," Jasper said with a glance at Grace. "I'm a great driver, right?"

Grace hesitated. "Uh, you are good at getting places fast."

"We aren't in a hurry," Detective Park said. "In fact, it's better we keep a low profile. We don't want Mechwell knowing we're coming."

"Fine, Detective Park can drive," Jasper conceded. "But I'm calling shotgun."

"As long as you don't play that goddamn musical soundtrack, that's fine by me." Detective Park said as they walked out of the precinct.

"How about 2000s pop music from Earth?"

"Never heard it, but I'm sure it's better than what I've been listening to."

Holly interjected. "Actually, it would be helpful if we got some details on Mechwell before we arrive."

"Good point." Detective Park handed his tablet to Jasper. "Here, you can read his file."

"Yippee," Jasper muttered.

They piled into the car, and Jasper scrolled through the file's text and photos while they drove. Ro Mechwell was a short, bald guy with pastel pink skin and big round ears. His demeanor in his ID photo was far from menacing. "He's got an office job at the Sagev Department of Transportation."

"Doesn't sound like the killer type," Alyow said from the back.

"You'd be surprised," Tary replied. "I saw this movie once where a guy—"

"Lives alone," Jasper interrupted. "We shouldn't have to deal with anyone else during the arrest."

"Don't get your hopes up," Detective Park said. "Civilians tend to get in the way. They hear there's a criminal on the loose and all come running to take pictures. Some like to play hero and try to catch the guy for us."

They pulled into the apartment complex parking lot not long after that. On their way into the building, Detective Park barked orders. "We'll split up, in case he tries to run. I'll knock on his door. Alyow, Tary, take the ground level exits. Jasper, Mud, Starling, I want you by the elevators and stairs on his floor. Someone on the east side, someone on the west. If anyone sees him, radio in so we can converge."

Alyow and Tary separated to guard the exits. The elevator took the other four up ten levels to the top floor. While Detective Park headed for Mechwell's apartment, Jasper turned to Holly and Grace. "One of you take the west side, one of you go east. I'm following Park."

"Why?" Grace asked.

"If Mechwell makes a run for it, I should be close. I'm the fastest one here."

Holly sighed. "Can't argue with that."

Jasper waited around the corner while Detective Park knocked on Mechwell's door. When no one answered, she switched to X-ray vision and scanned the apartment. Empty.

There was movement at the other end of the hall just seconds later. Mechwell came around the corner and froze when he saw Detective Park at his door. A moment later, he was gone.

Talk about bad timing.

Detective Park sprinted after Mechwell and grabbed his communicator off his belt. "I've got eyes on Mechwell. He's headed for the west stairwell," he said into the radio.

"I'll meet Officer Mud there," Grace replied.

Jasper ran the other way. She was fast enough to catch Mechwell before he reached the stairs.

Or, she would have been, if people hadn't poured of their apartments to see what was happening. "Coming through!" Jasper yelled. She slowed to navigate the crowd, fighting her instinct to shove people aside.

"What's going on?" a woman asked, waving her hand and trying to step in Jasper's path.

"I'm having a hard time moving," Detective Park said over radio. "Too many people in the way." Holly and Grace chimed in to say they were having the same problem.

"Same here," Jasper told them. Her voice rose. "Everyone get back in your apartments! This is official police business!"

"Are we in danger?" a man asked.

"You wouldn't be if you went inside!" Jasper *gently* pushed him out of her way. Squeezing her own police communicator, she said, "Ugh. There has to be some way to make these people listen to us."

"We certainly can't threaten them. And there's no way we could arrest them all," Detective Park replied.

Honestly, they probably could make questionable threats against civilians and get away with it, given Si Hera's track record as a functioning government. But Jasper didn't want to contribute to that.

Wait. Threatening them. There might be a way to make that work. Not as a police officer, of course, but as someone else.

Jasper darted through an apartment door someone had left open in their quest to glimpse the action. She located a closet and pulled out a long, black coat that looked similar to what she usually wore. It was a bit big, but it would work. She threw it on, took off her sunglasses, adjusted her hair, and checked that no part of her police uniform was visible.

After returning to the hall, she aimed her blaster at the ceiling and fired. "Out of the way, idiots! If you don't want to get shot, you better get back in your apartments."

"Van Terra!" someone screamed. People scrambled to get out of Jasper's path, some of them darting through the first open door they could find.

Jasper looked to the left and checked her X-ray vision. Past the apartments in the hall parallel to her, she could see Mechwell running. "He's almost to the west stairwell," she warned Holly and Grace over comms.

"We have a problem," Detective Park said. "Apparently Van Terra's here."

"Really?" Holly asked, her voice sharpening. "Well, isn't that interesting?"

"Oh, don't give me that tone," Jasper hissed through the team's comms. To the communicator, she said, "What about Mechwell?"

"Tary, Alyow, get ready to intercept," Detective Park replied. "Mud, Starling, I'll meet you at the stairwell. If we can't grab him there, you'll help me find Van Terra."

Detective Park came around the corner up ahead. His eyes locked with Jasper's. He pointed his blaster and fired. Jasper dove to her right, through another door that had been left ajar. She ran past the family hiding under the table and into the next room, where she threw open a sliding glass door and stepped onto the balcony.

Her communicator crackled. "Jasper, where are you?" Detective Park asked.

She climbed over the railing and dropped to the next balcony down. "I just hit the floor below you," she replied, suppressing a grunt of pain. "I think I can catch up to Mechwell."

"Meet me back at the top of the stairwell. We might be able to trap Van Terra instead."

Jasper tried the sliding door. Locked. She kicked it with her cybernetic leg. It exploded into a shower of glass. "Sure. Great. I'm on my way back up." She shrugged off the coat, rolled it up tight, and shoved it into the back of her waistband. Hopefully the police jacket would hide it well enough. On her way out of the apartment, she slid her sunglasses back on.

Detective Park met her at the top at the top of the stairwell. "I think she's still on this floor. Mud and Starling went that way, so if we go the opposite direction, we should catch her."

"Great." As they broke into a run, Jasper asked, "Shouldn't we send someone to help Tary and Alyow?"

"Van Terra's far more important. Besides, Tary and Alyow are capable of catching Mechwell on their own. I hope."

"Well, it sounds like the *other two* might run into Jasper *first* and hopefully she won't *get away from* them through *a window*, right guys?"

Detective Park frowned at her odd emphasis. "That...would be unfortunate."

They flew around the next corner and nearly collided with Holly and Grace.

"Where did she go?" Detective Park asked.

Grace's eyes met Jasper's. "She ran into someone's apartment. I think she jumped out a window."

Jasper grinned and winked at her. Grace flushed and glanced away.

"Then we're going down," Detective Park said. "Move fast."

Before the detective could add anything else, Jasper cut in. "Starling and I will take the west stairwell. You and Mud can go east."

"Fine."

Detective Park and Holly ran off while Jasper and Grace headed the other way. When they reached the stairs, Jasper grabbed the railing and vaulted over. She caught herself on the level below and steadied herself before dropping to the next railing.

Grace leaned over the railing and peered down at her. "Where are you going?"

"To catch Mechwell!"

Jasper was almost to the first floor when she spotted Alyow waiting by the exit. Mechwell must have been on the other stairwell, then. Jasper pulled herself over the railing onto the second-floor landing and ran into the hall.

People down here must not have gotten the memo that Van Terra was on the loose, because it was even more crowded than the tenth floor had been. She ripped off her sunglasses, threw the coat back on, and drew her blaster. "Outta the way! Van Terra coming through!"

Her path to the stairwell cleared. Jasper made it up a flight and a half before she saw Mechwell coming down. She pointed her blaster at him. "Freeze!"

"Van Terra!" Mechwell yelped.

Oh, right. She hadn't switched back. Wait, this could work. "That's right. It's me. Van Terra," she said, forcing a dramatic flair into her voice. "I'm here to kidnap you, and the police can't save you!"

Mechwell turned and ran up. "Police! Help!"

Jasper could have caught up with him, but she kept her distance until Detective Park appeared in the doorway. He grabbed Mechwell's arm and aimed his blaster at Jasper. "Van Terra!"

Jasper jumped over the railing to her left and dropped a few floors before grabbing on to a set of bars. The violent stop sent pain through her body that she ignored.

As she pulled herself up, Detective Park spoke over radio again. "I've got Mechwell. Van Terra's headed down the east stairwell."

"I'm on my way up!" Tary replied.

Jasper entered the hallway, tossed aside the coat, and put her sunglasses back on. She reached back and pulled her ponytail down into a lower position.

Alyow came around the corner and yelped in surprise. "Oh, Detective Jasper, it's you! I thought you were Van Terra for a second." Her eyes widened. "Wait, where is she?"

"I just saw her jump out a window," Jasper replied.

"Huh. She really likes jumping out windows, doesn't she?"

Jasper sucked in a sharp breath. "Yep. Sure does."

Chapter Forty-One
Hack It and Reverse It

The precinct computers must not have been very secure, because Thea was able to pull Dr. Prime's address in two minutes. Dax watched her work, occasionally glancing up to make sure no one noticed them.

"Got it. Let's go." Thea started toward the front entrance.

Dax caught up on her right. "How are we getting there?"

Thea held up a hand and wiggled her fingers. "I'll get us a vehicle."

One hacked police cruiser and fifteen minutes of traffic later, they were walking up to Dr. Prime's apartment complex. After the ease with which she was able to manipulate the cruiser's computers into letting them in and taking them wherever she pleased, Thea spent the drive giving one of her usual spiels about the unnecessary use of computers in machines that didn't need them, opening up opportunities for bugs in code to wreak havoc.

She especially liked to complain about appliances that could connect to the net, making it possible for her to hack them at any distance. Dax didn't quite see the logic in complaining about things that made hacking easier, but he nodded along.

She switched gears as they approached the building. "I say we go in the balcony," Thea said. "It'll be easier than dealing with building security and the front door."

"Sounds good," Dax replied.

"It's on the fifth floor."

"Sounds less good. But okay."

Thankfully, the building was easy to climb. They reached Dr. Prime's balcony quickly and found themselves facing a locked glass door. Thea looked the door over. "Stand back."

"Be careful," Dax warned as he backed up. He'd have offered to break through the door instead, but her boots were much tougher than the sneakers he'd thrown on today.

Thea rolled her shoulders and gave the door a hard kick. Cracks ran up and down the glass. A second blow shattered it.

As Thea stepped inside, she lost her balance. Her hands waved to balance herself, and her right palm grazed a glass shard poking out from the door frame. She winced.

Dax hurried in behind her. "How bad is it?"

Thea held out the hand. The gash was already spilling blood onto her skin. "Could be worse."

"Sure." Dax pressed his palm against hers. "It should close up in a minute or so." A faint blue light glowed between their hands, then faded.

"Thanks."

The two entered the front room and split up. Thea headed for a computer on the desk in the corner. She rested a hand on top and closed her eyes. The screen lit up. Dax, meanwhile, sifted through the drawers around the room.

"Got something," Thea said after a few minutes. "Messages between Dr. Prime and the mayor of Sera. He was letting her use a room in the basement of Moon Hall."

"Great. So glad I could help," Dax joked. He paused and frowned. "Do you hear something?"

They both fell quiet. The faint sound of voices passed through the front door of the apartment. The voices stopped after a moment, and the silence was interrupted by the sound of someone kicking down the door.

"They've got blasters," Thea warned, flexing her hands.

No time to run or hide. Dax and Thea could only watch as three men dressed in black entered the room. The first man took aim at Thea, but she'd already disabled the weapons.

"Damn it." The man smacked the side of the blaster.

"Mine's not working either," the second said.

The third chimed in. "Same here."

The first man shoved his blaster into its holster. "Fine. Grab them."

Dax barely had time to put his fists up before one of the men attacked. Dax blocked the first strike, then the second, but the third landed. He gritted his teeth against the pain and managed a hit to the man's jaw. The man retaliated with a hard blow to Dax's stomach.

Dax gasped and stumbled. The man took a step forward, his dark clothes and gray skin blurring in Dax's vision. He lifted his fist to strike again. Dax sucked in a deep breath.

"You're not a bad fighter, for such a young kid. Makes me feel less bad about—" The man cut himself off with a yelp. Dax's vision returned to normal, and he realized a gash had opened in the man's right palm.

Just like the one in Thea's palm that Dax had healed minutes earlier. Had…he done that? Reversed his power, somehow?

Dax took his chance to kick the man in the stomach, knocking him onto his back. Nearby, Thea stood up, eyed her attacker to make sure he wasn't getting up anytime soon, and turned to Dax. "Third guy grabbed the computer and ran."

"Should we chase him?" Dax asked.

"He's long gone. I tried to wipe the computer, but this guy kept me busy. If they're working for Ringmaster—and I'm pretty sure they are—they have a good shot at finding Prime's hideout."

Thea unmuted her comm and explained the situation to the others as she and Dax returned to the cruiser.

"Ringmaster's going after Prime's hideout then, right?" Holly asked. "To steal the warp research?"

Jasper sighed. "As soon as he gets the location, I'm sure he will."

"Why don't we contact the mayor and tell him?" Grace suggested.

"He's not going to listen to a bunch of criminals who broke into Dr. Prime's apartment," Jasper said. "And even if we did come up with a believable story, whatever security measures he puts in place won't stop Ringmaster. We'll just have to break into the highly secure government facility ourselves and steal the research before Ringmaster can. Ooh, this is starting to sound like an Earth movie I saw once."

"Sure, let's steal our ideas from movies," Holly muttered. "That'll work out great."

"How are we getting in?" Thea asked. "Moon Hall doesn't do visitors. I might be able to get us fake IDs, but their security guards are thorough, from what I've heard—"

"Don't bother with all that. I have a better idea. It'll be more fun, too," Jasper said. "Thea, I have a job for you."

Thea still had access to Starchatter's backend, which allowed her to sneak a few short articles onto the website. Even though someone caught and removed them by the end of the day, they were up long enough for

Jasper's idea to gain momentum. The fact that other sites quickly shared—or straight up copied—them helped, too.

That evening, Dax and the rest of the team stood in the center of the police station, gathered in a circle with the officers on the Prime investigation.

"The star system is calling for a celebration of Si Hera's 421st Precinct after articles detailing their competition with Van Terra for the dramatic capture of a dangerous killer spread around the net," Detective Park read from his tablet.

"How exciting!" Officer Alyow exclaimed.

Detective Park shook his head. "The original articles were full of fabrications, and they were deleted later."

"Don't worry about the minor details," Jasper told him. "You deserve all the praise for catching Mechwell."

"He basically surrendered himself to me."

"After a thrilling chase!"

"Good news, everyone!" Captain Prool exclaimed as he emerged from his office. "I just got off the phone with Sera's mayor. His phones have been blowing up all day with calls about our celebration, and he's decided to go ahead and host a party for us."

"Guys, check this out." Tary waved his smartsphere in the air, making the holoscreen flicker. "Top seven reasons Precinct #421 deserves a party right now, explained through pictures of felines. Oh, and there's another one that talks about the arrest using reaction images from Star Conquerors—"

Dax glanced at Holly, who had never looked more exasperated in her life. Grace's expression was more bewildered than anything. Thea was typing away on her tablet, undoubtedly still wrestling with net code.

Jasper looked amused, but there was a faraway look in her eyes that hinted her thoughts were elsewhere.

Chapter Forty-Two
Galactic Treasure

The shining white Moon Hall glowed under the endless black sky of Sera, beneath the transparent dome housing the moon's city. It wasn't the sort of place you just waltzed into. It was rarely open to anyone besides government employees, and security guards and cameras monitored every entrance.

The night of the party honoring Precinct 421, five wanted criminals strolled in without anyone batting an eye.

Well, four criminals and Grace, wanted as she may have been. Thea still had a surprisingly hard time thinking of her as anything other than the hero Starr paraded her around as for years, which was an impressive feat given that he'd rarely let her make public appearances.

Jasper adjusted her sunglasses. "Thea, Holly, you ready?"

"Let us get to the edge of the room, first," Thea told her.

"Okay, just make it quick. Ringmaster's probably going to use the party as a distraction to sneak in, too. He could show up at any moment."

While Jasper approached the mayor, Thea and Holly hurried through the crowd. They were nearly to the exit when Jasper began her speech.

"I'd like to make a toast to the precinct," Jasper said. "I was lucky to witness such an incredible display of teamwork so soon after joining the force."

Everyone turned their attention to Jasper, leaving Thea free to assess the electronic box by the door. She tapped a finger against it and sent a signal to trick it into thinking a badge had been swiped. The door unlocked.

Jasper was still rambling. "Also, the 421st Precinct should get to move up a rank!"

"The numbers are assigned by location, they aren't ranks," Holly muttered into her comm.

"Oh. Uh, well, as I was saying, these phenomenal officers—"

Thea slipped through the door. Holly followed. They entered a quiet corridor, took a few turns, and went through another locked door to find the staircase to the basement. Their police jackets came off as they walked, revealing their villain costumes underneath.

"I'm sensing a lot of electronics nearby," Thea told Holly. She rested a hand on the wall and let it slide across the concrete as they walked. "Through that door up ahead, on the right."

This door was locked, too, and the electronic locking mechanism was even more complex than the ones upstairs. It took Thea about a minute to trigger it. The door swung open.

Ringmaster stood with his back to them, facing a massive bank of computer monitors. His right hand held a red data stick.

He turned his head slowly, unconcerned with the intrusion. "Red Holly. Jolt. I knew someone was messing with my stuff, but I certainly didn't expect you two."

"Ringmaster," Holly hissed, doubling as a warning to the others.

The only response was static. Thea shot Holly a warning look. The walls of the room had been made to keep signals from going in and out. They might get a message out this close to the doorway, but comms wouldn't work deeper in the room.

"You two are small fish in a big sea," Ringmaster said. "Turn around now."

Thea eyed the data drive in his hand. They needed to steal it, and she needed to wipe the computers so Ringmaster couldn't make another copy.

"We're not letting you leave with it," Holly told him.

"Suit yourself." Ringmaster lifted his free hand and fired a blast of golden energy. Holly and Thea dove in opposite directions, narrowly avoiding the beam.

Thea hit the ground and rolled. As she sat up, Ringmaster sent three golden rings flying her way. They solidified into metal in mid-air. Thea dodged two, but the third smacked into her head. Stars flashed in her vision.

Holly drew her blaster and fired. Ringmaster dodged. While he was distracted, Thea stood and darted to the computer bank. She pulled out her own data stick and attempted to jam it into a port.

A metal ring hit her hand with a crack. Thea gasped in pain. Her yellow stick bounced off the desk and tumbled to the ground.

Holly lunged at Ringmaster and managed to get a few hits in. His own data stick slipped from his grasp as he blocked a punch to the face. Then he was swinging his fists, and Holly was knocked to the ground.

Ringmaster's data stick slid across the floor, stopping a few feet from Thea's. She reached for both of them.

Golden light turned to a blade in Ringmaster's palm. He rushed forward and stabbed at Thea's hand. She yanked it back just in time. The blade snapped on the concrete floor. Ringmaster summoned another and slashed at Thea as she stepped away, leaving a gash on her arm.

Holly was back on her feet, but she was stumbling. She swung her blaster and slammed it into Ringmaster's back. He grunted in pain and jammed his elbow backward, shoving Holly into the wall. It was a temporary delay, but it was enough for Thea to grab both data drives.

A ring of gold appeared around Thea's wrist. Cold metal pressed to her skin and tightened. Pain raced through her arm in warning. Tighter. She grimaced. She needed another second. Tighter.

Her fingers opened and the drives fell. Ringmaster snatched them up as the ring dissipated, freeing Thea's wrist. She hardly had time for relief before Ringmaster delivered a blow to her ribs.

Air left her lungs. The world spun. Holly was in a similar state, gasping for breath on the ground nearby.

Ringmaster summoned a long rod of energy. He swung it in an arc and smashed through the computer bank. Monitors cracked and shattered. Ringmaster delivered another blow. And another.

Then he left.

Thea crawled toward the door.

"It's no use," Holly gasped.

Thea winced. "I don't need to catch up," she managed. "I can access my data remotely if I can just get out of this room."

She dragged herself to the doorway, her pain worsening with every movement. She pulled out her smartsphere and reached through the opening.

No signal. Thea made it another few inches. *Almost.* She stretched her arm as far as she could manage.

The sphere buzzed, and she managed a weak smile.

Chapter Forty-Three
Villains Don't Start Parties, But We Can Crash Them

It was tempting to think the hard part was over, but Jasper knew better than to let her guard down.

"Should we have heard from Holly and Thea by now?" Dax asked.

Jasper grabbed a piece of blue fruit off a passing tray. "I don't know. How long did Thea say it would take to download the data?"

"She didn't," Dax replied. "But it's been almost half an hour. What if they ran into Ringmaster?"

Jasper was feeling a little uneasy herself. "Well, we can't access the basement without Thea." She popped the fruit in her mouth and swallowed. "Maybe there's another way in—wait, South Siren's here?"

Dax and Grace scanned the crowd. "Where?" Dax asked.

"Front entrance."

Grace frowned. "Isn't that Sarena Trench?"

"They're the same person!" Jasper rolled her eyes as the celebrity strolled into the crowd, a silver dress shimmering against her teal skin. Her long waves of brown hair rested in an updo on top of her head, exposing the gills in her neck. "Why would Sarena Trench be on this side of the star system if not for the races?"

"Maybe she's legitimately here for the party," Grace said with a shrug.

"Yeah, quite a few celebrities showed up," Dax added.

"Whatever." Jasper's shoulders sagged. "Let's take the stairwell we were planning to leave through. There might be a less secure way into the basement."

The three didn't make it far down the stairs before the sound of footsteps coming up reached their ears. Multiple sets of footsteps, mixed with the sound of metal thudding against metal. Jasper grabbed the railing and peered over the edge.

"Ha!" Jasper grinned. "Look at that. Five sirens coming our way."

"What?" Grace yelped.

"Why are you excited about that?" Dax asked.

"Duh. That must be why Sarena's here." Seeing the distress on their faces, Jasper said, "Never mind. Also, three of Grim Machine's henchrobots are with them. I wonder why he's mad. Or how they found me."

Jasper pulled off her police jacket and drew the sword strapped to her back. It was a smaller one from her collection, with an iridescent blade that had already taken a beating. Hopefully it would hold up through one more fight.

"Have you had the whole time?" Grace asked.

"Yeah."

"I want to try something," Dax said.

"Great," Jasper replied, only half-hearing him as she gave the sword a few test swings. "Just stay behind me."

"Wait, I think I can use my powers—"

Jasper charged down the stairs. The narrow stairwell would make it impossible for more than one, maybe two goons to attack her at once. This would be an easy fight.

She swung at the first siren with the flat side of the sword, and the siren went down. The second lifted her spear to meet Jasper's blade and fended off the first few blows. Jasper swung at the woman's head. While she moved to block it, Jasper landed a kick to her stomach, sending her crashing into everyone behind her. Jasper lunged and slashed at the next siren in her path.

Despite the wound in her abdomen, the siren swung her spear and smacked Jasper in the skull. Wincing, Jasper clapped a hand against her head and slammed the hilt of the sword into the siren's forehead.

While the siren collapsed, Dax rested a hand on Jasper's shoulder. The stinging cuts and bruises around her body glowed blue in unison with hands, then faded.

Then, Dax darted around her, taking her by surprise.

"What are you doing?" Jasper exclaimed, alarmed. Dax usually did fine in combat, but he didn't have any weapons.

Dax threw a punch at the fourth siren. She grabbed his wrist and pushed him into the wall. Jasper jumped in and kicked her into the last siren, sending them both tumbling. "You okay?" she asked Dax as he found his balance.

"Yeah," Dax said. He looked at his hands. "I'm still not sure how—"

The first of the grimbots—which looked like smaller, thinner versions of Grim Machine—stepped over the fallen sirens and fired a bright blue-green blast from its palm. Jasper raised the sword to block. It worked, but the blade exploded, sending iridescent metal fragments raining down on the concrete stairs.

"I need you two to brace yourselves," Jasper told Grace and Dax as she tossed aside the hilt.

"For what?" Dax asked.

Jasper grabbed him and tossed him over the railing, onto the landing a floor down. There was a thud, followed by an "ow" that was more annoyed than pained.

"You good?" Jasper yelled.

"Yeah!"

Jasper looked at Grace, who moved to the railing on her own. "I'll fly, thanks."

While Grace went over the edge, the grimbot in front fired at Jasper again. Jasper ducked and drew three small throwing knives. When the bot prepared to fire a third time, she flung the first knife into its blaster opening, interrupting its firing components. Then she hit the second bot, and the third.

Jasper climbed onto the railing. The nearest bot grabbed her leg, ripped her off the railing, and slammed her against the steps. Jasper rolled. The bot's fist smashed into the ground where her face had been.

The bot drew back its arm to strike again, but the one behind it toppled forward, knocking them both down. Grace's wings pounded against the air as she kicked the last bot to the ground.

"Hurry, before they get back up!" Jasper shouted as she climbed to her feet. She and Grace raced down the stairs to meet Dax.

"I think I found a way into the basement," Dax said when they reached him. He gestured to the door in front of him. "But it's locked."

Jasper looked back at the bots coming down the stairs. "Ugh. I have an idea. It's not great, but it'll be the fastest way in."

"What is it?" Grace asked.

"You two get out of the way. Get ready to help me knock the bots down." Jasper positioned herself in front of the door. "Their blasters are strong enough to destroy the lock. Maybe even the entire door."

"Yeah, and also your face," Dax pointed out.

"Yes. Also my face. Now get out of the way."

Dax and Grace reluctantly obeyed. As the grimbot leading the charge approached, it ripped out the blade Jasper had thrown into its blaster and took aim. She watched the bot slow, waiting for the first flash of light to appear in its palm. When it did, she would have a split second to move.

She almost made it out of the way. Almost. The blast grazed her upper arm, leaving her with searing pain. It also shattered the lock on the door.

Jasper hit the ground. Shrapnel shot over her head. "Now!" she yelled.

Dax and Grace each lunged at a bot. Jasper sprang to her feet and kicked down the third. Her next move was to throw open the basement door. "Hurry!"

Dax and Grace ran through. Grace paused on the other side. "Are you coming?"

"They'll chase us if someone doesn't distract them," Jasper replied.

"But—"

"I can get away from them! Let me know when you find Holly and Thea." Jasper threw the door shut, wincing as the pain in her arm flared up again. No time to focus on that. The bots were getting back up. She turned and flung herself over the stairwell railing.

The landing was one of the worst she'd had in a while. It took her a moment to catch her breath and get back on her aching legs. Bots thudded down the stairs above her, but she was only a few feet from the parking garage entrance.

She burst into the garage and scanned the vehicles. A sleek black motorcycle caught her eye. It was nowhere near as cool as hers, but it would do. She hopped on and set to work on hotwiring it.

The grimbots were almost to her when the motorcycle shot forward. Jasper moved fast enough to stay out of reach, but not so fast that she would lose them.

At the exit, she hopped up onto the concrete wall lining the road that spiraled out of the parking garage. One of the grimbots fired. Jasper hit the brakes. The blast missed, leaving a sizeable hole in the wall.

"Is that all you got?" Jasper taunted. She hopped off the motorcycle, leaving it to fall onto the road next to her. "Too afraid to fight me hand-to-hand?"

The grimbot in front stalked toward her. "You want to fight a robot, you sack of flesh?"

"Eesh, I didn't know you'd been programmed to be so rude." Jasper lifted her fists and took a step back toward the gap in the wall.

The bot charged. The other two followed. Jasper waited until the first was a few feet away before dropping, grabbing its legs, and chucking it as far as she could.

The grimbots were lighter than she expected. She'd feared the bot might not make it through the hole in the wall, but it went sailing off the parking complex. The other two stopped and stared.

"One of you gets to go that same route, the other gets to answer my questions." Jasper turned and rested a hand on her hip. "What's it gonna be?"

The bot on the right took aim. The end of its blaster glowed blue.

"You it is." Jasper grabbed the motorcycle and used it to shield herself from the blast. Once the light subsided, she tossed the vehicle's slightly melty remains at the left bot before grabbing the right one and throwing it off the complex.

Jasper walked to where the pile of motorcycle pinned the last bot to the ground. "Were you working together with the sirens, or did you just happen to show up at the same time?"

The bot didn't answer. Jasper rested a foot on the motorcycle and pushed. The grimbots might not be able to feel pain, but she was pretty sure they had some sense of self-preservation programmed into them.

"South Siren approached us!" the bot exclaimed, its robotic tone managing to sound frantic. "She asked Grim Machine if he wanted to help attack you. He agreed and sent us."

"How did you know I would be here tonight?" Jasper asked.

"Luck. She was here for the party, recognized you, and called us in."

"Anyone on comms?" Jasper asked.

Grace replied. "Is something wrong?"

"Oh, I'm fine." Jasper picked up the robot and flung it into the night with its brethren. "Just thought I'd mention that my new friend confirmed South Siren was here for the party—"

"Now's not the time for your stupid theory!" Holly snapped.

"Oh good, you're okay," Jasper said, straightening up. "I was beginning to worry."

"We're a little banged up," Thea said. "I downloaded the data, but Ringmaster got away with a copy."

Could have gone better. Could have gone worse. "Okay," Jasper replied. "I'll meet you all behind Moon Hall."

After regrouping, the team made their way to Sera's spaceport. Warped to Si Hera. Dragged themselves to the car. Drove to the shack.

Shortly after their return, they sat on the floor, gathered around Thea, watching numbers and text scroll down her screen.

"What does that mean?" Jasper asked.

"I don't know," Thea said.

Jasper pointed to a diagram. "What about that?"

"No idea."

Dax rested his arms on his knees. "If we can't understand it, maybe Starr and Ringmaster won't, either."

"Wait, look here," Thea said, pointing to a new box of text. "Dr. Prime included a summary of her findings." She frowned. "The warps output high levels of energy. Ridiculously high. She notes if it could be harnessed, a single spacetime warp could potentially power all of Kronos for half a starcycle during the time it's open."

"That's a pretty big 'if.'" Jasper's eyes narrowed. "How would you even go about harnessing that energy?"

"If it's possible somehow, that must be what Starr wants, right?" Grace asked. "To power Kronos?"

"Kronos has problems, but an energy crisis isn't one of them," Jasper replied. "It's certainly not enough of an issue to warrant messing with something so dangerous. I think Starr's after something bigger." Maybe it was connected to his lab experiments.

"There is one other thing I want to bring up," Thea said.

Jasper rested her hands behind her and leaned back. "Is it important?"

"Kind of." Thea tapped the screen, and a still from a security camera popped up. "This is the footage that shows Mechwell leaving the alley after the gunshot. At least, according to the timestamp."

"And?" Jasper asked.

"I sensed something off about the video file, so I went through the code. Turns out it was manipulated. Mechwell did leave the alley." Thea brought up an identical image, but the time was marked as ten minutes earlier. "However, he left the alley before Prime was killed." She looked up. "I'm pretty sure we arrested the wrong guy."

Chapter Forty-Four
Space is the Place

The woman found Jane Clarke in an alley one evening, just as Jane was bringing the spree of two violent bank robbers to an end by means of broken bones and concussions. The woman said her name was Commander Fields, and that she was from an organization that might have a place for Jane, should she prove herself in training and pass their tests. They were called Laika Academy.

"We operate underground, but we reach for the stars," Fields told Jane that night. She had graying hair that was always kept in a top bun and a perpetually stern expression on her wrinkled face.

Jane wanted to say that she'd been to the stars already, and that they were full of monsters. Instead, she said, "I'll join you."

"What's your name?"

"Jade Armstrong," Jane lied.

"How old are you?"

"Seventeen," she lied again.

"You got a family?"

"Not anymore."

Fields drove Jade to a laundromat with a hidden back room. The room held an elevator that went down forty floors, all underground.

Laika Academy was named for a dog who'd been plucked off the streets of Moscow and sent into orbit. She hadn't survived the trip, nor had she been intended to. Jade found this distressing. Fields used the story to go into a tangent about sacrifices for the greater good. Jade found that more distressing.

"We do testing once a year to allow new students into our program," Fields told Jade during her tour of the facilities. "They're coming up at the end of December. You won't have much time to prepare, but you're welcome to try. If you fail to make the 1976 class, there's always next year."

Jade nodded, already determined to pass. Fields explained that there would be a flight simulation, a physical, and a written exam. Jade was assigned a temporary dorm and given access to training rooms and a small library of textbooks.

The computer that gave Jade her lightning reflexes made flying easy. And after countless hours of studying, her mind finally activated a camera she'd had no idea existed. She quickly learned her storage space was limited, but she condensed her notes as much as possible, took images, and aced her exams.

On January second—her twenty-fourth birthday—she was formally inducted into the academy, along with twenty-seven other kids. Some were assigned to be pilots, like Jade, while some were assigned to engineering, others to research, and more.

Jade kept her distance from other students, putting all her focus into becoming the best pilot. It paid off. In December, Fields came to Jade and informed her she'd been selected for a mission. The launch date was set for March 1, 1977. Jade was moved to a new room so that she and the others on the mission could develop "strong team chemistry."

Holly Farr, the designated "astronaut" was a moody, angsty loner. Dax Cho, the medic, was shy and didn't talk much. Thea Smith, the engineer, was nice enough, though she spent most of her time focused on one of her many screens.

Jade had no hope of flying to Kronos in a simple spacecraft. But if she could find a warp station, the journey would be doable. She'd learned during her time on Kronos that warp stations around the galaxy allowed large ships to carry cargo between star systems. Once the team returned from the mission, and Jade had learned all she could about Laika's flight and security protocols, she could steal a spaceship and head to Kronos on her own.

Her initial plan was to keep her head down and count down the days until they went to space. That changed when she caught Holly shapeshifting in the bathroom.

Jade watched her for a long moment before speaking. "Your real family name is Faye."

Holly's eyes went wide. Her pale green skin changed to a more human color, her slitted pupils rounded out, and her ears lost their point. Her thick mane of red hair thinned out and fell around her shoulders. She spun around. "What the hell?"

"The Kronosian elite family. The Fayes. Shapeshifters."

"How do you know anything about Kronos?" Holly demanded.

"I've been." Jade leaned against the doorway and smirked, not entirely sure why she was so delighted. Maybe it was the realization that someone here might actually be able to understand a fraction of what she'd been through.

Then again, Holly wasn't exactly chatty. Jade wasn't sure there was a point in attempting to bond with her.

Holly shook her head. "You've been to the Janus System? And back? How?"

"I'll tell you," Jade replied. "If you tell me what you're doing on Earth."

"That's my business."

Jade shrugged. "Suit yourself." Before walking away, she glanced back and added, "Your secret's safe with me, though." She didn't care about the Faye family and had never given the missing child Hollixa much thought. Whatever Holly's reasons for running away, though, Jade had a feeling they were good.

The team was given new details as the launch date approached but still weren't told exactly what the mission was, beyond that it was an investigation into an anomaly.

The night before, no one could sleep.

Holly was the first one out of bed. Jade rolled over in a half-awake state and watched her move to stand by the window.

"Not much of a view," Jade said quietly as she climbed out of bed. She walked to Holly's side and stared at the concrete outside. Faint lights from other parts of the facility filtered in through the gap. "I mean, why even bother?"

Holly didn't answer. She rested a hand on the glass.

Jade watched her trace circles with her finger. "Are you trying to get back to Kronos?" Maybe they could work together.

Holly scoffed. "I'd rather die than go back."

Or not.

Holly's hand lowered. "I came here to escape, and I stayed because I didn't know where else to go."

"How'd you wind up at Laika?" Jade asked.

"They found me. I didn't do as well on my own as I thought I would, so I figured I'd work for them if they put a roof over my head."

"What's going on?" Dax mumbled as he pulled himself out of bed. He rubbed his eyes and yawned.

Thea sat up. "You guys can't sleep either?"

Jade leaned against the wall by the window and slid to the floor. "I wish they'd give us more details about the anomaly." She ran a hand through her hair. It reached her shoulders, now, and was finally even thanks to Laika Academy's barber.

"They probably don't know more than we do," Dax said.

"Sure, they don't know what it is." Jade rested her arms on her knees. "But they won't even tell us how they found it. Was it weird readings? Did they see something in a telescope? All we know is that it's past Mars."

Holly sat down next to her, and Dax and Thea formed a loose circle with them.

"Thea," Holly said. "You're good with tech. Could you hack into their system and find out what they know?"

"I considered looking into it, actually, but I've been busy with another project." Thea leaned over to reach under her bed. When she straightened back up, she held a small computer chip. "Meet Mia."

"What is it?" Jade asked.

Thea held up the handheld computer she'd built herself and slid the chip in. "She's an artificial intelligence program I've been working on for a couple years."

Holly frowned. "What does she do?"

"Pretty much everything. She's a real powerhouse." The barest hint of a smug smile touched Thea's lips as she pressed the on button. "Mia, what time is it?"

A feminine and slightly robotic voice responded. "It is two-fifteen a.m."

"Wow. Mind blowing." Holly rolled her eyes.

"She can do a lot more. I just have to put some final touches on her device integration code." Thea turned the handheld off and set it aside. "So, you guys scared?"

Holly scoffed. "No."

"Kind of," Dax admitted.

They all looked at Jade, who shrugged. "I've been in much more terrifying places."

Chapter Forty-Five
The Dog

The spacecraft Laika Academy had were advanced, far beyond what any Earth government had built. Jade never got to meet the people in charge that Fields alluded to. She wondered if they were all human.

The simulations didn't prepare Jade for how rough takeoff would be, but she got the team out of Earth's atmosphere in one piece. The pitch-black sky above the academy's remote hangar was quickly broken by the sun appearing on the horizon while Earth shrank beneath them. Gravity lessened. The takeoff engine—red engine—disconnected from the ship and drifted away.

Jade took a moment to catch her breath, to recover from the rough escape, to slide off her helmet. Her fingers drifted to her seat belt.

Click.

She floated out of her seat, grabbed the back of the chair, and turned herself around. "Welcome to space."

The others undid their seat belts. Thea pushed herself toward the cockpit to gaze out the front window. "Whoa," she breathed.

Dax drifted to her side, and Holly to his.

"Huh," Dax said. "All of Earth—all the geography and history we've ever learned—it's all right there."

"All of our problems are on that tiny rock," Thea added with a solemn nod.

Not all of Jade's problems. She shared a brief look with Holly, and a sense of understanding passed between them.

The radio in front of the pilot's seat crackled. "This is Laika to Tracker 1. Come in. Our monitors say you're stationary."

Jade grabbed the console and pressed a black button. "This is Tracker 1. We're outside Earth's atmosphere. Takeoff was successful."

"Activate the blue engine and proceed toward the target."

"Will do." Jade slid back into her seat. "Seat belts back on, everyone. At least until we're stable."

The others tore their gazes from Earth and returned to the back of the ship. Jade settled in. Helmet on. Seat belt on. She oriented the ship in the right direction. Monitors beeped. Numbers flashed on screens.

"Activating blue engine," Jade announced.

With the press of a few buttons and the flip of a switch, the team's journey began.

Over a month passed of eating weird food, performing periodic equipment calibrations and assessments, exercising in their limited space, reading the material Laika had given them, and sending updates back and forth. In the spare time they had between Laika's assignments and requirements, they talked. Shared theories about what the anomaly was.

And little by little, pieces of their lives slipped out. Dax had a little sister and loved taking pottery classes at school, despite not being very good at it. Thea had her school's record for typing speed and wanted a pet dog once she had a place of her own. Jade even found herself sharing stories from her time in elementary school, though she dodged any mention of her life after.

Holly—well, Holly remained a locked box, for the most part.

Jade was shaken from sleep one—well, there wasn't exactly night and day in the void of space. But her clock told her it was roughly three a.m. in New York when Holly woke her.

"Engines have started the auto shut off procedure," Holly said.

"We must be close." Jade rubbed her eyes.

"Uh, yeah. Come look out the window."

Jade hurried to the cockpit, where the others already waited, wide eyed. Outside, it looked as if the fabric of space itself had been ripped apart. The hole left behind glowed with shifting, iridescent light.

It was unsettling.

Jade recovered her train of thought and called Laika. "Tracker 1 to Laika. We've reached the anomaly." Maybe it was a space warp, a naturally occurring one. Did those even exist? And if so...where did it lead?

As the ship had moved farther from Earth, it took longer and longer for Laika to respond to messages. The academy may have been swimming in advanced spacecraft tech, but they lacked the warp networks that allowed instantaneous communication in other parts of the galaxy. Now, it took a few minutes for ground control to answer.

Finally, the response came. "Message received. Begin investigative procedures."

Holly pulled her spacesuit from the locker and put it on. Thea and Dax helped her hook up to the cord that would tether her to the ship. Meanwhile, Jade ran another engine analysis. And threw frequent glances at the anomaly.

"I'm ready to go," Holly announced.

"You've got all your equipment?" Jade asked.

"Duh." Holly held up the bulky computer box Laika had given her. The screen indicated it was powering on. It would transmit readings and photos to Laika as they were recorded.

"Great. Have fun."

Jade, Thea, and Dax watched through the front window. Jade turned on the camera at the front of the craft to take footage of Holly for Laika.

A number on one of the screens in front of Jade changed, catching her eye. She frowned and watched it change again. "Hey, Holly, are you picking up any gravity readings?"

"No." Holly's voice mixed with crackling interference. "I don't think this thing even has mass—wait. I do feel like I'm being pulled toward it."

"Ship's moving," Jade said. They should have been holding still. She tried to keep panic out of her voice. "We should pull her back in. Now." The numbers changed faster. "I want to back away from this thing."

Thea and Dax rushed to the airlock at the back of the ship. Jade sat down and started the engines. Minutes passed in what felt like mere heartbeats. She sent a brief update to Laika.

Jade glanced back and frowned. "Why are you guys putting on spacesuits?"

"Whatever force is pulling on her, it's stronger than us," Thea said. "The cord won't budge. We're taking the backup thruster packs."

"Okay." Jade swallowed. "Be careful. I'm moving us as fast as I can."

Thea and Dax appeared in the front windshield a minute later, attached to their own cords. They each grabbed one of Holly's arms and activated the thrusters on their packs. If they were moving away from the anomaly, it was too slowly for Jade to tell.

"Tracker 1, this is Laika," a voice said over the radio. "Pull back if necessary, but stay as close to the anomaly as possible for accurate readings. Make sure Farr keeps the box on at all times."

Holly, Dax and Thea were silhouettes against the bright light. Jade stared at the nearing tear in space until the engines finally came online. She turned the ship—cutting off her view of the team—and increased power. Their movement toward the anomaly slowed, but the pull was still strong.

"Jade," Holly said over the radio. "What's going on?"

"I don't know." Jade pushed the ship to full power. "It seems like the force is increasing. I've got the engines at their max."

"There has to be something else we can do!"

"Thea?" Dax tried.

"I'm working through the ship," Thea said. "I don't think there's anything my power can—" her voice cut out.

"Thea?" Jade frantically fiddled with the radio dials. "Hello? Can anyone hear me?"

There was one last one shot at gaining enough power to escape the anomaly. But it was also the only way home: the green engine. Without it, they might make it back, but it would take...months? Years? Would the regular fuel supply last that long? The food certainly wouldn't. Jade rubbed her forehead. Laika could intercept them with another spacecraft, right? Send more supplies?

"Tracker 1 to Laika. We can't escape whatever force the anomaly has. I'm activating the green engine. It's our only hope." No time to wait for a response. Jade started up the green engine.

The ship's backward speed gradually increased. Jade's fingers tapped impatiently against the dashboard as she waited for the green engine to finish prepping. The radio crackled a few times, but none of the team's voices came through. Probably interference from the anomaly. Jade wondered if the box was still sending signals to Earth.

She couldn't see the others, but they had to be nearly to the anomaly now. Or touching it. Or—

An alert signaled that the green engine was ready. Jade slammed buttons and flipped the activation switch so hard it snapped off. Warning lights flashed on the dashboard. Jade only understood half of them. From what she could gather, they were too close to the anomaly for anything to function.

Except the engine.

Slowly but surely, the ship's backward momentum slowed. Stopped. Reversed. Jade's hands tightened and loosened around the steering wheel with every shaky breath she took. She eyed the radio call button. She reached for it, pulled away, reached for it, pulled away—

The radio came on. "Tracker 1, this is Laika. Give us your status."

With a trembling hand, Jade undid her seatbelt. She had to go to the back window. She had to see if the others made it.

She floated to the back of the ship and pressed her hands to the window. The cabin lights flickered. The anomaly glowed menacingly in the distance. Jade swore it was brighter than before.

The team's cords had been severed.

It took a few minutes for Jade to overcome her paralysis, to swallow her nausea and return to the cockpit. She fumbled with the buttons for a few minutes more until she found the right one. "Tracker 1. This is Armstrong. The others were pulled into the anomaly. Green engine's gone. How should I proceed?"

Minutes passed without response. Too many minutes. Jade tried another message. "Should I start heading for Earth with the remainder of my fuel? Or wait? Can you send something to intercept me?"

They had the technology. Dozens of ships and probes ready for launch.

The response that eventually came wasn't promising. "Tracker 1, thank you for your work. The readings from the box before it entered the warp are coming in."

Shouldn't the green engine have lasted longer? Was the anomaly really that strong? Jade checked the fuel levels while she waited for a follow-up. She checked the records from the blue engine. No, no, the numbers were way off.

"Laika, I think there was an issue with the green engine. Fuel levels should have been higher." Five times higher, at least.

"Thank you, Tracker 1." It was a voice Jade recognized this time: Commander Fields.

Jade's hand hovered over the button. Choking, she pressed it. "We were the dog."

Minutes passed. "I'm sorry, Tracker 1, could you repeat that?"

"No more Tracker 1," Jade said. "It's just me. We were the dog. You didn't give us enough fuel."

Fields's next reply came after excruciating silence. "You might have made it. But giving you any more fuel would have made it impossible to get you there in the timeframe we wanted," she admitted. "In fact, without the others, you still have a chance. Bring the ship back and we can discuss options as you get closer."

There was a chance. A chance to get back to Earth.

There was also a spacecraft warp station to Kronos hidden somewhere in the asteroid belt.

"Fields, full offense intended, but I've got a destination of my own in mind." Jade began setting her course.

"Armstrong, if you aren't going to attempt a return to Earth, please leave Tracker 1 in its current location so that we can retrieve it in the future."

"Well, I would have preferred not to be sent on a one-way mission without my knowledge or permission, but life just doesn't work out sometimes, does it?" Jade examined the barely functioning radar screen, ready to head for anything that looked suspiciously un-asteroid-like. "Listen, Fields, I have a long list of asses to kick. You better hope I don't get around to your name. I'm muting this thing now, so don't bother replying. Over and out."

It took hours to reach her destination. Every passing minute heightened Jade's anxiety. She may have very well thrown away a slim chance at survival for an even slimmer one.

But, for better or worse, she found her way to the warp station.

Jade wasn't sure what she'd expected, but a massive metal ring floating in space wasn't it. No building, no structure—she'd envisioned some sort of spaceship parking structure, maybe, with a tiny booth and an alien attendant who'd charge her ten bucks to enter.

She approached slowly. Was she supposed to just fly through the ring? Was anyone going to—?

The radio crackled. "Hello? Hello?" a high-pitched voice asked.

Jade leaned forward. "Hello?"

"Identify yourself."

"Uh, this is Tracker 1."

"What is your purpose?"

"I'm—trying to get to Kronos?" Jade tried. "I was a part of an investigative mission. I'm my team's only survivor."

"Okay. Enter the warp."

That was it?

"Be sure to have your paperwork ready when you reach your port," the voice added.

Screw ports. There had to be somewhere relatively flat where Jade could land, right? "Thanks," she replied. She eased forward.

She was about halfway through the ring and still nothing had happened. She was ready to get back on the radio with whoever was watching when a flash of light blinded her. The entire world went white. Jade felt ripped from her body. No, ripped from reality. She was suspended in a dream.

Then, she was back in her seat.

The city lights of Kronos glittered below, interrupted in patches by dark seas. The entire ship shuddered. Clearly, the warp had exerted a little more force than the poor thing could handle.

Oh, and the fuel was gone.

Jade climbed out of her seat and stumbled to the storage locker, unused to the gravity that came with being in the sky over Kronos. The ship drifted through the air for a moment before gliding turned to falling.

One last spacesuit waited in the storage locker. Jade pulled it on and grabbed a thruster pack. She slid on her pilot's helmet before making her way to the rear door.

The sight of Thea's handheld computer lying on the ground made her pause. She picked it up, popped out Mia's chip, and slid it into an inner pocket that she hoped would protect it.

The airlock door crawled open, inch by painstaking inch. Wind whipped by, carrying the scent of the ocean and a warning that Jade wasn't far from smacking into water that may as well have been concrete. She dropped to her stomach and crawled to the edge. As soon as the door was high enough, she pushed herself out.

Thrusters activated, jerking Jade from a free fall to a somewhat controlled descent. They weren't meant to be used like this, and it was doubtful the pack would last long, especially with the added pressure of Kronos's atmosphere. She turned the thrusters back off.

The ship hit the water below. Freezing spray came high enough to make Jade yelp. Thrusters back on. Up a few feet. Off. Drop again.

She turned them back on one last time, and when she was only a few feet above the water, she turned them off for good.

The swim to shore was a breeze compared to that night after Naomi—

Jade shook the thought off as she pulled herself onto the docks. She tossed the thruster pack into the sea, along with her helmet. Then, ignoring strange looks from onlookers, she set off into the city.

Alone again.

Chapter Forty-Six
Going to Jail Speedrun

"Mechwell's trial date has already been decided. Three days. Courthouse is on Vala." Jasper tossed her coat onto a nearby chair, which promptly collapsed to the floor of the shack. "Someone guess the date and location of the next race."

"During the trial on Vala?" Grace guessed from where she sat on the floor.

"Bingo."

"Whoa, three days?" Thea asked, brow furrowing. "That's ridiculous."

"Yeah. The official statement is that they 'prioritized him' due to 'the nature of his target' and 'certain government connections.'" Jasper made quotes in the air as she spoke. "Oh, and the dude they were supposed to be trying during that time mysteriously died in jail. Ringmaster, and presumably Starr, want this wrapped up quickly. Before anyone can prove Mechwell's innocent."

"So, we have three days to do just that?" Dax guessed.

"Yup."

"We're helping Mechwell?" Grace sounded surprised. "Why do you care?"

"I need to know why Ringmaster decided to frame him," Jasper replied. "If it wasn't a random choice, that could mean he has useful information about Ringmaster." With a wave of her hand, she added, "And I certainly don't want the police getting away with this. I don't know much about Mechwell, but I'll gladly side with him over them."

"Can't we just show the court that the footage was tampered with and that Mechwell left the alley before the murder even happened?" Holly asked.

"I figured that out with my technopathy," Thea told her. "It's going to be difficult to explain to a jury of average people, let alone convince them. Especially with the prosecution's evidence."

"Let's talk to Mechwell," Jasper said. "See if he saw anything that day that might lead us to the real killer."

"Okay, so we go back to the police station—" Holly began.

"He's not there." Thea shook her head. "They already moved him to Vala. Only people talking to him now are his lawyers."

Holly groaned. "Let me guess. We're lawyers now?"

"Yep." Jasper clapped her hands together. "Pack your day bags, everyone. We're going to Vala."

Vala's atmosphere was technically breathable, although it was generally recommended people not spend too much time outside buildings with air cleaning systems, because it wasn't the healthiest stuff. This was mainly due to the *slightly* poisonous gas the moon's volcanoes put out on a semi-regular basis.

Mechwell was being represented by Arch & Archer, a small firm on Vala founded by Clover Arch and Clove Archer—no relation whatsoever, they met at university. While the firm's top lawyers were good, Thea's search of their system revealed that Mechwell's case had been handed off to the new guy: Mo Smits, someone Jasper identified as a "certified dumbass" with no won cases.

Smits barely had any experience at all. The other lawyers had likely realized the case was unwinnable with the absurd time crunch and pawned it off on him, not even giving him a mentor to work with like they ordinarily would have.

Not long after warping to Vala, the team sat in a stolen van outside the law firm and watched the bald, blue-skinned Smits enter. "Dax," Jasper said. "You mentioned that you've apparently unlocked a new ability."

Dax blinked in surprise. "Yeah, but you saw me in that fight. I still haven't figured out how to use it—"

"I need you to get on that. I have an idea." Jasper twisted around in the driver's seat to peer at the back of the van. "Holly, I need you to track down a sick person, and I need Dax to cure them. Thea, find a way to lure Smits out here."

"You want me to get him sick?" Dax asked.

"Not super sick. We don't want him to die or anything. Just, you know, maybe cough up an organ or too."

Holly threw open the door and climbed out. Dax followed. Thea pulled a laptop from her bag. "I'll see if I can get into his office cameras. Maybe there's something in there we can use."

"Great," Jasper said. "After Dax takes care of him, all that will be left for us to do is swoop in and offer to take the case instead."

Grace frowned. "Won't people know we don't work there?"

"No one wants this case. If we tell them we're handling it, they're not going to ask questions."

"Guy's got Sagev Sand Serpents merch all over his office," Thea said.

"What's that?" Grace asked, twisting in the passenger seat to try to catch a glimpse of Thea's screen.

"A sandsurfing team," Thea replied. "Jasper, wanna play radio announcer?"

Jasper grinned. "Always."

"Let me just get into his receiver." Thea held up a smartsphere. "I'll repurpose the audio input—and we're good. As soon as the station he's on goes to commercial, I'll put you on."

Jasper cleared her throat and took the sphere.

"Five seconds," Thea said. "Four. Three." She held up a hand and counted down on her fingers. *Two, one, live.*

"Citizens of Vala and loyal listeners of this station, I know you're just *dying* for opportunity to meet the Sagev Sand Serpents!"

"He's interested," Thea whispered.

"Our Sandsurfing Fan Van will be parked out front of Arch & Archer legal offices from twelve to thirteen in the a.m.," Jasper said. "Come on down and say hi to the team!" She gave Thea a thumbs up and lowered the sphere.

Thea tapped a few buttons and closed her laptop. "Great. That gives us an hour for Holly and Dax to find someone and get back."

Grace leaned against her door and peered out the window. "Should we do something about the fact that this van is clearly made for selling frozen fruit pops?"

"No worries," Jasper said. "We'll give it a paint job. There's a Mota Mart across the street."

Getting paint from the Mota Mart was easy enough, but making the van look even close to professional was a different can of neoworms entirely. Jasper haphazardly covered the fruit pop pictures with layer after layer of white spray paint, but they still peered through.

Jasper rested a hand on her hip. "I think we're going to have to cover it with red instead."

"The team colors are red and white," Thea said. "How are we going to do the text?"

"I don't see why it matters. We'll just do the words in black."

"Jasper!" Dax exclaimed as he crossed the street, Holly behind him. "We found something that should work. Also, Holly had me practice by giving her a bunch of papercuts. I'm getting the hang of it. I think."

Holly looked Jasper, Thea, and Grace up and down. "You look like you got in a fight with a graffiti artist," she said.

Thea turned around and began spraying red letters over top of the pictures of fruit pops. "We want to make this as obvious as possible for Smits. He's not the brightest."

"How did he get a job as a lawyer, exactly?" Grace asked.

"His dad is also a lawyer. A very rich one."

Grace's brow furrowed. Systemic corruption still seemed to be a new concept to her. *Not for long, if you stick around the Janus System,* Jasper thought.

"All right, I call drawing the serpent!" Jasper picked up a black can, shook it, and sprayed a wiggly line onto the van.

"Is that it?" Holly asked, folding her arms.

"Yeah. You got a problem with it?"

"You can't even tell what end's the head and what end's the tail." Holly picked up a green can off the ground. "Here, let me—"

"Whoa," Thea said, holding out a hand to stop her. "There's no green in the team colors."

"Then why did you guys get all these cans of paint?"

"I got a little carried away," Jasper admitted.

"It's almost twelve," Grace warned. Even though she'd stood a fair distance back from the van, specks of white and red paint dotted her face.

"You guys all get in line and pretend to be fans," Jasper said. She opened the passenger door and climbed in. "Dax, do your thing."

"What are we going to do when the team doesn't, you know, actually show up?" Thea asked.

"I'll handle it." Jasper pulled the door shut.

Smits came running out of the building right at twelve, nearly tripping over himself on the way to the van. Jasper cracked the window to watch and listen.

"Oh, this must be the Fan Van!" Smits exclaimed.

"How could you tell?" Holly asked sarcastically.

He pointed at the black squiggle on the van. "That's their mascot!"

"Right. Obviously."

Dax awkwardly stuck out his hand. "Nice to meet a fellow fan."

"Of course!" Smits grabbed his hand and shook it violently, nearly yanking Dax to the ground. "Sorry, I'm just so excited. None of my coworkers like sandsurfing."

"Oof." Jasper shook her head. "Dax, did it work?" Even if he had been able to replicate illness with the same bioenergy he amplified healing with, there was no telling how long it would take.

"I don't know," Dax whispered as Smits went on to aggressively shake everyone else's hands. "And like I said, I don't remember seeing a glow when I cut the guy's hand at Prime's apartment. I might have just missed it, but there might not be a visual cue when I reverse the energy."

"Well, did you feel anything?" Jasper asked.

Dax hesitated a moment. "I thought I felt something more when I did it the first time. But I was also about to get murdered."

"Maybe you need to convince this guy to try to murder you."

"That won't be necessary," Holly said. "He's already starting to look like the lady Dax cured. Red, watery eyes and paling skin. I bet any second now he's going to—"

Smits broke into a violent fit of coughing.

"Great!" Jasper rolled the window down all the way. "Hey everyone, I have some bad news. The Sand Serpents are stuck in terrible traffic and won't be here for a few more hours."

"Oh, that's too—" Smits sneezed. "That's—" Another sneeze. "Too bad." And another. "Guess I'd better get back to work."

He turned around and walked back to the building.

Jasper smirked. "Time for phase two."

Chapter Forty-Seven
Schrodinger's Arch(er)

"We're from emergency legal services," Jasper lied.

The gray-furred man behind the desk, either Clove Archer or Clover Arch, frowned. "I've never heard of that."

"We keep a low profile," Jasper told him with a wave of her hand. "Otherwise, legal offices would be calling us nonstop, asking for help with trivial things rather than real emergencies. Such as the one you find yourself in. I mean come on, you take on this client and then find out his trial's in three days?"

"It is ridiculous," Arch or Archer muttered. One of the small, rounded ears on top of his head twitched.

"And now the guy you've assigned the case to is too sick to do anything," Jasper added sympathetically. "That's where we come in. We'll pick up where he left off, handle all the paperwork, and credit for the case goes under your firm's name."

"Sounds perfect." Arch(er?) frowned. "Almost too perfect. How did you even know about this?"

"We have eyes everywhere in the legal world. We won't bore you with the details." Jasper placed her hands on his desk and leaned forward. "Just trust us. We'll handle everything."

"I just want to know we're in good hands. Our reputation is important."

Thea's fingers brushed the power cord connected to his monitor. "Completely understandable," she said. "We are listed in the Vala legal database, if you want to have a look."

Arch/er punched in a site address. As he scrolled, he asked, "What were you called again?"

"Vala Emergency Legal Services." Jasper shot Thea a glance, and she nodded in confirmation.

"Oh, well, here you are. I suppose that checks out." He sighed and pointed to a tablet sitting at the edge of the desk. "That's got all of the case info. Good luck. I think you'll need it."

"We're better than luck." Jasper grabbed the tablet.

As they left the offices, Jasper scrolled through the evidence in Mechwell's case file. "Prosecution's got the tampered footage, the DNA analysis, crime scene photos including the cup, and nothing that makes Mechwell look good."

"While I was in Arch—uh, maybe Archer's—system, I sent a message to the jail letting them know we're coming," Thea said. "We shouldn't have any problems talking to him."

They drove the graffitied van to the jail and parked as far from the security cameras as possible. Mechwell gave the team a startled look when guards brought him into the room where they waited.

"What happened to Smits?" he asked.

"He's sick. We're your new legal team." Jasper offered some jazz hands. "Yay!"

Mechwell wasn't as excited. He slid into the chair on the other side of the table. "What's the use? I'm screwed."

"Don't give up yet. We think we can solve this, but we need you to answer a few questions to steer us in the right direction." Jasper set down the tablet and brought up the image of the cup. "Did you drink from this?"

Mechwell's shoulders sagged. "It looks exactly like the one I had. I bought a coffee from the shop in the building I work at. But I tossed it inside the building, before I got to the alley!"

Jasper lifted an eyebrow. "And why did you go through the alley?"

"My office has an exit at one end," Mechwell explained. "The bus stop I use is down the street on the other side."

"And that's where you went after you left the alley?"

"Yes. And then I went home, only to get arrested the next day!"

"Okay." Jasper tapped a finger against the tablet. "We can work with this. You threw out the cup on your way out. Someone took it out of the trash, went into the alley, killed Prime while holding the cup, and tossed it aside. They probably entered the convenience store immediately after to erase security footage."

Thea folded her arms. "Should we try the cashier again?"

Jasper nodded. "Maybe we can jog his memory and figure out who deleted the footage. It will be helpful to have someone to point fingers at if we're saying Mechwell's innocent."

"The murder took place right after Mechwell left the alley, right?" Grace asked. "Maybe he saw the real killer at some point."

"Good point," Jasper replied. She looked at Mechwell. "Did you see anyone unusual on your way out of work?"

Mechwell grimaced. "I wasn't really paying close attention. Things have been more hectic than usual, lately. Not in my department, but in the one next door."

"And what would that be?"

"All I know is that they report directly Kronos, not Sagev or Si Hera. They're employed by Governor Starr."

Jasper raised an eyebrow. "But you're not involved with any of that. You work in Sagev's transportation department." Maybe this had simply been a case of him being in the wrong place at the wrong time, after all. He walked through the alley every day after work, and that made him an easy scapegoat.

Still, the department next door was something to keep in mind.

When the team returned to Sagev and found the convenience store, the same clerk sat behind the register, feet on the countertop, looking bored.

"Oh hey, cops are back," he said.

"We're not cops, we're lawyers," Jasper told him.

"Lawyers don't do detective work."

"These ones do." Jasper slammed her hands down on the counter. "Now, you were working alone at the time the murder happened. No other employees could have deleted the footage."

"Yes, I was working alone." He put his hands up. "But I swear, I didn't delete anything." Hesitation crossed his face.

"If you're really innocent, it would be in your best interest to tell us everything you know." Jasper leaned forward.

"Okay, fine, I left the store for a few minutes."

"Oh?"

"That illegal supervillain street race was happening outside. I wanted to watch. I was on the sidewalk out front when the gunshot went off." The cashier swallowed. "It was slow all day, so I thought it wouldn't be a big deal if I stepped out for a minute. When I went back in, a boy was leaving. I asked if he needed anything, and he said he'd only been looking."

Jasper frowned. "What did he look like?"

"He was human, I think. Light skin, curly blonde hair, kinda nervous looking."

"Aymes Bell?" Holly asked, lifting an eyebrow. "Maybe he is the killer, after all."

"Do you think he could have entered the store after the gunshot, deleted the footage, and then passed you on the way out?" Jasper asked.

The clerk shrugged. "Maybe. I don't remember how long—"

A sudden thought made Jasper cut him off. "The race!" she exclaimed.

Eyes wide, the clerk leaned back. "Uh, yes?"

Security cameras in the area may have been lacking, but the race would have resulted in a lot of civilian footage. "Thea, pull up any footage from the race you can find. Search social media. Net posts. News stations. Get anything that was filmed near the alley."

While Thea got to work on her tablet, the team left the convenience store. They found a nearby Bibi's to stop in for a break, which for Jasper meant pacing back and forth next to Thea and looking over her shoulder every few minutes. Or maybe a few times a minute.

Finally, Thea tapped the top of her smartsphere, opening a grid of ten different videos. "These are the most promising ones," she said. "You can clearly see Mechwell leaving the alley before the gunshot. They don't all have timestamps, but I can overlay the file creation time and the video length on the ones that don't."

"Great!" Jasper said.

"There is one minor issue, though," Thea added. She pointed to the right side of the projected screen. "These videos show Aymes on the street during the gunshot as well. He then enters the convenience store. He probably deleted the footage, but we can't pin him for the murder."

"Okay," Jasper said. "They also have the cup with Mechwell's DNA. If we can't prove that someone else took the cup and held it, that still doesn't look great for Mechwell."

"Did they take fingerprints on the cup?" Grace asked.

Jasper shrugged. "Even if they got reliable prints, Mechwell's would be on there, along with everyone at the coffee shop who handled it before him." Her face lit up. "Thea, could you get into the cameras at Mechwell's office? If there's a camera near the trash can he threw the cup out in, we could nab the killer taking it out later."

Thea sighed. "Maybe. But even if there is a camera in the right position, he works in a government building. Tech security will be tough."

"Couldn't we just ask them for the footage?" Grace asked. "I mean, we are the law. Sort of. Hypothetically, if we were going to present the footage in court..."

"Oh, right." Jasper frowned. "What do we need? A warrant? How do we do that? We're lawyers, not cops."

"We're neither," Holly reminded her. "And yeah, I doubt they'd let us take their footage without a warrant."

Thea laughed. "Oh, I could fake a warrant."

Chapter Forty-Eight
You're My Cup Of Tea But I'm Your Rat Poison

Jane quickly settled back into her old routine on Kronos. Rotating hideouts, stealing food, watching for pursuers. This time, though, she also sought out information.

It wasn't until late 1979—more than two years after her return to the city-planet—that she was able to track down Ybra during one of the hunter's occasional visits to Kronos. Jane found her late one night behind a motel in the Tide District and knocked her to the ground before she even realized Jane was there.

"Do you know who I am?" Jane asked, pressing a blaster to her forehead. "Earth? New York? About six and a half starcycles ago?"

"I—I recognize you," Ybra stammered. "I think."

"Do you know where Eriph is?"

"No, but I'll help you find him."

"Actually, I'll be the one helping you find him." Jane pulled the trigger.

The first ship Jane could afford passage on after that took her to Si Hera. She wound up in a small town called Blink, twenty or so miles north of Sagev, where she went by June Roswell and found work at a restaurant. The town was nestled between the base of the mountains and the edge of the desert, so it kept fairly busy in summer and winter.

June thought the small town would give her some time to clear her head and figure out what she wanted to do next. Instead, the restaurant stripped away what little strength and feeling she had left. She was given little training beyond a vague warning to look out for crawlers, which turned out to be a word meaning any large and horrifying bug that made its way into the restaurant. On one occasion, it referred to a large rodent.

That went on for nearly three years.

The endless cycle of waking and working and five-minute breakdowns in the freezer and sneaking out whatever food she could and going to bed in her tiny apartment was finally broken late one night in the fall of 1982—the beginning of summer, on Si Hera. June stood in the alley behind the restaurant, cramming leaky garbage bags into the dumpster, when she heard voices.

The restaurant owner—a pale, skinny, six-eyed man named Rakne—and a man June didn't recognize were in a heated argument at the end of the alley, apparently unaware of her presence. Rakne drew a blaster. The stranger lifted his hands, his tone turned fearful. Everything about his appearance was reptilian, from the bright green scales of his skin to his slitted pupils. His long black hair was slicked back and shiny.

June grabbed a bent pipe off the ground and stormed toward the man who ran her own personal hell. "Put the blaster down."

Rakne shot her a surprised look, then laughed. "What's your name again? Juice?"

"June." She lifted the pipe, ready to swing.

"You have no idea what you're walking into, June. And I hardly think a rusty pipe is the kind of thing you want to use against a blaster." Rakne's eyes narrowed. "Walk away, girl."

June's gaze flickered to the stranger, who regarded her with curiosity. When their eyes met, his expression switched back to terror, but it didn't seem genuine.

"I'm not walking away," June told Rakne.

"What, you think you're some sort of hero?" Rakne turned the blaster on her. "I'm not above killing kids like you. I've done it before."

Apparently done with attempting to negotiate, he fired. First at June, then at the stranger.

June barely avoided the shot meant for her. She shoved the stranger out of the way and swung the pipe. The blast snapped off the top half. June swung again with the rest and struck Rakne's head. She snatched the blaster from him. Fired. Green light pierced his chest.

Rakne was dead before he hit the ground.

"Impressive," the stranger said as he climbed to his feet. "Though you shoved me rather hard."

"Sorry," June replied lamely. She let her weapons clatter to the ground.

"I've wanted him dead a long time."

What had she walked into? A feud? Was Rakne in the wrong? Did it matter?

"I've been watching you for a couple seasons now," the stranger continued. "What are you doing getting ordered around in that little restaurant? There's clearly a lot more to you."

"I'm trying to take a break from…" From death? From running? June wanted to escape the chaos, but the chaos ran through her blood. It was fused to her bones and wired to her brain.

"Maybe you should come out of retirement. I have work you could do. And I could get you better living conditions." The stranger walked away from her before she could decide on a response. "I'll be in touch."

June showed up at work the next day expecting the place to have dissolved into disorder. To her surprise, things seemed to be running smoother than usual.

The stranger waited in the back room. He introduced himself as Mr. Scales and explained that he'd kindly offered to step in and take over the place after Rakne's tragic death. June got the sense he'd been waiting for a chance like this. He owned other businesses around town, and she quickly picked up on the fact that they were fronts for darker work.

June didn't care about all that. Keeping her head down hadn't done her much good, and Scales was offering her a change of pace. Maybe he was awful, but so were the targets he gave her.

Employees who must have been a little too loyal to Rakne disappeared. New ones took their places. One was a local Si Heran boy named Mylo with tough bronze skin, short waves of dark brown hair, and serpentine eyes. Mylo was completely uninvolved in any of the behind-the-scenes business. He was funny, kind, and the only person in Blink to take in interest in June for reasons besides her abilities.

She hid them from him. Hid everything she did at night.

One night, Scales told June to watch herself around Mylo. "He's ordinary. Doesn't know about the things that happen in this town at night. You're too powerful to get caught up with people that don't matter."

He was telling June she was too good for Mylo, she knew. But when she stood in the bathroom of her apartment that night—the newer, nicer one Scales had moved her to—she had a hard time feeling that way. If anyone deserved better, it was Mylo.

At this point, she was hardly more than a machine.

Chapter Forty-Nine
I'M GONNA TOUCH THE PLANETS WHILE NO ONE'S LOOKING

Jasper adjusted her tie with one hand and finished her can of Nova Cora with the other. "You guys sure you can handle this? I have to leave right after the opening statements."

"We've got it, Jasper," Holly told her. "In fact, I think we'll do better without you there to spout nonsense."

The team entered the courtroom and gathered around the defense table. Mechwell was a nervous, shaking wreck. He watched with wide eyes as the prosecution's lawyer gave a little spiel about how it was oh-so-obvious Mechwell committed the murder.

Their turn. Jasper rose to address the courtroom. "Jury and gentlelawyers," she said. "While the prosecution would have you believe Mechwell murdered Dr. Prime despite his lack of motivation and, to be honest, probable lack of capability, my team will demonstrate that he was framed. Whether this is a case of being in the wrong place at the wrong time, or something more sinister, is yet to be determined. But the defendant could not have killed Dr. Prime in that alleyway."

With a nod at the judge and a thumbs up aimed at the team, Jasper left the courtroom. It was up to them now.

Her motorcycle waited behind the building. She pulled off the nice, lawyer-y clothes she'd thrown on over her racing suit, put on her helmet, checked that her favorite sword was securely fastened to the side of the motorcycle, and hopped on.

Dark clouds choked the sky above, and they reflected the morning light into a blend of violets and oranges. Between the clouds, twinkling stars still lingered, and Si Hera hung large in the sky. Sera shone to the left of the planet, significantly smaller but still a striking sight.

Jasper wasn't thrilled to be breathing the moon's air with little protection, but as long as she didn't stay out for more than an hour, it wasn't likely to cause her many problems. Dax could always give her lungs a healing boost later if he thought she needed it, anyway.

People were already forming crowds along the streets as Jasper raced to the edge of the city, realizing that a race was coming. But despite their apparent excitement, the crowds ended abruptly at the flat metal bridges crossing the empty moat around the city. Jasper crossed one of the bridges and surveyed the landscape ahead.

The race's starting point was at the base of the low black mountains forming a semi-circle around the western edge of the city. At cruising speed, it took Jasper nearly ten minutes to reach the peak of the starting hill. She found a spot to wait at the edge of the pack. Roughly sixty racers were still in the running.

Ringmaster hovered overhead, staring intently at something in the mountains above them. Jasper followed his gaze but couldn't find anything of interest. She didn't have much time to look, though, before the ground started shaking.

Volcano. The mountain they were on was a volcano.

"Racers," Ringmaster said. "Get ready. Quickly, I suggest. The lava here moves fast."

Other racers scrambled to get as close to the starting line as possible. Jasper continued to hang at the edge of the fray. Better to give the others a head start if it meant not getting stuck in the crowd.

Ringmaster summoned a golden flag. The man was dramatic, sure, but seriously? He was really going to make them race down a volcano actively spewing lava?

When the lava neared the city, the bridges would go up, leaving the lava nowhere to go but into the moat that drained deep into the moon. Great for protecting the city, not so great for people trying to get in. Ringmaster's course map showed that he would allow racers to go either through or around, but anyone who got in before the city closed would be far ahead of the rest.

"On your marks. Get set." Bright orange lava oozed over the top of the volcano. Ringmaster waved his flag. "Go!"

The shaking mountain was a challenge to navigate. Cracks opened in the ground frequently, letting more lava escape from under the surface. To make matters worse, large boulders of black lava rock tumbled down the slope, shaken loose by the quakes. And, of course—

"I feel like I'm more of a target than usual," Jasper said, ducking to avoid a purple beam from a blaster.

"Huh. Do you think it's because you insulted a bunch of your opponents, or because you did well enough in the last race for people to see you as a threat?" Holly asked.

Ignoring the commentary, Jasper swerved to avoid a bomb that struck the ground behind her, leaving behind a small crater. She scanned the slope below. The crowd ahead was splitting around a ledge with a steep drop. *Cowards.*

Jasper picked up speed and aimed for the ledge. It'd be a rough landing at the bottom, but nothing she couldn't handle. And it would be worth it to get ahead of everyone.

She was almost to the ledge when the ground fractured beneath her. She gritted her teeth. The ledge was crumbling. Nearby racers glanced her way. If the ledge collapsed entirely before she reached it, she'd be in for a much harder fall.

If she beat it, she'd land in first.

A violent tremor shook the ground. A large chunk fell from the ledge. Jasper pushed her motorcycle to full speed.

She sailed over the edge, over the flow of lava spilling from the moon's crust, and landed so hard that for a heartbeat she feared she'd broken the motorcycle or herself or both. But the motorcycle kept moving, and the pain shooting through her wasn't enough to make her stop.

Jasper glanced back over her shoulder, at the racers falling over each other to get down the steepening slope. She laughed.

The city's sirens blared a warning of the approaching lava flow. The closest bridge was already lifting off the ground. Oh, this was going to be too easy. Jasper used the bridge as a ramp to launch herself onto Main Street.

She was halfway through the city when someone unmuted their comm.

"Jasper!" Grace hissed.

"Angel?" Jasper waved at a cluster of civilians as she passed. "What's up? How's the trial going?"

"I don't know. I went to the bathroom. There are Red Blades here!"

Jasper's blood went cold. Colder than usual. "What?"

"I think they're looking for me!"

"Holly?" Jasper tried. "Thea? Dax? Hello? Can someone help Grace?"

No response. "I don't know what's happening," Grace said. "The jury was about to deliberate."

Already? Valan trials were known for being snappy, but that was still a bit quick for evidence presentation. Had the judge been bribed to speed along the trial, too? Jasper sighed. "Okay, hang tight. I'm on my way."

Chapter Fifty
Law & Disorder

"The judge is moving things along quickly," Thea muttered, echoing what Grace had been thinking. "The case is pretty straightforward, but I didn't think he'd be handing things over to the jury so soon."

"Well, we did our best," Dax said. "All that's left to do is wait."

"Wrong." Holly stood up. "My turn."

"Where are you going?" Grace asked.

"I'm going to shapeshift into different members of the jury and convince them all that everyone else believes Mechwell is innocent." Holly shrugged. "What else would I be doing?"

"Oh. Okay." Grace stood, too. "I'm going to run to the restroom."

She made it halfway down the hall before realizing she had no idea which way she should be going. She continued to where the hallway split in two. Right, maybe? Which way had they come in? After a few more moments' hesitation, she ventured down the right hall.

The quiet air of the building was unnerving. It had been so busy earlier. The sound of distant footsteps only added to Grace's unease. She picked up the pace. Her gaze flickered around the walls, searching for signs to point her in the right direction.

She reached another split and started around the corner to her left. The group standing at the end of the hall made her dart back. Once she was out of sight, she listened for any indication that the Red Blades had seen her.

A faint command reached her ears. "Split up."

Footsteps started her way.

Running would make her location obvious. As quietly as she could manage, Grace hurried back the way she'd come and frantically searched for somewhere to hide. Her eyes finally found the restroom sign. She darted through the doorway and around the corner, pressed her back to the wall, and quieted her breathing.

It took her trembling fingers longer than they should have to unmute her comm. "Jasper!" she hissed.

"Angel?" came Jasper's response. "What's up? How's the trial going?"

"I don't know. I went to the bathroom. There are Red Blades here!" Grace threw an anxious glance at the door.

"What?" The shock in Jasper's voice made Grace's heart race even faster.

"I think they're looking for me!" Grace told her.

"Holly? Thea? Dax? Hello? Can someone help Grace?"

None of the others responded. What was going on? "I don't know what's happening," Grace said. "The jury was about to deliberate."

"Okay, hang tight. I'm on my way."

"But the race—"

"I said I'm on my way," Jasper insisted. "I'm way ahead of everyone, anyway."

Footsteps stopped outside the restroom. "Check in there. Seems the next logical place if she's not in the courtroom."

In a panic, Grace glanced to her left, where she spotted a closet. She grabbed the door handle and tried it. Locked. She gritted her teeth and pushed harder. Something snapped. The handle broke off and the door opened.

"I thought she was with Van Terra," another voice replied.

"Van Terra denied they're working together, apparently," the first Blade said. "But they have been seen in the same locations. And Van Terra was parked here. Whatever is going on between them, this is a good place to check for Alvarez."

Grace slid into the closet and pulled it shut. She peered through the hole in the door where the handle had been. A moment later, a man entered the bathroom. He stalked down the aisle of stalls, checking each one.

Grace was breathing too hard. Her heart beat too loudly in her chest. The man turned around, his gaze sweeping the sinks. Could he hear her? His eyes rested on the closet door. He started toward Grace. She backed away from the door and searched the small space for anything that could be a weapon.

When the Blade yanked open the door, she was holding a shelf panel, the contents of which she'd spilled on the floor. She swung at his head.

The Blade ducked, dodged, lunged forward. The next thing Grace knew, she was being thrown to the floor. Her head smacked against tile. Spots of light danced on the ceiling above her, and then on the Blade's face as he stood over her. He lifted a dagger.

Something made him pause. He frowned and looked toward the bathroom door. There was a sound in the hallways, getting louder. Relief washed over Grace.

It was a motorcycle engine.

People shouted in the hall. Jasper flew into the bathroom, dragging a second Blade by his shirt. She threw him into the first and sent them crashing into the closet.

Jasper slid to a stop and off the motorcycle in one smooth motion. "You okay?" she asked as she crouched next to Grace.

Grace watched her own reflection move in the visor of Jasper's helmet as she nodded. She hadn't completely caught her breath, but her vision was clearing. "Yeah, I—"

The Blades climbed back to their feet.

"Hold that thought." Jasper straightened up, grabbed her motorcycle by the handlebar, and swung, sending the Blades back into the closet. "How many more are there in the building?"

"I don't know," Grace said.

"Okay." Jasper climbed back onto the motorcycle.

"Wait!" Grace looked back. "What if they get back up? Or more come this way? Or—"

"Take a deep breath, Angel. You'll be fine as long as you're with me." Jasper jutted a thumb at the space on the seat behind her.

Grace scrambled onto the back. Jasper grabbed the sword strapped to the side. A pink sword with a wide blade that gave off a faint glow. "You ready?"

"Yeah."

They sped out of the bathroom. "I'm dropping you off in the courtroom. The others can handle any Blades that show up there."

As three Blades came racing around the corner ahead of them, all Grace could do was hope that Jasper was right.

"Hey Angel, are your wings ready?" Jasper asked.

"I can use them, if that's what you mean," Grace replied.

"Okay. I'm going to launch you out of harm's way. Ideally, you will land right in front of the courtroom doors."

"Ideally?"

"Yes. You ready?"

The Blades were drawing guns now. Aiming at Jasper.

"Okay!" Grace's voice came out panicked. "Do it!"

Jasper hit the front tire's break, lifting the motorcycle onto the front wheel and launching Grace into the air. She soared over the Red Blades' heads and spread her wings enough to slow her fall. Her landing was awkward but not too painful.

Jasper flipped over the front end of the motorcycle and flung it over her head at the Blades before any of them could attack Grace. They went down with the bike. She stalked toward them.

The first Blade jumped up. "We won't hurt you if you help us get Alvarez."

"You think I'm stupid?" Jasper lifted her sword.

The Blade fired three shots at her. She knocked them all out of the air with lightning-fast slashes. A second Blade climbed to his feet and pointed his gun at Grace.

Grace opened the courtroom door, ducking as she did. The bullet ripped through the dark wood above her.

"—find the defendant not guilty." The judge's gaze, along with the rest of the courtroom's, moved to the door. To Grace.

"Uh, security?" Grace yelled.

A Blade collided with floor behind her. "No worries," Jasper said. "I already did their job for them." With that, she hopped on the motorcycle and sped off.

Grace hurried to the defense table, throwing back glances to make sure no more Blades were following. "What happened?" she hissed as she slid into her chair.

"What happened to you?" Thea asked.

"Blades showed up! Jasper was the only person responding on comms."

"Sorry! I was having some problems getting signals in and out of the courtroom."

"Well, we won," Dax said. "So, yay?"

Chapter Fifty-One
Whose War Is It, Anyway?

The fracturing Si Heran government finally shattered in the middle of the hottest summer on record. Factions raced to recruit armies they could throw at each other in the middle of the desert wastelands. It didn't take long for people to call them the Waste Wars.

One of the early battles took place mere miles from Blink. June and Mylo sat on the roof of the restaurant and watched the distant flashes of light. The ground trembled with the brightest ones.

"I'm going to join Dune's army," Mylo said.

June didn't grasp what he meant at first. "Who?"

"Dune. The guy who ran for Si Heran governor last winter. He had the campaign to get Ryvon out of office. Maybe if he'd succeeded, this wouldn't have happened." Mylo picked up a pebble and tossed it off the roof. "I think he's got the best shot at fixing the planet."

June shook her head. She didn't want to get involved. She had little understanding of Si Hera's government, but with so many people vying for power, there was no way this was going to end well for anyone. "We should leave Si Hera."

"And go where? This is my home."

June looked to the apartment complex across the street. She was supposed to break in that night to kill one of Scales's enemies.

She didn't really feel up to it.

"Fine," June said. "But I'm coming with you to make sure you don't get killed."

Mylo laughed. "Funny."

"I'm serious."

Despite his "okay, if you say so," Mylo didn't seem to really believe June was joining him until they were marching to their first battle, which turned into a series of battles south of Sagev.

They built a shack to get out of the dirty, cramped barracks. It housed them for months. The army around them dwindled. Their enemies increased in numbers, surrounding them on all sides, closing in.

Between fights, they sat outside the shack and talked.

"When the war is over," Mylo said one night. "We can burn this shack to the ground together."

"I was thinking more along the line of explosions," June replied. "With fireworks. Take the thing out with a bang."

Mylo laughed. "I like that idea."

In the middle of winter, they were sent to ambush an enemy camp. The sandstorm took everyone by surprise. Carefully aimed gunfire and bombs rapidly devolved into a chaotic free-for-all.

Screw this. All of it. June switched to heat vision and grabbed Mylo. "Follow me!" she screamed.

She dragged him through the fray. They were going to make it. They would find the edge and keep running. They would leave Si Hera.

No matter how much he protested, she was going to get him out of here.

A bomb landed nearby and unleashed a violent explosion of light and energy. The blast didn't reach them, but the ground shook and the heat overwhelmed June's vision. She tried to make out something, anything in the white.

Another blast sent them flying into the sand. Mylo's hand slipped from June's. She coughed, trying to expel dust from her lungs, as she reached for him.

Her hand found something. An arm. A body. The blinding light cleared from her vision, showing her the heat signature of the young man lying in the sand.

"Mylo?" June pulled herself closer. "Can you hear me?"

She switched to X-ray vision. Her hand flew to her mouth. Her stomach turned. So many things broken, and that was only what she could see between the bursts of sand obscuring her vision.

"Mylo!" The wind stole the words from the air in front of her, whipping it away before even she could hear it. June placed a shaking hand on the side of Mylo's face. A terrible feeling had crawled into her chest to squeeze her heart.

She returned to her normal vision and forced herself to study Mylo. Eyes closed. Blood covering his face, though June doubted it was all his own. Shaking fingers touched his neck as she checked for a pulse.

Sobs ripped through her throat. She pressed her face into his chest and struggled for air. Every gasp felt as if it would crack her ribs or burst her heart.

Maybe the gunfire would take her. Maybe a bomb would land too close. She could drag herself away from the fight. She could escape. But where would she go?

She couldn't hear her own screams and useless apologies over the violence. And by the time the battle dwindled to a close, her throat was too raw to let anything out. If there were any other survivors, they were long gone by the time June opened her eyes and crawled out from under the sand piled on top of her. The world was red, a mix of blood and setting sun.

Her eyes burned the entire walk to the shack. She collapsed more than once, and each time it took her anywhere from a few seconds to a few hours to push herself back up. Carrying Mylo's body was excruciating, but she refused to set him down or drag him.

She buried him behind the shack.

Chapter Fifty-Two
I Bless The Rains Down In Si Hera

Twelfth place wasn't bad, considering the detour. Jasper was more concerned with keeping any more Blades from finding the team than how close she was to victory today.

Not that it wouldn't have been nice to rub first place in everyone else's faces.

She stopped outside the courthouse and leaned against her motorcycle, watching people stream out of the building. As Mechwell emerged, a free man once again, she pulled off her helmet. "Mechwell. I want to talk!"

Mechwell's eyes went wide. "Van Terra! Help!"

"I'm not going to hurt you." Jasper rolled her eyes. A few people looked her way as she approached him. She waved her sword in their direction. "Mind your own business!"

"What do you want with me?" Mechwell asked. He tugged at the collar of his shirt as sweat beaded on his skin.

Jasper stopped in front of him. "Just a few questions," she told him. "Do you have any idea why you were framed?"

"What? No!"

"Think." Jasper gave the sword a few casual swings. "Anything unusual happen recently?"

"Not that I—" Mechwell's eyes somehow managed to go even wider. "Well, there was the data drive."

"Data drive?"

"I don't know what it could possibly have to do with Prime's murder."

Jasper raised an eyebrow. "Why don't you tell me about it anyway?"

"Well, the building secretary was out sick, so my boss asked me to take some files to Kronos's department. Just some organizational stuff related to the building. He also told me to pick up a data drive with utility information. When I showed up, a manager told me to leave the files on a desk."

Mechwell's nervous gaze darted back to the courthouse. He continued. "There was a data drive waiting, so I took it. When I showed it to my boss, he said it was the wrong one, and that I should take it back before I left for the day."

"Did you?"

"No. I forgot and took the drive home."

"What was on it?"

Mechwell shrugged. "I never looked at it. I threw it on my desk somewhere and completely forgot about it."

"It's still there?" Jasper asked.

"No."

"For the love of—where is it?"

Mechwell winced at Jasper's exasperation. "It was on me when I was arrested. I was going to take it back to work and forgot about it again. It should still be at the police station, since I haven't collected my things from them yet."

"Great. Thanks." Jasper stepped around him and headed up the steps to meet the team as they exited the building.

"We have to make a stop," Jasper told them. "Police station. Mechwell had a data drive on him when he was arrested, and I think it's connected to Starr."

Holly groaned. "Do we all have to go?"

"I guess not. Are the police uniforms still in the car?"

"Yeah."

"Okay. Angel, Thea, and I will go into the station while Holly and Dax keep the car running. We'll swing by the shack when we're done to pack up. And I have one last thing to take care of."

"And after that?" Holly asked.

"The next race location is on Sa Ren."

Dax frowned. "Why would Ringmaster go there?"

"Well, it's where Aymes's school is, and it's about time we started paying attention to him anyway. He's the weakest link in all this, and our best shot at getting intel we can use." Jasper adjusted her grip on her sword. "You guys bring the van round front. I'll throw in my motorcycle."

Mechwell stared at Jasper as she stalked back down the steps. "Why were you talking to my lawyers?"

"You a cop or something? Mind your business." Jasper picked up her motorcycle with one hand and slung it over her shoulder, sword still in the other. Holly and the others pulled up in the van, and she tossed the vehicle in the back.

"Let's take the drive-through warp on Twenty-Seventh," Jasper said. "It'll be easier than getting out and going through a spaceport and grabbing the other car."

"Jasper, drive-throughs require a driver's license and vehicle registration," Holly said.

Jasper raised an eyebrow. "Thea?"

Thea sighed. "Give me ten minutes. I need to check out their database connections."

"It only takes five to get there." Holly pulled onto the road.

"Oh, good," Jasper said. "We can stop for food then."

After a quick detour to Bibi's, they made it through the warp and to the police station without trouble. Jasper, Grace, and Thea put on their uniforms and went straight for the evidence room.

Jasper had just grabbed the door handle when someone called her name. Sort of.

"Detective Jasper." Detective Park paused, his eyes darting between the three. "Officer Sparks. Officer Starling. What are you all up to?"

"We were asked to grab Mechwell's belongings," Jasper said as she turned the handle. "Get them ready for him to pick up."

"Weird to ask three people to do that, including a detective." Detective Park sighed and took a sip of his coffee. "Can't believe it wasn't Mechwell. We're basically back to square one."

"We have the footage of the guy who took Mechwell's coffee cup, though." Jasper nodded for Grace and Thea to go into the evidence room.

"He might be our guy, but facial recognition didn't find matches in any databases."

"Damn. Sorry to hear that."

"What do you think we should do next?" Detective Park asked.

"Uh, unfortunately, my team and I have been transferred. Again. There was this incident at our old station—anyway, we won't be able to help."

Jasper's gaze flickered into the room where Grace and Thea were sifting through cabinets. "But you should look into Ringmaster."

"Ringmaster?" Detective Park asked, frowning.

"I know, I know, it sounds crazy. But I think he was involved," Jasper told him. "Just look at the past couple locations of those races he's hosting. I think you'll find some clues. And the killer might work for him."

"Got the drive," Thea muttered into her comm.

"We have to go. Now." Jasper backed away from Detective Park. "I just realized we left our car—oven—car oven on."

Thea and Grace left the room and jogged down the hallway. Jasper followed.

"Who are you really, Jasper?" Detective Park called after her.

Jasper kept moving, faster now. "I don't know what you mean gotta go good luck with the murder case bye!"

She caught up to the other two. "I think we're in the clear."

"You sure?" Grace asked.

"Yes."

"Park seems pretty suspicious," Thea said.

"Well, we're leaving, so, whatever."

They exited the station and waited by the curb for Holly and Dax to pull up. "Thea, can you open up the data drive?" Jasper asked as she removed her sunglasses.

"No way am I plugging this thing into my good tech," Thea said, waving the drive. "It could have a virus protecting it. I have a spare sphere in the van I'll use."

"Okay." Jasper rose up onto her tiptoes, trying to spot the van over the other vehicles in the parking lot.

Grace looked up at the sky. "Is that a storm coming?" she asked.

Jasper followed her gaze. Sure enough, dark clouds loomed on the horizon. "Huh," Jasper said. "Looks like it. That's rare."

There was a thud behind them as the station doors opened. "Detective!" Detective Park started down the steps.

"Oh boy," Jasper muttered. She slid her sunglasses back on. "Okay, get ready to run. I'm going to try to convince him—"

"I wanted to thank you for your help before you leave." Detective Park stopped halfway down the steps. "Even though he ended up being innocent, we couldn't have found Mechwell without your team."

"Oh," Jasper said as she turned to face him. "That was really nice. You're welcome."

"Don't get me wrong, I don't trust you at all. I sincerely doubt you are who you say you are, and I don't understand your motives. But you did help."

"Thanks. I think." Jasper took a step back. "And hey, keep up the good work. You'll find the killer. I know it's tough when it feels like you're up against everyone else."

"Thanks."

The van pulled up moments after Detective Park disappeared inside— it was probably best he didn't see the stolen vehicle they'd vandalized. As the three climbed in, Grace said, "Did you really mean that?"

Jasper glanced at her. "Huh?"

"The nice stuff you said to Park."

"Eh. Guy's doing his best. I kind of feel bad for him." Jasper shrugged. "Then again, he works for an organization that's incompetent at best and corrupt at worst, so maybe he should try switching jobs if he's having such a bad time."

Jasper, Grace and Thea buckled themselves into the backseat. "Holly, take us to the shack," Jasper directed. "Thea—"

"Already on it." Thea plugged the data drive into a black smartsphere that was a few years old, at least. "Still, if this thing breaks, you owe me a new one."

"You have a dozen of those."

"Yeah, and?"

"You can steal as well as I can."

"Yeah, and?"

"Fine." Jasper leaned back in the middle seat and heaved a sigh. "Sa Ren's going to be so nice compared to this desert."

"This data drive's super secure," Thea said. "It's incredible, really, I don't know if I'll even be able to—ha, just kidding, I can get in. It will take a while though."

"Okay, miss 'I'm the greatest hacker.' Chill."

They were pulling up at the shack by the time Thea had an update. "I've got a couple of the files open," she said. "They're mostly hologram projections." She tapped the top of the sphere, and a 3D model popped up.

"What is that?" Grace asked, leaning in.

Thea spun the model around. "Design for a machine. Looks a bit like a big satellite dish." She frowned. "Not exactly the right shape for picking up standard signals, though. I think it's meant to absorb something more like…energy?"

"Energy?" Jasper repeated.

Thea tapped the right side of the sphere and it switched to a new diagram. "Oh."

Grace winced. "I'm guessing that's a spacetime warp?"

Jasper barely heard her. She stared blankly at the warp diagram. Despite the fact that it was a still image, she swore it was moving, throwing off light the way it did that day.

"The machine must be for absorbing energy from the warp." Thea flipped to a new diagram. "Here, they've designed a way to store it—"

"We won't let them," Jasper said.

"Huh?"

"No one's going anywhere near those things." Jasper rubbed her forehead. "Would the machine even work?"

Thea shrugged. "It could, but the only way to know for sure would be to test it. I think the one we just looked at is a prototype." She traced her thumb along the side of the sphere. "Also, I can sense more files on the drive, but I can't get them to open. They're either well hidden, or poorly deleted."

"If you find anything else, let me know." Jasper climbed out of the van. "You all have five minutes to get your stuff out of the shack. Then, I'm blowing this thing up."

"What?" Holly shrieked. "Why?"

"I promised I would."

"To who?"

"Doesn't matter. Now hurry."

Jasper walked to the back of the shack, to the small pile of rocks she'd left on the grave. She stood over it for a minute in silence before speaking. "Sorry it took me so long to come back," she said. "And for everything else."

The gray sky overhead darkened, warning of the oncoming storm.

"I wish you could have had a chance to leave. There's a lot of terrible things out there, but there's a lot of cool stuff, too. Anyway, I'm going to blow up the shack now. Like we said." Her eyes stung. "If you're somewhere, anywhere…I hope it's nice there."

A duffel bag waited by the back wall of the shack, exactly where Jasper had left it after the shopping—well, shoplifting—spree she'd squeezed in before they left for the trial. "Everyone in the van?" she yelled as she began dumping the contents of the bag into a loose circle around the structure.

"We're all in!" Holly called back. "Are you coming?"

Jasper pulled out a small container of fuel and went back around the circle. A single drop of water bounced off her nose. "On my way!"

She drew out a match. Lit it. Another raindrop hit her skin. She dropped the match and backed up.

The downpour started, but there was no stopping the explosives now. Or the fireworks.

Jasper grinned as her back hit the van. The storm soaked her, but she didn't climb inside yet. She watched and waited for the colors to stop bursting, for the shack to finish collapsing, for the last of the flames to die out.

IV. EAST MARINA HIGH

Chapter Fifty-Three
And They Lived Underwater!

The team stepped off the warp into a spaceport lobby bathed in soft blue light. Grace tipped her head back to examine the glass dome over their heads. "The spaceport's underwater?"

"That's not the only thing underwater." Jasper moved a hand from her motorcycle handlebar to point at something behind Grace. As Grace turned around, she said, "There's a whole city out that way. Blue Trench. It's not huge, but it's fun. I think there's a roller coaster."

Grace wandered to the nearest wall to examine the variety of colorful fish passing by outside. "What time is it here?"

"It's ten here, but they've got twenty-hour days, so it's basically noon," Thea explained as she tossed a smartsphere into the air, caught it, and tossed it again.

"Thea, did you get hotel reservations sorted out?" Jasper asked.

"Yep. We're gonna head north and take the escalator up to the boardwalk." Thea caught the sphere and slid it into her bag. "Hotel's a two-minute walk from the school."

"I want to stop by the school on the way and take a quick look."

The team took the longest escalator Grace had ever seen through a glass tube that broke the sea's surface and deposited them on a boardwalk. From there, they navigated a crowd of loud tourists and surprisingly aggressive hummingbirds to get into the city of East Marina.

"I've got a full download school's database and I'm scanning for anything related to Aymes. Should have his schedule in a minute here," Thea said. "Also, make a left." She looked up from her tablet screen. "We're going to pass behind the school. It's up there on the right."

Jasper paused and leaned her motorcycle up against the fence wrapping around the edge of the school's property. Grace peered through the fence's gaps. "What are those kids doing outside?"

"Sports." Jasper gestured to a nearby group. "Well, those ones are taking pictures of trees, but everyone else is doing sports."

Holly folded her arms. "Is there anything in particular you wanted to see, or can we go?"

"What class is Aymes supposed to be in now?" Jasper asked.

"Hang on," Thea replied.

Holly groaned. "You're not going to make us go inside and find him, are you?"

"No, but I would like to see if he's here today."

"He should actually be at volleyball practice," Thea said. She looked up. "The class is usually held in the gym, but the school map does show outdoor volleyball nets on the east side—"

"Oh, there!" Jasper rose onto her toes. "I can see him. Okay, good."

"Do you think Ringmaster came here specifically for Aymes's school?" Grace asked.

"Probably. If Aymes has been following Ringmaster this whole time, then he hasn't been able to go to school in a couple weeks. He can only miss so many days." Jasper stepped back from the fence. "All right. Hotel. Let's go."

When the team reached the adjoined rooms Thea had reserved for them, they all let their bags clatter to the floor. Jasper collapsed onto one of the beds and pointed to the opposite wall. "Thea, give us the rundown."

Thea set a sphere on the table and sent a projection onto the wall. "Aymes Nolan Bell. Here's his schedule, and a calendar with his upcoming events."

"I'll take over his first period biology class," Jasper said. "Can you get rid of the teacher? Maybe an email about a fake conference on the other side of the planet? Let her know the substitute's already been taken care of. Get her a bonus payment for the trouble, too."

Thea nodded. "On it."

Jasper pointed to a spot on the calendar. "Aymes is participating in that science fair? I'm putting you on that, too. See if you can talk to him."

"What am I supposed to do for a project?" Thea asked.

"You're smart. I'm sure you'll think of something." Jasper sat up. "Dax, I'm putting you in his third period."

"Volleyball?" Dax asked, frowning. "I'm not exactly good at—"

"Holly, you're going in second period," Jasper said.

Holly didn't look up from the bag she was sorting through. "And what would that be?" she asked as she pulled out a blaster charging cable.

"He's on the tech crew for the school musical."

"Fine."

"What about me?" Grace asked.

"You'll be in a group project with him in my class," Jasper said. "What I need everyone to do is talk to him. If we can get our hands on any of his devices, Thea might be able to access his conversations with Ringmaster. I want to know how he got involved with Ringmaster in the first place." She hopped off the bed and paced across the room. "We only have a few days before the next race, and god knows what Ringmaster's doing after that."

Chapter Fifty-Four
A Sequence of Unfavorable Happenings

Fluorescent green letters spelled out East Marina High's name across the top of the building. Students didn't pay Jasper and the others much attention as they entered, though one girl tried to hand them flyers for a dance.

"Home of the sea goats," Holly read off the wall as they walked in. "What the hell is a sea goat?"

"You know, like, a Capricorn." Jasper scanned the foyer for some indication of which hall they should take.

"A Capricorn?" Holly asked. "As in, the Capricornus constellation?"

"It's from the Earth zodiac," Thea explained as she handed Jasper a tablet. A map of the school filled the screen. The team circled around a fountain in the foyer's center and headed for a hallway entrance.

"What's a zodiac?"

"They say if you're born under certain stars, it affects your personality," Dax told Holly as the team began walking again. "The Earth zodiac has twelve signs."

Holly's brow furrowed. "Okay, but what's a goat?"

"That." Jasper pointed at the kid walking by in the school's green and black mascot costume. "Shame I never went to high school. I would have made a great mascot."

"You didn't go to high school on Earth?" Thea asked.

"No. I was an elementary school drop out." Jasper was forced to stop in front of a large cluster of kids in the middle of the hallway. "Uh, excuse me, coming through."

No one moved. Most didn't even hear her. One girl shot her a glare.

Jasper raised her voice. "Out of the way, people! Some of us have places to be!" She shoved her way through the group.

"Hey, watch it!" a boy exclaimed.

"If this school were a body, you idiots would be the blood clot that kills us. Move!"

They reached the classroom not long after that. Jasper threw open the door. "What do we have here?" She looked around the empty desks and lab area. The others filed in behind her and chose seats at the back of the room.

"Jasper, do you even know anything about biology?" Holly asked as she settled into a chair.

"Sure I do. The mitochondria is the powerhouse of the cell."

"Where did you hear that?" Thea asked. "It's not even grammatically correct. 'Mitochondria' is plural."

"What are you going to do to fill the class period?" Holly added before Jasper could respond.

Jasper shrugged. "I'll let everyone loose in the lab. Let 'em have fun with chemicals, or whatever. But I think the group project will do most of the work."

"I hate group projects," Holly muttered.

"Lucky for you, you don't actually have to do one. I'm putting you, Thea, and Dax in a group so that you can focus on your other classes with Aymes. Grace, I'm putting you with Aymes. You should probably use a fake name."

Grace hesitated. "I'm not good at coming up with names."

"Okay, then your name is Grace O'Paradise now. Talk to Aymes and find out anything you can." He'd apparently managed to recognize Grace at the mall despite her being out of the makeup she'd worn to Starchatter, so hopefully the look Holly had gone with today—combined with the wig of black hair—would be enough to prevent that from happening again.

"What am I supposed to say to him?" Grace asked.

The bell rang before Jasper could answer, and the door opened to let in the first few students. "I'll help you later," Jasper told Grace before walking to the front of the room.

One of the people entering the room wasn't a student, but a slimy purple man who extended his webbed hand to Jasper. "Nice to meet you. You must be the sub. Miss Elizab?"

Jasper frowned as she shook it. "Uh, yes." She shot Thea a confused glance. Thea shrugged.

"I'm Principal Price," he introduced himself. "Mrs. Marianas emailed me this morning and mentioned you'd be taking her place. I haven't heard of this conference before, it sounds pretty prestigious."

"Yeah, I heard that too." Hopefully they'd be done here by the time Marianas realized the conference was fake.

"Excuse me?" A girl raised her hand. She looked to be the same species as Principal Price, but with skin that was magenta instead. Waves of white hair tumbled down her back.

"Yes?" Principal Price nodded at her.

The girl gave Jasper a weird look. "Is it just me, or does this lady look like Van Terra?"

"Don't be ridiculous," Principal Price said. "Why would Van Terra be at a high school on Sa Ren of all places?" He waved his hand dismissively. "Besides, Van Terra has brown eyes and keeps her hair in a ponytail. Miss Elizab here has green eyes, and her hair's up in a bun."

"Couldn't she just change her hair and put in colored contacts?" the girl asked. "Besides, she looks too young to be a teacher."

"You do look rather young," Principal Price conceded, turning to Jasper.

"Thank you," Jasper said. "I drink a mixture of vinegar, fish oil, and diet Cora every morning."

"See? It all checks out. Be nice to the sub, kids." Principal Price waved and left.

Jasper folded her arms and looked the girl who'd questioned her identity up and down. "What's your name?"

"Ileen."

"Okay, Ileen, answer me this: do you know where Aymes Bell is?"

Ileen shrugged. "Why would I know? He hasn't been here since—"

The door opened. "Sorry I'm late," Aymes muttered as he made his way to an empty seat at the back of the class.

"We're just glad you're here." Jasper clapped her hands together. "Now, for the group project."

Half the class groaned, and the other half waved excitedly at their friends.

"I'm assigning groups."

Now everyone was groaning. Jasper ignored them as she herded people into sections.

"What's the project?" Ileen asked.

"Pick a topic and make a poster board or something. I don't care. Go wild." Jasper walked to Thea, Holly, and Dax and lowered her voice. "Thea, are you sensing anything on his devices?"

"Yeah, I can sense that they're all super secure." Thea glanced at Aymes in annoyance. "I'll need to get my hands on them to get anything, and it could take me an hour or so to get in."

"That's the goal then. Anyone who can get their hands on Aymes's stuff and get it to Thea gets an A."

Jasper wandered around the lab for a bit, making note of chemicals and supplies that might come in handy later. As she opened a freezer, she asked, "Angel, is Aymes talking?"

"He's not saying much," Grace whispered. "And my group isn't exactly being cooperative—"

"Don't worry about them. Just make small talk with Aymes." Jasper raised an eyebrow. "Huh, Marianas keeps a lot of dead birds." She closed the freezer and returned to the front of the classroom. "Anyone want to share what they're working on?"

Ileen raised her hand. "My group came up with a way to clean up the toxic algae on the southern coast that we think will—"

"That's nice. How about you, Aymes? What's your group doing?"

Aymes looked up, surprise flashing across his face. "Something with the nervous system, I guess."

"Okay, well you still have—" Jasper looked at the clock. "Uh..."

"Forty minutes," Ileen offered.

"Yeah, that. So, get back to work."

While the students returned to their conversations, Jasper stopped by Aymes's table. "Aymes, would it be possible for me to arrange a conference with one of your parental or guardian units? Preferably tonight."

Aymes hesitated a moment. "I think my mom could come tonight."

"Perfect," Jasper turned away. Under her breath, she muttered, "It's all coming together."

"What was that?" Aymes asked.

"Nothing. Don't worry about it."

Chapter Fifty-Five
This Group Project is a Crime

"Aymes," Grace said. "Could you find pictures for the poster board?"

"Sure." Aymes started typing on his tablet.

"And I figured the rest of us could each take a section from this chapter to summarize." Grace pointed to the open textbook in front of her. "Who wants what parts?"

None of the other three students looked up from their screens. "Uh, I'll do the first one," a guy said after a long moment. One of the girls showed the other something on her tablet.

"Okay, how about you do part two and you do part three," Grace said, trying to keep her tone light as she pointed to the girls.

"Yeah, sure, sounds good," one said. She tapped her screen, and a video started playing.

Grace turned and waved at Jasper.

"What is it? Did you find something on Aymes?" Jasper asked as she approached.

"No, my group won't cooperate," Grace told her. "Nothing's getting done."

"Don't worry about that. It's not a big deal," Jasper replied. "Focus on Aymes, and I'll give you an A no matter what. Also, you're not a real student and I'm not a real teacher. But I'll give you an A in spirit."

"I've never been to an actual school before. Starr had me take private lessons with tutors. I want to do well!"

Jasper lifted an eyebrow. "This is the mall job thing all over again, isn't it?"

"They're looking at articles on how to take care of a pet wolfoid!"

"Those are legal to own? Let me see." Jasper leaned over and peered at the boy's screen. "Oh, no, now they're taking Starchatter quizzes on what scent their aura is." She sighed. "Look, Aymes has been absent since the races started. Pretend you've been here the whole time and ask him where he's been."

Grace blew out a breath of air. "Okay."

As Jasper walked away, Grace inched her chair closer to Aymes. "How's it coming?" she asked.

"Pretty good," Aymes replied. "I've got a bunch of diagrams set aside. I just need to narrow them down."

"Oh, wow, you're actually doing work." Grace resisted the urge to shoot the rest of the group a glare. "Hey, I noticed you haven't been here in a few pentasols."

"Yeah, my absences were school-approved. I was doing an...extracurricular."

"What kind?"

"Uh, internship."

"Sounds like he's making it up as he goes," Jasper muttered over comms. "Keep pressing him. He's bound to let something slip."

"Oh, cool. I've been trying to get an internship," Grace said. "How'd you find out about it?"

"I was actually contacted about it. I did stuff online for about a season. Then recently I was asked to help with...field work."

Grace tried to find some way to make him elaborate, but the bell rang first. She stood up and looked at the others. "Did you guys get your parts written up?"

"I didn't quite get to it," one of the girls said. The other two mumbled something similar.

"That's fine." Grace forced a smile. "Maybe just print off some stuff for next time? Someone could bring a poster board."

"Yeah, sure, will do." The boy's tone wasn't convincing.

Chapter Fifty-Six
Break a Leg

Dragonworld, a classical-rap-meets-technorock musical, had been one of Holly's favorites as a child. Unfortunately, she never got to see it performed live. Her parents thought it was trash and only wanted her indulging in "high-class" art.

She doubted a high school performance was going to live up to her expectations, but maybe she could find some enjoyment in watching it anyway.

The school tech crew was a piece of cake to infiltrate. All Holly needed was a clipboard and confidence, and no one batted an eye. When Aymes took a seat at the lighting controls, she slid into the empty chair next to him.

She suspected based on Grace's interaction with Aymes that he was more likely to question himself than Holly if she pretended to recognize him. "You haven't been here in a couple of pentasols. Been busy?"

"Oh, uh, yeah." He frowned. "Got a lot going on."

"You're doing the science fair too, aren't you? And volleyball?"

"Yeah. I'm trying to get into a good university."

"His interest in university is a bit weird, considering Ringmaster's training him to be a villain," Jasper noted over comms.

"You got any schools in mind?" Holly asked. "Or careers?"

Aymes shrugged. "If I can get in, University of Kronos. I want to be a doctor."

The theater teacher turned off the tech booth lights, preventing any further questions from Holly. "We're going from the top, everyone!"

Holly slipped out of the chair and moved to the back of the room, to a dark corner where she could wait unnoticed for another chance to talk to

Aymes. The opening number started, and Holly found herself tapping her fingers against her arm to the beat. Before she knew it, she was mouthing the words.

"Excuse me."

Startled, Holly looked up at the teacher. Had he realized she wasn't one of his usual students? She could try to convince him she was new—?

"Do you know all the words?" the teacher asked.

Oh. "Uh, yeah, I do," Holly admitted.

"A few too many kids have dropped out of the ensemble, and your voice is great."

Oh no. She'd been singing? He'd heard her?

The teacher waved to a student nearby. "Could you grab her a costume?"

"Wait, what?" Holly yelped. "The show's the night after tomorrow—"

"You'll be fine! Just follow everyone else's lead. I'm sure you'll pick it up quickly. Good luck!"

Chapter Fifty-Seven
Lions And Tigers And Water Bears, Oh My!

Jasper had told Dax to do his best and he'd be fine, but his best at volleyball was pretty bad. The ball came his way too frequently for comfort, and with all his focus spent on not getting smacked in the face, it was difficult to come up with excuses to talk to Aymes.

To make matters worse, today's class wasn't practice, but an actual game. They were being visited by the Blue Trench Tardigrades, one of the top high school volleyball teams this side of the planet. And on top of *that*, it turned out that Sa Renian volleyball wasn't quite the same as Earth volleyball, which only made it harder for Dax to follow.

Aymes, on the other hand, was great at the sport. He did most of the work for the team, and had their opponents agitated only a few minutes in.

Partway into the game, a buzzer went off, and the teams left the court. Half time, maybe? Whatever was happening, Dax was eager for the break. He followed his team members toward the sidelines.

One of the opposing team members picked up the ball and chucked it. Dax, at the back of the group, was the only one to see. Eyes wide, he shouted, "Look out—!"

The ball hit the back of Aymes's head and knocked him face first to the floor. His teammates immediately started yelling at the kid who'd thrown the ball, until the ref stepped in and ordered everyone to calm down.

Dax darted to Aymes's side as he climbed to his feed. Blood trickled from Aymes's nose. Dax winced. After a quick glance up to make sure no one had looked their way yet, he lifted a hand. "Hold on."

The blue glow wiped away the injury. Aymes, stunned, asked, "You have healing powers?"

Dax nodded. Aymes grabbed his water bottle off the ground. "Follow me to that fountain."

Once they were out of earshot of the rest of the team, Aymes held out his palm. A small sphere of energy shimmered in the air, transforming into a silver ring. "Me too," he said. "A form of manipulation."

"Where'd you get it?" Dax asked.

Aymes shrugged. "Born with it. You?"

"Me too."

"Ah, now we're getting somewhere," Jasper said over comms as Aymes turned to fill his bottle from the fountain. "Dax is doing great work out here, everyone."

"Thanks!" Dax said. He was promptly hit in the face by a ball.

"Hey, watch it!" the ref shouted before returning to his conversation with the coach. The kid who had thrown the ball shrugged, picked up another, and threw it again in Dax's direction.

Chapter Fifty-Eight
[ASMR] Building a Robot for the School Science Fair

Science fair prep took place in a large gymnasium. Thea doubted she'd accomplish her full idea in the next few days, but she just needed something to work on while she spied on Aymes. And she was confident she'd at least finish a prototype.

Thea looked up as Jasper approached her table. "Do you think you could grab me some supplies?" she asked. "I have a list—"

"You're supposed to be talking to Aymes." Jasper looked at the table next to Thea, where Aymes was sorting through a box of vials.

Thea waved a hand. "Yeah, yeah, I'm building up to that."

"What are you working on, anyway?" Jasper picked up one of the scraps of metal Thea had snatched from various locations around the school.

"I'm building an android."

"An android? Can you do that in two days?"

"Not a good one, but the prototype of what I've really been wanting to make," Thea told her. "A body for Mia."

"Aww, really?"

Thea nodded. She'd felt a strange connection to the A.I. ever since first interacting with it, shortly after Jasper had rescued her, Holly, and Dax and taken them in. She couldn't think of any logical reason for it, so she'd never brought it up. Maybe it was simply the way her technopathy interacted with more advanced programming.

After watching Thea poke at her scraps for another minute, Jasper shot a pointed look at the back of Aymes's head. With a sigh, Thea scooted her chair toward Aymes. "Excuse me, do you by chance have a marker I could borrow?"

"I think so." Aymes turned away from the box he'd been digging around in and reached into his bag.

While he dug around, Thea reached for the smartsphere at the edge of his table. Her fingers had barely grazed it when Aymes popped back up, marker in hand. She accepted the marker and pulled her hand away.

"Ugh," Holly groaned through comms. "I don't know how, but I wound up in fourteen theatre kid group chats. I don't know these people. Or understand their inside jokes. My sphere won't stop buzzing. I'm going to throw it into that fountain in the middle of the foyer."

Thea sighed. "Please don't," she muttered. "I made a lot of programming modifications to our spheres—"

"Too late. It's in the fountain."

Chapter Fifty-Nine
Mom Said It's My Turn On The Tragic Backstory

Jasper made it halfway down the hall outside her classroom before bumping into someone. The woman adjusted her glasses with a blue webbed hand and looked Jasper over. "Oh, you're that new sub, aren't you?"

"Uh, yes," Jasper replied.

"How old are you?"

"Late sixties."

"No way! You look so young. What's your secret?"

"God is punishing me," Jasper muttered.

"What was that?"

"Goat cheese," Jasper said. "Now, if you'll excuse me, I'm going to go find a place that sells coffee, energy drinks, and Nova Cora."

"There's a cafe at the Twin Sunrise books down the street. They have everything. And I mean everything." The woman laughed. "I usually go between classes to get drinks. These kids can be hard to handle, you know?"

Yikes. "What was your name?" Jasper asked.

"Mrs. Metor," the teacher answered.

"Okay, well, I'm meeting with a parent soon, so—"

"Whose parent?"

Mind your damn business, lady! "Aymes Bell." Jasper attempted to step around Mrs. Metor.

"Oh, Aymes. He's a bit of a problem, isn't he?"

Jasper froze. "What do you mean?"

"I had him for a first period class last semester. He was always late, spouting excuses about taking his little sister to school because his mom had to work, or something. I don't know how he expects to get into a good school. Kid's gonna end up working at Bibi's."

"Uh, I don't have time to unpack all of that, so I'm just gonna go."

Jasper walked to the bookstore and into the cafe. A young woman stood behind the counter with her back to Jasper, organizing a shelf of flavored syrups. "I'll be with you in a moment," she said, barely loud enough for Jasper to hear.

Jasper frowned. The employee's voice was familiar. Too familiar.

She turned around. All Jasper could do was stare blankly.

"What can I get you?" the employee asked.

"I—uh—" Was this a joke? Why did this girl have Grace's face? Jasper leaned to the right, double checking that there were no wings sprouting from the girl's back. "I was just going to have a coffee, but you know what, go ahead and make a mix of equal parts cosmiotto, Nova Cora, and lunberry soda."

The girl gave her a weird look, but nodded and punched the order in. Her hair was similar to Grace's, too, except that it was cut to her chin and straightened. Jasper squinted at her name tag. Kora. A common name this side of the star system.

"You live around here your whole life?" Jasper asked.

"Uh, kind of," Kora answered. "Your total's five janos."

"Kind of?" Jasper handed her a few bills.

"I was adopted from some place off Kronos, but I've lived here as long as I can remember."

"Okay." Even if Jasper could keep asking questions without sounding like a complete weirdo, it sounded like there wasn't much else this girl could tell her. "Thanks. Sorry, I know it's a weird order."

Kora shrugged. "I've seen weirder." The gesture screamed Grace. *What the hell?*

Jasper really needed to see those lab records Ringmaster had been talking about.

She took her drink and walked back to the school, debating whether she should tell Grace. Maybe it would help trigger Grace's memory. Or maybe it would just distress her even more.

Grace, Holly, and Dax were waiting in the classroom when Jasper returned. Holly and Dax were deep in conversation, and Grace was still laboring over the text portion of her project.

Jasper sat next to Grace. "You've had your wings as long as you can remember, right?"

Grace shot her a weird look, nearly identical to the one Kora had given earlier. "Yes?"

"And you don't remember anything before wandering out of a secret lab and saving Starr?" Jasper asked.

"No." Grace frowned. "Did something happen?"

"Not—no, don't worry about it."

Grace went back to typing. "You said I was probably an experiment in Starr's secret labs specifically, right?"

"Yeah, I was just hoping you might remember…anything," Jasper said lamely. "I'd like to know what he wants winged people for."

"I'm sorry. I'll let you know if I do." Grace glanced at Holly and Dax. Lowering her voice, she said, "I've heard you guys mention it a few times, but what exactly happened with Holly and the others? How did they join you?"

Jasper sifted through the story, wondering what parts to tell Grace and what parts could be saved for another day. There were things even the others didn't know, of course, because Jasper still didn't understand them and couldn't possibly begin to explain. "Holly's real name is Hollixa Faye."

"As in the Fayes that run the Prism District?"

Jasper nodded. "I wouldn't be surprised if you hadn't heard her name, though. She's the youngest of a lot of cousins, and she ran away a long time ago. Almost fifty years."

Grace frowned. "Holly's eighteen."

"I know. She disappeared at age thirteen. Five years ago, she and the other two appeared as young teens on the shores of the Tide District, with no memory of how they got there." All five years younger than when they went into the warp.

"The Fayes took them in and ran all sorts of tests, trying to figure out what happened," Jasper continued. "Locked them up, really. And since no one had any idea what was going on, Starr kept it out of the news." She tipped her head back, moving her eyes from Grace's to the ceiling. "I broke into the Faye penthouse a few months later looking for information and found them being treated like prisoners. I told them I'd help them, if they came with me."

"You rescued them and turned them into criminals?"

Jasper grimaced at Grace's response. "I honestly just gave them a place to stay. But they all had powers, and they wanted answers, and I needed their help if we were going to get anywhere." She let her gaze drop. "The last thing Thea and Dax remembered was living their lives on Earth. They have no idea what led to them being dumped on an alien planet."

"Makes sense, I guess." Grace folded her arms. "Have you figured any of it out?"

Jasper blew out a deep breath. "Nothing new. Yet. All I know is that it has to do with the spacetime warps."

"How do you know that?" Grace asked.

"I mean, it makes sense," Jasper quickly said. "They were warped through space, and time was involved too. Obviously."

Grace raised an eyebrow. "But how did you know about the warps in the first place?"

"My search for information on Starr and his projects has yielded a lot of other stuff," Jasper told her. "I met a scientist who was studying them years ago. She was pretty sure there was an 'other side' to the warps."

Grace leaned forward, her voice low. "The others had never heard of spacetime warps before they came up during the Starchatter mission. Why didn't you tell them?"

"Because I still know next to nothing about them, except that they exist." Jasper didn't mean to sound so defensive. She felt a twinge of guilt. It wasn't fair that she knew the others had been through a warp. They were desperate for answers, and she had something, even if it wasn't much.

The alarm Jasper had set earlier beeped. Good, a way out of this conversation. "You guys need to clear out. Aymes's mom is going to be here soon," she said. "Grab Thea. I'll meet you all back at the hotel."

Jasper sank into the chair at her desk as the other three left the room. What information did she want from Aymes's mother? Whether or not she knew he was working for a supervillain? Did she even know he had powers?

Jasper muted her comm so the others wouldn't have to listen to the meeting. There was a knock on the doorframe, and a woman entered the room. Human. Her blonde hair was piled in a messy bun, while her green eyes darted around anxiously.

Jasper stood up to shake her hand. "Mrs. Bell?"

"Yes," she said. "You wanted to talk about Aymes? Is something wrong?"

"Not exactly. I just had a few questions. He's an interesting kid, and I want to make sure I'm giving him what he needs while I'm here." They sat down on opposite sides of the desk, and Jasper continued. "I know I'm only a sub and I won't be here long, but I noticed Aymes has a very ambitious schedule."

Mrs. Bell nodded. "He's trying to get into the University of Kronos." After a moment, she quickly added, "Of course, he's not just doing the extracurriculars for his application. He's genuinely passionate about them."

"Good," Jasper said. "I also noticed that he's been absent for a couple weeks, though. Is he okay?"

"He's just been off on his internship." Despite the attempt at a cheery tone, Mrs. Bell's gaze darkened.

Jasper furrowed her brow. "Is something wrong?"

A moment passed, then the facade cracked. Mrs. Bell sighed. "I—I just worry. When I ask about the internship, he's very vague about it. He's probably just being a teenager, but he's been acting weird for a few months now." She leaned forward. "I've been struggling since his father died, if I'm being honest. Aymes was just a baby when it happened, but he does his best to keep us going these days. I'm afraid he's going to sacrifice too much trying to help me."

"Oh. I'm sorry." Poor kid. Poor mom.

"I tell Aymes he should do what he wants, but I think he's determined to go to school for me." Mrs. Bell gave Jasper a sad smile. "It means a lot, you wanting to meet with me. Most of his teachers don't care. I really appreciate the ones that do."

Oh boy. Jasper tried very hard to ignore the way her heart squeezed in her chest. "Of course. I think we need more kids like him."

Chapter Sixty
Source: I Heard It In A Dream

If Ringmaster really was here for Aymes, Jasper supposed it made sense that the race took place the same day as the science fair and the musical. They were all scheduled for Reonsday, which served as a day off at the end of a pentasol. Hopefully, the day before would be the calm before the storm.

But maybe hoping for a calm was too much.

According to Holly, Aymes would set up his project at the fair, and then head out to do tech on the musical. At Jasper's encouragement, Thea offered to keep an eye on his stuff for him while he was gone.

The morning before the race, Jasper circled the classroom while students worked on their projects. She tried to grab Aymes's smartsphere while he was distracted, but other kids kept bothering her with annoying questions like, "Do you have a rubric for the project?" or, "When is this due?" and, "Can we use stuff in the lab?" And then, of course, "I spilled this chemical on myself and my skin is burning what should I do?"

"Grace, could you grab Aymes's sphere?" Jasper finally asked, straining to keep exasperation out of her voice.

"Aymes is the only one here doing any work!" Grace replied.

"Exactly! While he's distracted, you could—"

"Hey, did any of you ever learn how to cite your sources? It's not hard. I figured it out this morning because I took five minutes to look it up!" It seemed like Grace wanted to sound polite, but there was no way to make that statement friendly.

"Okay, Holly," Jasper tried. "I need you to try to grab Aymes's sphere during rehearsal. Or maybe his tablet, if you can get into his bag."

"I don't think I can," Holly replied. "He'll be in the booth and I'll be on stage."

"Well, Dax, you've gotten along with him pretty well. Maybe you can grab it?"

"Uh." Dax did not sound confident. "I guess I could try at the beginning or end of class, but we can't have our devices on us while we're playing."

"Ugh. Guys. The whole point of this mission is to spy on Aymes." Aymes. The poor kid who'd somehow gotten caught up with Ringmaster and only wanted to do well in school and help his mother. Jasper folded her arms and watched him scroll through his text for the project. She felt bad that he was doing all this work for a fake project, especially considering the rest of the group didn't care. Well, besides—

"Has anyone finished their summaries?" Grace asked.

"Almost. We're still picking a font," a girl replied.

"But you've written it?"

"Well, no."

"Thea," Jasper said. "I really need you to get into his stuff. I want to know how Ringmaster found him and convinced him to join him."

"I thought you wanted information on Ringmaster's plans with Starr—" Thea started.

"Yeah, yeah, that too. Just give me everything."

"I'll probably have a chance while we're working on our projects for the fair."

Jasper sighed as she watched a nearby student drop a vial of glowy chemicals onto the floor. Shattered glass and liquid splattered the tile. "I'm sure you will, assuming you don't get distracted by your own stuff."

"What's that supposed to mean?" Thea asked.

"You tend to get carried away," Jasper told her. "Oh, and don't forget about that thing I need for the race."

"What thing?" Holly asked.

"Don't worry about it. Thea's got it covered."

"I hope you're not wasting time on unnecessary—"

"I said don't worry about it," Jasper said. "It'll take Thea five minutes, and it'll give me a huge advantage." She paused. "I will need your guys' help stealing a vehicle carrier and parking it on the race course, though. No biggie."

Chapter Sixty-One
A Full Ride Scholarship To Clown College

Another ball narrowly missed Aymes. "I think that kid is targeting you on purpose," Dax muttered.

"Oh, definitely," Aymes replied.

"Why?"

"I was picked over him for an athletic scholarship." Aymes picked up the ball and tossed it back, only for a different one to bounce off his shoulder. He winced and rubbed the spot. "A lot of people are mad, actually. But mostly Mak."

"Sorry about that." Dax ducked to avoid another ball. "Also, I don't get the point of this. Is it supposed to help us with volleyball?"

"No, Coach Lerch just makes us play dodgeball when we don't have a game, instead of coming up with useful training exercises."

Dax lowered his voice. "I can do more than just heal people, you know."

"Really?" Aymes raised an eyebrow.

"Go ahead and take a water break, everyone," Lerch called from his chair.

Dax and Aymes slipped into line at the fountain behind Mak, a muscular student with lime green skin who towered over everyone else. Dax took a moment to focus on the various bruises and scrapes he'd healed over the past couple of days. When Mak walked away from the fountain, he didn't bother going around Dax, instead pushing past him.

As Dax stepped forward, Mak turned around, a sizable bruise running up the size of his face. "Hey!"

"What?" Dax asked.

Lerch looked up from his tablet. "What's going on?"

"He did this to me!" Mak pointed to Dax, then at the bruise.

Dax lifted his hands. "How could I possibly have done that?"

Lerch was already staring back at his screen. "This is a no bullying zone."

"Implying that there are bullying zones?" Dax asked, frowning.

"There is a bullying zone, and it's called your face," Mak said. "You better hope I don't find you outside of class." He stormed off.

"You okay?" Aymes asked. "I don't think he'd actually fight you, but—"

"Oh, I'd be fine if he attacked me," Dax assured him.

"You sure? He's a lot bigger than you."

"Yeah. I'll be fine." Elaborating on the fact that Dax had years of combat training from Jasper would just raise more questions.

"If you say so. Where are you eating lunch?" Aymes asked.

"Uh…" Dax and the others usually ate in Jasper's classroom, but eating with Aymes might give him a chance to nab one of his devices. "I don't know yet."

"I'm gonna head to the cafeteria after class, if you want to join me."

Dax nodded. "Sounds great."

Chapter Sixty-Two
This Ain't A Food Fight, It's A Goddamn Lunch War

Rumor had it that while the cafeteria was mostly awful, the school's Nova Cora machines dispensed a perfect ratio of syrup and soda water. So, Jasper was standing in line with a bunch of teenagers when the fight broke out.

Before that, she was surprised to see the others in the cafeteria as well. Thea and Grace were both glued to their tablets, deep in their work. Holly had a murderous glare on her face as she sat with a group of kids that broke into song every other minute. Dax and Aymes walked by, and Dax shot Holly a sympathetic look before he and Aymes stepped into line to get food.

"Nice work, Dax," Jasper muttered. "Whoa, who's that marching angrily towards you?"

"Huh?" Dax looked to the right, and his eyes widened. "Uh oh. Mak looks pissed."

Mak shoved Dax into the wall when he reached him. Jasper stepped toward them, but Dax muttered, "Wait."

"What was that?" Mak demanded. A few other kids who'd been trailing behind him—presumably his friends—formed a wall at his back.

Dax lifted his chin. "What do you want?"

"Leave him alone!" Aymes held out an arm between the two. "Dax didn't do anything."

"Really?" Mak asked, turning his burning gaze on Aymes. "Because I've got injuries all over my body, in the exact same places I hit you!"

"Nice one, Dax," Jasper said. "But seriously, do you need help?"

Aymes pushed Mak back a step. "Back off."

"It'd be a shame if you got injured and couldn't take the athletic scholarship, wouldn't it, Aymes?" Max hissed.

Jasper frowned. "What the hell, is this a school or a battle royale?"

"Dude," Aymes said. "Calm down. I never even said I was taking the scholarship. I don't plan on playing volleyball after this year."

"Yeah, right." Mak held out his hand, and one of his friends handed him a tray of food. "How am I supposed to know you're not just saying that to get me off your back?"

Before Aymes could respond, Mak dumped the food onto Aymes's head.

"Oh, no way are we letting him get away with that," Jasper said. She stormed toward the confrontation, grabbing a glass of juice off a kid's tray as she passed. As Mak turned around, she tossed the drink in his face.

"What the hell?" He wiped his face with his arm. "Who are you?"

"You a cop or something? Mind your business."

The boy at Mak's right stepped forward. "Don't worry, Mak, no one steps on us like that." He tossed the contents of his own tray onto Jasper.

"That does it." Jasper brushed vegetables off her shirt, annoyed to find the sauce they were soaked in had left a stain. "Someone get me a condiment!"

Aymes peered around Mak and his friends. "Miss Elizab? What are you doing?"

"Does it matter? Hand me that bottle of sauce on the counter behind you."

"Not so fast!" Mak held out his hand to the girl on his left. "Give me your tray."

"I paid ten janos for this!"

"Did I ask?"

Aymes grabbed the bottle of sauce and tossed it to Jasper. She pointed at Mak and squeezed the contents into his face. He yelped.

"Excuse me, Miss Elizab? I had a question about the project—" Ileen stopped just short of the chaos. "What's going on?"

Mak—blinded by the sauce—reached out, grabbed a sandwich off his friend's tray, and threw it into Ileen's face.

"Come on, Ileen! Are you going to take that?" Jasper handed her the sauce bottle. "Or are you going to fight back?"

"I don't know what's happening!" Ileen shrieked as she took the bottle.

"I'll tell you what's happening." Jasper hopped onto the nearest table. "Food fight!"

Instead of chaos breaking out like she'd hoped, the kids at the table stared at her. Students nearby spared a glance, unable to hear over the commotion of the cafeteria but intrigued by Jasper's presence on top of a table.

"Someone help me," Jasper muttered.

Holly climbed onto her own table. "You all heard the lady! Food fight!" She picked up a bottle of soda and poured it onto the table in front of her, sending the theatre kids into chaos. One by one, other tables joined in.

"A little eager there, but that works." Jasper jumped down.

"Jasper, what are you doing?" Grace asked.

"Creating a distraction. Would someone please grab Aymes's sphere and get it to Thea?"

"On it!" Dax said, before getting hit in the face by a piece of flying fruit.

Jasper eyed the bag slung over Aymes's back. While he lifted his hands to shield his face from a spray of salad ingredients, Dax reached into the back pocket and pulled out the sphere. He tossed it at Jasper, and she caught it.

She ducked in time to avoid a tray spinning end over end and crawled underneath the nearest table. "Holly, could you get ready to catch?"

"Huh?" Holly looked out from behind the textbook she held to shield her face. "Oh, yeah."

Jasper darted out from under the table, snatching up a tray off the ground as she did and raising to protect her face. She dodged a puddle, leaped over a table, and threw the sphere.

Holly caught it with ease before dropping to the ground to avoid an onslaught of rice. "Thea?"

"Bit busy protecting my stuff!" Thea yelled. She hid under a table, shielding her various devices.

"Okay then. Grace?"

"I'm ready." Grace climbed onto her chair, raising her hands.

"Hang on, you've got incoming," Jasper said, eyes on the small melon sailing through the air. She chucked her tray and sent it spinning. When it passed through the air in front of Grace, the melon smashed into it, and they both crashed to the ground.

"Now!" Grace yelled.

Holly chucked the sphere. Grace caught it and slid off the chair in time to avoid more fruit. She held out the sphere to Thea, who added it to her pile.

Before Jasper could commend the team for that incredible display of teamwork, students around her abruptly dropped their food and scrambled to get off the tables.

"What is going on here?" Mrs. Metor demanded from the cafeteria doorway.

"Aymes started it!" Mak yelled, pointing at Aymes.

"No I didn't!" Aymes protested.

Mrs. Metor started toward him. "Really, Aymes?"

Jasper stood up and hurried into the teacher's path. "I've been here the whole time. Aymes did nothing wrong."

"Oh, sure, the substitute's going to step in, like she has any authority." Mrs. Metor folded her arms. "Why should I listen to you, anyway? You're covered in food."

"These sauce stains are a badge of honor," Jasper said. "I've been out here on the front lines, and where have you been? Sitting in your comfy teacher's lounge, safe from harm?"

"I don't know how to respond to that. I'm done talking to you." Mrs. Metor turned to Aymes. "And as for you, good luck trying to start food fights in detention." Before Aymes could argue further, she stormed out of the room.

Jasper grimaced. "Sorry about the detention thing."

"It's fine. I'm used to it." Aymes plucked a grape stem from his hair. "Besides, there's no way Principal Price will let her single-handedly blame me for this whole thing. The whole school will probably get a stern lecture and maybe lose some privilege or another for a pentasol."

Aymes moved to return to the food line, and Dax hurried after him. Jasper leaned against the table next to her and spotted a half empty glass of Nova Cora. She picked it up and took a sip. "Thea, make sure you get Aymes his sphere back as soon as possible."

"Duh. We want to track his future messages," Thea said.

"Yeah, but do it quickly. Kid's got enough to worry about as is."

Chapter Sixty-Three
Don't Talk To Me Or My Robot Ever Again

Jasper eyed the two android bodies propped against the wall on either side of Thea as she approached her table. "That's a lot of typing you've got going on there. Is breaking into the sphere really that intense?"

"Huh? Oh, no, this is something else. I finished with the sphere a while ago." Thea pointed to where it sat at the edge of her table. Her eyes stayed on the laptop screen in front of her.

"Well, what was on it?"

"Give me three seconds." Thea tapped something on the screen.

"What are you doing?" Jasper's gaze moved to the androids. "And why are there two robot bodies instead of one?"

"I'm making another A.I." Thea turned the laptop to face Jasper. "But you wanted to hear about Aymes, right?"

"Why would you—okay, sure, tell me what you found."

"It starts a few months ago." Thea pointed to a spot on the screen. The start of a message log. "Here. Ringmaster sends Aymes a message saying he knows about his powers and is willing to train him if Aymes helps him out."

"How did he know about Aymes's powers?" Jasper asked.

"Aymes asked the same thing. Ringmaster said something vague about being able to sense people with his same power."

"Which begs the question: where did their powers come from?" Ringmaster was so determined to get his hands on the lab records that Jasper thought it could be related, but Aymes couldn't be a lab experiment, if he'd been with his mother since his birth.

"Oh, and we were right about this race being for Aymes's sake," Thea said, scrolling through the log. "He sent Ringmaster a message saying he had a math test and the science fair and whatnot, and that he needed to be here for a few days. Ringmaster actually tried to convince him to drop out."

Jasper's eyes narrowed. She scanned the screen. "He did?"

"Ringmaster told Aymes that he wouldn't need school if he stuck with him. But Aymes insisted. He said the only reason he was helping Ringmaster anyway was because Ringmaster agreed to get Aymes money for college. In fact, that was one of the first things Aymes asked about."

"Eh, can't fault him there." Jasper said. "University's expensive. Becoming a supervillain to pay for it is understandable."

Thea shrugged. "Anyway, Aymes's software isn't modified the way Ringmaster's stuff is, so I was able to sneak in a tracker we can use to read his future messages without triggering any alarms. It's unlikely he'll ever notice it."

"Great." Jasper looked up. "Oh look, here he comes now."

"Before you go, could I have Mia's chip?" Thea asked. "I'm ready to put her in the android."

"Promise you'll be careful with her." Jasper pulled out her sphere and ejected the A.I. chip. "And the new A.I., whatever you're calling it."

"Chloe," Thea said. "And yes, I'll be careful with them. Even though they're A.I., not living things that can feel emotion."

"They might not be able to feel bad, but I can and would if anything happened to them."

Aymes reached his table. Thea waved her hand to catch his attention, then pointed at the sphere. "This was on the floor by your chair. Is it yours?"

"Yeah, it is. Thanks." Aymes took it and frowned. "Weird, I thought I had it with me."

"Thea, are you going to come help me with the ramp thing?" Jasper asked after Aymes turned away.

"I'm already putting the flyers everywhere I possibly can on local net pages," Thea told her. "And do you really need more than two or three people for the job?"

"No, but I thought I'd invite you so you could spend some quality time with your family."

"Right. Quality time stealing a carrier vehicle with a ramp. That I will set up for you to control remotely so that only you can use it, in order to win a race that you really don't need to win, but insist on winning anyway because you have the desire to prove yourself to a bunch of criminals?"

Jasper blinked. "Okay. Have fun with your robots."

Chapter Sixty-Four
Theatre Kids Scare The Living !#@% Out Of Me

Grace wandered around the science fair with Dax, amazed by the variation in projects. And skill level. There were kids who had built mind-blowing inventions on par with Thea's androids, and kids who had clearly slapped together a poster the night before. Or possibly the morning of. Maybe even fifteen minutes before the fair started.

"Are we just going to keep walking around while Jasper races?" Grace asked.

Dax shrugged. "I was going to watch Holly in the musical when it started."

"You really don't need to do that," Holly muttered into her comm.

"Well, I am. We've been through the whole fair three times anyway."

"I'll come, too," Grace added. It had to be better than doing more laps.

They stopped by Thea's table on the way out. The two androids she'd built were now standing, and as Grace and Dax approached, their heads turned to watch. One was put together with mostly gold and black metal, the other with silver and black. The one with gold was taller and stockier than the silver. Both had massive gaps in their plating that exposed wire and circuitry beneath. And they didn't have much by way of faces at the moment.

"A little creepy, but cool!" Dax said.

"Like I said, they're just prototypes." Thea was typing on her laptop. "I'm going to redesign the bodies once I have access to better parts. And I want to work out bugs in the integration software, first."

"Well, we're headed to the musical, if you wanted to join us," Dax told her.

"I'm busy with an issue in Mia's navigation protocol." Thea pointed to the android with silver parts. "Mia, find me the nearest Bibi's."

"The nearest Bibi's is two-point-five light years away."

"Isn't there one down the street?" Grace asked.

"Yeah. And she's doing better than Chloe," Thea said. "Chloe, find me the nearest MoonCo."

The gold and black android spoke. "The nearest MoonCo is seven." Chloe's voice was feminine, like Mia's, but a bit deeper and a shade less gentle.

"Oh, I wanna try!" Jasper exclaimed. "Someone put a comm by Chloe."

"Isn't the race starting?" Thea asked.

"I have two minutes. Let me talk to Chloe!"

Grace pulled her comm out and held it toward the android. "Go ahead."

"Don't—" Thea started.

"Chloe, what is the powerhouse of the cell?" Jasper asked.

The android answered, "According to a net search, the mitochondria is the powerhouse of the cell."

"Uh, I don't know what you mean by bugs. Sounds like she's working just fine."

"Again, that's not grammatically correct," Thea replied. "Jasper, stop messing with—"

"Sorry gotta go the race is starting! Wish me luck!"

Grace slid the comm back in her ear. "I thought you said you didn't need luck."

"Yeah, but I'll take what I can get." Grace could practically hear Jasper winking.

Grace and Dax left Thea to her work and walked to the auditorium, where they found seats near the front. The lights dimmed moments after they sat down.

The cast was halfway through the opening number when Thea spoke over comms. "Guys? One of my monitor drones detected movement outside. Red Blades are entering the building."

Jasper groaned. "Of course they are," she said. "All right, hang tight, I'm on my way."

"Wait, how many?" Grace asked.

"Six," Thea answered.

"We can handle them, right?" Grace stood up. "Holly?"

Onstage, Holly moved in unison with a row of twirling dancers in old-fashioned astronaut costumes. "You'll have to wait for the musical number to end," she said through clenched teeth.

As it turned out, they didn't. The opening number was still going when three Blades stumbled onto the stage. It took the audience a moment to realize that the men with blasters who sent the ensemble running and screaming were not part of the show. Then, they joined in the screaming.

Dax sprinted to the stage. Grace tossed aside her jacket, flew up, and dropped onto the back of one of the Blades. Dax and Holly each took another. While they were able to quickly disarm their opponents, Grace struggled to get the blaster out of her Blade's hands. Someone's finger brushed the trigger, and a blast of red light blew a hole in the wall.

The auditorium lights went out, and the complete darkness made people scream louder. Three spotlights came on, each pointing directly at a Blade's face and blinding them.

"Aymes is on lights," Holly said. She saluted into the darkness before kicking her Blade in the gut.

Grace knocked the blaster from the hand of the Blade in front of her. She swung at his jaw and sent him down with it. He climbed back up immediately, but the spotlight stayed on his face, and shielding his eyes didn't seem to do him much good.

Apparently bolstered by the Blades being blinded, the fact that Grace and the others were fighting them, and probably a lot of iced coffee, the musical cast returned to the stage and joined the battle. They weren't exactly good, but they did have strength in numbers. Holly darted between moving legs and swinging fists to snatch up the three blasters.

While the theatre kids beat up the unarmed gang members, Grace and the others slipped off the stage and into the hallway.

"Thea, you good?" Holly asked.

"I'm being chased around the hallways by dudes with blasters, so, no."

"Where?"

"I don't know. These halls all look the same!" Thea exclaimed. "I'll try to head back toward the fair, but I left in the first place because I didn't want these guys catching anyone in the crossfire."

Grace, Holly, and Dax flew around a corner, and—

"Ow!" Grace smacked into someone and stumbled to the floor. "Sorry!"

"No need to apologize, I can't feel pain."

Grace looked up at the black and silver android standing over her. "Oh—I—what?"

She held out a hand to help Grace up. "It's me. Mia. Mitochondria."

"Yes, I see that." Grace frowned. "Wait, Jasper, is Mia short for Mitochondria?"

"Duh," Jasper replied. "I didn't name her, though,"

"Yeah, you did," Holly said, folding her arms. "You had her when you found us!"

"Never said I named her. Now leave me alone. I'm busy."

The taller android behind Mia waved. "Hi, I'm Chloe."

"Where's Thea?" Dax asked.

"Thea wandered off. We're looking for her," Mia explained.

"Uh, wandered off or ran off?" Grace asked.

"Yes, she was running."

"Look out!" Chloe shouted.

Grace, Dax, and Holly whirled around as a Blade came around the corner behind them and raised his blaster. Nothing happened. Frowning, he examined the weapon, searching for the problem. Then, he dropped to the ground.

Thea stood behind him. She shook out her wrist. "There are two more Blades around here somewhere—" She looked up. "Oh god, what are Mia and Chloe doing?"

"Helping," Chloe said.

"You gave us combat programming," Mia added.

"You did *what* to our children?" Jasper demanded.

"Jasper, aren't you racing? And yes, I thought they could be helpful." Thea walked toward the group and flung out her arms in exasperation. "But they're nowhere near ready yet!"

The last two Blades appeared at the other end of the hall, holding blasters.

Thea's fists clenched. "They're not close enough for me to—everyone get down!"

While everyone else dove out of the way, Holly went for the other Blade's blaster and held it up. "Thea!" she shouted.

Thea nodded. Holly fired. Her shot missed, but it forced the approaching Blades to slow down.

Grace climbed to her feet and tensed. Voices rose in the distance, joined by thundering footsteps. She frowned. "Do you guys hear that?"

Confused, the Blades halted and looked behind them. Their eyes went wide with confusion, then even wider with alarm.

The first kids of the stampede came around the corner, dressed in blue and white sports uniforms, carrying streamers and balloons, and screaming. Something blasted music.

"What is this?" Holly asked, gesturing wildly with her blaster. As the rest of the crowd emerged, so did the giant stuffed creature they were carrying. Their mascot.

"Oh, this is the invasion," Thea said calmly.

Dax stood up. "The what?"

"Are those kids from Blue Trench?" Grace asked.

"Yeah, it's all over the local media," Thea said. "There's a big inter-school sporting event next week, so everyone's trying to intimidate their rivals. These kids are basically planning to leave streamers and confetti and cardboard cutouts of tardigrades everywhere before their games against the sea goats."

"I love how schools have taken something as simple as teaching kids to read and count and turned it into an aggressive competition," Jasper said.

"Jasper, if you're not going to help, shut up," Holly snapped.

The Blades' alarm persisted as the stampede drew closer with no signs of stopping. Holly took the opportunity to shoot them both in the shoulders. A few kids at the front of the crowd slowed.

Before they could fully process what was happening, Grace pointed at the Blades laying on the floor. "Hey guys, let's grab those sea goats and, uh, put them on the roof!"

This earned cheers and applause from the rival kids as they scooped up the Blades and carried them off. The kids left a trail of blue glitter and white streamers in their wake. A few balloons drifted free of the pack, too.

One of the Blades, still holding his blaster, aimed at Grace and fired. Grace moved, but in the split second she had, she realized it wouldn't be fast enough. Her eyes widened and—

Something clattered to the floor in front of her.

"Chloe!" Thea shouted.

Grace knelt next to the android. "Is she okay?"

Thea raced over, dropped to her knees, and slid to Chloe's side. The android's chest plate had been blown open by the blast.

"I can't shoot at the Blades. I could hit one of the kids. But they're still armed," Holly warned. "We need to move."

"Hang on," Thea said. She opened a compartment on Chloe's neck and pulled out a chip.

"Thea, look out—"

This time, Mia jumped in the path of the shot.

"Wow, they're fast," Dax said as the android collapsed in a smoking pile.

"They have computers for brains, of course they're fast!" Thea moved to Mia and removed her chip. "And now I'm going to avenge them and kick that guy's ass!"

"Aren't their chips fine?" Holly asked. "You can just put them in another—"

Thea slid them in her pocket. "For Mia and Chloe!"

"For Mia and Chloe!" Dax exclaimed, pumping a fist in the air.

"Dax, don't encourage—ugh, fine," Holly said. "For Mia and Chloe! Even though they're fine!"

"For Mia and Chloe!" Grace repeated as they sprinted toward the crowd of kids.

The same Blade lifted his blaster again but struggled to aim with the kids bouncing him up and down. The other Blade—who was being dragged by a pair of athletes at the edge of the crowd—had lost his blaster. After a moment of fumbling, though, he managed to draw dagger from his side. Grace spread her wings and took to the air. She crashed into the Blade and tumbled to the ground with him.

He stabbed at her, and she barely managed to grab his wrist before the dagger reached her chest. She forced the wrist to the ground. While he fought to break free from her grasp, she punched him in the stomach. He grimaced but kept his hold on the weapon.

A kid marching by stepped on the Blade's arm. The Blade grunted in pain, and the dagger clattered to the ground.

Grace snatched it and pointed it at his throat. "How did you know I was here?"

The Blade chuckled. "Our network on other worlds isn't nearly as extensive as Kronos, but we do have eyes everywhere. We've been scouting race locations, since you seem to have developed a rivalry with Van Terra." With a cold smile, he added, "You can be as careful as you want. But sooner or later, we will get our hands on you."

The Blades had more resources than Jasper had expected, apparently. Grace rose to her feet and pointed at the Blade. "This guy just said that tardigrades suck! Are we going to take that?"

There was a chorus of no's as kids eagerly scooped up the Blade to carry him off. The rest of the crowd disappeared around the next corner, leaving Grace and the others standing in a hallway littered with confetti and glitter. While Grace had dealt with the Blade, Holly had managed to retrieve the blaster from the other one.

"I think Jasper had the right idea, dropping out of elementary school," Thea said.

Chapter Sixty-Five
Objects In Mirror Are Losing

Six Blades. The team could handle six Blades. Still, Jasper couldn't help feeling on edge as she navigated the first part of the race course. Her apprehension increased as the first racers entered the neighborhood she and Thea had crafted the fake flyers for. Even if her plan worked, she had to make sure no one else used the ramp. She let herself drift to the back of the pack, ignoring smug looks from people who passed her.

The blaring of horns, confused shouting, and angry yelling reached Jasper's ears sooner than she expected. She moved up onto the sidewalk, turned a corner, and grinned.

The street was packed with vehicles. More vehicles filling driveways blocked the path of racers seeking any gap in the crowd to squeeze through. It seemed that everyone in East Marina wanted to get their hands on the free electronics that were allegedly being handed out at this location.

Jasper headed for the carrier truck parked in a driveway at the edge of the traffic jam. The home's owners were out of town, and the fake construction tape was holding up just fine. Jasper burst through the tape, and once she was clear of the crowd, she pressed the button on the remote Thea had given her. The vehicle's ramp lowered. She shot across the yard.

It wasn't until she was in the air that people noticed her.

Other racers fought to get to the ramp first, but it was already lifting up out of reach. Jasper tightened her grip and braced herself for the landing. She slammed onto a roof, slid down the side, and drove into the less crowded street on the other side of the home.

This was the best idea she'd had in a while. By the time she reached the boardwalk, a few other racers had gotten through the heavy traffic, but they were far behind her. She reached the escalators to Blue Trench and turned on the motorcycle's antigravity, allowing her to move up onto the ceiling of the glass tube and shoot past everyone on the escalator.

She passed a group of roughly forty teenagers coming up on other escalator. Their faces were covered in paint, and they were blasting music and carrying a range of party supplies.

"Weirdos," Jasper muttered as she passed them.

The glass tunnel entered the sea, and blue light spilled onto the escalator. People behind Jasper screamed, prompting her to look back. She groaned. South Siren had reached the escalator.

"You're not taking first from me this time," Jasper muttered as she considered her array of weapons. She didn't want to hit any civilians, though she doubted South Siren cared as much.

The civilians didn't seem to care much either. Some scrambled farther down the escalator, but others paused to take videos and pictures. And scream the villains' names.

Jasper drew the biggest dagger she had and watched South Siren get closer. And closer. She could push her speed higher, but she wanted to take care of South Siren now, before they got close to the finish line.

South Siren's hekten—who'd made a speedy recovery from its neoworm infection—adjusted itself as South Siren raised her arm. Jasper reached the bottom of the escalator and twisted in the air to land upright to land on the tile floor of Blue Trench's main promenade. South Siren hit the ground next to her. Jasper slashed at her tires. South Siren swerved and dodged, and her hekten fired.

Jasper raised the dagger to block the blast, and the blade exploded in her hand. The hekten's beak opened to fire again, but a water fountain forced Jasper and South Siren to separate to go around.

The long, rectangular fountain stretched out to the next intersection. Jasper spotted a wet floor sign ahead. She drew a knife and threw it at the sign to knock it flat against the edge of the fountain. As she passed a table in front of a cafe, she grabbed an empty chair.

The sign worked as a ramp, but Jasper didn't get enough air to go over the fountain, instead flying straight through the spray of water. She came out the other side and swung the chair. It smacked into South Siren hard and knocked her off her motorcycle. The vehicle tipped and slid across the ground.

Jasper continued down Blue Trench's promenade, keeping an eye on the tiny map overlaid on her screen. Another escalator took her to an upper level of the underwater city, where she shot through the front doors of a circular restaurant and took a winding path through the tables and soft blue light.

She was halfway through when a shadow moved over her. A glance up revealed a massive golden fish passing over the restaurant's glass ceiling.

When Jasper burst out of the doors at the other end of the restaurant, she dropped off a balcony onto a walkway. A thud came from behind her a few moments later. South Siren was back up, and not too far behind. She had a good shot at catching up to Jasper before the end of the race.

Jasper's gaze flicked to the right, to the city below. And to the massive roller coaster standing between her and the finish line. She'd originally planned to go around, but it was technically marked as part of the path on Ringmaster's course map.

It gave her a terrible, terrible idea.

Numbers flashed in her vision, telling her how fast the coaster was moving, how long each section of track had before it would come rolling through. She hopped onto the walkway railing, waved at South Siren, and let herself fall off.

Jasper landed on the peak of the track's highest drop. She leaned forward, and the motorcycle rolled over the edge, sending her into a vertical drop. Laughing, she flung her arms out to each side.

As she neared the bottom, she hit the gas and shot up the next portion of the track. Up, down, around curves, and—

A loop. Small enough that Jasper hadn't noticed it in the initial survey of the ride. She glanced back. The roller coaster was speeding toward her. She glanced down. There was nowhere else for her to go. She eyed the loop again, wondering if she could move fast enough to make it.

Eh, maybe, but her second idea seemed slightly less risky. Emphasis on slightly. Jasper looked back again as she slowed down. The timing had to be perfect. *Three, two, one...*

She jumped the motorcycle with as much strength as she could muster, possibly setting a personal record in the process. The coaster shot under her. She flipped herself upside down in the air and reached out with her cybernetic arm to grab the back end. It could handle a lot, but this would be a new test of strength. Maybe she should have tried the first option. Oh god, what if ripped her arm off?

It didn't, but the pain was enough to make Jasper shout. Her eyes stung as her motorcycle slammed back down on the track. The coaster went around the loop and over another hill. As they neared the top, Jasper let go, gasping for air. Her entire body trembled.

She veered off the track and fell. Past another section of track, past a second coaster cart shooting by, past the balcony Ringmaster watched the race from, his expression unreadable.

Jasper drew her grappling hook and fired at a walkway. The hook caught. She sailed over a crowd of people yelling and pointing and let go. The landing was rough, and the grappling hook slipped from her hand, but she managed to keep herself upright. At least, long enough to cross the finish line.

First place.

She couldn't even manage a weak smile. Her hands shook violently. Even though other racers were approaching, she stopped and stumbled off the motorcycle.

"Status?" Jasper gasped. "Are you all okay?"

"We're fine," Thea said. "You?"

Jasper dragged her motorcycle through the outdoor seating of a cafe. She grabbed a bottle of Nova Cora right out of some dude's hand, ignoring his surprised cry. "I'm fine. I took first." She chugged the entire drink in seconds and tossed the bottle into a recycling bin as she passed.

"Good. All that work wasn't for nothing," Holly said. "I mean, that that was entirely unnecessary, and you've only made yourself a bigger target. But congrats."

Jasper didn't have the strength to come up with a response other than, "I'll meet you all back at the hotel."

She dragged the motorcycle into an alley between two shops, mentally planning a route back to East Marina. Something moved overhead. A figure jumped off one of the shop roofs and landed in front of her.

"You're insane," South Siren said. "What made you think you could pull that off?"

Jasper shrugged. "I'm Van Terra. Idiot." She put on a nonchalant front, but her hands tightened around the handlebar as she braced herself for an attack.

No attack. Not today, anyway. "One of these days, I'm going to kill you," South Siren hissed before turning and storming off.

Chapter Sixty-Six
Wounds You Can't Stitch Up

When Jasper first returned to the hotel room, Dax asked if she had any injuries she needed healed. She'd brushed him off, insisting she only had a few minor bruises. She'd believed herself, too, but she was still shaky as they ate dinner and every movement was hell.

"You sure you're okay?" Dax asked.

"I'm fine." Jasper absentmindedly watched Thea plug Mia's chip into a smartsphere and set it on the table.

Holly's stern gaze was on Jasper. "Hey, Jasper, what were you saying earlier about not naming Mia?" she asked. "Where'd you get her?"

Jasper rubbed her forehead, not quite processing the question. "Sorry, what was that?"

"No, no, it's fine, you don't have to tell us about your past." Holly took a bite of her roasted—whatever Dax had cooked. Some kind of bird?

"Holly," Thea warned.

"What did she ask?" Jasper asked. No one seemed to hear her.

"I just wish we would talk about the fact that she claims to be seventeen but looks the same as she did four years ago when she found us!" Holly threw her fork on the table. "She dodges so many questions. Even about why she rescued us."

Dax's eyes widened. He threw an anxious glance at Jasper.

"Either she was lying then, or she's lying now." Holly sounded less angry and more...disappointed? Jasper was having a hard time reading her. "You all know I'm right. I'm tired of not talking about it."

Grace leaned toward Jasper. "Jasper? You listening?" Something about the concern in her voice, her eyes, made Jasper's heart squeeze.

Jasper stood up. "What? I'm not—"

Grace stood too, eyes still on her.

"Holly, I want answers too, but I don't think now's a good time," Thea said. "She's clearly in one of her...weird moods."

"What? Tired? Hurt?" Holly asked. "Then why doesn't she tell us what's wrong!"

"Maybe we should try talking to Jade later—"

Jasper froze. "What did you call me?"

"I—" Thea frowned. "I don't know. I think my brain just slipped."

"Jade." Jasper's hands tightened at her sides. "You said Jade."

"We all say the wrong thing sometimes. It's not a big deal." Holly was standing now.

"Why is everyone standing?" Jasper asked.

"You stood first," Holly told her. "And Dax and Thea are still sitting."

"Jasper, is something wrong?" Grace asked, her voice dropping to a near whisper. She took a step closer to Jasper. The movement made Jasper's heart pound twice as hard. "You're acting weird."

"This is normal," Holly said.

"Why?"

Good question. Jasper walked away from the table. "I need some air." She stepped onto the balcony, not bothering to close the sliding door behind her.

Grace followed a moment later. After a long pause, she said, "Every time I start to think I've figured you out, there seems to be another layer."

Jasper wrapped her hands around the balcony railing, focusing on the cold metal against her palms. The cold metal under her skin, wrapped around her bones and racing through her blood. "Why are you still here? I'm going to get you killed." She'd already gotten Naomi killed. Gotten Mylo killed. Killed—

"No, you're not," Grace said. "And I'm definitely going to get myself killed if I run off on my own."

The others came out onto the balcony and gathered around Jasper.

"Oh, so you're all going to try to get answers this time?" Jasper asked, glancing back at them.

"We've been here for years, and you never bothered telling us anything," Holly replied. There was an odd strain in her voice. Almost as if she were fighting back tears. But that couldn't be right.

Jasper looked forward again. The city lights, the sunset sky, the distant horizon, it all blurred together in her vision. *Jade.* Had the name been lingering in Thea's mind the whole time, buried somewhere in her subconscious? Were there five years of memories locked in there somewhere?

Was there some way for Holly and Dax and Thea to remember everything they'd experienced at Laika before getting warped to Kronos?

Jasper turned around and sank to the floor of the balcony, her back against the railing. "I think I broke something. During the race." Multiple somethings.

Dax knelt next to her and rested a hand on her shoulder. "Feels like mostly cracks and fractures," he said after a moment. He grimaced. "Still, not great. Once I get everything healing, it'll take care of itself over the next day or so."

While the blue glow washed over Jasper's face, she said, "When they put the cybernetics in me, they gave me a serum that makes me heal faster."

"Who's 'they?'" Holly asked.

"Sky Labs," Jasper replied. "I was kidnapped from Earth when I was twelve and forced to work in the Governor's Palace for a few years, before they took me to the labs for their experiments." She rested her arms on her knees, turned her head, and kept her gaze glued to the traffic on the street below, not wanting to see the others' expressions. "I don't know what was in the serum, but that was—" She frowned. "What's sixty-eight minus seventeen?"

"Fifty-one," Mia answered through the sphere in Thea's hand.

"Thanks, Mia," Jasper said. "Fifty-one years ago."

"You're sixty-eight?" Dax asked incredulously.

Jasper swallowed. "There's a lot of stuff I haven't told you guys. Some of it—well, I haven't figured it all out yet."

After a long, painful silence, Holly said, "Sixty-eight? Do you know if the not aging thing is permanent, or…?"

"I don't," Jasper told her. "Which is why I'd like to get my hands on those lab records. If I can find out what it is they put in me, or track down other people they used it on…maybe I can get answers."

And, of course, there was the walking, breathing, nearly-identical-copy-of-Grace thing. Another secret.

Jasper pushed herself to her feet. She felt—better? No. The anxiety from earlier was gone, but an empty feeling had overtaken her, rather than any sort of relief. The others clearly still had more questions, but a few glances between them suggested that they all felt it best to give her some space, first. The rest of dinner was eaten with hollow conversation about the mission and the news and the city.

Jasper laid in bed that night, exhausted but unable to sleep. When she turned down her audio input, blocking out traffic and the others' breathing and voices in the halls, she could hear the faint hum of the computer in her skull. Her own heartbeat. Her lungs filling with air.

What was she doing? Where was all of this going? The only thing pushing her forward was the hope that when they caught up with Ringmaster, they'd find a way to expose Starr.

Jasper's cybernetics, Grace's clone, the investigation into the warps—they all had to be connected. Syrus Starr was pursuing *something*. What chance did the team have of stopping him? Jasper had been trying for years, and Starr seemed to grow more invincible with every passing day. And no one on Kronos cared.

She guessed she was still going because she would be in pain either way. Sure, chasing Starr meant fighting and falling and breaking, and she could run from that. But she couldn't outrun this ache that settled into her chest at night.

If she was going to spend her days burning with rage, she may as well put it to good use.

V. RINGMASTER'S CARNIVAL

Chapter Sixty-Seven
When The Moon Smacks Your Eye

Kronos was the proud center of orbit to two beautiful moons. Hedas was small, had a rocky terrain, and was covered in poisonous gas that kept it uninhabited. A bit of a problem child, but a pretty sight in the night sky all the same.

Iros, on the other hand, was the breathtaking bigger sibling. A few small cities dotted its glittering surface, and beyond their streets, crystals that formed on top of the moon's crust shimmered rainbow under the ever-black sky.

The smallest populated area was less a city and more a small town centered around a carnival. The Carnival of Iros appeared to be a reputable organization to the public, but anyone involved with crime on a serious level knew it was run by Ringmaster, both as a money-making operation and as a way for him to recruit young talent into his ranks.

Getting recruited was the team's plan.

"Remember, we're on his turf now," Jasper told the others as they exited the small spaceport at the carnival's edge. "Keep your guard up. We'll have to stay in disguise twenty-four-seven. Or how ever many hours are in a day here." She scanned the flashing lights and spinning rides in the distance. "I wonder why he's brought the race to his carnival."

Thea tipped her head back and raised an eyebrow. "It might have something to do with the giant hole in the sky."

Jasper followed her gaze. Her heart sank deep into the pit of her stomach, stirring up an all-too-familiar feeling of dread. "Oh."

Seeing the warp was somehow worse than she remembered. And it was alarmingly close to the moon. Not close enough for it to have any pull, though. Not yet.

"What are people saying about it?" Jasper asked. "Is it in the news?"

Thea projected a holoscreen from her watch. Multiple social media and news feeds popped up in a grid and began to scroll on their own. "No one has an explanation, but I guess that's not surprising. There's mostly just...jokes."

"Jokes?" Jasper's brow furrowed.

"Yeah. This guy posted a picture of it and said, 'anyone wanna go on a date with me in the giant hole in the sky?' And someone else said they hope it destroys Iros before their astrobiology test tomorrow."

"Kids these days." Jasper shook her head as she led the team onward. "What's happening in Aymes's messages?"

"He's on his way here to help manage the race, but Ringmaster hasn't given him any new information."

A thick layer of dirt had been laid over the carnival grounds, giving the patrons something softer to walk on than sharp crystals. There were also sparse patches of grass planted here and there. Flashing neon lights from the rides and game booths illuminated it all. Workers dressed as clowns wandered through the crowds, juggling and performing magic tricks to entertain people waiting in line.

At the center of all the rides and performers and wafting scents of carnival food stood a massive red and white tent where the circus shows took place. The smaller tent next to it was their destination. Jasper waved as she approached the worker standing outside the tent. "We have an appointment to audition," she told him. "We called earlier."

He jutted a thumb at the open tent flap behind him. "In there."

Roughly twenty other people waited inside the tent in a loose line. Carnival workers walked up and down the line, asking for names and basic information.

"Do all of these people have powers or something?" Grace whispered as a boy nearby lit a flame in his hand. The firelight reflected off the shiny gold wig she'd be wearing during her time on Iros, part of Jasper's attempt to keep her from being recognized.

"Either that, or they've been training for a long time," Jasper answered. "Ringmaster's only interested in people that can handle working for him. Or do him some favors, at the very least."

Thea leaned in and whispered. "I recognize some of the workers. That man by the front of the line attacked me and Dax at Dr. Prime's apartment."

One of the workers held up an arm to get the crowd's attention. "Listen up!" she shouted. "We'll take you or your group to the main tent one by one so you can audition. Most of you, if you're accepted, will be background performers. Work hard, and you can earn a bigger part in the show." She rested the hand on her hip. "You'll be given a place to stay in one of the outer tents, unless we decide to make you a bigger act, in which case you'll get a room in the main facilities building."

While she led the first person in line out of the tent, Jasper gestured for the others to huddle in a circle. "We need to get into the main building."

"It's not like we have much control over where they assign us," Dax said. "Shouldn't we just do our best?"

"No. We need better than our best. A few flips aren't going to cut it. Remember, they aren't just looking for a show, they're looking for abilities that will be useful to Ringmaster." Jasper lowered her voice. "I have a few ideas."

"You're going to come up with a new act for us ten minutes before we're auditioning?" Holly hissed.

"Yes." Jasper explained her plan, most of which she came up with as the words left her mouth. It was all based on the very quick X-ray scan she'd taken of the big tent as they'd walked past it.

The others stared at her. Holly folded her arms. "That's a lot to do without any practice."

"Can you do it?" Jasper asked. "If there's any part someone isn't comfortable with, we'll cut it. But displaying the extent of our abilities is the best way to impress them."

"My part will be easy," Thea said with a shrug.

Holly sighed. "I can do mine."

"Me too," Dax added.

Jasper glanced at Grace, who swallowed and nodded. "Me too."

"You sure?" Jasper asked, scanning Grace's expression for any sign of fear. "I know you've got a lot of strength, but you haven't had much practice using it."

Grace lifted her chin. "Yeah. I can do it."

Jasper grinned. "Great. I'm going to grab my motorcycle from outside and track down some glitter."

Chapter Sixty-Eight
Not Our Circus

It became harder and harder for Grace to hold still as they moved closer to the front of the line. She fiddled with her hands and hair as she ran through the messy plan Jasper had laid out again and again. Her fear wasn't that she couldn't do everything, but that she would forget what she was supposed to be doing in the first place.

"Don't stress if you have to improvise," Jasper had told them before hurrying off. "This is about showing off our abilities. As long as you look like you know what you're doing, we'll be fine."

Grace took a deep breath.

A worker paused next to Grace and the others and looked them over before returning her gaze to her tablet. "Next party, follow me."

"I've got control of their lights," Thea muttered as they approached the big tent. "And speakers." She turned a sphere over in her hand. "The music Jasper wanted was—oh, here we are."

Holly pulled her hair up. Dax shook out his hands.

Grace shrugged off her jacket as they entered the tent. Her wings stretched out, revealing a key component of their plan: temporary gold spray paint coating every last feather. It made it less likely that anyone would realize she was Governor Starr's biggest target. As Jasper had pointed out, she wasn't the only winged being wandering the Janus System.

Still, Grace could only hope that the spray paint—combined with one of Holly's makeup looks and the wig—would be enough.

Her heart quickened at the sight of carnival workers waiting for a show, the sight of empty stadium seating towering over them, the sight of the tent ceiling barely visible in the darkness above.

"Whenever you're ready," a man said.

Grace tossed the jacket to the ground. She only needed confidence for a few minutes. Like Jasper had promised, various props and parts were set up around the edge of the arena, including a ramp that needed to be moved next to the tent's rear entrance. Grace's job.

"Everyone ready?" Thea asked.

Holly, Dax, and Grace nodded. Thea snapped her fingers, and the lights went out. Music took over the tent's speakers.

Grace took to the air and flew to the ramp, having only her memory to guide her in the darkness. Her hands found it, and she dragged it toward the entrance.

Meanwhile, a spotlight fell on Holly, revealing she'd changed her hair color to purple. It went out and came back on to illuminate black hair, then flashed once more on her red hair. A second spotlight appeared on Dax.

"Jasper?" Grace whispered as she let go of the ramp.

"Ready," Jasper replied. "I've got eyes on all of you."

Grace swooped down, emerging from the black to grab Holly and Dax and throw them into the air. She winced at the strain on her arms, but her pain quickly shifted to apprehension. If Jasper wasn't fast enough—

An engine revved. Jasper shot in through the tent entrance. She hadn't donned her racing suit or helmet, but Grace supposed the costume would give away her identity.

The two spotlights combined and moved onto Jasper as she flew off the ramp and passed under Holly and Dax. She released the handlebar and reached out her arms, one to grab Holly and one to grab Dax. They both took hold of the motorcycle.

More lights came on, shining white and red on the three as they landed. Jasper slammed the front brakes, sending Holly and Dax back into the air. As they landed, Jasper flipped over the front of the motorcycle, touched down, and threw it over her head. Holly and Dax caught it together and barely kept it from touching the ground.

The white spotlights combined into one and moved up to where Thea stood on the trapeze tower. The drones she'd begrudgingly agreed to sacrifice for the show formed a swarm and flew toward Jasper, who stood alone in the red spotlight.

Grace's turn again. She dropped down to the motorcycle, grabbed the sword strapped to its side, and tossed it to Jasper. Despite Jasper's insistence she could catch it, Grace's heart refused to beat properly until Jasper had the sword safely in her hand.

Jasper took down the drones one by one, twisting and jumping and spinning as Thea sent them at her from every direction. Once she'd sent the last one crashing into the shadows, she strolled over to the motorcycle, raising up her hand as she walked. With her other, she rested the blade on her palm and made a cut.

Grace landed on the ground by Holly and Dax. She helped shoulder the motorcycle, leaving Dax free to step toward Jasper and lift his own hand. A blue glow wiped the wound from Jasper's skin. She tossed the sword to the healed hand and held up her other. The same cut appeared in this palm, accompanied by the glow.

"Finale time," Jasper muttered as the spotlight moved off her and the gash healed itself. "So far, so good."

The light illuminated Grace as she took the full weight of the motorcycle from Holly and threw it to Jasper. Her arms burned with the effort. She spread her wings and jumped.

"Ready?" Thea asked. A golden light moved onto her.

Grace nodded and held out her arms.

Thea jumped. Grace caught her, and they dropped halfway to the ground before her wings caught enough air to hover. Grace locked eyes with Jasper, who gave her the slightest nod. Grace dropped Thea.

Thea landed on the motorcycle still held high in Jasper's arms. Jasper hid it well, but Grace glimpsed a brief flash of pain cross her face.

Holly locked her fingers together. Dax stepped into her hand, and she lifted him above her head. Holly jumped. Grace grabbed her and lifted them both up.

"Strike a pose, please," Jasper said through clenched teeth.

The last note of the song played. Thea, standing on the motorcycle's seat, put a hand on her hip. Jasper pushed the motorcycle up higher, extending her arms to their full length, and forced a smile. Dax, seemingly out of sheer panic, threw up a peace sign. Holly shifted his weight into one of her hands and put the other in a fist under her chin. Grace couldn't do much with her arms, but she stretched out her wings to their full length.

It was at this moment that the small bomb Jasper had set went off, which she'd filled with...glitter. Rainbow glitter that rained down on all of them.

"If I find glitter on my body when this is all over, I'm going to kill someone," Holly muttered.

Thea turned off the spotlights and restored the tent to its ordinary lighting. Everyone dropped to the ground, and Jasper set down the motorcycle. Relief coursed through Grace's muscles.

The workers whispered to each other for a few moments before one stepped forward. The man's gaze swept over the five. "Who's in charge?" he asked.

"Me." Jasper stepped forward.

"Congratulations. You're in. We're going to make some adjustments, but we'd like to include you as an opening act. You'll stay in the main facility."

Jasper grinned and bowed. "Thank you."

"I'll escort you there and get you some costumes. Follow me." As they left the tent, the man asked, "What are your names?"

"I'm Jay." Jasper pointed to Holly, Dax, Thea, then Grace. "They're Red, Jack, Ten, and Lyre."

"You can call me Viper. I'm in charge of the shows this season, so I'll be overseeing your performance."

Viper was a big guy with plenty of muscle. His pale skin bordered on white, except for the places elaborately tattooed with pitch black ink. His eyes were red and glowed in low light, and his shiny gold hair was pulled back in a short ponytail.

He led the team into a plain white building behind the big tent. "This building isn't just performer rooms," Viper said. "There are offices and storage closets. They're locked for a reason. Don't go snooping where you shouldn't, keep to the living spaces, and you'll be fine." He stopped in front of a door. "This suite will be for your team. Drop off your stuff. I'll be back in a few minutes, and we'll get started."

White walls and floor tiled with a red-and-black checkerboard pattern greeted them. The suite's five beds were spread across two rooms connected by an open doorway. There was one attached bathroom, and not much by way of furnishings. But it was surprisingly clean, and the lone table in the middle of the room held a basket of fruit and nutrient bars.

While they had some time alone—and after Thea confirmed she couldn't sense any recording devices in the suite—Jasper explained that there were three types of people working at the carnival. There were the performers, of course, a.k.a. the wannabe villains using the job as a starting point. There were also legitimate employees, mostly teenagers who simply ran the rides or sold food and didn't know who their boss really was.

And the third type, the higher-ranking workers, were Ringmaster's henchpeople. She suspected that Viper was way up at the top of the food chain.

"So, why are they putting us in the main facility if there's sensitive stuff here?" Holly asked as she dropped her bag onto one of the beds. "Why not the outer tents?"

"I assume to keep a closer eye on people with more potential." Jasper shrugged. "Maybe it's a test to see if we go snooping."

Viper returned a minute later to collect them. Their next stop was a nearby building referred to as the Wardrobe. Everything inside was vaguely circus-themed and generally stuck to Ringmaster's color scheme, but there was enough variety to give them some freedom when it came to their costumes.

"I feel a little ridiculous," Thea said as she adjusted her gold jacket.

"More ridiculous than in your regular costume?" Jasper asked. "The one with the lightning bolt? And the yellow pants? And all the leather?"

"Don't worry, Thea," Holly said. "Jasper looks ten times worse than the rest of us."

Jasper shrugged as she looked herself over in the mirror. "That's showbiz, baby." If the black bodysuit, glittery tights, gold bow tie, red boots, and red jacket were excessive, she didn't care.

She clapped her hands together. "Now, listen up," she said. "I overheard a worker say something to Viper about the manager's office. Ringmaster's office, presumably. We need to get in there. Maybe Thea could hack the door while we distract everyone else at the show?"

Thea shook her head. "I ran a sweep of the security system while we were dropping our stuff off. No electronic locks—seems like everything is under old-fashioned lock and key."

Jasper shrugged. "I'll kick the door down then."

"From what I saw on cameras, all the interesting doors are a few inches of solid metal," Thea said. "Anything tough enough to get through that is going to alert everyone else in the building. I can stop the cameras from picking you up if you give me a few hours to get deeper into the system, but you're going to need an actual key from one of the workers."

"Fine. We'll have to work the act around that, then." Jasper waved her hand to flag down Viper as he walked by. "Hey, when's our first show?"

Viper paused. "We're giving you two days to refine the act and rehearse. You'll open for the show Renday night."

"That's the night of the race," Jasper muttered after he walked away.

"Why not break in sometime after the race?" Grace asked.

"Ringmaster might leave immediately after, and then we'd have to track him down wherever he goes next. The carnival is big but finding him in a city will be much more difficult." Jasper shook her head. "We're ending this here. Renday night, we catch Ringmaster."

Chapter Sixty-Nine
Nice (To Meet You)

After two days consumed almost entirely by rehearsal, Renday night finally came. The team sat outside the big tent, making their final preparations for the show. Grace stretched her arms and wings while she watched the others work. Holly was doing some final touches on Dax's makeup, while Thea did...whatever she was doing on her tablet.

Jasper moved into a handstand. "Shame we haven't had time to hang out at the carnival," she said. "I mean, I know it's run by a supervillain, but some of the rides look fun. We should come back one of these days."

Grace raised an eyebrow. "Won't the place get shut down if we succeed at stopping Ringmaster?"

Jasper laughed as she dropped out of the handstand. "Nah, there are plenty of rich people waiting around the buy this place up if the government seizes control of it." She raised her arms back in the air.

Grace moved her gaze past Jasper to a nearby roller coaster in time to watch a cart fly through its loop. "Well, I've never been on a carnival ride, but if they're half as fun as flying..."

"Well, I've never gone flying around on wings, so I'm not sure I can make a comparison," Jasper said. She flashed Grace an upside-down grin.

Grace laughed. "Well, maybe I can take you on a real flight some time. In exchange for a ride on a roller coaster."

Jasper sprang to her feet, her face flushed with exertion. "I suppose that's fair." She smiled, but something distant crept into her gaze. She turned and lifted her arms again.

Before Grace could think of something to follow up with, Thea picked up a smartsphere and groaned. "I grabbed the wrong sphere. I need the one with my light and sound program."

"Just go grab the right one!" Jasper said as she came up from a cartwheel.

"I'm in the middle of running a debugging on my master tablet. I can't—"

"I can grab it," Grace said. "I'm not doing anything else."

"It's in the front pocket of the bag on my bed," Thea told her.

"Be careful," Jasper added.

Grace walked to the main building. She didn't see anyone on her way to the team's suite, and grabbing the sphere only took a few seconds. On her way back out, though, she passed a group of performers standing in the hallway. She ducked her head and avoided eye contact. None of them paid her any attention.

"Where are you headed, then?" a woman asked.

"Anywhere outside the Janus System," another replied. "We haven't decided for sure yet, but the company we're going through has cheap fares to the Solar System, and we can pass for human without too much effort."

Grace stopped. Hesitated. Glanced back. "Sorry to interrupt," she said. "But did you say the Solar System?"

"Sure did," the second woman answered.

"That's where Earth is, right?"

The man next to her raised an eyebrow. "Yeah. You trying to go?"

"No. I mean, I don't—I was thinking about going." Grace nervously traced the edge of Thea's sphere with her thumb.

"You want to come with us?" One of the other women in th group folded her arms. "The bigger our group, the better our discount."

"When are you going?" Grace asked.

"Tonight."

Grace looked down at the sphere in her hands. She was taking long enough as it was. The team was waiting.

Ringmaster was waiting.

Governor Starr was waiting.

Grace shook her head. "I can't. I'm sorry. I don't know why I said anything—"

The man pulled a card out of his pocket and held it out to Grace. "If you do decide to go, this company's cheap. Plus, I get a bonus for everyone I refer."

After a moment's hesitation, Grace took the card. "Thanks."

Her hand tightened around the card as she walked away. Even if the fares were cheap, she had no money to speak of whatsoever. Jasper surely wouldn't help her get to Earth until after they dealt with Starr. And despite how terrifying her new life could be at times, Grace wanted to help take down the governor in any way she could. It was what Kara's endgame had really been, after all.

Kara had died trying to save Grace. The least Grace could do was see her mission through, even if it wasn't exactly in the way she'd intended.

Grace dropped the card in a trash bin on her way out of the building.

Chapter Seventy
The Okayest Show

Jasper had needed to walk a fine line with Viper, convincing him to let the team incorporate all of the elements she needed for the plan to work without being too pushy.

One, she had to swing by the front row of the audience, specifically the section where Ringmaster's henchpeople sat. This came with the added bonus of getting to use a grappling hook.

Two, she needed a blackout.

Three, she needed a very loud distraction.

The team waited in the wings at the back of the circus tent as their time neared, listening to the announcer warm up the audience, watching from the shadows.

"Are you guys ready?" Jasper asked in a low voice.

"You've asked us that twenty times," Holly replied.

"Just making sure."

Grace glanced at Jasper. It was a little surprising how well she managed to pull off the borderline ridiculous gold wig Jasper had found for her. "Are you going to race?"

Jasper shrugged. "I'm going to try to find Ringmaster before the race starts, but if I don't, I'll have to show up to the race to find him."

Thea folded her arms. "And what is the plan after that, exactly?"

"We're going to catch him," Jasper said, injecting more confidence into her voice than she actually felt. "He's powerful, but not so strong that we can't knock him out and lock him up. All we need is to stop him from helping Starr, figure out what they're planning with the warps, and find physical proof that they're working together." *Easy peasy.*

"Why take Ringmaster alive?" Holly asked. "It's not like he's going to cooperate with us."

"I'd like to see what he has to say about the matter," Jasper replied. She gave a slight shrug. "Who knows? Maybe he'll be willing to expose Starr. I doubt he's loyal to anything other than the man's money and protection."

"Would you let him go in exchange for helping you?"

Before Jasper could figure out her response to Holly's question, a worker approached the team. "You're on."

The lights in the tent dimmed. Music started. One large spotlight landed on the five as they emerged, then split in two. One beam followed Holly, Dax and Thea, while the other stayed on Grace as she grabbed Jasper and flew into the air.

Holly and Dax linked their hands for Thea to step on and lifted her into the air. Thea raised her arms. Scrappy robotic birds darted out from where they'd been hidden among the audience to form a flock circling the arena.

Grace released her hold on Jasper's wrists. The spotlight followed Jasper as she fell and grabbed the first trapeze with one hand. With the other, she sent a knife flying toward Thea. She released the first trapeze and grabbed the second.

A bird swooped down to snatch the knife before it could reach Thea. Then, it turned and flew toward Jasper. Jasper tuned out the gasps from the crowd, the hum of the bird's machinery, her own heavy breathing. The only sound in the world was a ringing in her ears as the bird sliced through the trapeze rope with the knife.

She twisted in the air and lifted her hands. Grace tossed her the grappling hook. They'd practiced the throw countless times, but the fear still flashed in Grace's eyes as it sailed through the air.

Jasper caught it, aimed at a distant rafter, and fired. The hook caught. She glided a few feet over the ground before moving into the air over the audience. As she swung back, she neared the bench where Viper sat in the front row, supervising the show.

Thea snapped her fingers, and the lights went out. Jasper switched to night vision and located the ring of keys on Viper's belt. She slipped a tiny knife into her hand.

"Three, two, one," she whispered into her comm.

Thea set off the bomb. The ground trembled as Jasper sliced through the belt loop and hooked a finger through the key ring. The fireworks going off at the center of the arena, small as they were, hid the sounds of clinking metal.

Jasper released the grappling hook at the peak of her swing. Grace soared through the air to grab her. Jasper's heart skipped a beat as they collided, but Grace managed the catch perfectly.

"Good job, Angel," Jasper whispered. She offered Grace a reassuring smile.

"Oh, um, thanks," Grace stammered. Her heart pounded fast enough in her chest that one of Jasper's various sensors made note of it. She brought them to the floor of the arena in a smooth landing and let go of Jasper.

That was the end of the opening act. As the man lights came back on, more performers entered the tent and hurried into the arena, mostly by means of flips or somersaults or dancing. The plan was for the team to fade into the background for a few minutes and leave when the next act came on.

Jasper would be slipping out a little early.

After Grace released her on the ground, she and the others joined a line of dancers. Among the torch jugglers and music and streamers and ribbons and gold-painted animals, they faded from the center of attention. Jasper performed some twirls with far more enthusiasm than necessary and caught Grace restraining a laugh at the sight.

Not scared of me anymore, I hope. Jasper winked at her.

In the low light at the edge of the tent, Jasper ducked and rolled, passing under a small elephant and narrowly avoiding its feet. She popped up on the other side, darted to an exit flap and slipped out.

Jasper walked to the main facility building, periodically checking if Mia's sphere was in range. She passed by the side of the building where their rooms were located, and her brain finally linked to the A.I. "Mia, call contact one," she whispered. "Leave the message I recorded."

She circled around to the front door and paused to look up. Most stars in the black sky were overwhelmed by the lights of the carnival. A golden songbird flitted across her view and landed on top of a nearby ticket booth that had closed for the night. It looked like one of the painted animals performing in the show.

Though…it could have been the lights, but Jasper swore the bird was emitting a faint glow. She frowned.

There were no voices, no footsteps when she entered the white building. She headed for the offices, her hand tight around the keys she'd stolen from Viper. When she stopped in front of the door to the manager's office, she inspected the lock and compared an X-ray scan to the keys on the loop to find the right one. She stuck it in, turned it, and pushed the door open.

The room was empty. White floor, white walls, white ceiling, and nothing in between.

This was the office they were supposed to stay out of? The most secure place in the carnival? There had to be a secret door or something. Jasper walked to the center of the room and turned in a slow circle. No cracks, no buttons. X-ray and heat vision revealed nothing.

"You're not the first to break in here."

Jasper whirled around. Viper stood in the doorway. "It makes a great trap," he continued. "To weed out the recruits trying to spy on or steal from Ringmaster."

Jasper could handle Viper. It wasn't the dagger in his hand that sent her heart racing, but the realization that the rest of the team was in danger.

Viper threw the dagger. Jasper dodged, but it gave him the chance to rush forward, grab her, and shove her against the nearest wall. "What are you looking for?" he demanded. "Who are you, really?"

"You'll have to do better than that if you want information from me," Jasper hissed, hoping to alert the others to the danger.

Viper's grasp tightened. Jasper struggled for a moment before feigning defeat. He relaxed ever-so-slightly, and she kneed him in the stomach. The blow was enough for her to break free and duck out of his reach.

She snatched the dagger off the floor and drove it into Viper's arm when he tried to grab her again. He staggered away, leaving her free to sprint out the door.

"Guys, can you hear me?" Jasper asked as she ran. "Viper found me. Our cover's blown."

Nothing.

Footsteps signaled Viper was following. Jasper headed to the team's suite, threw her coat and helmet on over her carnival uniform, and grabbed the motorcycle from where it rested against the wall. Viper entered the room. She knocked him into the wall with the motorcycle.

Then, she climbed on, raced out of the building, and headed for the big tent.

Chapter Seventy-One
Why Does Nothing Ever Go As Planned?

Jasper must have reached the main building by now. Grace and the others stood in the shadows behind the tent and after nearly ten minutes of silence, Holly asked, "Jasper? Everything okay over there?"

Thea frowned. "Something's wrong with the comms. They aren't sending any signals out."

"You're not the only technopath around here," a woman's voice said. The carnival worker it belonged to emerged from a flap in the tent, flanked by two others.

Dax frowned. "Were you just waiting by the exit for a chance to step out and say that?"

"You cut our comms?" Holly asked, louder. "Why?"

A new voice answered behind them. "Why don't you tell me why Van Terra acts like some sort of mastermind when she only has a handful of low-level villains working for her?"

Grace turned slower than the others, afraid to see the owner of the voice.

Ringmaster studied them carefully before speaking again. "Red Holly. Jolt. I wondered what you could possibly want with Dr. Prime's spacetime warp data. And it would seem Van Terra lied about her affiliation with Alvarez, too."

Holly raised her fists. "Why don't we have a rematch."

"Four against one hardly seems fair," Ringmaster said. He waved his hand. Glowing golden bars rose from the ground, surrounding the team. A roof appeared overhead, and the cage became solid. "Maybe if Van Terra were with you, it'd be a fair fight, but she's busy walking into a trap right now."

Ringmaster circled the cage. "Grace Alvarez. What *are* you doing, helping Van Terra? Has she really turned you to the dark side so quickly?"

Grace lifted her chin. "I'm only trying to make Starr pay for what he did to me."

Ringmaster laughed. "You're fighting an uphill battle. Don't worry, I won't tell the Red Blades you're here. I may be on good terms with Starr, but I know better than to hand someone as valuable as you over to him."

A golden bird darted down from the sky and landed on Ringmaster's shoulder. "You know," he said. "I made the animals we use in our shows myself. It requires a lot of energy, but it's easier than training live beasts."

The bird dissolved into energy, and Ringmaster frowned. "It would seem Viper failed at his task."

"You sent one person to catch Jasper Van Terra?" Holly barked out a cold laugh.

Ringmaster's eyes narrowed. "He's not the only one. My employees are scouring the grounds for her as we speak." He sighed. "I'm sure she'll be here any minute to rescue you all. I'll have to move you."

The cage lifted into the air. Grace stumbled forward and wrapped her hands around the bars.

"What are you going to do with us?" Holly demanded.

Ringmaster raised an eyebrow. "You think I'm just going to tell you my plan?"

Two golden elephants emerged from the tent. In the shadows outside, the faint glow they emitted was more obvious. Ringmaster lowered the cage onto their backs. "Take them to tent seven. It should be empty," he ordered his henchpeople. "Van Terra might be able to handle my employees, but she's going to have a much harder time with me."

Chapter Seventy-Two
Mirror, Mirror

Jasper circled the big tent. No sign of the others. Still nothing on comms. She ducked inside to see if they'd wound up staying in the show longer than they were supposed to, but they were nowhere to be seen.

She walked back out and climbed onto the motorcycle. Ringmaster had to have a base—a real one—that he could monitor the park from. And with the race starting soon, it seemed the most likely place for him to be.

Jasper sped through the carnival, scanning structures with her X-ray vision. The crowd slowed her progress. The warp in the sky kept her on edge. She was running out of time.

She passed the entrance to a funhouse and hit the brakes. "Silver Hands Fright House," the sign out front read. There were several metal panels in the front of the building covered with what appeared to be intentional graffiti, mostly words that were vaguely horror or carnival related. There were a few random names as well, and one in particular caught her eye.

"Interesting," Jasper muttered. The building fit in with the rest of the carnival on the surface, but she could see rooms extending below ground, and a figure moving in them. She hopped off the motorcycle, left her helmet on the handlebars, and ran in.

She made it a few feet before smacking into one of the mirrors lining the walls. A mirror maze was certainly a great place to hide a secret room. She checked her heat vision and found the figure again. The entrance to the lower rooms seemed to be somewhere on the other side of the maze. Maybe the doorway was hidden behind a mirror?

Jasper elbowed her way through groups of visitors. A man dressed as a clown jumped out from behind a corner and screamed. Jasper screamed back, louder, and walked past with her chin held high, only to collide with another mirror.

She reached an intersection. Screams came from somewhere nearby, followed by laughter. Jasper went the other way, moving into a quieter part of the funhouse.

Chainsaw noises came from her right. Jasper strolled by a girl in a creepy mask. "Sorry to disappoint," she said. "But I'm not here to get scared. I'm looking for someone."

"Me too."

Jasper spun around in time to get smacked in the face by the fake chainsaw. She stumbled into a mirror. Blood trickled from her nose. She wiped her face with the back of her hand and ducked as the girl swung again.

"You can't beat all of us, Van Terra." The girl tossed aside the chainsaw and drew a dagger. A real dagger. The blade glinted in the low light as the girl lunged.

The weapon sliced Jasper's arm, sending blood splattering across several mirrors. Jasper hissed. She grabbed the girl's wrist and threw her as far as she could before running in the other direction.

A man appeared, reflected dozens of times in the mirrors around her. She stopped and spun in a circle, trying to identify which was the real one. Before she could figure it out, he landed a blow to her back.

Jasper hit the floor face first. As she pushed herself up, the man kicked her again. She rolled and drew the first knife from her coat that her hand found.

The man laughed and moved to stand over her. "You gonna kill me with that tiny thing?"

"It's not about size, it's about how you use it." Jasper sent the knife spinning into his neck.

She staggered to her feet as the man collapsed. Without giving him so much as a second glance, she sprinted down the hall. She hadn't been running for long when a flash of red light caught her eye. She paused and scanned the direction it had come from, wondering if she'd imagined it.

It flashed again. The blinking light helped her locate the tiny box in a corner where two mirrors met. There was a pad—a fingerprint scanner. Jasper studied the mirror hiding the basement entrance. She had no way of forcing the fingerprint scanner to let her in.

So, she checked her coat pockets, assessing what other weapons she had on her. A blaster would be best, but she'd neglected to grab one. She went with her largest dagger and jammed the hilt into the mirror.

Cracks fractured her reflection. With a roar of exasperation, she swung again. The mirror spiderwebbed into countless tiny shards. One final blow sent them raining to the ground.

"Oh, cool," Jasper muttered when she saw the opening behind the mirror. "A secret tunnel to hell." The staircase on the other side was narrow, illuminated only by a faint red glow at the bottom. The light came from under a door.

The door's handle was unlocked.

Jasper stepped through and entered a small room. Screens filled the walls from floor to ceiling, showing live security footage from around the carnival. One was an exception: it showed an aerial view of the moon's glittering surface. Instead of the word "Camera" followed by a number, the bottom right corner of the screen read "Satellite A."

Above the moon's horizon, at the center of the screen, was the spacetime warp. Jasper swallowed and pulled her eyes from the warp to scan the rest of the monitors. Villains were arriving for the race, riling up crowds of civilians. Her gaze flickered to the bottom rightmost monitor. Her heart skipped a beat.

A golden cage held the team.

Jasper leaned in, scanning their surroundings, trying to identify their location. She could see the top of the big tent in the background, and part of the Ferris wheel to the right—

Ringmaster announced his presence by sending a golden knife flying into Jasper's shoulder. She cried out and grabbed her arm.

"Believe it or not, I don't want to kill you. Yet." A golden ring of energy materialized in the air above Ringmaster's palm and turned in slow circles.

Jasper straightened up as she turned to face him. "Silver Hands Fright House, eh?" She rested a hand on the desk behind her to steady herself. "Named after anyone? I noticed the name Nolan in the graffiti..."

Ringmaster's eyes narrowed. "Why are you trying to fight me?"

"Nothing personal, dude," Jasper said. "My real enemy is Starr. But you seem to be his biggest asset right now, so you have to go." She glanced back at the screens. "What does Starr want with the spacetime warps? I'm guessing that machine we saw in Prime's data is for channeling energy, but

I have a hard time believing you missed all the documents describing how dangerous the warps are."

"If you're trying to get me monologuing about Starr's plans, you're going to be disappointed." Ringmaster flicked his wrist, and the ring above his hand twisted itself and solidified into a long dagger. "You're clearly invested in this warp thing. I suppose I'll have to deal with you and your friends after I've handled that."

Grimacing, Jasper held up the dagger she'd used to break into the room. "You have no idea what I'm capable of."

"I have a few ideas." Ringmaster lunged. He slowed with every passing second. The sound of Jasper's heart slowed. Distant voices slowed. Her lungs filled and she dove forward, swinging the dagger.

She slashed across Ringmaster's legs. Time resumed. He hissed in pain and whirled around.

Jasper kept running. Let him think she was a coward. The thought made her jaw clench, but she forced herself up the steps. She had to find her team.

She stumbled through the maze, spilling blood and leaving red stains on the mirrors she stumbled into. People inside didn't pay her much attention, likely assuming she was a funhouse actor, but she did turn a few heads when she staggered out the entrance and to her motorcycle.

Helmet on. Engine on. Jasper looked over her shoulder and spotted the Ferris wheel and the big tent. She was on the wrong side of the carnival.

A car nearly collided with her as she turned the bike around. She slammed the brakes, and the flame-painted vehicle shot by with a roar, accompanied by the driver's angry curses.

South Siren's motorbike was right behind the vehicle, and she slowed as she passed to laugh at Jasper. "Wrong way, Van Terra!"

The race was about to start. Had Ringmaster given up on the thing entirely, now that he had the warp to deal with? Or—

"Racers, start your engines!"

The Apprentice—Aymes—stood on a silver platform, dressed in an outfit similar to Ringmaster's. A silver masquerade-style mask covered the upper half of his face. He hovered over the starting line on the other side of a small concessions building. The race would begin in less than a minute.

Jasper headed the other way, toward her team.

Chapter Seventy-Three
Self-Care Is Dropping Out Of School To
Become A Supervillain

Jasper stumbled off the motorcycle and over to the cage, not bothering to remove her helmet. "Is everyone okay?"

"Behind you—" Holly started.

Jasper ducked, narrowly avoiding the crowbar in the carnival worker's hands. But the woman swung again before Jasper could fully recover, and the crowbar struck her in the stomach. She staggered backward but kept upright.

Four more of Ringmaster's henchpeople approached, falling in line with the first woman. Jasper lifted her dagger. "Who wants to get stabbed first?"

"Looks like you already did." The lead woman nodded at the small knife still protruding from the back of Jasper's shoulder.

"Better than bleeding out." Jasper lunged. The woman dodged and came at Jasper with a roundhouse kick. Jasper hopped over the leg and stabbed the dagger into her stomach. While the woman dropped to the ground with a scream, crowbar slipping from her grasp, the other four swarmed.

Jasper jumped at the last second to flip over the two to her left. As she moved through the air, she drew throwing stars and sent them spinning into limbs. The pain wasn't enough to deter her opponents. The closest slammed a foot into Jasper's chest as she landed, knocking her into the dirt.

Another yanked the star from his upper arm and threw it back at Jasper. Jasper rolled to dodge, sprang to her feet, and landed a blow to the man's jaw. "What did I say about bleeding out?" she exclaimed as the worker hit the ground, frantically clutching at his arm in a futile attempt to stop the blood from pouring out.

Another henchman drew a blaster and took aim. "Okay, that's enough."

"I agree." Jasper kicked the blaster from his grasp and slammed her foot into his ribs. She ducked to avoid the blast from the next woman's weapon, and the laser struck the guy getting back up. Jasper snatched up the blaster she'd knocked to the ground.

The woman fired again, and Jasper fired a heartbeat later. The beams collided with each other and exploded in a shower of red sparks. While the woman shielded her eyes, Jasper drew a knife and drove it into her shoulder. She dropped.

Jasper hurried to the cage. "Everyone okay?"

"Are we okay?" Grace yelped. "You're the one with a knife in your shoulder!"

"Oh. Right." Jasper yanked it free. "Dax?"

Dax reached through the bars and rested a hand on her arm. "Be careful, it'll still be easy to reopen for a while," he said once the glow faded.

"In that case, it's definitely going to get reopened. But thanks." Jasper took a step back and assessed the cage.

"I'm not sure we can get out of here without Ringmaster's powers," Thea said.

Jasper's face lit up. When no one reacted, she remembered her helmet was still on. "I have an idea. There is someone else here with Ringmaster's power."

"If we had enough heat, maybe a blowtorch—" Holly began.

"No, no, this will work." Jasper took a few steps backward. "I'm going to find Aymes and convince him to help us."

"I can't imagine how you plan to do that," Thea said. "But you better figure it out quick, because he's right behind you."

Jasper spun around. Sure enough, Aymes was coming her way, carried through the air by his platform. For a moment she thought he was following the racers—but no, his eyes were definitely on her.

His platform brought him to the ground before dissolving. He lifted a hand, and blast of silver energy fired from his palm.

Jasper narrowly dodged the blast. As she straightened up, she shouted, "Wait!"

A silver staff took form in Aymes's hand. He stepped forward and swung. The staff smacked into the side of Jasper's helmet.

She staggered sideways. Lifted her hands. "I just want to talk!"

"Ringmaster told me all about you, Van Terra. Don't think you can fool me." Aymes swung again, this time hitting hard enough to make lights flash in Jasper's vision. Something cracked, and it her took a moment to realize it was the helmet. A piece of the visor fell to the dirt.

"Aymes! Please!"

Aymes paused. "How do you know my name?"

Jasper slid the cracked helmet off her head. "It's me! Miss Elizab!"

Aymes lowered the staff, but his expression was still apprehensive. "Why are you dressed like that? And why are you here?"

"I'm Van Terra, idiot."

His eyes narrowed. "Then we're enemies."

"Why? Because Ringmaster said so?" Maybe she shouldn't have called him an idiot. Usually, the people she felt the need to inform of her identity *were* idiots.

"I work for him. So, yes." Aymes swung.

Jasper ducked. The staff passed over her head. Her right hand shot up and grabbed it. She winced in pain as she attempted to pull it from Aymes's hands.

The staff vanished into thin air. Aymes stepped back, summoned a new one, and swung again. He hit Jasper's side and knocked her to the ground.

"Come on, Jasper!" Holly exclaimed. "Just knock the kid out!"

Groaning, Jasper sat up. "Aymes, I don't want to—"

A sound like thunder shook the sky, drowning out the world for a moment. Jasper tipped her head back. Her eyes went wide.

The warp glowed brighter than it had before, and space distorted around it. A blast of white energy shot out, then another, and another, each accompanied by a loud boom. The blasts were all moving in the same direction: toward the Ferris wheel.

The prototype machine they'd seen in Dr. Prime's research drive sat on the top of the wheel's hub, sucking in the energy.

"Ringmaster has no idea what he's messing with," Jasper shouted over the next boom. "We have to stop him. Everyone on this moon could die!"

Hesitation crossed Aymes's face. He lowered the staff. "Why should I trust you over Ringmaster?"

"He's manipulating you into being a criminal!"

"Like you?" Aymes asked, his tone turning accusatory. "Why were you at my school, anyway? What were you doing?"

Jasper grimaced. "We wanted information on Ringmaster's plans, and we knew you were working for him."

Aymes's voice rose. "You were spying on me the whole time?"

"Listen, Aymes, you're new to all of this. Please believe me when I say it's nothing personal." Jasper climbed to her feet. "Ringmaster's involved in a complicated web of…stuff. I actually don't care much about him. Starr's the one I'm really after. But…" She trailed off and shook her head. "It's not too late for you to get out, Aymes. You have a lot of potential."

"Yeah, a lot of potential and no money," Aymes spat. "Ringmaster's my only shot at getting anywhere in life."

"No, he's not. There are other ways."

"Like what?"

Jasper's mouth opened, closed, and opened again. She sighed. "I don't know. Maybe you're right. But Ringmaster doesn't care about helping you with school. You know that. He's trying to persuade you to join him full time, isn't he?"

"Yeah, but he's not forcing me to do anything." Aymes waved a hand, and his staff transformed into several hovering spheres. "And he does want to help me. In his own…twisted way, I guess."

"I want to help you too." The sky cracked again, and the moon shuddered with it.

"Why should I believe you?"

"I tried to help you at East Marina, didn't I?"

"You were spying on me!" Aymes swung an arm, and one of the spheres flew at Jasper's face. She barely had time to throw her arms up and shield herself before it hit her and knocked her onto her back.

Jasper sat up and looked back at the cage, at her team whose worried gazes flickered between her and the sky.

Heart quickening, her attention returned to Aymes. "Okay. Don't believe I want to help you. I wouldn't blame you." She pushed herself up. "But you can't deny that we're in danger. Whatever Ringmaster's trying to do with the warp, it's going to rip the moon apart. People will die. Steal, break things, run Ringmaster's errands, whatever. But you don't want all these people to get hurt, do you?"

Aymes's gaze darted to the warp. "Of course not. But—"

"You're in over your head, kid."

"And you're not?"

Jasper laughed. "I've been in over my head for a long time. You learn to swim." Her head tipped to the right. "Did Ringmaster tell you anything about the warps? About what that machine's supposed to do?"

"No. But I don't think even he knows what Starr wants with them."

"I've been close to one before. Way too close." Jasper shook her head. "Starr must be after something big if he's willing to mess with something so dangerous."

Aymes's head turned to study the cage Ringmaster had made. After a moment's hesitation, he said, "Ringmaster was talking about evacuating if things went bad with the machine. He knows this is dangerous."

"And you're going to let him run off while people die?"

Another long moment passed. Finally, Aymes lifted a hand. The golden bars at the front of the cage glowed and shimmered before disappearing entirely. The team staggered out.

"Thank you," Dax said.

Aymes glanced at him briefly before returning his gaze to Jasper. "I'm not doing this for you. But you're right. I shouldn't have let Ringmaster get this far with the warps." He sighed. "I just wanted to learn to use my powers."

"Don't sweat it, kid," Jasper said. "But if I were you, I'd get out of here. Or at least get out of the costume. Police are on their way."

Aymes frowned. "How do you know?"

"Because I called them."

"Most of the police who are trained to handle villains know not to touch Ringmaster," Aymes warned. "And some of the other villains here are on Starr's good side, too."

"Trust me, these guys aren't corrupt," Jasper told him. "Starr thinks they're too stupid to be of any use to him."

"Are they?"

"Uh, yeah. They're really just backup, and a threat to the lesser villains. I plan on catching Ringmaster myself."

"Well, I'm not running yet," Aymes said. "You'll need my help to stop him."

Chapter Seventy-Four
Good Enough

The team—and Aymes—returned to the funhouse. Well, they attempted to. After fighting their way through the crowds of people running and freaking out about the violent turn the hole in the sky had taken, they were stopped by the golden elephants and lions and bears patrolling the building.

Jasper sighed. Why couldn't Ringmaster's creations be more…stabable?

"They're huge. And made from Ringmaster's energy," Thea said. "We don't stand a chance."

Aymes stepped forward. His fists clenched. "I do."

The ground trembled. "We'll have to split," Jasper said. "I'm going to climb the Ferris wheel and see if I can disable the machine. Aymes, fight your way into the funhouse and bring Ringmaster out."

"We're coming with you, I'm assuming?" Holly asked. "Because it sounds like—"

Jasper shook her head. "Ringmaster is a priority. You all need to work together to catch him." She turned around. A hand grabbed her arm. She expected to see Holly, or maybe Dax, but it was Grace she found when she glanced back.

"What if you die?" Grace asked.

Jasper laughed, as if the sound could mask her uncertainty. "I don't die."

"You—this team is all I have, now."

"Maybe you should get a hobby." Jasper couldn't bring herself to yank her arm free. "Seriously, Angel, I'm going to be fine."

Grace's gaze flickered to Aymes, who was already starting toward one of the lions. "Ringmaster's going to be pissed at Aymes. What if he kills him?"

"He won't. Trust me." Jasper frowned. "Do you think I don't care what happens to Aymes?"

Grace didn't answer. She did release Jasper's arm, though. "Maybe I should come with you. I can fly."

"None of you are going near the warp. That's an order."

Leaving the team behind—and hoping they stayed that way—Jasper sprinted toward the Ferris wheel. Its passengers had abandoned it, but it was still moving. In fact, it was spinning abnormally fast.

Although visitors scrambled to leave the park, the racers were still going strong. Maybe they assumed the moonquake was just another obstacle Ringmaster wanted them to overcome. Most of them had probably never heard of spacetime warps.

Jasper reached the base of the Ferris wheel. Without slowing, she jumped, pushed off the structure's base, and grabbed onto the bottom rung of the maintenance ladder. The entire Ferris wheel shook violently as another blast hit the machine.

The warp was expanding.

Jasper forced herself to climb as fast as possible, only pausing when the trembling became too much. Finally, she reached the top of the ladder. She looked the machine over and searched for any cracks, any weaknesses she could use to take it apart.

Nothing. She pulled out the blaster she'd nabbed from one of the henchpeople and slammed it against the thing. Then again. And again. Even aiming for the weaker-looking parts around the machine's dish didn't appear to do any good.

The energy coming in from the warp fluctuated. The wheel shuddered again. Jasper lost her balance and nearly fell, only barely managing to keep her grip on the hub.

She glanced down. Maybe if she couldn't break the machine, she could break the structure holding it.

Jasper scrambled back down the ladder. Where had she left the motorcycle? By the cage? That wasn't far. She sprinted across the main path running through the carnival. Passing racers swerved and honked and yelled at her.

When she reached the motorcycle, Jasper momentarily considered the helmet lying on the ground nearby, but it was too broken to do much good. And what she was about to do was far too dangerous for the thing to make a difference if it did end badly. She started her engine and headed for the racers, pulling up the course map as she did.

She cut in near the front of the race, next to South Siren. South Siren glared at her. "Where have you been? You can't just show up in the middle of the race!"

"Who's going to stop me?" Jasper grinned. Others had taken notice of her and were shooting her dirty looks as well. She couldn't wait to tell Holly that making everyone hate her was actually going to be useful.

"Ringmaster won't allow it," South Siren said. "You may as well leave now."

"But the fun's just getting started." Jasper drew the blaster, acting as if she might fire. "Besides, Ringmaster and his Apprentice seem to be otherwise occupied."

"I don't have time for this." South Siren's hekten lifted itself off her shoulder.

Jasper dodged the blast. "Come on, surely you've got more firepower than that thing."

"You trying to get me to kill you?" South Siren asked. "I'll hit you with everything I've got."

"Do it."

South Siren lifted a hand and snapped. A powerful shockwave rolled from her fingers. Jasper swerved out of its path and headed toward the Ferris wheel, setting her gaze on the biggest racer nearby: Grim Machine.

While South Siren reached for something on the other side of her motorcycle, her hekten fired again. Jasper veered right. The blast hit Grim Machine. A massive gun lifted off Grim Machine's hood to fire back at South Siren.

Jasper waved her hand. "My bad!"

The gun swiveled toward her.

More and more racers took notice as she zig-zagged through the crowd, laughing and yelling. "Would someone shut that dumbass up?" one of the villains yelled.

South Siren procured a grenade. Jasper cut across an empty stretch of grass and neared the rapidly spinning wheel. The world slowed. She glanced back, and her gaze drifted from the grenade leaving South Siren's hand, past the various guns and blasters aimed her way, to Cutthroat, who watched her carefully from the edge of the pack.

Jasper's hand inched through the air to point at the warp. Her head tipped toward the Ferris wheel.

Understanding crossed Cutthroat's face. The cannon on the front of his cart joined the other weapons pointed in Jasper's direction.

The only way for her to avoid getting blown to pieces was to go through the wheel. Time reduced to a crawl as she approached the spinning seats. The humming in her skull drowned everything else out, louder than it had ever been.

Jasper released the gas. Her mind spat calculations at her. A fence that once guided the line to the ride, partially collapsed from the moonquakes, worked as a ramp. She took to the air.

She passed between two Ferris wheel compartments. The one above inched closer and closer. Jasper leaned forward, lowering her head to avoid getting hit. Her front tire emerged on the other side. Almost, almost…

She was nearly free when the seats coming down grazed the back of the motorcycle, sending her spiraling toward the ground. Time abruptly returned to its usual pace, and Jasper's stomach jumped into her throat. She let go of the motorcycle and slammed hard into the dirt, rolling as best she could to redirect the force of the landing.

The Ferris wheel shook, not from the warp this time, but from taking blow after blow from the angry villains. Something exploded on the other side, and the structure groaned. Creaked. A cannon ball came flying through, smashing up metal bars in its path.

The carnival ride began its fall.

Jasper forced herself up and back onto the motorcycle. The wheel's collapsing shadow moved over her. She gunned it.

Behind her, the Ferris wheel crashed to the ground.

Chapter Seventy-Five
Lightning May Not Strike Twice, But These Fists Sure Do

There was no sign of the team outside the funhouse. Ringmaster's animal guards were gone, too. Jasper sprinted through the building's entrance but didn't make it far before the shaking ground knocked her off her feet.

As she slammed into the floor, a nearby wall collapsed. Mirrors exploded and shattered glass sprayed in every direction. Jasper raised an arm to shield her face. Light spilled in from the gaps opening up in the ceiling.

Relief washed over Jasper when she lowered the arm and spotted the team picking their way through the rubble.

"Van Terra!" Ringmaster emerged from behind a half-collapsed wall, closer to Jasper than the team was. Aymes came running after him. "I said I didn't want to kill you. Not that I wouldn't." Golden energy swirled around his fists in glowing streams.

Jasper climbed to her feet and pointed her blaster at Aymes. "I'm sorry, what was that?"

Aymes froze, his eyes widening. A couple of gasps came from the team's direction. Was one of them from Grace? Jasper forced herself to keep her eyes locked with Ringmaster's.

"Why would I care if you kill him? He betrayed me." Still, Ringmaster lowered his hands. If he was trying to mask his hesitation, he wasn't entirely succeeding.

Jasper raised an eyebrow. "Don't bother. I know the truth."

"What truth?" Aymes asked, glancing at his mentor. "What is she talking about?"

"Oh, I bet you didn't tell him," Jasper said. "Even better."

Uncertainty faded from Ringmaster's face, turning to a slight smile. "All right, Van Terra. You're not the only one with information. I got my hands on Starr's lab records."

"Great. That'll come in handy when I steal them from you. After I catch you and get all your employees arrested, that is."

"You and what police?"

Jasper pointed up to the sky. "Those ones."

Small police ships descended on the moon's surface, red and yellow lights flashing and sirens blaring. The number 421 was plastered on the side of each one.

"Thank goodness," Jasper said. "I was afraid my timing would be off and I'd look like an idiot."

"You already look like an idiot," Ringmaster told her.

"Are those your last words before I shoot you and tie you up?"

"Whatever you say, *Jane*."

Jasper's hand tightened around the blaster. Determined not to let him get to her, she asked, "How'd you figure that one out?"

"Like I said, lab records. But I'd like to make you an offer. You want to know where my powers came from?" A ring appeared above Ringmaster's hand, and he twirled it around his finger. "I'm like you. Taken from Earth. Brought to the labs. I never got around to being experimented on, though. My powers were the result of an accident with some other project of theirs. It allowed me to escape."

"Then why are you working for Starr?"

"Unlike you, I'm grateful for my abilities."

Jasper's jaw clenched. "Grateful to be ripped from your home?"

"It wasn't exactly a good one." Ringmaster shrugged. "And I'm working with Starr because it benefits me. You want to take him down? Join me. We can take over his empire together."

"I don't want to take his empire. I want to destroy it," Jasper hissed. "You might not be the dictator he is, but how many innocent people have you hurt doing what he tells you?"

"Who cares?" Ringmaster laughed. "I thought you were a villain, Van Terra. And all of those 'innocent people' contribute to the society that ruined your life. They all serve Starr, in a way."

"It's not their fault," Jasper said. "Not all of them. There's nothing they can do." Her gaze flickered to the team, who watched her with wide eyes.

"Starr's the bigger fish. Work with me. I'll let you see the lab records. There are more things in there that would interest you." A cold smile crawled onto Ringmaster's face. "Think of your team, if that's what really matters. What's best for them?"

Jasper's hand trembled. All she could see on the team's faces were concern and apprehension. What did they want her to do? Starr would be a challenge even with Ringmaster imprisoned. And every day he was in power, Grace was in danger.

"Trust me," Ringmaster pressed. "If we work together, Starr will be easy. Especially with what I know about the spacetime warps."

"Oh, hell no! We're shutting down that machine and throwing out everything related to the warps." Jasper shot an anxious glance toward the sky, as if mentioning the warp might make it act up again. The fact that a low rumble filled the air as she looked up didn't help her nerves any.

Ringmaster's nostrils flared. "Are you insane? The warps are the greatest source of power the universe has ever seen!"

"Trying to drain the energy from that one nearly ripped this moon apart! And you have no idea what happens if you get too close."

"And you do?"

"We're running out of time," Jasper said. "Police are going to swarm the place any second now."

"I agree." Ringmaster folded his arms. "So, what's it going to be?"

Jasper looked at the team. At the kids she'd lost to a warp. At the girl she'd sworn she'd protect, even if for her own gain in the beginning.

Jasper lowered the blaster.

"That's what I thought—"

Jasper fired at Ringmaster's foot. He shouted in pain and dropped to one knee.

"Not going to kill me?" he gasped. "What, you're too good for that?"

"I'm keeping you alive as long as there's a chance I can use you as evidence against Starr." Jasper drew a dagger and stalked toward him.

"I'm not going down that easy." Ringmaster summoned a blade twice the size of Jasper's. In the blink of an eye, he lunged. The weapon grazed the side of her face.

"Jasper!" Grace exclaimed. She and the team surged forward. With a flick of his wrist, Ringmaster threw up a shimmering, semi-transparent wall to stop them.

Gritting her teeth, Jasper plunged her dagger into Ringmaster's side. He swiped. She tipped her head back. The blade missed her face by inches. Another slash left a wound on her shoulder. She hissed.

"I know more about you than you do," Ringmaster growled. He grabbed her wrist. "All the plans they had for you. All the things they put in you. Right arm, right?" He stabbed his dagger down.

Jasper cried out as the blade sank in. Ringmaster twisted it. She screamed.

When he pulled the blade free, it glowed and transformed into a whip that wrapped around Jasper's forearm and yanked her to the ground. She immediately pushed herself upright. As she did, a new layer of pain settled over the sharp sensation of the knife wound. She glanced at the arm.

White arcs of electricity danced around the bleeding gash. Her muscles clenched under the pain of electric shock. Pain that coursed through her veins. Her nerves. Her bones.

"Ringmaster!" Aymes yelled. "We need to leave. The moon—"

"You can go. I'm not done here." Ringmaster's whip changed again, this time into a staff. He swung.

Jasper's left hand flew up to grab the staff. The sting of it hitting her palm was nothing compared to everything else. The electricity leaping across her skin spread farther across her body. "What is this?" she gasped.

"Seems they were right about the pain." Ringmaster yanked the staff from her grasp. "Though with some modifications—"

Jasper sprang to her feet and grabbed Ringmaster by the shoulders. Lightning jumped between them. He hissed in pain, and when she released him, he dropped to his knees. She threw a punch at his jaw.

The electricity reduced to scattered sparks and faded, offering Jasper some relief. Her shoulders sagged. Now, they just needed to contain Ringmaster—

With one swift movement, Ringmaster formed a dagger and slashed at Jasper's legs. She jumped backwards. He was on his feet and running in an instant.

"Oh, come on!" Jasper sprinted after him.

Ringmaster stumbled, giving her hope for that she could catch up. That hope lasted about five seconds. A massive gold eagle swooped down from above and knocked a racer off their motorcycle. Ringmaster grabbed it, hopped on, and sped off.

Jasper's lungs were burning by the time she made it to where she'd left her motorcycle. Still, she scrambled on and followed. She was faster than Ringmaster, but not by much. The gap between them closed inch by inch.

The air ahead shimmered. A shining ramp rose from the ground, into the sky, toward—

"Have you lost your mind?" Jasper screamed.

Ringmaster looked back. "There's another side, isn't there?" he called over the wind. "That's where Hollixa Faye went and came back from."

"Yes." Jasper's hands tightened. "But wherever you end up—it'll be another place and time. And you might not—"

Ringmaster sped up.

Jasper gritted her teeth. "You're not getting away."

At the end of the ramp, the warp had returned to its usual appearance, save for the fact that it was much smaller now. Ringmaster drove onto the ramp, and while every instinct screamed for her to stop, Jasper followed. She drew closer. Closer. She stretched out an arm. She could almost reach him…

Ringmaster reached back and fired a blast of energy from his palm. The beam struck Jasper's motorcycle head-on and sent her spinning. Energy coursed through her, golden light blinded her, and she screamed in pain.

She fell.

As the wind whipped past her falling body, her vision returned in time for her to watch Ringmaster fly into the warp. A heartbeat later, the warp collapsed. Vanished.

Jasper reached for something, anything. Where had the motorcycle gone? The ramp had disappeared with Ringmaster. There was nothing to stop her from hitting the ground—

Something slammed into her. Hands grabbed her. Grace's wings spread to catch the air.

The two collided with the ground a moment later. Grace stumbled, and Jasper slipped from her grasp. She hit the dirt with a grunt of pain and rolled onto her back, desperately fighting to get some air back into her lungs.

"Jasper!" Grace knelt next to her. "Jasper? Are you okay?"

The rest of the team was already gathering around. Dax dropped into a crouch at Jasper's side. "Hold on," he said. His hands glowed blue.

As soon as Jasper could speak, she gasped, "I'm sorry."

"What?" Grace rested a hand on her shoulder.

Jasper pushed herself up, ignoring Dax's protests. "I failed." She shook her head. "I should have taken Ringmaster's offer."

Thea shook her head. "I don't think that would have been a good idea." Next to her, Dax mumbled something that sounded like agreement. Grace was still wide-eyed, still looking Jasper up and down as if she feared she would drop dead at any moment.

"Why didn't you?" Holly asked. "I mean—for a moment I really thought you would."

Jasper trembled violently, and even though the electricity Ringmaster had somehow triggered was gone, she could hear her inner systems crackling with static. "I couldn't. I couldn't let him keep messing with the warps. Not after what happened to you guys."

Something flashed in Holly's expression. "What are you talking about?"

Jasper closed her eyes. "Thea. I need you to fix—whatever's wrong with me. My system's all screwed up."

Thea rested a hand on Jasper's shoulder. An appalled expression overtook her face. "Stars, Jasper, what happened?"

"I'm still figuring that out," Jasper muttered.

"You're overloaded. It's okay, I can fix it." Thea's eyes closed. "Hang on. Breathe."

"What do you mean what happened to us?" Holly pressed, her voice strained. "What happened with the warps, Jasper?" She sounded…closer to tears than anger.

Jasper was relieved to find her internal buzzing was lessening by the second. Thea stepped back and folded her arms as she looked Jasper over. Concern still lingered in her gaze.

"Earth," Jasper said, finally meeting Holly's eyes. "I met you three on Earth, in 1977. There was an academy. They recruited us and sent us into space and we found a warp and—" She grimaced. "You all got pulled in. I barely got away. And then, decades later, you all showed up five years younger on Kronos."

The team stared at her with stunned expressions. Before anyone could muster a response, footsteps approached. Aymes.

"Ringmaster went into the warp?" Aymes asked.

Jasper nodded. Rubbed her forehead.

Emotions and fatigue warred on Aymes's face. "Maybe it's for the best." He pulled a data drive from his pocket. "I grabbed this from the funhouse basement. I think it's got those lab records he was talking about, and the warp research."

Jasper held out a hand, and Aymes tossed her the drive. "Thanks," she said. "Do you know if there are communication logs in here with Starr?"

"Not sure. Sorry."

"Stop! Police!" a voice shouted.

"Oh, great," Holly said under her breath. "More running."

If they had to run, Jasper was screwed. Even with Dax's healing boost, every part of her ached. "Wait," she said. "I know that voice." She climbed to her feet and turned around. "Detective Park!"

Detective Park stopped, blaster in hand. "The hell?"

"It's me! Detective Jasper! From Dr. Prime's murder case!" Jasper forced a smile and weakly waved her hands.

"I knew there was something off about you. But Van Terra?" Detective Park's gaze moved to the others. "And let me guess, your team?"

"Yes. Look, I called you, remember?"

"You did. I'm guessing that wasn't to get yourself arrested?"

"No," Jasper said. "See, I was hoping in exchange for helping you get your hands on so many other villains here, you could maybe let me and my friends go. Just this once. As a tiny little favor." She made a gesture with her thumb and forefinger pinched together.

"I do have to admit, this has been a great night." Detective Park kept a tight grip on his blaster, but he did lower it a little. "We've already made a lot of arrests. I even found the guy who really killed Dr. Prime. You were right about him working for Ringmaster. Name's Viper."

"Huh. That doesn't surprise me," Jasper said. "Did you guys get South Siren?"

"I don't think so. Someone on the radio said something about her getting away earlier."

Damn. Jasper sighed. "Well, what's it going to be?"

Detective Park's face was unreadable as he assessed Jasper, undoubtedly realizing what terrible condition she was in. Finally, he said, "I don't understand you. After everything with the precinct..." He shook his head. "All right, I'm only letting you go because I'm outnumbered, understand?"

Jasper grinned. "Right. I'm just so terrifying that you knew you didn't stand a chance against me."

"I'll be sure to leave out the various stab wounds that seem to be plaguing you." Detective Park holstered his weapon and walked away.

As he left, Jasper turned and surveyed the crumbling carnival. "Oh no!"

The alarm in her voice sent fear into the other's faces. "What's wrong?" Holly asked.

Jasper pointed to the wreckage twenty feet away. "My motorcycle! It's completely destroyed!"

The others groaned.

Chapter Seventy-Six
More To Bury

The team stumbled into the apartment on Kronos at around two in the morning.

"I think I'm going to sleep for a week," Thea said.

Holly tossed her bags unceremoniously onto the ground. "Are we just going to gloss over everything Jasper said about knowing us on Earth? Because we should talk about that."

"What is there to talk about?" Jasper asked through a yawn. She pulled her sphere from her coat and set it on the counter. "Whatever happened in the warp wiped away five years of your memories. I don't know anything more than you do about how the warps work or what's on the other side."

"I want to know what I did in those five years. What the four of us did. What things were like at that academy you mentioned."

"I'll tell you," Jasper said to Holly, though she glanced at the others while she spoke. "After we all get some sleep." She didn't have the emotional capacity for that conversation right now. She doubted she would tomorrow, either. In fact, she'd probably wind up putting the conversation off for as long as possible.

They deserve better. Jasper was surprised by the sting that thought brought to her eyes.

Holly, Thea, and Dax entered the hallway. Jasper moved to follow.

"Jasper," Grace whispered.

Jasper turned around. "Something wrong?"

"I just have a question." Grace hesitated, waiting for the sound of three doors to close before continuing. "What did you mean about Ringmaster not hurting Aymes? What secret were you talking about?"

"They have the same powers," Jasper said. "I didn't think much of it at first. There could be any number of reasons for that. But then there was the Silver Hands Fright House, and Nolan was one of the random names graffitied on the building—that's Aymes's middle name. I made a guess, and Ringmaster confirmed it." She paused. "He's Aymes's father."

Grace's eyes widened. "Why didn't you tell Aymes?"

"I was going to, but then Ringmaster disappeared and—what would be the point?"

"Doesn't he deserve to know?"

Jasper shrugged. "Was it my place to tell him?"

"Well, it's not like Ringmaster can anymore." Grace sighed. "But I guess he gets to go back to a normal life, now. Maybe that's better."

"Do you think I was right to keep the warp thing from the others, too?" The words came out before Jasper could stop them.

A moment passed. Another. "I don't know," Grace said softly.

"I had no explanation for it. And it was so hard to think about losing them to that thing, let alone talk about—" Jasper's throat tightened. She swallowed. "I feel like I failed them. Twice now."

"You didn't fail us by letting Ringmaster get away. We have his data drive." Grace folded her arms and glanced away. "And—I don't know about the others, but I'm glad you didn't join him."

"Me too," Jasper replied. "I am sorry, though. It might take longer than I thought to bring down Starr. But I promise you I will, and then you'll be free to go—wherever you're going, without worrying about him or Red Blades."

"Right." Grace started toward the hallway, passed Jasper, then paused. Turned around. "Sorry, one last thing. Did you look at the lab records yet?"

"I skimmed them on the way here," Jasper replied.

"Anything interesting?"

The window behind Grace spilled city lights over her, illuminating the wings relaxed behind her, her dark waves of hair, her skin. Jasper's heart quickened. She thought of the diagrams of cybernetic wings, the memory wipe procedures, the list of test subject after test subject. Grace's name. The numbers.

That girl in the cafe. How many more were there?

And which one was Grace, if not the original?

"No," Jasper lied. "Nothing yet."

"Okay. Good night."

Grace disappeared into the dark hall. Jasper's heart still pounded, even after Grace was gone, and she silently cursed its unsteady rhythm. There was too much going on for her to start another battle with her own emotions.

Why not? Why not tell everyone everything? Maybe Jasper thought she could spare them from the repercussions of the truth if she carried it alone. If they never knew the terrible things that had happened to them, they could live in blissful ignorance indefinitely.

Not like Jasper, who had every memory burned into her mind forever.

Forever. God, she hoped the serum wouldn't keep her alive that long. It had to wear out eventually, right? Would she resume aging normally, or would she drop dead all at once?

"Mia," Jasper whispered.

The response came through the sphere on the counter. "Yes?"

Jasper swallowed. "Can you tell me who made you?"

"Thea made me. She doesn't remember."

"And you've never told her."

"You told me not to."

Jasper nodded. "Good."

She opened the fridge and grabbed a Nova Cora. Drank it. Move to the window to stare out at the city.

"I'm coming for you Starr," she whispered.

Not just Starr. His villains, his gang, the Fayes, the other elite families that kept him in power. She didn't know who would replace the people in charge, and right now, she didn't care.

The next morning, the team gathered around the counter to look at the data drive. Jasper had already hidden parts of the lab records in a different drive and deleted them off Ringmaster's, careful to use all the procedures Thea had once shown her that would ensure they were gone for good.

Even without all that, there was a lot to sort through.

"I think we have some concrete stuff tying Starr to Ringmaster," Thea said as she scrolled through one of the documents. "Our primary concern is making sure it can't be disputed as fake. We need to be sure people will believe it. And, of course, make sure they see it in the first place."

"How are we going to do that?" Grace asked.

Jasper grinned. "I have a few ideas."

Thank you for reading
VAN TERRA

To get updates and find out how you can be the first to read new books,
find me at:

www.rorynorth.com

If you enjoyed the story, please help support this indie author!
Tell a friend, leave reviews, request the book at your local library, and talk
about it on social media! #vanterra

Villain Complex: After defeating the city's biggest hero, supervillain Julian Godfrey finds himself in over his head when he attempts to train the woman who took on the hero's powers as part of an elaborate scheme.

Plague Saint: In a frozen city in the distant future, Winter Pierce kills the hospital's Plague Saint to save her mother after discovering his corruption. When she steals his identity, she quickly finds herself tangled up in a government conspiracy.

A Drop of Haunted Blood: After a magician kills his family, Felix discovers his latent ability to bind ghosts to his soul and wield their magical abilities.

Be the first to know about new stories and upcoming releases! Sign up for my newsletter at:

rorynorth.com/starchatter